Dear Reader,

Once again, it is [our] [pleasure] [t]o bring you our annu[al Christmas col]-lection. This year, [Patricia Potter, Ruth Langan, Theresa Michaels] and Bronwyn Will[iams have stories that wi]ll warm your heart [this holiday season. Yo]u won't want to miss a single page from the streets of New York City, to the faraway English countryside, to the dark days of the Civil War, in this special collection.

The editors would like to take this time to thank all of the readers who have helped to make 1992 a wonderful year for Harlequin Historicals. With your support, during the upcoming year we will continue to bring you four new titles every month full of romance and adventure.

Our best wishes to you and your family this holiday season and throughout the New Year.

Sincerely,

Tracy Farrell
Senior Editor

HARLEQUIN HISTORICAL

CHRISTMAS

• STORIES • 1992 •

MAURA SEGER
ERIN YORKE
BRONWYN WILLIAMS

Harlequin Books

TORONTO • NEW YORK • LONDON
AMSTERDAM • PARIS • SYDNEY • HAMBURG
STOCKHOLM • ATHENS • TOKYO • MILAN
MADRID • WARSAW • BUDAPEST • AUCKLAND

Harlequin Historical first edition November 1992

ISBN 0-373-83245-1

MISS MONTRACHET REQUESTS
Copyright © 1992 by Maura Seger

CHRISTMAS BOUNTY
Copyright © 1992 by Susan McGovern Yansick and Christine Healy

A PROMISE KEPT
Copyright © 1992 by Dixie Browning and Mary Williams

CONTENTS

MISS MONTRACHET REQUESTS

Maura
Seger

For my parents, Ann and Brendan Jones,
and all the memories of happy Christmases.

Maura Seger's Family Fruitcake

1 cup dried apricots
¾ cup butter
1 cup sugar
1 tsp lemon extract
4 eggs, separated
1 lb candied fruit
½ cup slivered almonds or other nuts
1 cup raisins
2 cups flour
1 tsp salt
½ tsp baking soda
Irish whiskey or rum

Cover apricots with cold water, bring to boil for one minute, drain, slice coarsely. Beat butter, sugar, lemon extract, egg yolks and apricots until light and creamy. Dust candied fruit lightly with flour, then stir into mixture along with nuts and raisins. Sift flour, salt and baking soda in separate bowl. Add alternately to mixture with stiffly beaten egg whites. Pour into well-greased two-quart casserole and cover. Place casserole in large pan half-filled with water. Steam in slow oven, set at about 275°F, for 1½ hours. Remove from water pan and bake for an additional hour or longer, depending on thickness of cake. Mixture can be divided into smaller loaf pans. Cake is ready when cake tester comes out dry. Reduce cooking time as needed. Cool on rack. Wrap in cheesecloth. Place in tins. Cover with one ounce Irish whiskey or rum. Two weeks later, open tins and add another ounce. Seal until Christmas.

Chapter One

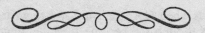

Alanda turned toward Lord Randall with tremulous joy. She could not quite yet believe the great good fortune that had befallen her since the discovery of Lady Margaret's duplicity. The smile on his rugged face assured her that all misunderstandings between them were at an end. When he opened his powerful arms, she went into them without hesitation. Together, they gazed out across the manor gardens as the sun rose over a new day.

The End

Miss Cornelia Montgomery sat back in her desk chair, put down her pen and sighed with relief. *Cornwall Encounter* was finished and, in her opinion, it wasn't half-bad. Still, she was glad to be done with it. Her publisher had been pestering her for weeks to deliver the manuscript. Loyal readers were panting for another Luciana Montrachet romance and she could hardly let them down.

A small smile played over her heart-shaped face as she absently flexed her fingers, easing the cramp from them. She was really quite fond of Luciana, even if the lady did cause her occasional disquiet. Originally a mere figment of Cornelia's imagination, Luciana was becoming more real with each passing book that bore her name.

Nowadays when Cornelia sat down to write, she almost felt as though she became Luciana, a woman of fire and drama, far freer than her own modest self. As Luciana, she traveled great distances, had fascinating adventures, met extraordinary men, survived dastardly dangers and ultimately emerged safe, beloved and bound for a lifetime of happiness. And all without leaving the quiet of her lavender-scented boudoir overlooking Gramercy Park in the heart of New York.

Outside her windows, carriages rattled by, the horses' hooves muted on the cobblestones slushy with remnants of the previous night's snow. Newsboys shouted the headlines about Goulds, Astors and Vanderbilts. Ladies nestled in their winter pelisses, high buttoned boots gleaming, strolled by on their way to the stores lining the Ladies Mile along lower Broadway. In the park surrounded by the high wrought-iron fence, well-bundled children played under the watchful eyes of their nannies while dreaming of what Father Christmas would shortly bring them.

All was sweet normality, the same comfortable, predictable life Cornelia had always known. The life she, her mother and her two younger brothers had come perilously close to losing.

Her smooth brow furrowed as she briefly recalled those days four years before when a sudden financial panic brought on by excess and greed had all but destroyed the country's banking system. In the terrifying confusion that followed, there had been many casualties. Among them was the banker William Montgomery, her father, who had succumbed to heart failure upon confronting the destruction of his life's work.

Dear Luciana had been born then, in those frantic days, out of desperation and a reckless bid for survival. Incredibly, she worked. Luciana Montrachet's first book captured the imagination of the public, sold copiously, and kept the debt collectors from the door of the family's Gramercy Park house. Her subsequent offerings had assured the family's financial security. All done in secret, mind, so as not to distress Cornelia's very loving but very proper mother. Happily, Melanie Montgomery believed her late husband's prudent stock investments were seeing the family through.

Strictly speaking, there was no necessity for Cornelia to continue writing, but the fact of the matter was that she enjoyed it. Even now, as she rubbed the back of her neck and reflected ruefully on her ink-stained self, she knew that she would be loath to give it up.

But there was little time for such ruminating. Her mother expected her downstairs for afternoon tea and she could hardly appear in her present state.

Half an hour later, suitably scrubbed, Cornelia hastened down the steps. She was above medium height for a woman, slender but not overly so, with rich chestnut hair, a complexion distressingly given to freckles, and a ready smile that reached her azure blue eyes.

At twenty-six, she was older than most unmarried women, but that did not trouble her. She had been surprised to discover that she actually enjoyed assuming responsibility for her family and found satisfaction in caring for those dependent on her. To give that up for the passive role of wife and helpmate was more than she could contemplate.

Yet neither could she shirk her duties as a good, obedient daughter. Her mother awaited her in the front parlor. It was Melanie Montgomery's "at home" day, when she received callers. Custom required her daughter to join her.

Cornelia did not overly mind the duty. She enjoyed meeting people and found that among her and her mother's friends the conversation tended to be a good deal livelier then the usual polite drivel about the weather.

Entering the parlor, she detoured around a rubber plant, turned right at the piano covered with a fringed shawl and stopped to give her mother a quick kiss before settling herself on the horsehair-and-velvet couch.

Melanie had been playing with tarot cards, which she swiftly swept out of sight as the doorbell chimed.

"You look tired, dear," she said, patting the couch pillow back in place. "You really should get more rest."

"I'm sure you're right," Cornelia said agreeably. She saw no reason to burden her mother with the knowledge that her late nights were not spent snuggled in bed reading but rather at her desk, writing. Luciana was a closely held secret.

Her mother, on the contrary, looked well rested and at peace. For that, Cornelia was infinitely grateful. She loved the woman who had given her birth and charted her through the rocky shoals of childhood with gentle strength. There was truly nothing she would not do for her or, for that matter, for her younger brothers, scalawags that they were.

The maid, a bright-faced Irish girl, entered the room. She was crisply turned out in a black dress, white frilled apron, a white cap topping her scarlet hair. Her manner was properly subdued despite the humor lurking in the curve of her mouth. Her name was Sophia, bestowed by a mother much taken with the notion of a goddess of wisdom. Former employers had insisted on calling her Bridgit or Mary—names appropriate for those in the servant class—but Mrs. Montgomery used Sophia's proper name, treated her with respect and was rewarded with prompt and diligent service.

"Mrs. DeWitt, ma'am," Sophia announced. She stood aside for a plump, gray-haired lady decked out in a satin damask day dress of blue and gold with a bolero jacket and leg-of-mutton sleeves. With it the woman wore a feathered bonnet complete with net veil, which she properly rolled up as she entered the room.

Cornelia knew without having to be told that Mrs. DeWitt would have left her outer coat, probably her favorite good wool with the ermine trim, in the entry hall. It was perfectly permissible for old friends to remove such garments upon coming to call. Less intimate acquaintances retained their outer garments as a signal that they did not intend to impose very long on one's hospitality.

There were many other such niceties to the art of calling. Indeed, so many that one had to be trained in the etiquette of it from childhood to be confident of not making a mistake. It was rather like the Japanese tea ceremony Cornelia had been reading about not long ago, a seemingly simple exercise concealing subtle complexities that revealed who really belonged and who didn't.

But enough of that, she thought, as she gave her attention to Mrs. DeWitt.

"Too lovely, Cornelia, dear," the matron murmured as she kissed the air beside the younger woman's cheek. "You really should get out more. That poor Bartlett boy is still devastated that you rejected him."

"I thought he went off to Europe and had a roaring good time for himself," Cornelia replied. She liked Davey Bartlett and certainly wished him no ill, but she wasn't about to marry him, either. Never mind his pleasant nature, his fortune and his family's standing. There was something missing between them that she couldn't quite define but wasn't going to do without. That certain something Luciana's heroines always managed to find despite seemingly insurmountable odds.

"All pretense, my dear," Mrs. DeWitt said as she settled herself more comfortably on the couch. "I have it on the most reliable authority that he is still carrying a torch for you."

"Then he had best snuff it out," Cornelia said with a hint of acerbity. "Or he's liable to get his fingers burnt."

Mrs. DeWitt shot her a look of mild reproof but it faded fast. She had other more important matters on her mind.

"Speaking of torches, have you seen today's *Journal?*"

Mrs. Montgomery shook her head. She leaned forward slightly, sensing an amusing bit of gossip. Dear

Muffy—a nickname derived from an excessive child-hood fondness for muffins—read everything and knew everyone. She could always be counted on to be entertaining.

"That absolutely dreadful Peter Lowell." Muffy said it as a compliment. "He can be so provoking. This time he's used his column to lambaste the penny dreadfuls. He says trees shouldn't be cut down to make the paper for printing them. Says they're all poppycock and rot, and that people should be encouraged to read real books. Now mind you, I never touch the things myself but—"

"Really?" Mrs. Montgomery interjected with a smile. "I thought you never missed the latest Reginald Wells mystery, or—what's that other one?—the romance lady, Luciana Montrachet."

Muffy rolled her eyes in dismay. "Mel, I'm surprised at you. You know my tastes are far more enlightened. I positively live for my Chaucer. But never mind. The point is that Mr. Lowell has the most cutting wit. He can be terribly funny but this time he's rather scathing, particularly about poor Miss Montrachet. What he said was really too cruel. I must say, I would hate to ever come under his sights."

As this was hardly a likely prospect, it was passed over without comment. The conversation turned to other matters. Cornelia followed it as best she could, but inside she was seething. As soon as she could, she excused herself and slipped away.

The paper was on the side table in the entry hall along with the morning mail. Cornelia took a cursory look at the letters. There had been a time when she dreaded seeing the bills come in, but no longer. Thanks to Luciana, she need never fear them again. That was something Mr. Peter Lowell—he of the silver spoon—would be incapable of appreciating, never having known a day of want in his gilded life.

She picked up the paper and slipped into the morning room that overlooked the back garden. The warm, comforting scent of toast from breakfast still lingered on the air. Cornelia ignored it as she sat down at the table and hastily paged through the newspaper.

Ordinarily she enjoyed reading the *Journal*. In a city with almost a dozen daily newspapers, it was one of the saner and more reliable. But not today. Today, the *Journal*'s august publisher had seen fit to rip into those he considered *"debasers of our culture, panderers to the unfortunate human urge for the simple, the pat, the nonsensical."* And, if he was to be believed, *"befoulers of our beloved national treasures in that majestic trees, some centuries old, are felled in service to their drossy jottings."*

Cornelia closed the paper with a snap. Her cheeks were flushed and her eyes flashed dangerously. Of all the inane, pretentious, arrogant twaddle she had ever heard, this took the cake!

The nerve of the man. Who did he think he was to criticize the honest work of herself and writers like her who provided innocent entertainment and escape from the rigors of daily life? What service did Mr. Peter Lowell provide except to exploit the labors of his long-suffering employees, those individuals who were actually responsible for getting out the paper each day and who were forced to endure the ill-timed, ignorant and insolent ravings of a man who had never had to do an honest day's work in his life.

In short, Miss Cornelia Montgomery was not well-disposed toward Mr. Peter Lowell. In fact, he made her spit nails.

For a brief but satisfying time, she considered how she might respond to his attack. With very little effort, she could craft a letter of such scathing denunciation that it would be a veritable call to arms against the publisher.

But to write such a letter she would also have to sign it and that she could not do. Her spirits fell as she realized the impossibility of taking such a public stance. It would embarrass her mother, draw attention to herself, and worse yet, risk revealing her true association with she whom the despicable Mr. Lowell chose to dub "Queen of the Penny Dreadfuls."

Really, it was too frustrating. The unfairness of it and her own inability to respond rankled. Reluctantly Cornelia put the paper away and left the morning room. She had things to do—a manuscript to deliver and Christmas presents to buy. It would be foolish for her to dwell on Mr. Peter Lowell and his supercilious notions of what made for the proper use of trees.

Yet, as she set off on her errands, he continued to occupy her thoughts. The man seemed to represent what she had come to dislike most about her own social class, the narrow-minded presumption that individuals endowed with privilege from birth somehow knew best how to order the lives of their less fortunate brethren. For, as she knew all too well, they were also capable of making horrendous mistakes out of greed and stupidity with the direst repercussions for those least able to bear them.

Which was much too grim a thought for this most joyful of seasons. Doing her best to forget it, Cornelia set out on her rounds. She walked because she preferred that to being jostled in a hired carriage. Keeping a private carriage in New York was, to her mind, the height of both extravagance and inconvenience.

At that precise moment, Mr. Peter Lowell's thoughts were tending in a remarkably similar direction. He was seated in the back of his polished black brougham, safely above the slush-strewn streets but was going nowhere fast. Traffic was in its usual snarl as carriages and wagons fought for space in the too-narrow streets. Horses whinnied, drivers cursed, pedestrians squeezed in between as best they could, and what had started out as a pleasant ride downtown from his Fifth Avenue mansion threatened to become a test of endurance.

Mr. Peter Lowell cursed under his breath. Those who knew him as a man of culture and refinement—the ladies of his family, for instance—would have been surprised by the breadth of his vocabulary, not to say shocked. But those who knew him in other ways—the sparring partners at Gentleman Jim's Boxing Club or the habitués of the Red Horse Saloon not far from the stock exchange, for example—would have taken it in stride. They knew a different Peter Lowell, one whom they would never want to go against but would be delighted to have at their back in any fight.

But it was not of the boxing club or the saloon that Lowell thought as he gazed out the window impatiently. Rather, he was remembering the wide-open spaces of the Western frontier from which he had only recently returned. There, where a man could ride all day without ever seeing another human being and where the canopy of stars was the only roof any sane individual would ever desire, he was free of all the responsibilities and demands that had been his lot since earliest manhood. But only temporarily.

As soon as he returned to the city, reality crowded in. His father's death when Peter was barely out of his teens had required him to grow up swiftly and decisively. He had done what was expected of him, taking over the *Journal* and running it with diligence and vision. So, too, had he taken his place in New York society, subscribing to the proper charities, accepting an important role in advising the city's government, and otherwise fulfilling his obligations as a man of standing and substance.

Nor had he neglected the care of his mother and sisters, to whom he was unfailingly patient, gentle and gracious. A slight smile touched his hard mouth as he considered that the only disappointment he had ever inflicted on the ladies of his family was his failure to add another to their numbers. Only that morning his mother had seen fit to remind him yet again that she was not getting any younger and that she longed for grandchildren. That her daughters could, and undoubtedly soon would, provide her with an ample supply did not deter Georgette Lowell from doing her utmost to convince her son to wed. It was a recurring theme with her, which explained, in part, why he maintained a discreet apartment some distance from the family residence to which he could adjourn alone or with suitable company as his mood required.

The patience he had earlier demonstrated with his mother, however, did not extend to New York traffic.

Abruptly he rapped on the roof of the carriage. As it came to a complete halt—having been moving only at the slightest pace—he thrust open the door and got out.

"I'll walk the rest of the way, Fergueson," he said to the gray-haired man in the driver's seat.

"Very good, sir. Shall I return for you this evening?"

Peter shook his head. "It hardly seems worth the effort. I'll make my own way back."

Fergueson nodded, unsurprised. He had known Mr. Peter long enough to be accustomed to his consideration for servants. Which was not to say that he didn't still appreciate it.

"Wind's changed, sir," he commented as he sniffed the air. "Could be a bit more snow tonight."

Peter nodded. "I'll keep that in mind." He strode off down the street, automatically avoiding a pile of steaming horse manure. The wind was fresh, the sky streaked by thin clouds coming from the north. Freed of the carriage, his mood improved. It felt good to stretch his long legs and feel the sun—such as it was— on his face which was still burnished by his days on the high plains.

Had he been asked, Peter would have described himself as a man of average looks. That he could see himself each morning in the shaving mirror and believe that was testament to his innate lack of self-regard. In fact, his strong, chiseled features, thick black hair and green eyes would have been sufficient to draw the attention of any woman even without the added inducement of his tall, powerfully muscled and graceful body. He was not oblivious to the fact that women liked him, he simply didn't think much about why that should be.

Aside, of course, from the obvious consideration of his wealth and position. Although he could deny that he was a cynic, he took it for granted that most of the society women who placed themselves across his path—or were placed there by his mother—had as their primary concern the manner of life to which his wife would automatically be entitled. He didn't blame them for that; it was the way of the world. He simply had no intention of going along with it.

The doorman saw him coming and had the door to the *Journal* building open as he approached. The paper was housed in an elegant four-story structure of Graeco-Roman design built in the earlier years of the century after fire had destroyed much of the old Wall Street area. Recently Peter had startled his employees and excited some comment from the public by installing one of Mr. Otis's electric elevators. Being well pleased with it, he was now prepared to electrify the entire *Journal* building. It would be expensive, but he was convinced electricity was the wave of the future. Just as there were certain other innovations that he did not hesitate to accept.

One of these awaited him as he passed beyond the mahogany-and-glass walls that separated the third-floor newsroom from his inner sanctum. Mirabel Everard was a female of some forty years, a graduate of Miss Stewart's College for Young Ladies, the mother of two daughters, and a widow. She was also a secretary, thanks to Peter's willingness to hire a woman for a job commonly reserved for men. Granted, he had been startled to have her turn up while he was interviewing, but she had quickly impressed him with her intelligence and competency. He had decided to take a chance and had been glad ever since that he had. She kept his professional life in order, showed absolutely no interest in his personal affairs and was unfailingly pleasant.

Except for this morning, when he thought he detected a slight frown as she brought in the stack of morning mail.

"Is something wrong, Mrs. Everard?" he inquired as he glanced through the pile of messages.

Although austerely dressed as always with a high-collared dress of sensible blue serge, Mirabel Everard was not an unattractive woman. When not at work, she enjoyed an active life with her daughters and a certain gentleman of her acquaintance for whom she might eventually be persuaded to give up her widowed state. She was also a devoted reader whose taste encompassed everything from the love sonnets of Shakespeare to the writings of Miss Luciana Montrachet. While not precisely willing to advertise her allegiance to Miss Montrachet, neither was Mrs. Everard entirely able to overlook the dreadful slight done to her favorite authoress's name.

She cleared her throat and said, "Not at all, sir. I was merely somewhat taken aback by your column this morning."

She did not elaborate, but then she didn't have to. One look at her shuttered face was enough to inform Peter that he had done something regrettable. But his conscience was clear and he didn't waste time worrying about it. Whatever small inconsideration he might have committed, he was certain she would forgive him quickly enough, and in the meantime it would never be permitted to affect the performance of her duties.

Mrs. Everard took herself off a short time later, leaving Peter to glance through the mail. Several items caught his eye, among them a note from his good friend Teddy Roosevelt asking when they were once again going to shake the dust of the city from their boots and head back out West. Teddy was biding his time serving on the Civil Service Commission, which was attempting to put an end to the greed and corruption that plagued the city's government. At thirty-four, he was stouthearted, brash, and the best companion in adventure a man could ask for. Everyone agreed Teddy was going places, although no one—including Teddy himself—had any idea where.

Peter was tempted to have Mrs. Everard place a telephone call to Teddy using the instrument lately installed on her desk, but he decided a note would suffice. Regrettably, he couldn't suggest they forget everything else and leave immediately. Duty demanded otherwise.

He discarded several other letters and made notes on a few for Mrs. Everard's action. Near the bottom of the pile was a brief message from the publisher Jonathan Withers, reminding him of a holiday soiree Withers was giving at the end of the week. Peter planned to attend, indeed, was looking forward to it.

His correspondence finished, he settled himself more comfortably behind his large oak desk, loosened his tie and got down to work. Steadily and methodically, he read his way through all the morning papers, mentally comparing each to the edition of the *Journal* he had read before leaving for work. In general, he was satisfied that his own paper led the pack, but he wasn't about to rest on his laurels. There was always room for improvement.

Take his daily column, for instance. In retrospect, it probably hadn't been necessary to call Miss Luciana Montrachet both a "purveyor of false sentiment" and an "unrivaled example of the deterioration of popular literature." One such phrase would have been enough.

Beyond that, he gave no thought at all to the woman he had savaged in print across hundreds of thousands of breakfast tables. So far as he was concerned, the matter was over and done with.

He was wrong, of course, but only one individual knew that and he wasn't talking. Indeed, at the moment, all Jonathan Withers was doing was listening.

Chapter Two

"I really didn't mean to get into this," Cornelia said. She was seated in the guest chair across from Jonathan's desk. Her hands were neatly folded in her lap. Beneath her long skirt her ankles were properly crossed. Her back was as erect as anyone could wish. Nothing in her manner revealed anything more than the mildest disquiet.

Jonathan was not fooled. He had known Cornelia most of her life and had worked with her for almost four years. The slight tremor in her voice and the shadows behind her normally bright azure eyes told him more than he really wished to know.

Silently he cursed Peter Lowell. Never mind that the man was his friend and that Jonathan genuinely admired him, Lowell's opinions on popular literature were, at the very least, regrettable. Even more unfortunate was the fact that he had seen fit to declare them so publicly.

"It's quite all right, my dear," he said. "You have every right to be upset. Lowell's attack was unfair and, I dare say, the result of ignorance. It's an odd thing, but otherwise intelligent and honorable people who wouldn't dream of expressing an opinion about a subject they know nothing about will waive that consideration when it comes to something like popular literature. They will make the most astounding assertions completely without evidence, and they won't think anything of doing so. I must say, I can't understand that.''

"I can," Cornelia replied. "Let us be honest here, Jonathan. Mr. Lowell didn't attack Mr. Reginald Wells for his mysteries or Mr. Paddy O'Shea for his adventure stories or any of a dozen other male authors I could mention. He attacked the books women like to read and he did so with utter contempt for our sensibilities. Clearly, Mr. Lowell is a misogynist."

Jonathan winced. He ran a hand through his thick, silvered hair and blinked twice, a sure sign that she was making him nervous. "That's a bit harsh. He's really quite a decent fellow."

"To other men, perhaps. Not to women."

And that, so far as Cornelia was concerned, was that. She had considered Mr. Lowell, found him wanting, and catalogued him neatly in her mind. And what a mind it was, Jonathan thought with just a hint of discomfiture. Was it possible that proper Miss Cornelia Montgomery, who by this time in her life ought to be married with a nice proper husband and several very proper children, was instead bidding fair to become—he shuddered at the thought—a *suffragette?*

Now that he thought about it, there was an undeniable streak of independence in her more recent heroines, something that had not been so evident at the beginning.

And now that he further thought about it, sales of her books were steadily increasing. Women who had never deigned to read them before were beginning to do so, if only secretly. Quite a few were even writing in to say that the books influenced their lives.

For a moment, he felt a flicker of concern that he might, all unknowingly, be helping to spread radical notions of female emancipation, however prettily packaged and sugarcoated. Knowing Cornelia as he did, he couldn't dismiss the notion out of hand, but he could put it in its proper perspective. Luciana Montrachet's books made money, a great deal of it. And that, so far as Jonathan was concerned, automatically made them good. They helped him to run a publishing company that actually turned a profit, no small feat when most such firms were owned by rich men whose sole objective was to demonstrate that they were—all other evidence to the contrary—gentlemen of culture and refinement.

"I'm sure the new book is splendid," Jonathan said, and he meant it. After getting over his initial shock at discovering that William Montgomery's maiden daughter possessed an imagination more suitable to a woman of the world, he had come to accept her reliability. This Luciana Montrachet would be at least as good as the others, it would sell at least as well, and all would be well in the world. At least so long as Cornelia chose to continue exercising her particular talent.

Which raised an unsettling question in Jonathan's mind. Given that the Montgomery family's financial condition was once again healthy, did Cornelia intend to keep on writing? Especially in light of the hurt inflicted on her by Lowell's attack, she just might decide to give it all up.

The possibility worried him, and not merely because of the financial implications.

"My dear," he said gently, "don't let this sorry business get you down. There is nothing to say that Mr. Lowell couldn't be persuaded to change his mind."

"Please don't attempt to do so," Cornelia said. She stood, smoothed her skirt and gave Jonathan a smile. "I am quite reconciled to the ways of the world, even if Mr. Lowell thinks me woefully ignorant of them."

Jonathan frowned. He did not like to think of any woman as young, beautiful and blessed as Cornelia being reconciled to anything. Although he was thirty years her senior and had known at least his share of disappointments, he still believed that life was full of marvelous possibilities. Cornelia seemed in danger of forgetting that.

But not, he thought, if he had anything to say about it. He owed his favorite authoress that much.

As he walked her to the door, his hand lightly guiding her elbow, he asked, "Shall you be joining us Friday?"

"Of course," Cornelia replied, surprised that he'd had any doubt. Her mother had accepted the invitation on behalf of all of them.

"Excellent," Jonathan said. He smiled. "Till then, my dear, and do try not to think too badly of Lowell. He does have some good points."

Cornelia didn't disagree, but privately she was convinced that nothing would ever change her opinion of the despicable Mr. Lowell. Nothing whatsoever.

By Friday, Cornelia had succeeded in putting all thought of Peter Lowell and his opinions out of her mind. Christmas was a scant two weeks away. The streets were thronged with holiday shoppers. Skaters abounded on the Central Park lake. Along the road north to Bloomingdale Village, sleigh bells rang as festive parties set off for a day in the countryside barely a few miles beyond the city.

Cornelia was looking forward to Jonathan's party. After the months of laboring over her new books, she was enjoying a brief respite before beginning her next one. She had gone so far as to indulge in several new outfits for the holidays, to the surprise and delight of her mother, who feared that Cornelia lacked sufficient interest in such matters.

Her dress for the evening was a concoction of white India silk with violet flowers around a narrow waist, from which they fell in profusion to encircle the hem. Froths of Bruges lace spilled from the elbow-length sleeves and along a bodice that was rather more daringly cut than any she had worn before. Her mother would undoubtedly think it too daring for an unmarried woman, even one of twenty-six, but Cornelia did not let that worry her. The dress made her think of spring. It reminded her that life was always there, even if hidden beneath the surface, only waiting to be released.

Sophia oohed and aahed over the dress when she saw it. "You'll be the belle of the ball, miss," she said as she dressed Cornelia's hair. She was delighted that her young mistress had agreed to dispense with her usual sensible chignon. Instead, Sophia arranged her hair in ringlets interlaced with violet ribbons that tumbled over the smooth alabaster skin of her bare shoulders.

"Hardly that," Cornelia said. "I'm far too old, for one thing. And besides, to be a belle, one needs a certain presence I could never manage."

"A certain silliness is more like it, if you ask me. I've friends working for some very high and fine society ladies, the sort we're all supposed to admire. Think the world revolves around them, they do. Don't give a fig for anyone else's feelings.''

Cornelia nodded. She knew the type well enough, having encountered them all her life. At six, they were the little girls who refused to dirty their hands, took no part in roughhousing and looked down their pert noses at anyone who failed to meet their exalted standards. By twelve, they were bunched together in remorseless cliques, whispering behind their hands about the shortcomings of this girl or that. At eighteen, they were lethal, utterly devoted to the single, all-important task of making a Brilliant Marriage, considering only wealth and position; the man himself was regarded as unimportant, whatever his virtues or lack of them.

But by the time they reached Cornelia's age, she had observed that a certain brittleness began to set in. They were constantly on the lookout for any slight—imagined or otherwise—to their self-importance, constantly striving to reassure themselves that they were still beautiful, still desirable, still important. Their husbands they saw rarely, their children even less. They had numerous female acquaintances but no friends. Their only close relationships seemed to be among a small group of men—attractive, sophisticated, witty, yet ultimately aloof—who made it their business to escort the ladies to parties, decorate their homes and advise them on virtually everything. All well and good, Cornelia thought, but not to her own taste.

When Sophia was finished, Cornelia thanked her. Alone again in her room, she stood in front of the full-length framed mirror and studied herself. Having already seen the dress several times while it was being fitted, she wasn't prepared for the quiver of surprise that went through her as the woman in the mirror stared back. Was that really her, that creature of unabashed femininity and grace? She looked utterly different from sensible Miss Cornelia Montgomery and rather shockingly like one of Luciana's own heroines.

How ridiculous to entertain such a notion, she thought with a shake of her head that set the chestnut curls to bouncing. No matter what she looked like, she was still very much herself. She would go to Jonathan's, have a good time and come home at a sensible hour. In a few weeks, the holidays would be over and she would be back to work.

Her life was well-ordered, peaceful and much to her satisfaction. Had the thought occurred to her that she was about to walk out of her bedroom and into another life entirely, she would have dismissed it as absurd. No such possibility clouded her mind as she picked up her skirts, gave a final glance around the room to see if she had forgotten anything and walked out the door.

Jonathan's residence was one of the newer brownstone houses along Madison Avenue, not far removed from the stretch of Fifth Avenue where the very rich were busy building palaces to rival anything seen in Paris or Rome. His was a more modest dwelling by far but still ample for a single man of taste who liked to live surrounded by his books and his friends. He had moved to the house several years before from the downtown residence where he had lived for several decades with his wife. Upon her death, finding the memories too hard to bear, he chose to start afresh. The result was an abode that, though unabashedly masculine, was also comfortable and welcoming.

Lights shone in all the windows and a long line of carriages waiting outside spoke to the early success of the gathering as Peter arrived. He was late, having been held up at the paper by a breaking story concerning an escape from the Tombs prison. New Yorkers would awaken to the news that three suspected murderers were once again loose among them. Undoubtedly, they would take it in stride, as they did all else.

A butler, hired for the evening, greeted him at the door and assisted him out of his topcoat. Beneath, he wore severely cut evening dress, the trousers and coat of black worsted, the waistcoat of white silk over a white shirt devoid of the usual frills other men favored. His black hair was brushed back from his forehead and left free of pomade. The whiteness of the shirt and waistcoat accentuated his tan. As he stood in the entry hall, surveying the crowd, several women cast surreptitious glances his way. He was bigger than the other men but more than that, he lacked their urbane softness. There was a hard strength about him, a certain relentlessness that was both appealing and threatening at the same time. Eyelashes fluttered behind lace fans, cheeks flushed slightly, and rare was the feminine heart that did not beat more swiftly at the sight of him.

Peter exchanged nods with several gentlemen of his acquaintance as he made his way into the parlor where his host was greeting guests. Jonathan saw him at once and came over to welcome him. The publisher looked particularly well that evening, his silver hair gleaming in the gaslight. The soft hiss of the lamps was drowned out by the chatter of the guests. The scent of pine drifted on the air from the big Christmas tree set up in one corner and the many wreaths hung about the room. A roaring fire and the clink of glasses completed the impression of a happy gathering well prepared to celebrate the holidays.

"Good of you to come, Peter," Jonathan said as he held out a hand. "How are things at the *Journal?*"

"Busy as usual. A friend of mine was saying the other day that barely had the Old Dutch settled here than they began complaining that the city was growing too fast, people were always getting into trouble, and that there was no peace anywhere. It seems nothing has changed."

Jonathan laughed as he accepted two glasses from a passing waiter and handed one to Peter. The men toasted each other. "But if they did," Jonathan said when he had taken a sip of the good French champagne, "you'd have nothing to write about."

"True enough," Peter agreed. He took another sip of the wine and was just lowering the glass when a sudden flash of color ahead of him caught his attention. His eyes narrowed, hardening as they came to rest on the woman who looked as though she had stepped from a spring garden. She was laughing at something the man next to her had said. Her face was beautiful without artifice, her enjoyment spontaneous and genuine. Against the red brocade wallpaper, her bare shoulders and the visible swell of her full breasts looked like cream touched by honey. His gaze moved over her, observing the riot of chestnut-hued curls tumbling over her shoulders, the narrow waist and gently swelling hips. She was taller than the other women, slender, with an erect carriage and a proud but not haughty tilt to her head. Laughter danced in her eyes. Looking at her, Peter felt as though a window had suddenly blown open in his mind, admitting a breeze redolent of sun-drenched fields filled with wildflowers, newly mowed hay and the sweet, tantalizing scent of a woman's skin close against his own.

For a moment, the sensation of suddenly standing in another time and place, utterly apart from the everyday world, was overpowering. He shook his head to clear it and realized he was gripping the delicate champagne flute so tightly it was in danger of cracking. Carefully he set it down on a nearby table and turned to Jonathan.

"Who is she?"

The question was stark and to the point. It was also not unexpected. Jonathan was far too shrewd and worldly a man not to realize immediately that his young friend was in the grip of what the French so aptly called a *coup de foudre,* the sudden and utterly unexpected attraction that could not be resisted.

Here he had spent the past few days wondering off and on what would happen when his two friends, one of whom had managed all-unknowingly to mortally offend the other, crossed paths in his parlor. He had told himself not to worry, that they were both civilized individuals who would behave properly under any circumstances. But he had been concerned all the same.

And now this.

He cast a wary glance in Cornelia's direction, marveling once again at how very well she looked. She had always been a lovely young woman, but tonight she positively glowed. In hindsight, it was not at all surprising that Peter should be interested in her.

Mentally girding himself for whatever might come, Jonathan said calmly, "She is Miss Cornelia Montgomery. Her father was the banker, William Montgomery. He died several years ago. Cornelia resides with her mother and her two younger brothers at their Gramercy Park home. I have the honor to consider them my friends.''

Peter nodded slowly, his eyes still on the radiant Miss Montgomery. In a few succinct sentences, Jonathan had told him a great deal. Namely, that the woman in question was a member in good standing of their own social class, well-off if not necessarily rich, eminently respectable, a person Jonathan cared about and would not wish to see treated lightly.

And women claimed only they could communicate reams with a few well-chosen words.

''Would you like to meet her?'' Jonathan inquired, observing that his friend's preoccupation had in no way lessened.

Peter hesitated an instant. He had spent the better part of his manhood avoiding the snares set by eminently respectable young ladies of his social class. It was not his habit to deliberately put himself in their path. But as he watched Miss Cornelia Montgomery's eyes sparkle and listened again to her delightful laugh, he had no doubt he was about to do exactly that.

''Yes,'' he said.

Jonathan suppressed a sigh. He had a sudden sense of being about to walk into the lion's den.

Or more correctly in this case, the lioness's.

''As you wish,'' he murmured, and began making his way through the crowd toward where Cornelia was standing.

She saw him coming and smiled a greeting. But her gaze rested on the man with him. ''Hello, Jonathan,'' she said. ''It's a lovely party.''

"Thank you, my dear. I'm delighted that you are having such a good time and I hope you will continue to do so."

Cornelia cast him a puzzled look. That seemed an odd sort of thing to say, as though he thought she might suddenly stop enjoying herself. Odder still was the way he was clearly hesitating to present the man at his side. Ordinarily she wouldn't have minded, being something less than a stickler for etiquette. But she found herself wanting to know who he was, this man who had suddenly seized her attention so that she barely heard one of the other guests when he said, "Lowell, good to see you. I thought you were still out in the wilds somewhere. When did you get back?"

"About a month ago," Peter said quietly. He turned his attention to the other man long enough to be polite. When he looked back, Miss Cornelia Montgomery was staring at him most peculiarly.

Jonathan laid a gentle hand on her arm. "As I was about to say, my dear, this is Mr. Peter Lowell. He is the publisher of the *Journal,* as I believe you are aware."

"Yes," Cornelia murmured. Her voice sounded strangled even to her own ears. *This* was the despicable Peter Lowell? This tall, powerfully built man with the chiseled features and the compelling eyes? This man who made her breath catch in her throat and whom she had only to glance at to feel the strangest warmth curling deep within her? What dreadful joke was this that Nature should arrange for her to be so affected by the one man she had reason to hold in the utmost contempt?

"Miss Montgomery," Peter said. He inclined his head.

"If you would excuse me," she replied coolly, "I see someone I really must speak with."

Without further ado, she gathered up her skirts and departed. Peter stood stock-still, attempting to absorb what had just happened. Unless he was very much mistaken, Miss Cornelia Montgomery had just cut him. His slanting brows—raven's wings, one female of his acquaintance had called them—drew together ominously.

Jonathan cleared his throat. "You must excuse Cornelia," he said. "She is actually rather shy."

Peter looked at him skeptically. "Really? I thought she was merely rude."

"She has been out in society less than most young ladies, in part because of her father's untimely death. But there is more to it than that. She is singularly lacking in the ambitions common to her sex."

"Such as?" Peter asked, still curious despite himself.

Jonathan hesitated. Prudence dictated that he say nothing more, yet he found the urge to do so irresistible. Cornelia and Peter happened to be two of his favorite people, individuals he admired and respected. Both of them refused to be ruled by the conformities of their age. Both were intelligent, spirited and utterly honorable. And neither had yet found that special person with whom they might properly share their lives.

He thought of his own happy years with his wife and of how much he still missed her. At the rate they were going, his young friends would never know such sweet, life-enhancing pleasure.

Although he had never aspired to the role of matchmaker, Jonathan found himself seriously considering it. He eased his doubts by reminding himself that he was not the first agent to bring them together. In an odd sort of way, that had already been accomplished by the controversial Miss Luciana Montrachet.

"Marriage," Jonathan said simply. He hid a smile at the effect the word alone had on Peter. The younger man flinched. As though blithely unaware of the impact of what he was about to impart, Jonathan continued.

"I have never heard her speak against it, but neither have I seen any evidence that she desires it. Davey Bartlett proposed to her last year and she turned him down. Did it perfectly nicely, I'm told, and they do remain friends, but there could hardly be a clearer indication that she is of a more independent turn of mind. If I'm not mistaken, Bartlett is considered a plum catch."

Thinking of what he knew about the young Bartlett, Peter had to agree. The family was almost as wealthy as his own and he had never heard of any blot on the gentleman's character that would discourage a lady from accepting his suit. Whatever else she might be, Miss Cornelia Montgomery was clearly no fortune hunter.

He looked in her direction, observing her speaking with two young men who were standing near the buffet table. Once again, she looked relaxed, congenial and utterly charming. It seemed she was that way to everyone except himself.

Standing tall and dark, his sea green eyes glinting as he surveyed the scene, Peter accepted a second glass of champagne. He barely tasted the crisp wine as it slid down his throat. All his attention was focused on the chestnut-haired beauty who had defied him.

A slight smile curved his hard mouth. He was behaving in a thoroughly predictable fashion, but he couldn't seem to prevent it. After a lifetime of being indulged, fawned over and generally spoiled by the women of his social class, he had discovered one who would not even deign to engage in casual conversation with him. Naturally enough, he found her irresistible.

A low laugh broke from him, drawing startled looks from those standing nearby. He ignored them and continued to study the young woman who had, all-unknowingly, aroused his hunter's instinct.

It made no difference that they were standing in a formal parlor surrounded by all the trappings of civilization. The urges stirring within him were as ancient as time itself.

The only question was what to do about them.

Chapter Three

Cornelia woke the following morning uneasy in her conscience. She knew she had not behaved well the previous evening and that troubled her. Not that the despicable Mr. Lowell didn't deserve the coldest of shoulders; he most certainly did. The problem was that he didn't know why he did and she was in no position to tell him. Beyond that, Jonathan had deserved better than to have two of his guests so at odds with each other, particularly in a season where it was incumbent upon all to show charity and forgiveness.

She would write Jonathan a note of apology first thing, she decided. It was the least she could do.

With that accomplished, she bathed and dressed, arriving downstairs to find the morning room deserted. It was only a little after eight o'clock but her brothers—taking advantage of the holiday from school—were still abed, as was her mother. Melanie Montgomery needed her rest. She was out of practice regarding the strenuous round of social engagements that characterized Christmas in the city. This was the first year since her husband's death that she had fully taken part. Cornelia was delighted to see her mother emerge from her semi-isolation, but she hoped she wouldn't overdo.

As for her brothers, the amount of food and sleep required by two teenage boys never failed to astound her. They never seemed to have enough of both.

A light snow was falling outside as she finished breakfast. She lingered over a cup of tea, reading the morning *Globe,* to which she had recently begun subscribing. The Montgomerys continued taking the *Journal*—Cornelia could hardly request that it be stopped without raising questions she did not care to answer—but she no longer read it. Whomever Mr. Peter Lowell had chosen to pillory on this particular morning, he would have to do it without her.

Regrettably, the *Globe* simply did not hold her attention as well as the *Journal* had always done. She finished it too quickly and sat staring out the window, watching the fluffy white flakes drift by as she tried to decide what to do with the day.

Her mother would be paying calls later and she could go along, but the idea had little appeal. She felt unaccustomedly restless and unable to settle on any of her usual pursuits. Her thoughts kept returning to Jonathan's party and most particularly to Mr. Peter Lowell. Try though she did, she could not banish the image of his tall, muscular body, his burnished features, the flash of his smile, the . . .

"Damnation," Cornelia muttered under her breath. It was as strong a word as she ever used, but under the circumstances she thought it apt. She was acting like one of Luciana's heroines instead of like her own sensible self. In another moment, she would find herself wishing that she might see the gentleman again, might even be afforded another opportunity to make his acquaintance.

Clearly she was in need of some restorative to clear away whatever was befogging her mind. Plain old hard work, that was the thing. She'd help Sophia polish the silver and then perhaps tackle the attic, which was in sore need of straightening.

But the silver was already done and the attic, when she climbed the stairs to peer into it, was so uninviting that she couldn't bear the thought of sequestering herself there. As she climbed back down, dusting off her skirt, the younger of her brothers emerged from his room. Ted rubbed his eyes, grinned sleepily at her and said, "Is breakfast ready yet?"

"Of course it's ready, you lout," she replied, not unfondly. "It's almost nine o'clock. If you wait a bit longer, you can have lunch."

"That's ages off," Ted claimed. He ran a hand through rumpled blond hair, shot her another grin and ambled on downstairs. As he did, the door next to his opened and his twin appeared.

Jed was the older of the two by all of ten minutes and never ceased to remind Ted of it. Although they were not identical, both were blond haired and blue eyed, and they shared the same engaging smile. At seventeen, they were far removed from the endearing little boys Cornelia had helped her overwhelmed mother to care for.

The twins had arrived after the Montgomerys had been married for almost ten years, at a time when they had come to believe they would be blessed with no children other than their beloved daughter. The discovery that there was to be another had been met by great joy by all concerned including Cornelia. The revelation that there was not one but two and that both were boys had provoked dumbfounded amazement. Even now, Cornelia would occasionally catch her mother staring at her two tall, stalwart sons with a look in her eye that suggested she had never quite figured out how they came to be.

"Are those cinnamon buns I smell?" Jed asked hopefully.

"Only if you hurry. Ted's already down there."

No further encouragement was needed. Jed hurried down the stairs as Cornelia followed at a more sedate pace. By the time she reached the morning room, her brothers were at the table. Their appetites did not make them forget their manners. They rose as she entered and Jed held out a chair for her.

"Good party yesterday," Ted said when they were all seated. "It was decent of Mr. Withers to include us."

"He knew Father very well," Cornelia replied, "and he has remained a good friend. Besides," she added with a smile, "you are old enough now for civilized company."

Jed shot her a reproving look. He was the more serious of the two and consequently more concerned with his dignity. "Of course we are. It's not as though we were still in short pants."

"There are lads our age fighting with the cavalry out West," Ted said. He looked as though he relished the thought.

"You'll be off soon enough," Cornelia said, not a little wistfully. They were both bound for Princeton in the coming year, their father's alma mater. The house would be very quiet once they were gone.

"But in the meantime," Jed said as he speared a sausage, "we've actually got a few days off. We thought we'd go for a jaunt up Harlem Lane. Want to come?"

"Isn't it a bit late in the year for that?" Cornelia asked. The lane—actually a fairly broad road running north out of Central Park—was one of her favorite parts of New York. At its base, closest to the park, was a collection of inns whose deep porches offered the perfect venue for observing the goings-on along the road.

And what goings-on they were. The elite of New York's horsey set gathered there to race their elegant equipages past the open fields and farms that covered the upper part of Manhattan Island. The road ran as far as 168th Street, where it intersected the old Bloomingdale Road, more commonly called Broadway. That was far out in the country indeed. The numbered street designation was misleading, as it existed only in the minds of mapmakers and developers who had gone so far as to grid the entire island from the Bowery to the Harlem River.

"The snow is stopping," Ted observed as he glanced out the window. "I can see a patch of blue. Should be a perfect day for the country."

Cornelia was tempted. As much as she loved the Christmas season, she was tired of struggling through the teeming streets. The crush of people, horses, carriages and wagons made her head throb and the noise left her ears ringing. Ted was right. A day in the country would be just the thing.

"I'll only need a minute," she said as she got up from the table.

Her brothers grinned, knowing it would more likely be half an hour or so before she was ready. Even their sister, a model of sensibleness and practicality among womankind, needed at least that much time to appear properly in public.

By the time Cornelia returned, the snow had stopped and the sky was clearing. She wore a simple day dress of daffodil-yellow wool with a high collar, modestly puffed sleeves, and one of the newer bustleless skirts that were so much more comfortable than the older style. Over it, she donned a bright blue coat with velvet collar and cuffs. Her hair was swept up and partially concealed by a pert black trilby decorated with a sweep of black feathers. She carried an ermine muff, a gift from her brothers the previous Christmas. Her eyes glowed with anticipation and a faint becoming flush warmed her cheeks.

The boys were ready and waiting. They each sketched a bow before offering their arms. She exited the house with one on either side, calling over her shoulder for Sophia to tell their mother where they had gone.

Two blocks away were the Stuyvesant Stables, where they quickly secured the use of a coach drawn by a pair of fast trotters. Ted took the reins and they were off. Going north along Fifth Avenue, they passed the impressive marble edifices of the Astor, Vanderbilt and Stewart mansions among others, those mammoth monuments to wealth and enterprise that were helping to lead the march north from what had been the city's limits.

Now there seemed to be none. Rows of neat brownstones were under construction everywhere. Three or four would be standing linked together, surrounded by cleared fields awaiting those yet to come. After a space of half a block or so, there would another cluster in a slightly different style. Eventually, Cornelia supposed, they would all be linked together, the pitted and rutted dirt roads would be paved, and people would flock to live in them. But she still had a hard time realizing that the city was truly destined to become that big.

By contrast, the Central Park remained a blessed enclave of peace and civility. Skaters could be seen gliding over the pond near the park's southern entrance. They continued at a brisk pace and were shortly in much lighter traffic as the buildings and vacant lots thinned out, giving way to squatters' shanties, the occasional old farm house, and here and there a tumble-down barn, some still in use.

At the tip of the park, near Harlem Lane, they drew rein in front of Toppy McGuire's Clubhouse, a rambling white clapboard structure that even at this time of year attracted a fair share of patrons. The bright day had coaxed others out with the same idea. They had to wait in line for several minutes before hitching the trotters to one of the posts in front of the building.

Once inside, they were immediately engulfed in warmth and good companionship. A log as big as a man's chest burned in the stone-manteled fireplace. Pine boughs scented the air along with mulled apple cider simmering in vats on the potbellied stove that stood near the bar. McGuire's was unusual in that it was a man's place that nonetheless admitted women. But then, Cornelia thought wryly, without the fair sex there would be no one to show off for and the entire exercise would be made that much less satisfying.

They had warmed their hands by the fire and been shown to a table near the window when Cornelia realized that it would be prudent to visit the ladies' retiring room. She excused herself as her brothers were ordering a luncheon of smoked duck, sausage, roast potatoes, applesauce and, of course, the justly famous mulled cider. All this despite the breakfast they had devoured scarcely two hours before.

The ladies' convenience was hardly as well fitted out as those found in establishments more congenial to the fair sex—it lacked a maid, for one thing, to assist with minor repairs to one's costume or coiffeur. But Cornelia managed all the same. She was returning to the table when her path crossed that of a portly red-faced gentleman who lurched toward her, somewhat the worse for whatever he had been drinking.

Cornelia frowned and stepped out of the way. Unlike many ladies of her acquaintance, she did not subscribe to the notion that drunkenness was a problem restricted to the lower orders. Therefore she was not particularly surprised to encounter it. She presumed the gentleman would move on as best he could, freeing her to do the same. But there she was mistaken.

Instead, he stopped suddenly and peered at her. A slow, lopsided smile spread across his florid features.

"What's thish then?" he inquired loudly. "A li'l bird. Canary, I warrant. Give us a song, swee'heart."

Cornelia ignored him and attempted to pass, but the space was too narrow and the gentleman—if that was the word—too persistent. He stepped in front of her, his smile taking on an unpleasant quality as his eyes ran over her.

"Pretty bird," he said.

Despite herself, Cornelia flushed. This was really going too far. It was absolutely unthinkable that a man would address an unknown woman of her class in such a way. In public, men of sensibility avoided making even eye contact with women they did not know, and women did the same. To prevent her passage, speak to her without permission, and subject her to such a lewd appraisal was more than she could possibly tolerate.

"Step aside, sir," she said firmly, hoping that he could not hear the suddenly rapid beating of her heart. Although she was by no means easily intimidated, the situation was sufficiently outside of her experience to concern her. The sooner it was over, the more relieved she would be.

But the man in question apparently had no intention of ending it quickly. On the contrary, he seemed to find her predicament much to his liking.

"Regular li'l bluenose, aren't you?" he said, his leer deepening. "Somebody ought to teach you better manners. I'm just the man to—"

Whatever else he had been about to say was lost. One moment he was directly in front of Cornelia, just about at her eye level, and the next he was considerably higher. Instinctively she glanced down. His feet were no longer on the ground. Instead, they flopped helplessly in the air.

The experience of levitation appeared to do nothing for the man's equanimity. His already florid complexion turned an alarming shade of purple. The garbled sounds coming from his throat communicated acute distress.

"Good afternoon, Miss Montgomery," Peter Lowell said pleasantly. "Is there anywhere in particular you would like me to put this?"

Cornelia took a quick breath, pressed her hands into the folds of her skirt to conceal their trembling and said, "The gentleman appears somewhat the worse for wear. Perhaps it would be best if he left?"

Peter nodded cordially. In the shadows of the hall, his ebony hair appeared almost blue-black. The burnished planes and angles of his face appeared more harshly carved than usual. There was a hint of censure in his voice as he said, "I presume you are not here alone?"

"Of course not," Cornelia replied coolly. His assistance—as regrettably necessary as it had been—did not give him leave to stand in judgment of her.

"I accompanied my brothers," she said. "They are at a table further inside." A strangled sound drew her attention. Matter-of-factly, she said, "His eyes are beginning to roll up in his head. I think you should put him down."

Peter scowled but saw that she was correct. He loosened his grip. The man's legs gave way and he collapsed to the floor, gasping for breath. Fearfully he looked up at Peter. What he saw saved him the trouble of even trying to rise. On hands and knees, he scurried toward the back door.

"I owe you my thanks," Cornelia said when he was gone. She spoke courteously, but her reluctance was evident.

A faint smile lifted the corners of Peter's mouth. He was pleased to discover that he could find some humor in the situation. The terrible rage that had engulfed him at the moment when he looked toward the back of the inn and saw her being accosted was beginning to abate. He no longer felt the urge to commit murder. Rather, what he most wanted now was to satisfy his curiosity about the lovely and defiant Miss Cornelia Montgomery.

"Allow me to escort you," he said. It was, in fact, far more of a command than a request and Cornelia did not mistake it for anything else. Peter offered his arm. With as much grace as she could muster, she took it. She felt a tremor of shock at the hard, unrelenting strength beneath her fingers. For a moment, she had an overwhelming sense that the finely tailored broadcloth she touched was no more than the thinnest veneer of civilization barely concealing something far more primal and dangerous. With a concerted effort of will, she thrust the thought aside and allowed him to lead her to her brothers' table.

The twins saw them coming and jumped to their feet. Both frowned as they saw their sister in the company of a stranger. "Is everything all right, Cornelia?" Jed asked, his eyes not on his sister but on the tall, powerful man beside her.

"Perfectly," she said. "May I introduce Mr. Peter Lowell? He was kind enough to assist me with a small problem."

She felt a twinge of guilt at so minimizing what had in fact been a very unpleasant situation, but her rescuer didn't seem to mind. He merely smiled and extended his hand to each of the brothers. "I believe you were at Jonathan's party yesterday, weren't you? There were so many people I didn't get to speak with everyone."

"Indeed we were, Mr. Lowell," Jed said, sounding very grown-up. Cornelia cast him a quick glance. Her normally unruffable brother looked inordinately pleased. It didn't take long to figure out why.

"I've read all your articles," Jed said. Indicating his brother, he added, "We both have. I hope you won't mind my saying that they were brilliant, particularly your dispatches from the frontier. You have had some extraordinary experiences out there."

"Nothing really unusual," Peter assured him. "It's an extraordinary place."

"We have every hope of seeing it for ourselves before too much longer," Ted said, drawing a startled look from Cornelia, who knew nothing of any such plans. She made a mental note to inquire about them, but not just then. Her brother appeared far too preoccupied. He clearly shared Jed's pleasure in meeting a man for whom they both might be accused of harboring a case of hero worship.

Cornelia repressed a sigh. This was too typical. Never mind about her, the poor beleaguered female, the men were off and running.

"You will join us, won't you?" Jed inquired. "It seems everybody and his cousin decided to come to McGuire's today. There aren't many tables left."

It was difficult to argue with this observation, although Cornelia suspected that Toppy McGuire would manage to accommodate Mr. Peter Lowell under any circumstances. Rather than point this out, she said mildly, "Mr. Lowell may have other plans, Jed."

Indeed, she most fervently hoped that would be the case, but Mr. Peter Lowell disappointed her. The look in his startlingly green eyes suggested he knew exactly what she was thinking as he said, "None at all. My rig's tied up outside and, truth be told, I'm starving. I'd be delighted to join you."

Nothing could have pleased the twins more. They positively preened at the notion that a man of his stature and reputation accepted them as equals, worthy of dining with. It was enough to make Cornelia wonder—not for the first time—at the intelligence of the male sex, but she managed to conceal her annoyance. He had, after all, done her a service and it would be churlish not to recognize that.

Nevertheless, she had not bargained for what the response would be when, toward the end of what turned out to be an unexpectedly congenial lunch, Mr. Peter Lowell kindly suggested that her brothers might like to try out his pair of trotters. It seemed that all the city, failing herself, knew Lowell's grays were the fastest and most daring to be found. They had won some race or other the previous year that had everyone talking. The twins were at first dumbfounded and then ecstatic that he should make such an offer.

That left only the small problem of their sister, whom they were clearly not anxious to take on whatever madcap dash they were contemplating. "Perhaps Miss Montgomery would care to accompany me in your hired rig?" Peter suggested helpfully.

Which was how Cornelia came to be seated alone in a carriage next to the man whom she had sworn only scant days before to despise forever. Under such disconcerting circumstances, was it any surprise that she found herself wondering how the far wiser and more worldly Luciana would handle the situation?

Chapter Four

Luciana would undoubtedly have turned the situation to her own advantage, but Cornelia could not begin to imagine how to do that. It was not entirely improper for her to be alone in a carriage with Peter Lowell—they had been formally introduced. But it was damnably disconcerting.

Barely had they left the hitching yard in front of the club than her brothers vanished from sight, gone in a cloud of dust up the lane. The hired rig followed more sedately.

"I hope you don't mind," Peter said. He was seated beside her, his long legs stretched out in the driver's box. A small smile played around his eyes. His large hands, the fingers blunt tipped, held the reins lightly. "The grays can use a good run and I wasn't in the mood myself."

"Indeed?" Cornelia asked. She held on to the edge of the box with one hand, having contrived to put as much distance between them as was possible. It wasn't much, given the limits of the carriage's dimensions, but it would have to do. She shot him a sidelong glance that was plainly skeptical. "What prompted you to bring them out then?"

"That sky," he said, indicating the wide swath of blue above them dotted with the remnants of the morning's clouds. "The air, the light and the conviction that if I spent much more time inside, I would become intolerable to myself and everyone else."

His honesty took Cornelia aback. She was not accustomed to gentlemen speaking so frankly. "I see," she said slowly. "You prefer the outdoors?"

He nodded. "Put any group of people inside four walls and they will waste no time complicating everything in sight. They will call the results etiquette, or society, or civilization, and they'll be quite proud of it. But what they will really have done is gotten everyone worrying about things that have absolutely no significance."

"An interesting theory," Cornelia said dryly, thinking that she had not been wrong to suspect that the veneer of civilization was very thin indeed on Mr. Peter Lowell. A small shiver ran down her back that had nothing at all to do with the brightening day.

"Have I just heard tomorrow's column?" she asked.

He looked disconcerted. "My apologies, I didn't mean to pontificate."

"Not at all, I found it quite provocative. In your view, people should avoid being inside buildings, which breeds an overreliance on the correct use of forks, an excessive interest in guest lists and a fondness for rather tiresome paintings. Is that correct?"

Sunlight danced off his ebony hair as he threw back his head and laughed. The sound was rich, deep, utterly masculine. It caused Cornelia to catch her breath.

"I wouldn't have put it that way myself, but I suppose you're right. And what about you, Miss Montgomery? What are your thoughts on society?"

"That while it can be very tiresome it does give people something to do and it even on occasion manages to achieve some good. At any rate, I'm not about to go live in a cave, subsist on mammoth meat, and hope that my neighbors over the next hill never decide to drop in for a visit."

"Very sensible of you," Peter said. "But if you find society tiresome, what do you prefer instead?"

Cornelia hesitated. She was reluctant to reveal too much of herself. It was hardly possible, for instance, to tell him that she spent much of her free time penning the novels he had so recently skewered. While the thought of how he would at react at finding himself seated beside the "Queen of the Penny Dreadfuls" was amusing, the consequences would be anything but.

"The company of friends and family," she said. "I am quite lucky in that regard."

"In all regards, I should say," he murmured.

She warmed under the sudden scrutiny of his eyes and remained silent for several minutes thereafter until, rounding a corner, they found her brothers by the side of the road. The grays were tethered to a tree nearby and appeared no worse for the wear. The same could not be said for the small, disreputable-looking animal Jed was kneeling over.

"What happened?" Peter asked as he swung down from the carriage. He turned and offered Cornelia a hand as she followed.

"Don't know," Ted said. His cheeks were flushed and he looked dangerously close to tears. "He was in the road as we came up. Barely managed to stop in time. Looks as though some rotter hit him and kept going.''

Cornelia's throat tightened as she looked toward the injured creature. It was a dog of some sort—or many sorts—with matted gray hair, huge dark eyes and small, floppy ears. As she watched, Jed lifted it in his arms. Despite his care, the animal gave a whimper of pain.

"We can't leave him," Ted said defiantly, though no one had suggested they do so.

"Of course not," Peter replied quietly. "I have a good man who looks after my horses. We'll take him there."

Rather than waste time changing places, he handed Cornelia back into the hired rig and climbed up beside her. Jed carried the dog to Peter's rig as Ted hurried to untie the reins.

Traffic was light enough that they were able to reach the offices of Dr. Gregory Zimmer without delay. They were located on Madison Avenue not far from the lower reaches of Central Park in an area populated with many stables and riding rings. Dr. Zimmer had a shingle hanging in front of his door. It announced him to be a veterinarian.

Cornelia had heard of such personages, although they were rare. She was curious to see his establishment and was mildly disappointed to discover that it was little different from the rooms occupied by her own physician.

Dr. Zimmer bustled out, wearing a long white coat over his suit. He was a youngish man, not above forty, with a sumptuous black beard and twinkling eyes.

Seeing Lowell, he smiled, but his good humor faded when he spied the dog in Jed's arms.

"What happened?" he demanded without preamble.

"We don't know," Peter said. "My friend here found him lying up on Harlem Lane. He appears to have been struck."

Zimmer shook his head angrily but his hands were gentle as they reached for the dog. "People ought to be horsewhipped. Too many of them don't give a damn what they do to animals."

Belatedly remembering himself, he nodded curtly to Cornelia. "Your pardon, miss. Very well then, let's see what we're dealing with. This will take a while, Lowell. Shall I telephone you?"

Peter nodded. "If you would. Do what you can for him, Greg. He seems a good sort."

The doctor assured him that he would and disappeared into the back with his patient. Peter turned to the twins. "I will contact you as soon as I hear. Are you on the telephone?"

Jed nodded. He had, with much difficulty, convinced their mother to install the contraption the previous year. She had complained that it would explode and kill them all, most likely in the middle of the night, but to date it had done nothing more than occasionally interrupt their conversations with its shrill ring.

"It is very good of you to do this," Cornelia said as they left the offices. Indeed, she was quite surprised to discover that he had such a compassionate side to his nature. But then, mongrel pups were clearly in a class above romance novelists, so far as Mr. Peter Lowell was concerned.

"Not at all," he said, shrugging off her praise. "I only hope the news is good. In the meantime—" he turned to the twins "—my mother is giving a skating party tomorrow. I'm sure she would be delighted if you would all come."

Jed looked startled. He was not so young that he didn't know an invitation from the Lowells was to be prized. First the loan of the grays and now this. He was at a loss for words.

Ted suffered no such lack. He positively beamed. "We'd be delighted."

No one thought to consult her, Cornelia thought sourly, but then no one would. Peter Lowell had behaved with perfect correctness in proffering the invitation to her brothers. They were, after all, the men in the family and therefore its head.

They were also quite thrilled to be acknowledged as such. It was only much later, after the three of them had left Lowell and were riding in the hired carriage back home, that Jed thought to say the obvious.

"Mr. Lowell seemed to enjoy your company, Cornelia. I suspect that may lie behind this invitation to the skating party." He seemed pleased with the notion.

But his pleasure faded when Cornelia turned away from her scrutiny of the passing scene, lifted her chin and said, "How unfortunate, since I will not be accompanying you."

"Of course you're going with us," Melanie Montgomery said. They were seated in the parlor a short time later, sipping mulled cider and warming their hands by the fire. The twins had just finished explaining to their mother how they came to encounter Mr.

Lowell, and his kindness to them, culminating with the invitation. The news could not have been received more delightedly.

"The Lowells," Melanie murmured. Her cheeks were slightly flushed and her eyes flashed. "I can hardly believe it. They are, as I am sure you all know, one of the oldest and most respected families in the city. Without wishing to sound crass, they are also fabulously wealthy. No one has more influence. Why, not even Mrs. Astor can hold a candle to them, although heaven knows, she tries." She pressed a hand to her breast as visions of social pinnacles danced in her head.

"I'll wear the maroon velvet, I think," she continued. "Cornelia, you will look lovely in the blue. But do restrain yourself, dear. I know how you enjoy skating, but some of the more daring figures are not quite the thing for a party of this nature."

Cornelia put her cup down, took a deep breath and said, "Mother, I really do not wish to go."

Melanie frowned. She shook her head in bewilderment. "I don't understand. Why would you possibly decline?" Her color deepened as a sudden suspicion flitted through her mind. "Mr. Lowell didn't...that is, he wasn't improper in any way, was he?"

The twins, who had been lounging near the fire, stiffened. Belatedly—very belatedly, in Cornelia's opinion—it occurred to them that perhaps they had been less than wise to leave her in the newspaper publisher's company.

"Did something happen?" Jed asked anxiously.

He all but sagged with relief when she shook her head. "Certainly not. That isn't the point."

But then what was? Their faces clearly showed that they were bewildered by her reluctance to attend what promised to be a thoroughly enjoyable event.

Worse yet, there was no way she could tell them the truth about why she did not want to be in Mr. Peter Lowell's company without also revealing the truth about herself. She was trapped.

"All right," she said with palpable reluctance, "I'll go."

That settled, Melanie threw herself into the preparations. She summoned Muffy DeWitt to help. They ensconced themselves in the parlor with tea and sandwiches, and proceeded to analyze every aspect of the coming evening. Muffy put aside her pardonable envy to rejoice in her friend's good fortune. Not only was Melanie finally getting back into society, she was doing it with a vengeance.

Cornelia endured it as long as she could before slipping away to her room. If she heard anything more about the Lowell lineage, the brilliance of Mr. Peter Lowell, his mother's futile efforts to interest him in a proper wife, and so on, she would be in no condition to attend the skating party.

For a time, she toyed with the idea of starting a new book, but the spirit simply wasn't in her. Whenever she tried to envision an appropriate hero, the image of Mr. Peter Lowell floated into her mind. Exasperated, she gave up the attempt.

By evening, a liveried footman had called, bearing the actual invitation. Melanie handled the engraved vellum card almost reverently as she scrutinized the style of lettering and the precise wording with undisguised interest. The twins teased her about it but she was unrepentant. To her way of thinking, there was simply no greater arbiter of society than the illustrious Georgette Lowell. To actually be holding in her hand an invitation from that lady was almost more than she could bear.

"Refreshments will be served," she informed them all as she consulted the invitation for perhaps the dozenth time. "At 7:00 p.m. I do so hope the weather holds. Muffy says that last year Mrs. Lowell's skating party was rained out and she was most vexed."

"I'm sure it won't happen again, Mother," Cornelia murmured. "Mrs. Lowell undoubtedly took the Almighty to task for such a lack of consideration."

"My dear," Melanie exclaimed, "don't be sacrilegious."

"To whom?" Jed whispered behind his hand. "God or Mrs. Lowell?"

"They aren't the same?" Ted whispered back.

"Hush, both of you," Cornelia said. "You got us into this. If it's absolutely dreadful—and I'm sure it will be—I shall expect recompense."

"Will a week of obeying your every whim do?" Ted asked with a grin.

"More likely a month," she informed him sternly. "We have nothing in common with the Lowells or their friends, and you can be sure they know it. I only hope they will not make themselves too intolerable."

"I daresay it won't matter," Jed said speculatively. He cast his sister a glance that took her by surprise. Suddenly he appeared not quite so young and inexperienced as usual. "Mr. Lowell doesn't impress me as a man who would tolerate rudeness toward those he has chosen to befriend. I suspect his mother and her circle are already well aware of that."

Cornelia was not reassured, even though she admitted to herself that Jed was probably right. The despicable Lowell was far too high-handed to brook any opposition from the women in his family. Indeed, now that she thought about it, she could only feel sorry for them. It couldn't be easy living with so overbearing and autocratic a man.

Very well, she would go, but she wouldn't have a good time. On that, she was absolutely certain.

As it happened, so was Georgette Lowell, who, having received the footman back with the Montgomerys' acceptances, frowned and went looking for her son.

"I did as you asked," she said, even though she privately thought that it had been less a request than an order, however politely phrased. "The Montgomerys will be joining us tomorrow evening. Not that I can understand for a moment why you should wish them to do so. The name wasn't entirely unfamiliar to me, you know. The father was William Montgomery, as I recall, a banker. There was some unfortunate business a few years ago regarding the mismanagement of funds. He died shortly thereafter."

Peter smiled wryly. He had long since reconciled himself to the fact that his mother was a snob.

"There was a great deal of mismanagement of funds a few years ago," he reminded her gently, "by a great many people. We were fortunate enough to be spared the consequences. Others weren't so lucky. At any rate, William Montgomery is dead and will not be joining us. His family will be and I expect them to receive every consideration."

Georgette inhaled sharply. She was used to her son's forceful ways, having had to endure them most of his life, but this was unusually blunt even for him. There was something at work here that he wasn't saying. She was suddenly looking forward to meeting the Montgomerys—mother, sons and, most particularly, the daughter.

Beneath her carefully coiffed silver hair, her brows drew together in a frown. Her son might not realize it yet, but he was going to make a brilliant marriage, one in keeping with his own wealth and stature. As his mother, it was her responsibility to see to it that he did so, no matter how difficult that might prove to be.

Miss Cornelia Montgomery simply did not qualify. The sooner the young lady realized that, the better for all concerned. Perhaps it was just as well she would be in attendance the following evening.

"Of course," she murmured thoughtfully. "They will receive every consideration. Indeed, I can promise you, it will be an evening they never forget."

Chapter Five

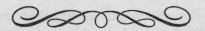

The sight that greeted Cornelia's eyes as she entered the park could have been a scene out of fairyland. Hundreds of colored lanterns hung from the trees and on poles set up around the ice-covered pond. Nearby, silver candlesticks gleamed with the fire of tall white tapers. The light reflected off dishes of fragile porcelain, beaten gold and crystal. Benches heaped with burgundy velvet cushions provided comfort for the gloriously dressed ladies and more austerely garbed gentlemen busy strapping on their skates.

Several pairs were already floating across the ice to the strains of the orchestra stationed nearby. Waiters and footmen moved among the hundreds of guests, offering toasts, canapés and mulled wine or cider. Snow had fallen in the morning. Several inches covered the ground, providing the perfect finishing touch to what was an almost ethereal setting.

"Exquisite," Melanie said as she tried to look in all directions at once. Her hand tightened on Jed's arm. "Look there," she said, indicating a tall, stately woman who appeared weighted down by the luxuriousness of her costume. "That is Mrs. Astor and the gentleman with her is Mr. McAllister. They almost never attend any but the most formal events but, of course, not even they could miss this." She cast a speaking glance at her daughter as though to further drive home the extraordinary good fortune that had brought them into such company.

Cornelia regarded the pair curiously. Only a few months before, Mr. McAllister had yielded to the public's clamor—or so he said—and published the list of the sacred Four Hundred who had received invitations to Mrs. Astor's annual ball. The list, drawn up with his guidance since he advised the lady in all things, was said to represent both the precise number of people who could fit into Mrs. Astor's ballroom and the only people worth knowing in New York. The Montgomerys, naturally enough, had not been mentioned. The Lowells, on the other hand, had been featured most prominently.

Wondering what could possibly make people care about such things, Cornelia allowed her attention to be diverted to several other illustrious beings her mother had spotted among the guests. Indeed, there was a veritable flood of them as the names of New York's social *glitterati* came trippingly off Melanie's lips. Vanderbilts, Martins, Stevenses, Johnstons, Huntingtons and the like abounded. Cornelia found herself thinking that if a capricious deity happened to pick that moment for a lightning strike, a great deal of the country's wealth would find itself in new hands. But the sky remained clear, the music played and good manners decreed that they present themselves to their hostess without further delay.

That was easier said than done. In the swarm of guests, it would have been difficult to locate someone they already knew. As none of them was acquainted with Mrs. Lowell, the task was doubly difficult. Cornelia did, however, manage to spot Peter. She credited this to her keen eyesight. Never mind that he was a good thirty yards away, in partial shadow and surrounded by a group of other people. It wasn't that she was particularly attuned to him in any way. There was nothing special about him. The feat was due solely to all those carrots she had obediently consumed in childhood.

Reluctantly she drew her brothers' attention to his whereabouts and was promptly dragged along. Lowell greeted them cordially, inclining his head to the ladies. Cornelia told herself she was imagining that his gaze lingered on her. Obviously she had been reading too many books of the Luciana sort—purely from professional interest, of course.

As her mother started in on how pleased they were to be invited, Cornelia allowed herself a surreptitious glance in the despicable Lowell's direction. She had to admit he was looking very well, dressed in an unadorned black overcoat open at the throat to reveal a plain white shirt with the usual high collar and a conservative Windsor tie. His head was bare, his hands gloveless.

Compared to most of the other men, who had garbed themselves as though for the frozen tundra, he was underdressed. Nonetheless, he looked perfectly at ease and appeared to be enjoying himself.

In fact, the impression was misleading. Having only just arrived at the party a few minutes before, Peter had already discovered that his mother had seen fit to invite no fewer than a dozen of New York's most eligible young ladies, all of whom seemed to have taken it into their heads that this particular evening was the proper time to call themselves to his attention.

He had only just managed to dodge the latest one when he spotted the Montgomerys. Courtesy alone required him to take them in hand, but he didn't mind that they also provided protection. While the humor of his predicament did not escape him—he had, after all, faced down charging buffalo—it also annoyed him. His mother was really going too far. He would have to clarify the matter with her.

But first he preferred to turn his attention to Miss Cornelia Montgomery. He kept thinking that if he saw enough of her, the sudden, shocking desire he had felt from the first moment in Jonathan's parlor would lessen, as it most assuredly must.

She was a woman of his own class and as such eligible only for marriage, in which he had absolutely no interest. She was undeniably beautiful but he had known women who were more classically lovely. There was nothing in the least charming about her, much less coquettish.

Indeed, there was a distinct chill in her attitude toward him. That might be enough of a novelty to explain why he could not get her out of his mind. But it certainly didn't account for the fierce rush of desire that tore through him whenever he happened to glance her way. It was no exaggeration to say that had their circumstances been different, he would have been tempted to sweep her into his arms and carry her away.

Instead, he was forced to puzzle over why she should have such a singular effect on him. The intelligence in her azure eyes might explain some of it although, to be honest, intelligence wasn't the first thing he looked for in a woman. More than that, he sensed a feminine strength and tenderness in her unlike anything he had ever encountered before. It aroused his most possessive instincts.

She looked quite well in the blue thingamajig she was wearing. He was happily ignorant of women's fashions and intended to remain so, but he knew what he liked. Gleaming chestnut hair piled high under a pert cap with a few stray tendrils drifting in the breeze fit the bill perfectly. So did flashing azure eyes, petal-smooth cheeks and a mouth—

He stopped abruptly. That train of thought was not adding to his self-control, which at the moment seemed perilously shaky. Determined to take himself in hand, he addressed the smiling but watchful woman at Cornelia's side.

Mrs. Montgomery was something of a surprise. She came to just above Cornelia's shoulder, was plump where her daughter was slender, and had soft brown eyes that seemed made to look at the world with gentle approval. Yet as excited as she was to be there, she was not overawed. Indeed, she held herself with decorous pride and impressed him with her quiet dignity.

"We do so admire the *Journal,*" she said. "It gives one by far the best sense of what is truly happening in this city and elsewhere as well."

"Thank you," Peter replied. He took the compliment seriously, for nothing had mattered to him quite so much as raising the standards of the paper he had inherited. "We are occasionally criticized for dwelling too much on the more sordid side of life."

"Only by people who do not wish to admit that it exists," Mrs. Montgomery said firmly. "There is a great deal of inequity that must be dealt with. The poverty and suffering of much of the immigrant class, for instance, wrings one's heart. It also simply doesn't make good sense. We would all be better off if everyone was allowed to live and work to their fullest potential."

Peter nodded slowly. He looked at her with even greater interest. "I see you have given the subject considerable thought."

"As we all should. Our people are our greatest resource. The future of this country—"

She broke off as Cornelia laid a gentle hand on her arm. "Mother, Mr. Lowell may not wish to—"

"Nonsense," Peter said. "I find your mother's opinions fascinating. It's regrettable that so few ladies of your stature take the trouble to think about such matters, Mrs. Montgomery."

Melanie blushed. Her audacity in speaking as she had left her shaken; she could still hardly believe that she had done it. But something in her had sensed that Mr. Peter Lowell would not think badly of her. He was a kindred spirit of sorts, a man who actually cared about others and was not inclined to condemn them merely for the circumstances life had thrust upon them.

Having herself experienced a terrifying brush with financial disaster, Melanie was more inclined than most to give the poor the benefit of the doubt. She was delighted to see that Mr. Peter Lowell felt the same. Silently she filed away the information that this devastatingly attractive, enormously rich and almost frighteningly powerful young man also possessed a heart.

"It was good of you to telephone about the pooch," Jed said. The call had come earlier in the day while Cornelia was out. She had returned to the news that the injured dog was improving and would be able to leave Dr. Zimmer's in a week or so.

"I wish we could take it," Ted said, casting a quick glance at his mother.

"Sadly, dogs and I do not get along well," Melanie said. "I tend to sneeze excessively in their presence."

"Don't concern yourself," Peter told her kindly. "I've been wanting a dog. I'll keep her."

"You will?" Cornelia asked. She couldn't keep the surprise out of her voice. Knowing as she did that her mother could not have a dog in the house, she had been worrying about the animal's fate ever since they found it. Now it seemed that had been for naught. Pooch— surely she would have a better name soon—would be going to live in a Fifth Avenue mansion. The poor dog might be pardoned for thinking that she had died and gone to heaven, after all.

"Wouldn't a pedigree spaniel be more appropriate?" Cornelia asked teasingly. "Perhaps of the sort Prince Edward favors." The heir to the British throne had a great fondness for King Charles spaniels and went nowhere without them. He had even brought them with him during a visit to New York several decades before. People still talked about the prince and his court of spaniels.

"Yappers," Peter said. "Always underfoot, no one's ankles are safe. Give me a good old mongrel, a dog who knows his way around."

"Her way," Cornelia corrected with a smile. Heaven help her, she was feeling a spurt of liking for the despicable Lowell. How dare he be so *nice?*

"Her way," he agreed. He had a sudden mental image of the battered gray dog racing about his mother's drawing room, jumping on the silk settees, ricocheting off the brocade-covered walls, perhaps tipping over one or two of the tables laden with porcelain snuffboxes and the like. His smile deepened.

So it was that Georgette Lowell saw her son as she happened to glance in his direction. He was standing next to a beautiful young woman in an azure ensemble, her chestnut hair swept up beneath a pert cap and her cheeks delicately flushed. Three others were standing nearby—a woman of approximately Georgette's own age and two young men—but she hardly noticed them. All her attention was focused on the girl and on her son.

Peter looked different from his usual formidable self. He appeared younger somehow, more relaxed, even . . . happy. No, that couldn't be right. It wasn't as though he customarily looked unhappy. On the contrary, he was far too self-confident a man to be prey to that emotion, and his life was, after all, sufficiently surrounded by privilege and comfort to be found congenial by even the most demanding men. Yet there was no denying that he seemed to have suddenly found something that pleased him greatly.

Much as Georgette would have liked to believe that it was the party itself, which she had arranged with her usual painstaking vigilance, or better yet, one of the very eligible young ladies she had taken care to invite, she did not even attempt to do so. Beneath her patrician exterior was a solid New England conscience that would tolerate small social falsehoods but no actual lies.

There was no getting around it, Miss Cornelia Montgomery was the cause. As such, she would require even firmer handling than Georgette had anticipated. She took a deep breath—or as deep a one as her corset would allow—and set off to join the small group.

Several minutes passed before she reached it, stopped as she was every few steps by guests anxious to greet her. By the time she reached Peter's side, he had seen her coming. The element of surprise was lost but Georgette didn't really need it. She inclined her head regally, ignored everyone but him, and said in a firm, clear voice, "Peter, dear, Miss Longines has arrived and she is so looking forward to meeting you. Do take just a moment to greet her."

Listening to her, Melanie frowned. She had always admired Georgette Lowell, at least in so far as she had read about her in the newspapers and ladies magazines. Standing at the pinnacle of elegance and style, she was also a well-known patron of the arts and of several women's colleges. Painters, composers, writers and scholars flocked to her twice-monthly salons. She was regularly consulted on all manner of pressing issues from the correct seating plan for a dinner party that included royalty to the proper role of the female in the coming century.

She was, in short, a person Melanie did not expect to behave rudely, yet that was precisely what the exalted Mrs. Lowell had done.

Not that it was a terribly dramatic or overt rudeness. No words had been exchanged, no formal gestures made. Yet the social snub was all the more potent for being subtle. One simply did not walk up to a group of people and immediately begin addressing a single member without even acknowledging the existence of the others. Not if one had any claim to true gentility.

Forced into a hasty reassessment of the woman she had regarded as a social paragon, Melanie frowned. For the second time in the space of only a few minutes, she found herself being uncommonly assertive.

"Excuse me," she said quietly but with a certain implacableness, "I do not believe we have met."

The look that accompanied this statement strongly suggested that there was no reason to change that. Peter, however, disagreed. Annoyed though he was by his mother's behavior, he was also amused. Swiftly he made the introduction, then stood back to see what would happen next.

The two women eyed each other cautiously. Georgette had not missed the undertone in her son's voice as he presented the Montgomerys. He possessed a ruthless will that was never very far below the surface, for all that it could be covered over by a surface congeniality. It was that will which lay behind the single great frustration of her life, his continuing refusal to make a proper marriage. Her late husband had not possessed anything similar nor, so far as she knew, had his father. Peter appeared to be a throwback to a time generations distant when the Lowell men had been swashbucklers and brigands, carving an empire for themselves by any means necessary. All that raw male power should have been safely stowed away in family legend, not reemerging in the present time to make itself damnably inconvenient.

Her smile was thin as she acknowledged her unwelcome guests. It narrowed even further as Peter said,

"Mrs. Montgomery is very interested in the plight of immigrants in New York. Professor Rasmusson would find her ideas most stimulating. He is here this evening, isn't he?"

Reluctantly Georgette nodded. Rasmusson was her latest conquest; she had competed with Mrs. Astor herself to add him to her salon. He was a brooding scholar of mixed Russian and French ancestry whose opinions on Western civilization titillated and shocked the upper class. As such, he had become their latest darling, the most reliable antidote to the boredom of having everything imaginable without having to make the least effort. Part of his charm was that it was impossible to predict what he would champion next. If there was any chance of him being taken with Melanie Montgomery, Georgette would have no choice but to tolerate her.

Melanie, who was familiar with the scholar's standing, was dumbstruck at the thought that she might actually meet him. That possibility alone was enough to convince her to go along with her hostess, who, however grudgingly, offered to present her.

Ted and Jed remained, but not for long. With dizzying ease, Peter plucked from the crowd several young ladies and gentlemen of the twins' own age who quickly took them up. Before she could quite comprehend what was happening, Cornelia found herself standing on the edge of the pond, alone except for her host.

"Care to give it a try?" he asked, gesturing to the shimmering expanse gleaming like polished marble in the lantern light.

"Don't you have an eccentric scholar I should meet?" she inquired, struggling to hide her sudden nervousness. "Or a collection of young people it would be pleasant for me to know?"

His eyes met hers. Softly he said, "If I have, they've slipped my mind."

Without giving her a chance to delay further, he held out his hand.

Without letting herself think of all the reasons why she should not, Cornelia took it.

Chapter Six

Gliding in Peter's arms across the ice, Cornelia was overwhelmed with feelings she was utterly unprepared to confront, which seemed to be happening all at once and on all levels of her being. To begin with, there was the simple fact of being touched by him and touching him in return. Even through the layers of their clothes she was acutely aware of the strength and power in him, the sheer vitality and even—this must be Luciana thinking—the sensualness of the man.

Tiny ripples of pleasure and awareness moved through her as the music gathered speed, sweeping them along with it. It all felt so right, being in his arms, letting the rest of the world fade into the half-remembered distance—so very, terribly, frighteningly right.

She looked up momentarily and saw through the bare fringe of the trees the night sky, streaked with fleeing clouds that veiled the crescent moon. As a child she had dreamed of swinging on such a moon, riding it higher and higher into the starlit sky. Now it felt as though she were doing exactly that.

His arm was strong across her back, guiding her at the same time it made her feel infinitely protected. How long had it been since she had felt any such thing? She had become so used to depending on herself, first to resist the conventions of her society that decreed she should have no concern but acquiring a suitable husband, and then to save her family from financial disaster. She could not remember the last time she had simply relaxed and let herself go.

The sensation was both terrifying and exhilarating. She lowered her eyes, the thick fringes concealing them, and studied Mr. Peter Lowell. He was, by any measure, an extraordinarily handsome man, yet he completely lacked the male prettiness and self-absorption of the beau ideals drawn by that arbiter of fashion both masculine and feminine, Mr. Charles Dana Gibson.

His nose looked as though it had been dented, if not actually broken, in some fight or other. There was a small white scar across his left cheek that looked as if it could have been made by a knife. His skin was weathered and burnished. When he smiled, the lines around his eyes deepened most provocatively. He smelled not of perfumed hair liniments, after-shaves and pastilles but of soap, good wool, fine cigars and something intrinsically male she could not identify but which a part of her seemed to recognize nonetheless.

He was also an excellent skater and, she suspected, an equally good dancer. He moved with the easy strength and grace of the natural athlete. Although in recent years she had danced little, and rarely skated with a partner, she was certain there were few to compare with him. He commanded the ice as he commanded everything else.

A wry smile touched her mouth. Peter saw it and slowed slightly. "Something amuses you?"

She nodded. "I do. I amuse myself."

He frowned, sensing she would not tell him more yet wanting to know everything about her. That need to bridge the gap between them took him by surprise. He was no stranger to physical desire, but this was different. Or more. He wasn't sure which was the case, much less why. The confusion he felt was not like him. He found it annoying.

"How nice for you," he said sardonically. "You must never be bored."

She ignored his obvious skepticism and shook her head. "Rarely. I find there is always something to do."

"Something uplifting and improving, no doubt?"

"Good heavens, no." She laughed at the thought. "I am not such a bluestocking as that. I merely meant that life tends to keep one busy. Don't you find that, too?"

He did most definitely, but he was surprised that she knew it. In his experience, most women like Miss Cornelia Montgomery lived lives he could only call indolent.

But that presumed there were other women like her and he was beginning to have doubts on that score. What had started out as a simple turn around the ice was becoming far more. He had thought to cure himself of this woman by being with her more, but that wasn't working. Each moment he spent with her in his arms, he desired her more.

The music played, the lights glowed, the moon rose in the sky and Cornelia and Peter stayed on the ice.

Other couples joined them but they were hardly aware of any presence apart from their own. Not until the gong rang to announce that dinner was ready did they reluctantly come back down to reality.

The moment they did, Cornelia realized something of significance had occurred. As she stepped off the ice, before she had even had a chance to remove her skates, she became aware of several young ladies sending glacial stares her way. Had they been able to tear frozen shards from the pond and launch them in her direction, the effect wouldn't have been much different.

Yet not everyone seemed displeased with her. Her brothers were having too good a time to notice much of anything while her mother, when Cornelia finally managed to spot her, appeared to be in deep discussion with a bearded gentleman who was hanging on her every word.

That was small consolation, given the fact that Mrs. Georgette Lowell was bearing down on them with a look in her eyes that suggested trouble.

"Dear boy," she said when she reached Peter, "how kind of you to remember the rest of us at last. Miss Longines will be your partner at supper. Do excuse us, Miss Montgomery."

Cornelia was perfectly prepared to do so, presuming that she had no alternative. In similar circumstances, her brothers would have done as they were told. But Peter Lowell was not seventeen and even when he had been, his temperament had never been so biddable.

The look he gave his mother was genuinely puzzled, as though he could not imagine what was going through her head. He did not remonstrate with her. Indeed, he did not complain in any way. He merely looked at her and said, "You are mistaken."

It was enough. Before Cornelia's fascinated eyes, Georgette appeared to retreat. She was not pleased with the situation—not at all—but even she had sufficient sense to know that she could not cross her formidable son.

As Peter took her arm and led her away, Cornelia asked, "Are you always so abrupt?"

He paused to consider that. At length, he said, "Only when it's appropriate."

"Your mother means well. She undoubtedly believes me to be a bad influence."

The look he gave her went clear through Cornelia. His mouth lifted in a taunting smile. "And are you?"

"I don't know," she said honestly. "I never have been, and I'm not absolutely certain I could manage it."

"I, on the contrary, have frequently done things I shouldn't have, at least by the definition of proper society. It isn't all that difficult once one learns how."

"Indeed? I would imagine one has to have a certain talent for it even to begin."

Her audacity left Cornelia all but breathless. She could hardly believe that she was engaging in so flirtatious a conversation with any man, much less the despicable Lowell. Except it was very difficult just then to remember why she had found him despicable in the first place.

Supper turned out to be an elaborate sit-down affair at damask-covered tables replete with silver candelabra. Bonfires roared nearby, giving off waves of heat to keep the guests comfortable as they sipped champagne, nibbled on pâtés, and worked their way through *boeuf* Wellington, duck in cherry sauce, winter vegetables, various cheeses and a variety of desserts, each more elaborate than the last. Champagne flowed between the courses, with several fine red wines accompanying the main dishes. At the conclusion, the gentlemen did without their brandy and port as the ladies remained at the tables with them, thereby signaling that, despite all evidence to the contrary, the affair was actually informal.

Cornelia had eaten little and drunk even less. Nervous flutters in her stomach increased as the meal wore on. She was discovering that it was difficult to be the censure of all eyes, however discreet the glances. The sheer sumptuousness of the evening astounded her.

Central Park was, after all, a public place, yet Mrs. Lowell had taken over the most popular part of it as though it were her own drawing room. The ring of large, rough-looking men who encircled the entire area around the pond had not escaped Cornelia's notice. Anyone wishing to skate that evening but lacking an invitation would have to go the extra distance to the Boathouse Pond or give up the idea entirely.

Such enormous power so casually displayed drove home how different the Lowells were from the rest of New York. Not even Mrs. Astor, who was looking unabashedly out of joint, would have attempted such a thing.

Supper was at last over, the servants were clearing up and the guests were beginning to depart. Some of the lanterns had already been extinguished. Long shadows crept across the ice-shrouded pond.

Cornelia felt a pang of regret as she realized the evening was ending and steeled herself against it. Whatever unexpected effect Peter Lowell had on her, it would not last anymore than his sudden interest in her family would. Granted, he had been kindness itself to them, but it was no more than the whim of a man well accustomed to indulging himself. He would forget them as soon as something new seized his attention.

She reminded herself of that firmly as he rose to escort her to her carriage. The hired rig was somewhere in the swarm of conveyances awaiting the guests as they made their farewells. Her mother and brothers appeared to have gone on ahead; she could find no sign of them in the group still lingering beside the pond. Undoubtedly her mother was weary after all the excitement and in need of rest.

As they left the area where the tables had been set up and walked around the rim of the pond, Cornelia said quietly, "Thank you. I had a lovely time."

Her grave politeness amused Peter but it vexed him, as well. The hours were too fleeting and Miss Cornelia Montgomery was too elusive. One moment, they were laughing together like old friends and the next he could feel her floating away like a dream that might never have been.

The memory of her in his arms remained so vivid that it blocked out a good deal else. Common sense, for one thing. Self-restraint, for another. To give him credit, he did hesitate. To be honest, it was only for the briefest moment.

In the sheltering darkness of a fragrant pine, he drew her close. Cornelia was too startled to even protest.

Nothing like this had ever happened to her. None of the men she knew would dare such a thing.

But Peter Lowell did not live by other men's rules. He made his own.

His arm was gentle but insistent as it closed around her. With his other hand, he lifted her chin. A startled exclamation began in her throat but got no further.

The first tremors hit her with the first touch of his mouth. His kiss was warm, coaxing, almost tender. There was nothing at all frightening about it except for the barely restrained passions she sensed just below the surface. She felt as though she were being drawn into a world she had never known, one carefully shaped to fit her present needs but in which vastly more was possible.

Cornelia had been kissed several times before, most recently by Davey Bartlett in the garden of his mother's house on Forty-ninth Street. Unlike some young women who spoke of the experience with distaste, she had found it pleasant. Not this time, though. Pleasant was far too weak and innocuous a word to describe the hot, coiling sensations stirring to life deep within her.

Peter made a low, guttural sound and drew her even closer. He became less gentle, more demanding. She could feel the hard, tensile strength of him along every inch of her body. When his lips parted hers, she gasped. His tongue brushed hers, igniting a sweet languor that swept aside all resistance.

Thoughts rioted through her mind, tumbling one after another. Who was this woman so unlike herself? This wanton being who permitted such boldness? Luciana would have recognized her, of that Cornelia had no doubt. Indeed, Luciana could have *invented* her.

But what was permissible within the pages of a romance was a different matter entirely standing in the midst of a public park where anyone might see them and most surely would if matters went on a moment longer.

Just as she thought she would have to somehow find the strength to resist, Peter raised his head. His sea green eyes glittered dangerously as they swept her heated face.

Huskily he said, "You are a surprise."

Cornelia's only reply was a low, disconcerted murmur. Heedless of her manners—singularly useless things under the circumstances—she gathered up her skirts and fled. She did not run, for that would only have drawn unwanted attention, but she did walk very quickly until she at last saw the hired rig up ahead. A sob of relief threatened to break from her but she repressed it as Ted caught sight of her.

"There you are," he said as he bounded down and offered her a hand. She took it gratefully. "We were getting worried about you."

"I had a bit of trouble finding my way through the crowd," she said, praying they would think her breathlessness was the result of her efforts.

Jed looked doubtful as she stepped into the carriage, but he said nothing. Beside him on the padded seat, their mother had already fallen asleep. Not wishing to disturb her, the three younger Montgomerys completed the ride home in silence.

Cornelia fell into bed a short time later, hoping that she would fall as easily into sleep. Although she was worn out in mind and body, she tossed and turned into the wee hours until she thought she could bear it no longer. Not long before dawn, she slipped at last into uneasy slumber, pursued by dreams of an ebony-haired man who laughed as he deftly closed her up within the pages of one of her own books.

In the clear light of morning, she awoke, bleary-eyed but firm in her resolve. She would not see Peter Lowell again. It was that simple. No matter what anyone said or did, she would have some excuse for staying well away from him.

Having come to that conclusion within her mind, she rose and set about the business of the day, not suspecting that the despicable Lowell had come to a decision of his own.

Chapter Seven

"Tell me about her," Peter said. He was sitting in Jonathan's office, comfortably ensconced in a leather armchair with his long legs stretched out in front of him and a glass of port at his side. It was late Tuesday afternoon, a week after the skating party. He had rung Jonathan up first thing that morning and arranged the meeting without telling the publisher what it was about. The older man could be pardoned for showing his surprise.

"Her," Jonathan repeated. He cleared his throat, more to buy time than for any other reason. "Miss Montgomery."

Peter nodded curtly. He had already covered this ground. "Cornelia."

Jonathan's eyebrows rose slightly. His gaze was shrewd and interlaced with humor as it ran over his young friend. "I take it she has given you permission to use her Christian name?"

Peter thought back to the night in Central Park, the hours beneath the stars, the kiss they had shared. She had given him a great deal, at least to ponder, but none of it had to do with society's dry etiquette. "Not in so many words." His exasperation showed as he continued, "She also does not return my telephone calls or respond to my invitations. I am given to understand that she is otherwise occupied."

"Perhaps she is," Jonathan suggested. He was making no effort now to hide the fact that he was enjoying himself. The great Peter Lowell, despair of dozens of proud mothers and their ambitious daughters, hoisted on his own petard. Truly, there was such a thing as justice.

"Cornelia is a delightful young woman," the publisher went on, seeing no harm in rubbing salt into the wound. "I have been privileged to know her since she was a child and I can honestly say that few people stand as high in my esteem. She is intelligent, honorable, thoughtful, considerate and free of those vanities and ambitions which plague some members of the gentle sex. Wealth and position have no lure for her. She values a way of life that is both simpler and at the same time far richer."

"Truly a paragon among women," Peter said. "Yet when I am in her company, I have the sense that there is something hidden, some conflict within her that she does not wish to reveal."

Jonathan looked away. His young friend was far too perceptive. He took a sip of his own port and tried to decide what to say. On the one hand, he had an obligation to Cornelia not to reveal her secret. On the other, he had a genuine and even fatherly concern about her future. He did not want to see her spend it alone.

Slowly he said, "Frankly, I am surprised you would concern yourself to such a degree. She isn't your usual style."

Peter grimaced. The publisher had him there. He could hardly deny that he had spent his adult life avoiding young ladies such as Cornelia Montgomery. Yet here he was, frustrated because one of them chose to avoid him.

"She...interests me," he said. It was as close as he would come to declaring his intentions. Slowly, as though just coming to realize it himself, he added, "I am concerned that her reluctance to be in my company may indicate that I have offended her."

"Indeed," Jonathan said. "How might that be?"

It might have something to do with the extreme impropriety of the kiss they had shared, but Peter wasn't about to admit that. He had certainly broached the bonds of respectfulness on that occasion, yet he had not been alone. Proper Miss Cornelia Montgomery had been a willing participant.

"Any number of ways," he said finally. "As you pointed out, she isn't in my usual style. I haven't troubled myself to learn much about young ladies of her sort."

"I'm not sure any such effort would have availed you much," Jonathan said. "Cornelia is...different."

That was as leading a comment as Peter was likely to get. He did not hesitate to follow it. "How so? Besides being a paragon, I mean."

"She can be rather...unconventional."

Peter's eyes narrowed. It wasn't a word he would have thought of to describe the proper Miss Montgomery, but considering that kiss, perhaps he shouldn't be so surprised.

"How so?"

Jonathan did not reply immediately. He sat back in his chair and twirled the crystal snifter between his fingers. Outwardly he looked like a man perfectly at peace with himself. But inwardly, his conscience was at war with itself. Did he do as Cornelia would most surely want him to do and keep silent, or did he follow his own instincts and, heaven help him, play Cupid?

The temptation was simply too much. He took another sip of the port and yielded to it.

"When William Montgomery died, his family was left in difficult circumstances. It is no exaggeration to say that their entire way of life was threatened."

"Then how...?"

Peter half expected Jonathan to confide that he had helped the family out. He was completely unprepared when the publisher said instead, "Their current prosperity is due entirely to Cornelia. Had it not been for her efforts, I shudder to think what might have happened to them."

Feeling suddenly at sea, Peter tried to conceive of how that might be. He had never really thought about it before, but there were very few jobs for women, and of those only a tiny handful were considered acceptable for a woman of the upper class in the grip of dire misfortune. She could become a governess, for instance, or a companion, but neither paid more than a pittance. Of course, there was always one alternative, but the thought that Cornelia could possibly have...

"What exactly are you telling me, Jonathan?"

The older man shook his head chidingly. "Not what seems to have just flitted through your mind. You didn't really think that—"

"No, of course not. Get on with it."

"Not so fast. I am under certain restrictions."

"Under what? What are you talking about?"

"Only that I stand in a position of confidence so far as Cornelia is concerned and I do not care to violate that."

"You mean," Peter said with deadly calm, "that you won't tell me?"

"I mean that you are going to have to figure it out for yourself."

Before Peter could respond, Jonathan stood up and went to a bookshelf behind his desk. From it, he selected half a dozen paperback novels.

"Your trouble," he said as he turned back to his guest, "is that you take life too seriously. Not surprising, really, considering the responsibilities you have had to bear. But it might do you good to relax a bit, indulge in a little light amusement."

Peter glanced at the books. There was quite a selection, everything from the latest Reginald Wells mystery to a Paddy O'Shea adventure, even one of Miss Luciana Montrachet's romances. "With these?" he asked derisively.

Jonathan nodded. "Won't do you any harm at all and you might even find them edifying."

Beyond that, he would say nothing. Peter left the office half an hour later, no better enlightened than he had been when he arrived. But he did have plenty to read. Passing a trash can, he considered chucking the books in. Only a reluctance to do that to any book—no matter how lowly—stopped him. Perhaps Mrs. Everard would like to have them.

But as it happened, his secretary was extremely busy that afternoon and he had no opportunity to offer her the books. So it was that they were still on his desk when it came time to depart. Seeing them, he grimaced and wondered for the dozenth time what Jonathan could have been thinking of. He had gone to him for help about Cornelia and instead the publisher had . . .

Publisher. Jonathan published books. In point of fact, he published the books he had given Peter. A quick check of the spines confirmed that. Jonathan's business was profitable. Somebody paid good money for the things and that meant—

The possibility that suddenly began to dawn in his mind was so outrageous that he almost dismissed it. Almost, but not quite. What he did instead was sweep the books into his briefcase and take them home with him.

He did not return to the Fifth Avenue mansion that night but went instead to the apartment he kept several blocks away. It took up most of the top floor of one of the large residential buildings that marked the northward march of the city. All the amenities expected of a wealthy man's home were present, including a staff of three highly discreet servants.

After serving a light supper in front of the fire in the parlor, the butler vanished. Peter was left to himself. He was tired but not excessively so. The thought of bed had no lure. He parted the heavy velvet drapes and glanced outside. Stray flakes of snow drifted past the windows. A lone carriage made its way along Madison Avenue.

At the sight of it, restlessness stirred in him. Briefly, he considered calling downstairs for one of the hired rigs that always lingered in the wealthier districts even at such a late hour. In short order, he could be at one of his clubs or availing himself of various other forms of amusement the city offered to discerning gentlemen. But the idea had no appeal.

Wryly he thought he must be getting older if the thought of a night on his own had more appeal than the amusements of his youth. He poked the fire, chose a book of natural history from the nearby shelves and settled down to read. The book had been recommended by his friend, Teddy Roosevelt, who praised the author as being unusually insightful. That proved to be true, yet the book could not hold Peter's attention. He gave up after half an hour or so and put it on the table beside him.

His briefcase was propped up against the wall near the parlor door. The butler, mindful that his employer often worked when he was in the apartment alone, had left it there. Telling himself he was being a fool, Peter got up and retrieved the small stack of books.

He got halfway through the Reginald Wells mystery before deciding that if he should ever take a mind to do so, he could write the things himself, so patently obvious was it who the villain was supposed to be. A quick glance at the end showed that he was, in fact, completely wrong; the murderer was a character he had not suspected at all, but with hindsight the chain of clues did indeed point in that direction.

Annoyed at having been taken by surprise, he turned to the Paddy O'Shea only to give it up in disgust a few minutes later. If Mr. O'Shea had ever been west of the Hudson River, he did a damn good job of concealing it. There were several other selections, which he browsed through. One was a mystery by a woman that he found a little stiff but actually not bad. He put it aside thoughtfully.

That left the last book in the pile, an offering by the redoubtable Miss Montrachet entitled *Devon Sum-*

mer. He picked it up reluctantly, expecting to give it no more than a cursory glance.

Two hours later, he closed the book and raised his eyes to stare into the fire. His features were tautly drawn, and a faint smile played over his hard mouth.

"Remarkable," he murmured under his breath. "Absolutely remarkable." He glanced again at the book before giving it a fond pat. He had wronged Miss Luciana Montrachet and would have to make it up to her.

But first he had a score to settle with the stubborn, elusive and all-too-tantalizing Miss Cornelia Montgomery.

Cornelia sat down wearily on the edge of her bed. She had just returned from an afternoon musical given by Mrs. DeWitt's daughter and son-in-law. The event should have been pleasant and relaxing, one of the less hectic outings of the holiday season. And so it would have been, had not Peter been there.

No, not *Peter.* She must not think of him so familiarly. *Lowell* was there, as he had been everywhere in the past week. At every soiree, every ball, every theater party, everywhere she set her foot and turned her head, there he was, thrilling the hostesses who had never thought to bag such a conquest and giving every appearance of enjoying himself.

How naive she had been to imagine that simply refusing to see him would solve the problem. Anywhere she went he was sure to be welcome. It was getting to the point where she was reluctant to set foot in her mother's parlor for fear of finding him there.

She sighed and rubbed the back of her neck. There was a soft knock at the door. "Come," she said.

Sophia entered and shut the door behind her. The maid frowned. "You look all in, miss. Not feeling well?"

"I'm fine," Cornelia insisted. She stood up and tried to still the nervous fluttering in her stomach. "It's only that the holidays seem more frantic than ever."

"You could stay in this evening," Sophia suggested. She began to undo the buttons down the back of Cornelia's day dress.

"We've been promised to the Lancasters' sleighing party for more than a month. I can hardly fail to turn up now. Besides," she added firmly, "I love sleighing and I have no intention of missing it."

"As you wish, miss," Sophia murmured. "But if you ask me, something's eating at you and it won't get any better until you set it to rest."

Cornelia sighed. The maid was right, but she wasn't about to admit it. "I'm merely tired. A bit of sleighing will cheer me up." Particularly if her prayers were answered and Lowell failed to attend. Surely there was a limit to how many social events he could stomach in quick succession. She had every right to expect at least a brief reprieve.

Not that it would do much good. Christmas Eve was only three days off and with it the famed Lowell Christmas Ball. The gilded invitation to that event lay in a place of honor on the hall table downstairs. It had arrived several days before. Her mother could not pass it without reaching out a hand to convince herself it was real. Naturally, it had been accepted at once. And just as naturally, there was no possibility of Cornelia being allowed to remain at home. The one suggestion she had made regarding that had brought such a shocked response that she dropped it at once.

Since she was doomed to attend the ball, she should at least be able to go to the Lancasters' sleighing party without constantly being drawn to Peter. Lowell. Him. Heaven help her, she could think of nothing else. She had to be mad to be in such a state, yet every time she remembered that kiss beside the pine tree, she . . .

She wouldn't remember it. She would block it out of her mind and pretend it had never happened.

She would flap her wings and fly to the moon.

"The red velvet, miss?" Sophia asked.

"Perfect," Cornelia murmured without thinking. She hardly noticed what Sophia was doing as the maid helped her to dress and did her hair. But she did remember to thank her when she was done.

Sophia smiled gravely but humor danced in her eyes. She was hardly ignorant of the rumors surrounding her young mistress. Indeed, only Cornelia herself seemed unaware that all New York was talking about her and Mr. Peter Lowell. They would be talking even more when this evening was done, if appearances were anything to judge by.

"Have a nice evening, miss," Sophia said. She watched as Cornelia left the room on a whiff of honeysuckle and a whisper of velvet.

Honeysuckle, Peter thought. She was wearing honeysuckle. And velvet, deep crimson velvet that looked as though his hand could crush it. Her hair was swept up in a loose confection of curls that tumbled over her shoulders and drew attention to the full curve of her breasts beneath the snugly fitted jacket. The jacket, in turn, was trimmed with black braid that indented sharply at her narrow waist before flaring again at her hips. The long skirt was cut in a bell shape that swayed gracefully as she moved.

"I've put you in with Mr. Lowell," Penelope Lancaster was saying brightly. "He was kind enough to bring his own sleigh with those marvelous trotters." Her smile was arch as she added, "You do so enjoy this sort of thing, I'm sure you'll have a marvelous time."

"I'm sure," Cornelia murmured. She dared a quick glance at Peter. He was bareheaded as usual. Snowflakes glinted in his ebony hair and along the thick fringe of the lashes shielding his sea green eyes. Despite that, she could see the amusement in them, as well there might be, for he knew she would not make a scene.

His arrogant assumption that she would have no choice but to comply stirred Cornelia's temper. On impulse, she said, "A great deal is said about your trotters but truth be told, I've seen little of their performance. Perhaps you are not truly confident in their handling?"

To her chagrin, the suggestion that his abilities as a horseman were in doubt only deepened his amusement.

"I'll tell you what," Peter said as he handed her into the sleigh. "Since you aren't sure I can give the grays a decent run, why don't you take charge?"

Her eyes widened. Momentarily forgetting that she had intended to maintain a cool distance between them, she said, "You aren't serious?"

"Why not? To be truthful, there isn't all that much to do. You ride, don't you?"

"Of course."

"Then you already know how to handle a horse. Handling two isn't all that much different. Besides, the grays are well trained. They don't need much coaxing."

Cornelia still looked doubtful. Not that she didn't want to take him up on it; the mere possibility thrilled her. But ladies simply did not do that sort of thing. Such a break with convention would put her further in his debt.

And yet, when would she ever get such a chance again?

In the end, the decision was made for her. As the other sleighs began to move out into the street, Peter lifted the reins and placed them in her hands.

"Go on," he said. "Live dangerously."

Warmth touched her cheeks. She could feel her heart beating more quickly as she brushed the reins lightly across the horses' backs. The sleigh surged forward.

Chapter Eight

The sleighing party went up the Bloomingdale Road. Because of the weather, there was almost no traffic except for others like themselves out to take advantage of the hard-packed snow. Harness bells jangled in the clear, crisp air. The moon was rising over the Palisades on the New Jersey side, casting its silver glow over the frozen river.

The rush of the runners over the snow sent crystalline flurries wafting over the sleigh. Cornelia touched her tongue to her lips, catching a flake even as it melted. She laughed with delight as a heady exhilaration filled her. The horses' effortless speed brought a glorious sense of freedom.

Beside her, Peter murmured, "Shorten up on the left for the curve...that's it. Good."

His approval and encouragement warmed her as much as the exciting ride. She could still hardly believe he was allowing her such liberties. The gentlemen of her acquaintance would have quailed at the mere notion that they entrust their beloved horses to a female. Yet he did it without apparent qualm. Honesty forced her to admit that he was a generous man and kind in a way that far transcended society's notion of proper behavior.

None of which meant he was a paragon, she reminded herself. He was also more than willing to use social courtesies to get his own way. She would be foolish indeed to forget that.

And yet, flying over the snow with him, she could forgive a great deal. If only he were anyone other than Peter Lowell. If only she and Miss Luciana Montrachet were not one and the same. If only he hadn't so cruelly mocked the work in which she took great pride and which was responsible for her family's survival.

Snow continued to dust her eyelashes, concealing the sudden sheen of tears in her azure eyes. So preoccupied was she with the sudden, wishful turn of her thoughts that she failed to note that the horses were changing direction slightly. Instead of staying to the main road, they veered to the left, toward what was at other times of the year a greensward beside the river.

Nor was she alone in her preoccupation. Full, ripe lips, the most delightful profile ever conceived by the Almighty, and the heady sense that his life was spiraling out of control all conspired to distract Peter most effectively. He, too, missed seeing the horses' intent until almost the last moment.

"Pull up," he said urgently, shaking Cornelia from her reverie.

She gasped and tried to do as he said, but the trotters were too swift and she too inexperienced. Before she could stop them, they careened into the park. Seeing that they could not be halted, she should have let up on the reins. But there, too, the lack of practice betrayed her. The horses went straight, she pulled to the left, and the sleigh tilted dangerously.

Instantly Peter's steely arm was around her. He took the reins, did something quick and expert, and the sleigh steadied back down. But not before they were deep into the surrounding trees.

All was silence, hushed darkness and blowing snow. Despite the march of progress, the city had not yet installed gas lamps in the park. Only moonlight shone off the soft white drifts and along the delicately etched branches of the trees.

Cornelia's breath caught in her throat. The sudden danger and its equally swift disappearance were as nothing compared to the shock of awareness she felt at being in Peter's arms. No mistake, that was exactly where she was. With the horses calm, he had let go of the reins and was holding her close against him. The warmth of his big, hard body engulfed her. His embrace was tender and protective yet undeniably possessive. She felt surrounded by raw male strength that could as easily be both danger and delight.

Snow continued to fall, glittering diamondlike in the silver swath of the moon. Somewhere far beyond them the city rumbled on, but here in the winter glen time and place had no meaning. Nothing mattered except each other.

Truly, Cornelia thought dryly, dear Luciana could not have managed it better. The sudden sense of being transported into a scene in one of her own books had a blessedly sobering effect. She drew back slightly from Peter's embrace and regarded him steadily.

"Sir," she said, her voice low and husky, "you presume a great deal."

A corner of his mouth twitched—that marvelously taut yet unexpectedly gentle mouth that had already proved capable of wringing such pleasure from her.

Gravely he said, "That has always been a failing of mine."

"You do not sound as though you regret it," she pointed out, and was pleased, not to say surprised, by how sensible she sounded, almost as though her heart were not beating at a most alarming rate and her breathing becoming quite erratic.

"That is true," he admitted, "and yet there are one or two things I wish could be different." Chief among them that he had met this woman without having first hurt her so badly that she inevitably was wary and distrustful of him.

"Indeed?" Cornelia murmured on a breath of sound. He was so very near. She could feel the snow lying chill on her face, but all else was heat and a strange, melting lightness of being—pure as the moon on the pristine drifts—growing deep within her.

The question was an invitation but one he chose to ignore in favor of the greater enticement of her eyes and her mouth, the delicate curve of her cheek, the shell-like perfection of the earlobe he glimpsed peeking out from behind a chestnut curl and...

Hellfire, what was happening to him? Passion he understood full well, and its plainer cousin, good old-fashioned lust. But this was different. He ached with need for this woman and yet the thought that he might do her an injury, however inadvertent, was so repugnant to him that he knew in that instant he would do anything necessary, to the extent of laying down his own life, to keep her from harm.

Which helped in no way whatsoever, for by all the ordinary measures of society, what he was doing at that very moment was harm enough. Did love come then with some share of hypocrisy that enabled the lover to blot from his sight the full enormity of the hunger within him? To allow him to pretend that all was sweet languor and gentleness when in fact it was the raging life force, ancient as the moon itself, that drove him?

Woolgathering, he thought, and grimaced, for he had never been prone to such lapses. Indeed, the ladies—using the word loosely—of his acquaintance would have agreed that his powers of concentration were nothing short of legendary.

He had sought this moment, conspiring to secure some time alone with the elusive Cornelia. His intent had been to soothe her ruffled feathers—and quite possibly her frayed nerves—so that she would agree to see him again and he could set about the business of courting more properly. But this encounter in the snow-secluded glen was more than he had anticipated, and more than he could resist.

"I'm sorry," Cornelia said.

"What for?" he murmured, hardly aware of what he was saying or, for that matter, what had prompted it.

She drew back and looked at him oddly. "For not managing the horses better. I could have caused us to be seriously hurt."

"Oh, that." He brushed it off. Not for a moment had it crossed his mind that he wouldn't be fully capable of handling any problem she might encounter. He would never have turned the reins over to her if that hadn't been the case.

"No harm done," he assured her.

Cornelia wasn't convinced. She took a deep breath and said what duty required. "Shouldn't we be getting back to the others?"

She was right, of course, Peter thought reluctantly. The curve of the river where they found themselves was not far from the sleighing party's destination. Just to their north the trees had been cleared and work begun for what would eventually be the tomb of the late President Ulysses S. Grant. At present, the site was deserted, construction having been suspended for the winter. However, immediately beyond, he could make out the lights of the gracious Claremont Inn gleaming through the trees.

The Lancasters and their guests would be arriving there shortly, if they weren't already there. It would take very little time for their absence to be noted—and commented on, no doubt at length. Such things did not trouble him in the least, but he suspected Cornelia would not be so immune.

"I suppose we must," he said, but with such palpable reluctance that a little thrill of anticipation curled through her.

Vainly she tried to repress it. This was not one of her novels; it was real life and she would be a terrible fool to forget that, even for a moment. Ignoring the bolder urgings of her nature, she pressed a hand against his chest and said, "We must go."

To her credit, she did manage to get the words out, but the effort was a mistake all the same. The moment she touched him, her resolve fled down the long corridor of her mind, tumbling willy-nilly over far more urgent emotions. She tried to pull her hand away, but it appeared suddenly disconnected from all reason. Rather than obey, it lingered against the broad wall of his chest.

Worse yet—or better, depending on which side of her shockingly contrary nature was consulted—the look in his eyes left little doubt as to how he regarded the matter. His hand, bare despite the chill, covered hers. Gently but implacably, he lowered her until she half lay on the carriage seat.

"Don't run from me anymore, Cornelia," he murmured in the instant before his mouth claimed hers.

Far in the back of her mind, the rational side of proper Miss Cornelia Montgomery took note: her mother had been right. She should have paid more attention to the dictates of fashion, not to mention of propriety. A decorously corseted young woman could not be stretched out in so sublime a position without risking fainting, at the very least, if not outright asphyxiation. But not her, oh, no. She didn't care for tight lacing, she didn't see the sense of it, she was convinced it was injurious to the health. And, to be honest, she was also well aware that nature had so endowed her that she did not require the benefits of it. Therefore, she—sensible, proper Miss Cornelia Montgomery—could be placed in so shocking a position with practiced ease.

Very practiced, if the exquisite torment of his kiss was anything to judge by. She gasped as his hand slipped beneath her fitted jacket to brush lightly over the rigid tip of her breast. He caught the soft sound she made and followed it with the slow, deep thrust of his tongue.

Whatever resistance had remained in Cornelia vanished as swiftly as the fragile snowflake plummeting into flame. She was lost, whirling away into darkness where diamonds danced in a velvet sky and the moon looked down, wisely, over all.

Peter felt her surrender and summoned all his strength. His need was desperate; not ever could he remember feeling so fierce a compulsion to possess a woman. But he could not—would not—take her there in his carriage, in the open, without the slightest pretense of consideration. She was a virgin; despite her exquisite responsiveness, he was quite sure of that. But more, she was Cornelia, whose proud courage enchanted him as much as her intelligence and beauty. She deserved far better. The question was whether he would be able to give it to her. He should stop immediately before matters got entirely out of hand, but the temptation to sate his thirst—and hers—just a little was irresistible.

The fur coverlet had slipped to the floor of the carriage. He gathered it up, drawing it around her. His long, blunt-tipped fingers fumbled over the small pearl buttons of her blouse. He parted the fragile lace to reveal a silk camisole trimmed with tiny rosebuds and beneath it, high, firm breasts darkly tipped.

"Perfect," he said as he held her, wrapped in fur, warmed by his breath. Her skin smelled of summer, lilac and roses tinged with honey. She was satin smooth beneath his mouth and hands. Heat coursed through him. He had a sudden, dazzling sense of the sun burning behind his eyes, denying the night. Urgently he pushed the camisole aside and let his mouth close over her nipple, suckling the rosy crest. She arched against him, her hands tangling in his hair as his name broke from her lips.

Sheer male satisfaction drove him to stave off restraint, if only for a few precious moments. "Promise me," he murmured, raising his head.

Her eyes, clouded with passion, met his. "Promise . . . what?"

He cupped her breast, his thumb rubbing back and forth over the hardened crest. "You won't deny this . . . or me."

She trembled convulsively and he felt a moment's guilt for driving her so far. But in the next instant, he saw her grow calm again as her pride slipped back into place. "I am not a hypocrite," she said steadily.

He drew a ragged breath and closed his eyes tightly for a moment, fighting for control. Her honesty was more than he could have hoped for, and surely more than he would have received from any other woman. She made no protestations, indulged in no hysterics and demanded no declarations. That last part worried him a little, but he pushed it aside for the moment.

Gently he drew her upright. She turned away to rearrange her clothing but not before he saw the bright flush staining her cheeks. When she was done, she avoided looking at him. Her confusion, however she tried to mask it, gave him a certain wry satisfaction. It seemed only fair, considering how she had turned his life upside down. But no more. Now that he understood the source of her vexation with him, he had the upper hand. He would enjoy drawing out his proud and prickly Cornelia, teaching her the delights of pleasure such as the inimitable Miss Montrachet had never dreamed of, until she was as sweetly compliant as any woman could be. He would shape her to his hand and then . . .

Such pleasant thoughts distracted him as he took up the reins and expertly turned the horses back toward the road. So complete was his preoccupation that he did not notice the determined set to Cornelia's features, nor the decidedly stubborn gleam in eyes no longer dazed by passion but lit instead by the clear light of determination. She desired Peter Lowell; heaven help her, she might even be falling in love with him. So be it. She had spoken the truth when she told him she wasn't a hypocrite.

But neither was she a fool. He needed very little encouraging—indeed, none at all—to dominate her completely. That she would never allow.

Her back straightened as she sat, looking straight ahead into the night. Accustomed as he was to the ladies of the upper class who measured the success of their lives purely in terms of who their husbands happened to be, it would undoubtedly shock him to realize he had encountered a female of far more independent mind.

The discovery would do him good, she decided, when and if she eventually allowed him to make it. But for the moment she was more than content to keep her secret to herself. Knowing that she had an entire identity apart from anything he credited her with made her feel far better able to deal with him than she would have done otherwise.

The more she thought of it, the more she decided that she quite liked knowing something he did not. He was far too overwhelming as it was. Without dear Luciana to buck her up, she would feel utterly at a loss as to how to deal with him. And if that ever happened . . .

It didn't bear thinking of. Better to settle back as the smooth gait of the trotters carried them swiftly over the snow. The inn was just up ahead. Light poured from its many windows. Laughter rang on the crystalline air. The pungent smoke of the bonfire on the front lawn and the leaping shadows cast by its flames swirled around the elegantly dressed men and women.

Peter drew the sleigh to a halt and stepped out. He stood tall and graceful, the fire behind him and the night all around. Silently he held out his hand.

Cornelia remained where she was, regarding him steadily. Not a flicker of doubt showed in his gaze. His confidence in the outcome could not have been clearer.

Nor could the challenge he represented. She was playing a dangerous game with a man her better judgment told her she ought to have nothing to do with. Yet the contest drew her irresistibly. Or was it the man himself who did that?

Mr. Peter Lowell was too damn used to having his own way, that was the problem. But not this time. Not with her.

She slipped her hand into his and heard, in the imagined distance, the clarion call of an ancient battle joined.

Chapter Nine

Three days later, Cornelia stepped from the carriage near the Lowell mansion, holding the skirt of her gown up with one hand while with the other she steadied the hood of her evening cape. It was almost eight o'clock, the appointed hour at which the gala was to begin. The press of carriages along Fifth Avenue and the adjacent side street was so severe that many guests were getting out and walking. Being fashionably late was all well and good, but even the most sophisticated were anxious not to miss anything. Cornelia did not share the general enthusiasm, but she could not dissuade her mother and brothers from abandoning their hansom and joining the stream heading toward the house.

A glimpse of the imposing structure was enough to heighten the nervousness that had been growing in her all day. On an avenue that was rapidly earning the name Millionaires' Row, where magnificent structures vied for attention one after another, the Lowell mansion stood out. It surpassed even Mrs. Astor's breathtaking chateau on the next block and utterly eclipsed the twin Vanderbilt residences not far away.

Designed in the Roman manner around a central court, the house and its adjacent gardens took up an entire city block. The walls and domed roof were of white marble. Ceiling-high windows emitted dazzling light from crystal chandeliers so large that they could be clearly seen from outside. The double doors of beaten bronze that formed the main entrance stood open to the steady stream of arriving guests.

Footmen garbed in silk and velvet, wearing powdered French wigs, stood by to check invitations and provide directions as needed to the various cloak-rooms. In one of those set aside for the ladies, Cornelia and her mother parted with their capes. As they joined the flow heading toward the main reception rooms, Melanie murmured discreetly behind her fan, "Incredible, absolutely incredible. I don't want to sound like a hayseed, but nothing one hears quite prepares one for the reality, does it?"

Cornelia shook her head, utterly at a loss for words. The house overwhelmed her. Besides its sheer size and wealth, it was extraordinarily beautiful, decorated in the best of taste, in every way truly regal. Had she visited it as a stranger, she would have delighted in it in an impersonal sort of way. But the house belonged, like so much else, to the man who filled her waking thoughts and turned her dreams to a torment.

For three days, since the sleighing party, she had rarely been out of Peter's company. He had called at the Montgomery home each morning, spending a pleasant hour or so chatting with her mother and brothers before escorting Cornelia to some suitable place or event. Suitable, that is, for a lady and gentleman just beginning the process of establishing whether or not they might deal congenially together. Considering what had actually passed between them, Cornelia thought she could be pardoned for feeling a tad befuddled and, much as she hated to admit it, just a wee bit chagrined.

So far, they had been to Wallack's theater for a performance of *Twelfth Night,* to a concert at Steinway Hall, an exhibit at the Art Students League, and—the most interesting in her opinion—an ice-fishing expedition on the Hudson at which she was the only female present and where she had, with just a little help from Peter, caught the largest fish.

Through three days of almost ceaseless activity, they had behaved with perfect propriety. The encounters in the sleigh and earlier in the park might never have taken place.

Indeed, there were times when she wondered if she hadn't imagined them. Only the blunt conviction that her creativity did not extend that far kept her from thinking she might be going mad.

In the center hall, they rejoined Ted and Jed. Cornelia felt a surge of pride as she regarded her brothers. They looked handsome, upright and blessedly unfazed by the grandeur of their surroundings. On their arms, the Montgomery ladies proceeded into the ballroom where their host waited to greet them.

What appeared to be an entire orchestra was tucked into one corner of the vast expanse. An immense Christmas tree stood at one end, festooned with hundreds of glittering lights. The windows looked out into the gardens awash with lanterns illuminating the gravel paths and the fountains in which water splashed. Cornelia stared at the water for a long moment before she realized why it captured her attention. Fountains in winter? It was below freezing outside.

"How...?" she murmured.

Beside her, Jed said, "They heat the water underground before it enters the fountains."

Cornelia looked at him disbelievingly. "You aren't serious?"

"Absolutely. How else would they manage it?"

"But that's absurd. What a terrible waste."

"It's only for this evening," he assured her. Lowering his voice a notch, he added, "Although I understand that *la grande madame* Lowell feels she ought to be able to keep the fountains flowing all year round."

"Who stops her?"

"Why Peter, of course. Make no mistake, everyone toes the line where he's concerned."

Not everyone, Cornelia thought, although she kept it to herself. They were moving up the receiving line. She could see him directly ahead of her, looking devastating in evening dress as he always did. His mother was at his side. With her were two young women Cornelia took to be Peter's sisters. They both caught sight of her as she approached and did not conceal their interest. But their mother managed to ignore Cornelia entirely until she was standing directly in front of her. Only then did Georgette deign to acknowledge her presence.

Her glance touched on Cornelia frostily, slid away and...

Returned. The eyes that it was said could determine the exact lineage of any human being—and come within five percent of his bank balance—widened as they regarded Cornelia. Beneath such scrutiny, a lesser woman would have shriveled. Cornelia merely smiled. Never mind that inside she quailed.

She had brought this upon herself. The gown she wore, while far from shocking, was not the sort customarily worn by young, unwed girls of good family. It was, however, stunning, a glorious design of azure silk draped low over the creamy smoothness of her shoulders and breasts, the sleeves concealing scant inches of her upper arms, the waist tapered and the skirt noticeably less full than usual so that when she moved, the long, lithe line of her legs was not so much revealed as hinted at. With it she wore no jewelry, no frilly fan, no little evening purse, nothing to draw the eye from the stark, unmistakable fact that only a woman of flawless confidence would dare to appear before the world garbed in such daring simplicity.

No member of her family had seen the dress before; Cornelia had taken care to appear downstairs with her cape already in place. And until this moment, they had been too concentrated on the activity going on around them to pay her much attention. Her mother gasped softly, pursed her lips and lifted her head defiantly. Jed paled slightly before stiffening his back and glaring at Georgette Lowell as though to dare her to make any comment other than the most complimentary. Ted, on the other hand, looked frankly delighted. He leaned closer to his sister, smiled and said, "About time, Corney. Thought for a while there that you weren't taking the whole thing seriously."

She gave him a little smile in return, but her attention was distracted. Peter took a step forward, gave her a grin in which admiration and desire mingled equally, and said, "Would you care to dance?"

That was enough to restore Georgette to her senses. Sputtering, she said, "We haven't finished receiving." Indeed, they had not. Although a hundred and more guests were already mingling in the center of the ballroom, accepting flutes of champagne being carried around by the waiters and chatting animatedly among themselves, several hundred more were either still in line or streaming through the doors.

Peter shrugged lightly and took Cornelia's hand. "I know who they all are," he assured Georgette, "and they know who I am. That ought to take care of it."

Before his mother could object that it most certainly did not, he led Cornelia out toward the center of the ballroom. The slightest nod of his head was enough to command the orchestra conductor's attention. Instantly the musicians straightened in their chairs, the baton rapped, and the glorious strains of a Strauss waltz filled the air.

"With your permission," Peter said, and took her in his arms.

They danced. Cornelia lost all sense of time and place. The ballroom faded from her mind and all the people in it. Nothing existed except the music and the man. His hand resting lightly on her waist was the sole anchor in a world suddenly without constraint. His eyes holding hers touched to the very core of her being and made her feel gloriously, giddily free. The other guests drew back, the better to observe their heedless flight. Tongues wagged, heads nodded, and off in the corners of the ballroom, a few discreet wagers were swiftly placed.

And when at last the strains of the waltz died away, they were left standing in the center of the room, surrounded by several hundred pairs of eyes, yet looking for all the world as though they were utterly alone.

Peter tucked Cornelia's hand into the crook of his arm and led her gently to the side. He, far more than she, understood the implications of what he had done. Had he climbed to the roof of the mansion and announced to all the world that she was his and his alone, he could not have driven the point home more effectively. Now he had only to hope that Cornelia had gotten the message as clearly.

Grimly he considered what he would do if she had not. Three days of socially acceptable courting had left him on a keen edge of frustration so acute he had to wonder how much longer he would be accountable for his actions. If not for that damn Luciana Montrachet business, he would have settled the matter before ever letting her get out of the sleigh.

Only the concern—not to say the fear—that his inadvertent abuse of Cornelia's pride required amending before matters could proceed between them had led him to go slowly. But no more. Tonight he no longer felt compelled to refrain from taking full advantage of her exquisite sensuality. On the contrary, he was determined to do exactly that.

But first, he wanted to soothe the nervousness he sensed within her. A footman approached. Peter removed two flutes of champagne from the man's tray and handed one to Cornelia. She accepted it without a word and before his startled eyes drank it in a single swallow.

''Thirsty?'' he asked matter-of-factly as he took the empty glass from her, set it back on the tray and handed her another.

She was sufficiently surprised by her own actions to answer honestly. "I must be. It is rather warm in here, don't you think?"

In fact, Peter had a particular dislike of overheated ballrooms and saw to it that his own was kept comfortably cool, no mean feat considering that several hundred guests produced the heat equivalent to a fully stocked furnace. The servants had standing orders to keep sufficient windows open to assure fresh air and a pleasant temperature.

Rather than say any of this, he merely nodded. Her cheeks were delightfully flushed, her eyes sparkled, and the rapid rise and fall of her breasts suggested that the waltz had been effective. His smile deepened. "Come and meet some people."

It was his intention to introduce Cornelia to several of his friends, men like himself with whom he shared the particular camaraderie of shared adventures and commitments. Teddy Roosevelt was somewhere in the crowd, undoubtedly craning his neck to get a better look at the woman everyone was by now talking about. And there were others; not many, for he was a selective man, but enough.

Before he could begin to do that, however, a gaggle of his mother's acquaintances surrounded them. Georgette herself was nowhere to be seen, having judiciously removed herself with the beginnings of a migraine. Lying upstairs in her gilded bedchamber with a cold cloth over her eyes, she was struggling to come to terms with the fact that Miss Cornelia Montgomery was not some bit of fluff who could be sent packing from her son's life. Indeed, she gave every evidence of having a spirit that was nothing short of formidable.

With Georgette missing in action, it fell to her allies to carry the flag. Some had daughters of their own and were not at all pleased to see New York's most eligible bachelor paying court to an interloper. Others were merely fascinated by the spectacle. They clustered around, sharp-eyed, mouths moving behind the concealment of their fans.

"Dear Peter..."

"Marvelous affair..."

"Such music..."

"Poor Georgette... headache..."

"Extraordinary gown, Miss...?"

"Montgomery," Peter said smoothly, though he understood full well that every one of them knew her name and in all likelihood a great deal more about her. Her lineage, including her father's bank failure, was undoubtedly a prime topic of conversation. The thought angered him.

"Of the Chicago Montomerys?" one of the ladies asked archly. There were no Chicago Montgomerys, or at least none of any account.

The others tittered, but their amusement died when they saw the look on Peter's face. He was the son of one of their own, and they had known him when he was in short pants. It was tempting to think of him as being very like their own children, sharing their parents' prejudices, or—if they did ever think for themselves—mindful enough of their inheritances to keep quiet about it.

But the tall, formidable man before them was different. To begin with, he was a man, not a boy in a man's suit. He had long ago recognized that if he lived by the rules and restrictions of his social class, he would end up not having lived at all. Instead, he devised his own code, a harsh one to be sure and one many could not have abided by. He lived with passion and with honor. He was never deliberately cruel, especially not to women, but neither would he tolerate cruelty in others.

Above all, he protected what belonged to him. His arm tightened around Cornelia's waist. He was about to speak when she unexpectedly forestalled him.

"The County Kerr Montgomerys," she said evenly. "My great-grandfather left there early in the century one step ahead of a British hangman's rope. I understand several of you can claim Gaelic heritage. Mrs. Hollister, your family's name was O'Houlighan originally, wasn't it? And Mrs. Gerard, the name was Fitzgerald, I believe?"

"How would you...?"

"My word..."

"I never..."

Cornelia smiled. "It's true the Montgomerys have only been in New York a few generations, nothing compared to the rest of you, I'm sure. However, we have managed to learn our way around well enough."

No one appeared ready to dispute her on that score. Instead, the ladies viewed her with new respect—and caution.

"That being the case, Miss Montgomery," one of them said, "you are surely aware of the lamentable state of the city these days. It is a constant struggle to prevent the lower orders from pulling us all down."

"How true," another chimed in. "Why just the other day I was reading Peter's column in the *Journal*—" she inclined her head in his direction "—the one about the dreadful state of popular culture. How insightfully you analyzed the problem. We can hardly expect our inferiors to behave with decency when they are allowed to wallow in the worst sort of trash masquerading as entertainment.''

Cornelia's breath caught. For a horrible moment, she thought her secret had been exposed, that the women knew who she was and were merely baiting her before moving in for the kill. Panic filled her, but in the next moment she realized that she was wrong. The woman who had spoken appeared to have no understanding of the impact of her words. She sought only to flatter Peter, as she undoubtedly did every powerful male she came in contact with. It was an instinct they all shared.

Not that the choice of topic was completely innocent. It was designed to drive home the difference between the daughter of a failed banker who had never been of much import to begin with, at least so far as they were concerned, and the possessor of one of the oldest and most honored names in the country, a name not incidentally accompanied by one of its largest fortunes.

If it mattered so much to them, Cornelia thought, they could drive home all the points they liked. But she did not need to listen to them. An opening appeared in the crowd. Her hand tightened on Peter's arm, hoping he would spot the opportunity to escape and take it.

But instead, he looked down at her and frowned. The sudden turn in the conversation took him aback. He was worried about Cornelia's response. She looked pale, and the way she held on to him suggested she was in distress. As well she should be, given the unfairness of the attack. Worse yet, it was his fault. In his thoughtless arrogance, he had derided her work and held her up to public contempt.

The key fact that he wasn't supposed to know he had done it slipped from his mind. Without thinking, he said, "I must disagree. In hindsight, I realize that I was unduly harsh. Many of the books published by the popular press have a surprising amount to recommend them. Had I looked into the matter properly before writing about it, I would have said so."

The ladies stared at him in surprise but their reaction was nothing as compared to Cornelia's. She was dumbfounded. Did he really mean what he said? Was it possible that her work might not be an insurmountable barrier between them? Certainly he no longer seemed the arrogant and presumptuous man she had thought him to be. On the contrary, she could well believe that he possessed a rare sensitivity, a generosity of spirit, a...

A guilty conscience. The thought sprang unbidden into her mind the instant she looked at him. The way his eyes met hers and what they communicated left no doubt. *He knew.*

Horror filled her. Images of them together darted through her mind. No wonder he had become interested in her, sought her out, showered her with attention. What a fool she was not to have seen it before! Everyone knew Peter Lowell was not the marrying sort. He avoided proper young ladies like the proverbial plague. But a woman who violated the strictures of her class by writing books of a certain sort, and who then went even further and allowed liberties normally permitted only of a husband, that woman could be considered fair game.

Her cheeks flamed as she considered the wantonness of her behavior. Surely she had given him every reason to believe she would succumb to whatever arrangement he proposed.

No thought remained in her mind except to flee. She could not possibly face him now. Turning, she murmured something about visiting the cloakroom and hurried away.

Peter watched her go with concern. He understood that she might need a few minutes to herself, but he would have preferred to waste no time putting the matter to rest. Once she understood that he was genuinely sorry, they could move on to other, happier matters.

But first he had to wait for her return. Long minutes passed. He excused himself to the ladies, who were glad enough for him to go, having a great deal to discuss. Several people spoke to him but he did no more than acknowledge their presence. Standing off to one side of the ballroom, he sipped a glass of champagne without tasting it and kept his eyes on the doors through which Cornelia would return. When a quarter hour had passed with no sign of her, his impatience got the better of him. She could have some time alone later. He needed her.

But there was no sign of Cornelia, not in the entry hall still crowded with arriving guests, nor on the stairs leading to the ladies' cloakroom, nor in that sanctum itself where he drew shocked gasps when he dared to glance inside.

The servant in charge of collecting wraps looked startled when his master suddenly appeared before him, demanding the whereabouts of a certain young lady. He thought fast and said, "Chestnut hair? Blue dress? Right you are, sir. She just left."

"Left?" Peter repeated disbelievingly. "What do you mean, left?"

The man looked nervous. It seemed plain enough. "She asked for her cloak, sir. Usually when they do that, they're leaving."

"Was she alone?"

The man nodded. "Aye, and come to think of it, she looked upset. A shame that, for she spoke right nicely, even said thank you, which plenty of them never bother with." He eyed Peter narrowly, interested to see what response this would bring.

He was not disappointed, for the look on his employer's face was such that had the footman himself been on the receiving end of it, he was certain he would have been turned to ash. As it was, he could already look forward to the attention he would command when he described the moment to his fellow servants. Too bad it was so fleeting, for in the next instant, Peter was gone, his broad back disappearing into the crowd.

It parted before him swiftly, no one being foolish enough to detain a man who looked so grimly determined. Cold air struck him as he stepped beyond the double bronze doors and looked quickly up and down the street. Fifth Avenue was a mess, jammed with carriages that were going nowhere quickly, or even slowly for that matter. The snow had begun to fall in greater earnest. It swirled in the gaslight, drifting over horses, drivers and pedestrians alike.

Ordinarily he would have been touched by its beauty, but now it was only an inconvenience and a concern. Where could Cornelia have gone? If she had entered one of the carriages, she was still sitting there unmoving. But he doubted she had done any such thing. Serious as she obviously was about putting distance between them, she would be on foot. Alone in the darkness and snow. His mouth set tautly. When he got his hands on her . . .

He began to run, long legs eating up the distance. Instinctively he headed south in the direction he believed she would have gone. Her own home was that way, if several miles distant, and she would have stood a better chance of finding an empty hansom farther downtown. Not that there would be many of them around on Christmas Eve. The streets were thronged with last-minute shoppers, party goers and the less savory types who were drawn out by both. To any of this last group, a beautiful woman alone, unprotected and in distress would seem like manna from heaven. He had to find her.

In the end, it was his height that served him best, for he was a full head taller than most of the crowd. Without that, he would not have been able to see far enough ahead to the feminine shape standing near a gas lamp, the sudden gleam of black velvet as her cape swirled about her, the familiar tilt of her head as she looked anxiously around.

He was at her side in an instant, having come close to trampling several people in order to reach her. "Cornelia," he said as he took her arm.

She started and for a moment her eyes were filled with relief and something that looked perilously close to joy. Until the realization of the true situation between them slammed back down on her.

"Leave me," she said, her voice choked.

Leave her? Did she think him mad? "Don't be ridiculous," he said. It was hardly loverlike, but under the circumstances it was the best he could do. "We have to talk."

With sudden fury, she wrenched her arm away and rounded on him. "How dare you? Of all the mendacious, duplicitous, low-life deceivers ever to crawl out from under a scum-covered rock, you take the cake. I don't know how you discovered the truth about me and I don't care, but I'll have you know that I'm a damn sight more honorable than those jumped-up society biddies your mother keeps trying to foist off on you. I'm a Montgomery and I'm proud of it. I *like* the books I write and so do plenty of other people. If you weren't so all-fired arrogant and presumptuous, you wouldn't be so quick to—"

"Be quiet," he said, and kissed her. It was far and away the most interesting thing any of the passersby had seen that evening and they all stopped to stare. Not that it mattered. Peter and Cornelia were oblivious to the attention they drew. Nothing existed for them except the incandescent passion flaring between them and beneath it, a lifetime's worth of tenderness.

When at last he raised his head and looked down at her, his eyes were a bit dazed. Fondly he said, "You idiot."

Proof positive, if any were needed, that he was a flesh-and-blood human being and not the hero of a pulp romance, who would absolutely have known better.

"Idiot?" Cornelia said. The seesaw effect of her emotions overcame her. From despair to relief, from dread to passion, from joy to anger, she simply could not stand it anymore. She did what no Luciana Montrachet heroine would ever have done—she swung back her foot and landed Peter a good one right on the shin.

Of course, it would have been a good deal more effective if she had been wearing something other than silk dancing slippers, rather tattered ones and soggy from her flight. Still, he let out a satisfying yelp and reached for his leg even as she moaned and took hold of her aching foot.

Their heads bumped, their balance threatened, and they only just managed to remain upright as they fell into each other's arms.

"Give him what for, love," offered an obliging young woman as she observed the scene. "They've all done *something* to deserve it."

"Start as you mean to go, friend," replied an older man, "or she'll have the upper hand forever."

The crowd fell to debating the various approaches to dealings between the sexes as Peter and Cornelia managed to make their way to the shelter of a nearby building entrance. There, in the shadows of a stone arch, they looked at each other cautiously.

"I'm sorry," Peter said at length.

"As well you should be," Cornelia said. She took a deep breath and straightened her shoulders. "I don't care what my books may have encouraged you to believe, I won't be your mistress."

His mouth dropped open. It was comical, especially in a man who was normally so self-possessed. But the fury building in his eyes suggested it would be a mistake to laugh.

"My what?" he demanded.

"You heard me," Cornelia replied. She absolutely would not back down now, no matter how he made her feel. She would say goodbye, walk away and never see him again. Never mind that her life would be overwhelmingly barren, somehow she would—

"You thought I wanted you to be my mistress," Peter said. It wasn't a question; he had gotten the message loud and clear. "You thought," he went on with dangerous exactitude, "that I sat in your mother's parlor making polite conversation with her and your brothers while plotting to whisk you away to a bed of sin."

Cornelia flushed. The way he put it made her seem like . . . like an idiot. But she knew what had happened between them and she wasn't about to forget it. "What else could I think?" she demanded.

"What else? Don't you ever read your own damn books? I've only read one of them and I know what's supposed to happen at the end."

Her eyes widened, reflecting the swirling snow falling like dancing stars over the street, the city, the world. He couldn't possibly mean—

Cornelia gasped. Her feet had left the ground. She was floating, held tight in Peter's arms as he carried her effortlessly off.

"Where are we going?" she demanded. It seemed the proper thing to do.

"To an apartment I keep around the corner from here," he said matter-of-factly. He strode along with perfect ease, ignoring the good-natured laughter of the people who saw them, as well as Cornelia's own half-hearted struggles. She knew she ought to do a better job of resisting but she just couldn't manage it.

"You aren't serious?" she suggested.

"I've never been more so," he assured her. "It's clear to me that you have an unruly turn of mind, probably the result of too much novel reading, not to mention writing. I'm not risking any more misunderstandings between us. We're going to settle this once and for all."

"And just how," she inquired, "do you intend to do that?"

"By compromising you, proper Miss Cornelia Montgomery," he said. The look of sheer, overwhelming love that he gave her undermined whatever sinister implications might have lurked behind those words.

"And then," he added for good measure, "by marrying you. Any objection to that?"

"None that I can think of," Cornelia murmured. She thought she did rather well to get that much out, considering that her heart was pounding and she had no breath. Dimly, in the far reaches of her mind, she was aware of a startled doorman holding a door open for them, a vast expanse of marble lobby, a gilded elevator, another door and a servant who disappeared with impressive speed. Then there was only a shadowed bedroom, soft murmurings, soaring heat, tender passion and the promise of love everlasting.

Luciana would have been pleased. Not surprised, of course, for she was never that, but most definitely pleased.

Epilogue

Decorum demands that we draw the curtain but open it again on a crisp January day when Jonathan escorts Cornelia down the aisle of Saint Thomas's on Fifth Avenue with all society in attendance. Forgive Jonathan if he looks a bit distracted. He's trying to decide what to do now that Luciana Montrachet seems destined for early retirement.

Or is she? Only Cornelia knows for sure, and she isn't saying. But there is the little matter of the untouched notebook waiting in her suite of rooms at the Lowell house. And the advertisement Peter showed her for something called a typewriter, which he says she might find useful. Not to mention all the marvelous inspiration she's been getting...

Goodbye, New York of 1892. Goodbye, Cornelia and Peter. Long live Luciana!

* * * * *

Dear Reader,

Christmas is without doubt my favorite time of year. I start looking forward to it months ahead of time, and the closer it gets, the more excited I become. We actually start our celebration right after Thanksgiving, when we bake fruitcakes. As soon as that's done, it's time to get into the attic. The Advent calendars come out first, along with the wreath. Each day, the children count off for Christmas, and each Sunday we light another candle. We cut our own tree at a farm near our house—an excursion that involves much debate and discussion, a hayride and hot chocolate around a bonfire. Having young children (ours will both be six when you read this) adds to the fun as we plan what to ask Santa to bring.

The days start to rush by, and before we know it, the presents are wrapped, grandparents have arrived and there's nothing left to do except enjoy those last few, precious hours of Christmas Eve, when the world lies hushed with waiting. For us, Christmas is a chance to put aside the concerns of everyday life and remember what really matters, that love is the greatest gift we can all share. I hope your holiday will be a time of rejoicing and renewal, and that the coming year will bring you much happiness.

Maura Seger

CHRISTMAS BOUNTY

Erin
Yorke

To Elsie and Jenny Ampuja,
whose hearts are always
filled with the spirit of Christmas

and
To Dad, Mom, Peggy, Peter, Veronica,
Gloria, Francis and Helen,
who fill my heart with Christmas memories

Scottish Shortbread

1 cup sugar
1 lb butter (creamed)*
1 egg yolk
4½ cups sifted flour

Cream butter and sugar together; then add egg yolk and continue mixing well. Gradually add flour, kneading thoroughly.

When all flour has been used, remove mixture from the bowl and knead on a wooden board or table until batter is smooth.

Either form mixture into a round and put on an ungreased cookie sheet or place in a shallow 8" × 12" pan.

Use the rounded side of a teaspoon to form depressions around the edges of the shortbread. Use the tines of a fork to make indentations in its surface.

Bake in a 350° F oven for one hour.

Remove from oven and allow to cool five minutes. Cut into pieces. Remove from pan to finish cooling. Store in airtight container. If you can keep your family away, the shortbread will keep for weeks.

*Substitution of margarine will seriously alter the result.

Chapter One

Scotland 1858

The weak December sunlight struggled against the darkness, which crept forward earlier now that winter had arrived in the small Highland village of Glenmuir. Deepening shades of grey blended with the color of the rough-hewn stone used to construct the simple houses huddled together along the rutted and frozen mud of the town's primitive roads. Despite the approaching Christmastide, a casual outsider would see no reason for rejoicing in such a desolate area. Yet to the observant eye, Glenmuir was not a bleak place at all.

The smoke of peat fires curled cozily from chimneys, and small paned windows allowed the softness of isolated candlelight within to spill out unto the hamlet's main thoroughfare. Delicious aromas wafted through the air as the local baker worked overlong to fill the gentry's demand for delicacies. They were mouth-watering dainties most of the local inhabitants could no longer afford. Nevertheless, it was evident that seasonal cheer had infected the small cluster of townsfolk standing before MacGregor and Son, the local mercantile.

Their marketing baskets were almost as empty as their pockets, but their faces were aglow with an expectancy quite out of place for middle-aged souls in so poor a region of Scotland. It was as if those who called Glenmuir home were immune to their poverty, viewing the village through a haze of hope, warm memories and possessive pride.

Certainly these were the feelings of the young female who left the house of the local seamstress and stepped out into the raw dampness that was December in the Highlands. At twenty-four years of age, Blair Duncan was a bonny lass indeed, the kind of woman whose fine looks demanded a second glance. Her reddish brown hair and clear blue eyes complemented a pretty face that, in spite of its delicate features, spoke of strength if not actual stubbornness.

Though her medium-height frame was wrapped in a faded but still serviceable plaid, there could be no doubt that there was a womanly shape beneath it. Despite the fact that the ancient garment was worn atop a frayed brown frock, the villagers nevertheless viewed her with respect when they spied her at the end of the street and watched as she made her way along the cobblestones to the establishment of MacGregor and Son.

"Och, 'tis young Blair, a wonderful lass she is," crooned Mrs. MacNab, a motherly sort, her silver hairs ample evidence of the nine boisterous sons she had raised.

"Aye, and a plucky one as well," Ian Ferguson murmured, a smile lighting the farmer's usually dour face. "She takes after her father. Other Highland lairds may have sold their birthrights, but Jaime Duncan was not one to succumb to the temptations of English riches. A fiery and proud Scot, the old laird was. Why he fair equated accepting English pounds for his estate with surrendering to the enemy."

"It's only too bad we dinna realize, until after he had died, what his struggle cost him," Ian's cousin Charlie lamented. "Poor Blair, left with little more than the Duncan lands and that near empty house."

"Even had we kenned, Charlie, what could we have done?" Ian asked, shaking his head, hard put to maintain his former cheer as he contemplated the situation. "There's little enough to go around, and that's the pity of it. Thank God, Blair continues to resist putting Duncan holdings into the hands of some English aristocrat! There are too many of them around as it is...."

"Aye, Glenmuir has lost half of its population these last few years," Charlie Ferguson agreed. "Imagine turning out entire families so that one English aristocrat can hunt. It's only too bad Queen Victoria has such a fondness for the Highlands. If she dinna like the place, these intruders would have stayed in England where they belong."

"Aye, then Scots wouldna have to leave their own homeland in order to survive."

"But we've hung on, haven't we? And just like young Blair, we manage," Mrs. MacNab said, coming closer to her companions and lowering her voice as the young woman in question continued in their direction. "It's hard for the lass, making do with so little after living a better life as a child. Still, she's a strong one. Of course Blair has turned down bids to purchase

the lands but do ye ken that she has spurned other offers as well?''

"What sort of offers?'' Charles asked.

"Why marriage, of course! And what young lass her
age doesna dream of her own household and pretty
gowns?''

"Things of that sort do na mean much to our lass,''
Ian insisted. "It's the Duncan pride which makes her
heart beat, not the desire for fripperies. She is, after all,
one of us. What would she want with an English husband?''

"Ian, you're showing your age if you canna recall
what a lass as bonny as Blair would want with a brawny
young lad, English or no,'' Charlie baited, enjoying the
sour expression that fleeted across the other man's
features as the remark hit home.

"Blair Duncan is too bright a female to fall for a
hottening of the blood. Don't ye think she learned a
lesson from seeing the results of Mary Connery's marriage to that English thief, Montgomery?'' Ian retorted as he brought his face closer to his cousin's,
daring him to disagree. "After they were wed, Mary
allowed him to christen the home they had built on the
Connery estate Lindsay Hall, placing an English name
on good Scottish ground but as soon as poor Mary was
laid to rest, he took off for England and the lad with
him. And not a word from them Montgomerys until
the land was sold. English blood doesna warm, no
matter how hot the passion.''

"Now stop it, the both of ye! I canna believe you're
so near to brawling with the Christmas season close as
it is. Besides, 'tis not right for the lass to hear talk such
as this, especially seeing her feelings for the lad once

upon a time," Mrs. MacNab scolded in a fierce whisper as if the men beside her were two of her own brood of wayward bairns. Then, in an effort to put an end to the argument, she turned with a smile and called out greetings to the young woman who by now had reached the merchant's door.

Returning their hellos with a graceful wave, Blair noticed with amusement that though Mrs. MacNab doubtless had years of practice in stopping clashes between obstinate males, she had never learned to do so discreetly. The woman's benevolent smile contrasted sharply with the glare she sent her companions so that the scowls of the two men disappeared instantly as they doffed their hats to the old laird's daughter.

Blair reached for the polished brass handle of the shop's door and wondered what it was that could have upset Ian and Charlie Ferguson now. The two of them had become scrappier. But then life had turned harder for all of them these past few years, and she supposed that even the approach of Christmas, Hogmanay, and the Daft Days in between, couldn't completely erase the problems besetting the inhabitants of Glenmuir.

The realization strengthened her resolve as she stepped across the threshold of MacGregor and Son and scanned the shop's well-stocked shelves. MacGregor was one of the few villagers who didn't mind the English invasion. The business of the outlanders, with all their demands, had been a great source of income to him. If the man could profit by others' misfortunes, the man could afford to be charitable, Blair decided as she stretched to her full height in preparation for battle with the proprietor.

Impoverished as Blair might be, she was still a Duncan, and there were the old traditions to uphold. She might have little more than they, but the young woman was determined to distribute Christmas baskets to the villagers and other locals as her family had always done, though each successive year made it harder to gather what was needed.

Of course, she had put by what she could, but her own resources were meager. It wouldn't hurt MacGregor to part with some merchandise, and unless she could make the shopkeeper see things her way, the holiday season might very well be less bright for many of her neighbors and tenants.

True, that mysterious benefactor known as the Spirit of Christmas had been quite evident and most generous in Glenmuir these past few years, and she, herself, had been the recipient of his generosity. But the young Scotswoman had learned in recent times not to depend upon unknowns. What if there were no Spirit this Christmas? Certainly it was better to swallow her pride and bully MacGregor into making a donation for her baskets. Then she could rest assured that she had brought some joy to Glenmuir's celebration of Christmastide.

With this thought in mind, Blair adjusted her full mouth into her most winning smile, a dangerous determination glinting in her deep blue eyes as she stalked forward and engaged an increasingly wary Amos MacGregor in conversation. He'd been the victim of her charitable bent before, and he'd not part with his goods without a fight.

A scarce ten minutes later, Blair emerged from the shop, genuine contentment lighting her pretty features. She had almost giggled at MacGregor's sigh of relief as he had ushered her from his place and then locked the door and pulled the shade, afraid the relentless Miss Duncan might well change her mind and decide he could afford to give more to her charitable enterprise.

However, despite MacGregor's reluctance, it had been a profitable visit. Surely her present mood reflected the satisfaction her raiding ancestors had felt after they had stolen a few head of cattle from another clan, she mused as she shifted her basket, weightier now, from one arm to the other. The wicker groaned under the strain placed upon it by two sacks of sugar, one of tea, blocks of salt, a pair of scissors and a few small mirrors. These treasures had joined the scraps of ribbon contributed by the seamstress, and the heaviness of the load made Blair's heart considerably lighter as she began to walk towards the villagers still huddled together in gossip.

There was time for a bit of conversation and friendship before she made her way back to her quiet home, and after the day's success, Blair deemed a few moments of idleness a deserved reward.

She had only taken a step or two, however, when she was hailed by a voice coming from behind her, the rich vibrancy of the tones bringing an unwelcome warmth that flushed her cheeks and made her exceedingly angry.

"Miss Duncan," the deep, cultured voice called again, much closer now, its insistence halting the young woman immediately. Squaring her shoulders under the voluminous folds of the plaid, she turned around, needing no words to convey her displeasure at being thus accosted.

"Milord," she responded, her polite reply at odds with the stubborn set of her jaw.

"It's good to see you, too, Blair," the man replied, amusement shining in his engaging hazel eyes, a peculiar mixture of greens and golds. "Have you met Lord Haverbrook?" he asked by way of introduction. "Harry, this is Miss Duncan, a childhood friend."

Harry Rogers, Lord Haverbrook, stood in marked contrast to his companion, Cameron Montgomery, Earl of Lindsay. Whereas Haverbrook was fortyish, short and portly, with wisps of grey peeking from beneath the brim of his hat and playing around a rather bland face, Montgomery was no more than in his late twenties, tall and muscular. His thick head of dark hair enhanced the quality of his aristocratic yet pleasing features, animated now at happening upon Blair Duncan in the streets of Glenmuir. In truth, the only thing this handsome man shared with Lord Haverbrook was the precision of his English diction, perfected by the best schools that country had to offer.

"I cannot say as I have had the pleasure," Haverbrook stated, his appreciation of the beautiful woman before him quite evident in his differential manner, the dimming daylight helping to hide the shabbiness of Blair's attire. "But you did say, Cameron, that you were acquainted with this fetching woman in childhood? I must confess that I had quite forgotten your mother was a Scot."

"So has milord Lindsay, I vow," Blair murmured demurely, even as her flashing blue eyes chided Cameron and issued him a silent challenge.

He answered with a smile, though he felt nothing but frustration at the beautiful and fiery Highlander's reception of him. Baffled, he once again addressed Haverbrook rather than respond to Blair's none-too-subtle insult, his unperturbed tones hiding his dismay.

"Yes, Harry, my father married a Connery, and I remember many a delightful summer spent here, frolicking with Miss Duncan. As a boy I always thought that one day I'd settle on the Connery estate and marry Blair."

"Which only proves childhood dreams are nothing but idle foolishness," Blair rejoined adamantly, glad that the deepening dusk veiled the blush burning her usually creamy skin. How dare he be so impertinent as to mock her memories, to remind her of their childish vow? And in front of a stranger, too!

Not trusting herself to remain any longer, Blair decided to forgo a visit with the villagers, interested though they had become in her present conversation with Cameron Montgomery, Earl of Lindsay. For her, his appearance had entirely changed her mood. Now, more than anything, she wanted to return home, a place that seemed, at this moment, a sanctuary of blessed solitude rather than its usual source of loneliness.

"If you will excuse me, gentlemen, I must be getting along," she said, her voice cold, revealing no trace of the laughter and warmth Cameron remembered from years gone by, years that were all too long ago.

"May I offer you a ride in my carriage, Blair?" Cameron asked solicitously, moving to block her path and unwilling to see her leave, even if it meant subjecting himself to more of her ill humor.

"That will not be necessary. The walk is not a long one, and I find I enjoy the fresh air," Blair replied over the murmur of the villagers who had stopped pretending to be unaware of her present situation.

"Do you enjoy the cold, too, Blair?" Cameron asked, raising a well-arched eyebrow in skepticism even before she replied.

"'Tis most invigorating."

"Still, put my mind at ease, and allow me to escort you," he pressed, not entirely successful at keeping overtones of exasperation from creeping into his voice. "It's almost dark, and I want to be certain you arrive home safely."

"As if I'd be in danger from anyone born in these parts, Lord Lindsay," Blair laughed, lifting her chin stubbornly. "Foreigners are the only ones I have to fear, and I usually make it a practice not to talk with them."

"Now see here, Blair," Cameron began, his patience straining under his concern for her welfare in the chill night air.

"There's no need to trouble yourself, your lordship. I'm going in that direction and I dinna mind seeing Miss Duncan home," Ian Ferguson interjected, coming forward. Reaching for Blair's basket, the farmer wondered if Cameron Montgomery had spoken to Blair of marriage more recently than childhood and been spurned for his efforts. That might explain his rude persistence, though of course his father's blood could do that, as well. Whatever the case, Ian smugly offered Blair his protection against this outsider, though as an old man, he could offer her little else.

"Thank you, Ian," Blair said sweetly, her smile at the aged Scot setting Cameron's teeth on edge, while for him she reserved a defiant tilt of her head. Then, before Cameron could object, the two began to trek out of Glenmuir.

"Goodbye to ye. If I do na see you beforehand, I hope the Spirit of Christmas is with ye," Charlie Ferguson called with a laugh.

"Aye, I hope the Spirit visits you as well," Ian replied, glancing over his shoulder, a wicked gleam in his eyes.

"Nice that the locals can be so cheerful about the holidays," Cameron muttered, forgetting Haverbrook's presence in his frustration at watching Blair walk away from him yet again.

"Don't be absurd! You know what it is they're talking about. The Scots don't celebrate the Yuletide as we do. Why I've heard that many of their businesses are open on Christmas Day," Haverbrook grumbled.

"That's in the Lowlands, Harry. Hogmanay may be a bigger holiday, but the Highlanders have always kept Christmas."

"Be that as it may, those blighters are not talking about the holy day. Surely you must know they're making a thinly veiled allusion to the thievery that goes on hereabouts during this time of year. Thievery aimed at us! It's no secret that the villagers call the villain the Spirit of Christmas because he comes and goes without ever having been seen, like some wraith in the night. What audacity to mention his name in our presence!"

"You're talking of the sort of Robin Hood who has plagued us these past few years, stealing from us rich and making gifts to the poor?"

"Bloody right I am," the nobleman replied indignantly. "Why we English have lost so much to that cur that a number of us are going to stay here over the holidays rather than return to London."

"It will be rather dull for you, don't you think?" Cameron asked, turning his attention to the man beside him now that Blair Duncan and her self-appointed guardian had disappeared from view.

"Well, you've done it, staying after the hunting season and remaining here until early January before you come back to London. How dreadful can it be?"

"It's not all that bad, actually. But then I must warn you that my presence has neither safeguarded my property nor helped to net the thief. Let's hope you and the others have better luck," Cameron drawled as he signaled for his carriage, which started immediately down the street to meet him.

"I am certain we will," Haverbrook announced, settling comfortably into the coach. "I think your problem, Cameron, is that you've had other things on your mind these past few seasons. Miss Duncan, perhaps?"

"I've hardly seen her during my sojourns in Scotland," Cameron protested.

"Hmm, though I doubt it's through any fault of yours. Can't say as I blame you for trying," Haverbrook continued with a grin. "The young lady certainly has a lovely piece of property. Imagine the hunts you could have on her lands! If I were free, I'd court her myself. In fact, now that I think of it, one of my brothers has a suitable son. Perhaps I should have him up for a visit."

"Save your money, Harry. I have the distinct impression Miss Duncan isn't interested in any of us," Cameron stated emphatically as he propped a muscular, boot-clad leg on the seat opposite.

"Why, Lindsay, you have to be more persistent. The fox never invites the hound to begin the chase," Haverbrook reproached. "Why not keep up the hue and cry, old boy? I daresay most ladies would find you have a certain degree of charm. Surely Miss Duncan will eventually capitulate to your attentions if you just stay at it. I'd say that as you have Scots blood, you'd have a better chance than any of us in winning Miss Duncan . . . and her lands."

"Maybe you're right," a brooding Cameron muttered, so deep in thought that he paid scant attention to Harry's last words. "Perhaps I've not been aggressive enough."

"That's what I've been trying to tell you," Haverbrook said with a laugh. From the dangerous look emerging on his companion's face, Harry Rogers was certain that the pursuit was about to begin in earnest. Between their efforts to apprehend the thief and Cameron Montgomery's wooing of Blair Duncan, he thought happily, it could be that Christmas in Glenmuir would not be so dull after all.

Chapter Two

The following morning Blair bustled about in the rambling kitchen of Duncan House. The rattling of pot lids seemed much louder than usual since she was all alone in the once-magnificent residence built by her family so many generations ago. But perhaps something other than her solitude and the sleepless night she had spent nettled the lively brunette as she prepared to make marmalade with MacGregor's sugar and a crate of overly ripe oranges sent to the parish kirk by a former neighbor who now made his living working a cargo ship.

Washing the oranges and setting them out to dry, Blair winced as she poked at one of the fruits and felt the rind give all too easily. Heaven only knew how long it had taken the crate to reach the isolated Highland village. Still, she decided thriftily, attempting to find peace by immersing herself in her task, the oranges would provide a tasty treat to be included in the Christmas baskets, and she was thankful for their appearance. Some of the rinds might even be dried and candied as sweets for the children.

Brushing a rich, reddish brown curl away from her face, Blair poured herself a cup of tea as she waited impatiently for Old Robbie and Mrs. Brown, her housekeeper, to return from errands in Glenmuir.

Once there would have been servants in abundance to aid in the assembly of the Christmas baskets, Blair sighed. Now, however, there was only Mrs. Brown and Robbie left, and since their salaries had all but disappeared, they remained with her solely out of loyalty.

Concluding that she could proceed no further until Mrs. Brown returned and rendered assistance, Blair decided to indulge in a late breakfast of porridge, an ever-present staple warming on the huge cast-iron stove.

The proud mistress of the diminished estate deftly set her meager meal on the scarred kitchen table. She rarely ate in the formal dining room anymore, only now and then at Mrs. Brown's insistence when some guest dined at Duncan House. At other times, Blair much preferred the warm conversation of her tiny staff to the loneliness of taking her meals as lady of the manor.

Continuing to feel restless as she seated herself at the table, Blair was oblivious to her first few spoonfuls of porridge, tasting them not at all in the struggle to find some tranquillity in her morning. Gingerly sipping the hot tea, she forced herself to admit the reason for her present unsettlement and her lack of sleep the night before—her meeting with Cameron Montgomery.

Heavily fringed hazel eyes shot with haunting greens and golds called to her from some rebellious portion of her mind, while once-beloved laughter echoed in the recesses of her memory, causing further discomfort.

"Damn him!" Blair mumbled crossly, setting her mug onto the table so roughly that some of its contents sloshed over its sides. "And curse the luck that brought me face-to-face with him yesterday."

At his sudden reappearance during the hunting season three years ago, Blair had told herself that she didn't want to see him and had evaded him almost completely during his sojourns in the Highlands. It was a simple enough feat; she had instructed Mrs. Brown and Robbie to say that she was not at home whenever Cameron called, and she herself had ignored whatever invitations he had sent. At Glenmuir festivities, she had always arrived late, long after he had grown bored with village pleasures and departed, or else she had refrained from attending some celebrations altogether.

But yesterday... yesterday, blast it, the nearness of the man had been a more heady experience than a pint of whisky. The very sight of Cameron Montgomery had warmed her insides, and the sound of his voice had been nothing short of seductive. But what had bothered the old laird's daughter most was that after all these years, she had to avert her glance and fight against the memory of that beckoning mouth of his—the mouth that had so sweetly taken her own when they had been little more than bairns.

Shoving the half-eaten porridge away from her in disgust, Blair knew that seeing the traitorous love of her youth yet again might prove her undoing. Each glimpse of his comely face would wear away at her resistance, weaken her anger, and eat at her distrust of him. She didn't want to have to make a decision concerning Cameron Montgomery, suspecting she still harbored tender feelings for him within her own heart.

Why couldn't Cameron leave her alone and return to London where he belonged? Surely with his wealth and title, there were women enough seeking after him.

Caught up in such churning rumination, Blair didn't hear the footsteps that stopped just outside the kitchen. Nor did she realize what a pretty picture she made for those eyes that feasted on the sight of her, despite the old green gown and enormous apron she wore. She had no idea of how vulnerable she appeared in this unguarded moment, nor did she have any concept of the way the sunlight settled upon her deep brown hair, igniting its red highlights so that her head fairly shimmered with a copper cast. The only thing of which Blair was aware was that she had to avoid Cameron Montgomery at all costs.

"What's this, poppet, enjoying a leisurely breakfast?" came a deep, familiar voice, which Blair feared her brooding reflections had conjured from the depths of her imagination. But when she turned her head, she saw that this was not a trick played upon a tired body by an overly active mind. There was Cameron standing in her doorway.

It had been many years since she had seen him in that spot, and his virile adult frame filled the entranceway so that he appeared almost larger than life and a hundred times more dangerous than she had ever thought him.

"What are you doing here?" Blair asked, hiding her work-roughened hands on her lap while Cameron, taking in her worn dress and the sad state of the kitchen, struggled to keep the sympathy he felt from manifesting itself in his expression and embarrassing her.

"Why I've come to see if you actually still live here," the handsome Englishman replied in a light and casual tone, pretending it did not hurt him to see her in such circumstances. "The last few times I've called, I was informed that you were not here. I'd begun to think perhaps you'd had a change of residence."

"No, I'm one of the fortunate ones," Blair stated dryly.

"So I see," Cameron replied, bending his head to avoid hitting it as he made his way into the kitchen. "However, you can't fault me for being uncertain as to your whereabouts, Blair, what with the way Mrs. Brown guards you. So when I saw the old dragon on her way to the village with Robbie, I thought this might be the perfect opportunity to come for a visit. But what has become of your famous Highland hospitality? Aren't you going to ask me to breakfast?"

"You shouldn't call Mrs. Brown such names," Blair rebuked the man who had intruded into her home much as he had her thoughts. "I warrant she could still take a strap to you if she heard such talk."

"Then we won't tell her, will we?" Cameron said, leaning forward to whisper in conspiratorial tones.

The nearness of him greatly unsettled the already distressed Blair. Without replying, she jumped up, walked to the stove and fetched him a cup of tea. Then she began to spoon some of the oat mixture into a bowl. Dishing out a large portion, she wondered if she had complied with Cameron's demand for food because Highland courtesy dictated she extend the hospitality of her household, poor as it might be, or because the commanding Englishman's presence at her table made her want to flee.

Placing the porridge before him, Blair returned with another bowl.

"You'll be wanting sugar, won't you?" she asked all too sweetly, placing it on the table beside her unwelcome guest.

Her subtle insult was not lost on Cameron. The Scots used salt on their porridge; only the English flavored it with sugar. Under the guise of courtesy, the brat was making the point that she considered him an outsider. The idea brought a smile to Cameron's well-formed lips. Blair hadn't lost her fiery nature. Poverty had not broken her spirit.

"Come and join me, won't you?" the dark-haired Englishman asked, patting the seat beside him when Blair continued to stand on the other side of the room. There was something in his words, however, that made the invitation more suggestive than it should have been, and Blair noted a predatory glint in Cameron's piercing eyes. She remained where she was, hoping fervently that Mrs. Brown and Robbie would return soon.

"It's impolite to leave me all alone at your table, and there's no reason for it...unless you're afraid of me," Cameron challenged softly.

"The day will never dawn that will see me afraid of an Englishman," Blair retorted, quickly taking a seat before she could have second thoughts, though she chose to sit opposite this stranger she had known so well, keeping the table between them.

"I'm glad to hear that," Cameron replied, smothering a chuckle in a spoonful of porridge.

Silence fell over the room while Cameron continued to lustily attack the simple meal she had placed before him. From beneath lowered lashes, Blair studied her visitor, his self-possessed mien telling her things words never could. Finally Blair could stand no more.

"I've fed you, Lord Lindsay, and you've—"

"If you'll recall, you used to call me Cameron," the nobleman interrupted.

"As I was saying, you've yet to inform me what has brought you into my kitchen unannounced," the un-amiable Blair continued, focusing on the now-cold mug of tea she held within her hands in order to still their trembling.

"Why little more than to tell you that I think it's time for two old friends to have a cozy visit. Do you realize that this is the first opportunity I've had to really talk with you since I've been coming back to the High-lands?" he asked quietly, finishing his hot cereal with relish and moving the bowl aside. "In fact, I've deter-mined that we should do it more often. I've come to ask you to a small party I'm hosting. Since all of my previous invitations have gone unanswered these last three years, I decided to deliver this one in person."

Blair blushed a deep red, though not from shame at callously disregarding the attempts Cameron had made to renew their friendship. Instead, thoughts concern-ing other unanswered correspondence ran round her head, and her reaction was pure anger.

Yes she had ignored his invitations just as he had ig-nored the girlish letters she had sent him after Cameron had left Glenmuir that last time, twelve years ago, re-turning to school in England. But she refused to tell him, to give Cameron the pleasure of knowing how much his silence over the years had wounded her. All that was in the past, and like anyone residing in the vi-cinity of Glenmuir, Blair had enough to do worrying about her future, a future that could not include Cameron Montgomery.

"I'm afraid I'm busy," Blair replied, hiding behind her mug as she took a swallow of the horridly cool tea.

"Busy? You don't even know the date!" Cameron protested, his eyes narrowing dangerously as he regarded this beautiful but infuriating woman closely.

"True, but I have little time to socialize before the holidays," Blair countered. She stood once more to clear the table, an action which she hoped would signal Cameron that both the conversation and the meal were at an end, and that he should be on his way.

"Surely you'll be attending services Christmas Eve," the dark-haired man persisted as Blair occupied herself at the sink. "If the party is out of the question, allow me to escort you to the kirk, and then just the two of us can enjoy a light supper at Lindsay Hall. You must admit your charity work will be finished by then, and if not, I can give you some help."

"I'll admit nothing to you, Cameron Montgomery," Blair said, her voice rising as her appreciation of his masculine beauty warred with her sense of righteousness, stretching her already taut nerves further.

"Blair, lovely Blair, have you forgotten the friendship we once shared?" Cameron asked gently, leaving the table and walking to stand behind her while she set the dishes to soak in a pan of water.

The hot whisper of Cameron's breath on the nape of her neck was more than the Scottish beauty could stand, and she whirled around, ready to channel her aroused passion into anger rather than give it the release it sought.

"Is it friendship we're speaking of, Cameron?" she began hotly. "There are many friends I knew once whom I'll never see again, friends who were forced to move overseas just to survive when huge tracts of Connery lands were sold and there was no longer a place for them here. I hardly think it loyal of me to associate with the man who caused their problems. After what you've done, how can you talk to me of friendship?"

"Blair, I had nothing to do with what happened here," Cameron protested vehemently, willing the blue-eyed vixen who stood fixing him with such disdain to have faith in what he told her.

"How can you deny it? 'Twas after your father's death, after the lands and title were yours that the Connery estate was parceled out and a good many Scots displaced in the process."

"But it wasn't done at my direction. The land had been lost years before, markers given by my father to settle his gambling debts. His friends and acquaintances were merely kind enough not to embarrass him by collecting their winnings until after his death, when the land could legally be divided up. All I was left with was the house and a small amount of acreage. I couldn't have stopped it, Blair."

"You could have tried," she shot back fiercely.

"Believe me, I wasn't aware of the situation before it was too late. Could you think I wanted such a thing to happen?"

"Then why didn't you buy the parcels back?" Blair asked, gliding away from him to the other side of the table in an effort to escape the compelling intensity of Cameron's stare.

"I tried, love, I tried. But no one would sell. An estate in Scotland, a hunting or fishing lodge in the Highlands, all are quite fashionable at present. Not one of my father's acquaintances would part with his prize. Not even Haverbrook, though I offered him much more than the land is worth."

Blair studied the rugged-looking male before her. His hands were on the table as he leaned towards her, his perfectly sculptured face only inches from hers. In the earnestness of the man's expression, the lovely Highlander saw the boy she had once loved, pleading with her to understand. The impact of the vision was all too powerful, and Blair's first reaction was to deny it by denying him.

"I don't believe you," she said hotly.

Anger surged in Cameron's breast. How could she say that to him?

There was new purpose in his darkening eyes as he stalked Blair, cornering her and towering over her, his stare capturing hers and refusing to relinquish it.

"Don't you realize that despite the years I am still the Cameron you knew, and not another Haverbrook? Or do I delude myself in thinking that you ever really trusted me?" he demanded, his voice for all its softness unable to conceal the rage he felt at the thought that Blair Duncan had never truly cared for him.

"If you aren't like the rest of the English, tell me why you ignored Scotland for so long, Cameron," Blair contested, fighting back desperately, refusing to be intimidated by either his nearness and strength or swayed by his passionate words. "Why did you wait until three years ago to come back? Your disregard sealed the fate of dozens of families and I don't know if I can ever forgive you for that."

"I wanted to see Lindsay Hall again, but I couldn't, Blair," Cameron explained in a quieter tone, his own turbulent emotions abating in the swell of this woman's deeply felt sentiments.

"Why not?" she asked insistently, all too conscious of the fact that it wasn't his failure to return to Scotland she was questioning, but his failure to return to her, instead.

"I couldn't come back, love," Cameron responded, reaching out to her as one would a frightened woodland creature. Tenderly he brushed a burnished tendril of hair from her cheek. "Until he died, Lindsay Hall belonged to my father. The house had been closed since the year that saw my mother's death. My father couldn't bear to come back to the place where my mother had died. And in his sorrow, he denied me access to the place as well."

"You still could have made your way to Glenmuir once again," Blair persevered.

"There isn't any inn for miles. Where would I have stayed?" he asked, fighting the urge to take this woman in his arms and find his home at last.

"You could have lodged with us! My father wouldn't have turned you away."

"Be reasonable. How could I have known that? How many years had passed with no communication between you and me? I couldn't have just planted myself on your doorstep and expected to be taken in."

"You should have known that we would have welcomed you with open arms," Blair rejoined stubbornly, tears beginning to well in the corners of her lovely blue eyes.

"I'm here now, Blair," he said with compelling tenderness. "Open your arms to me now."

"It's too late for that," Blair cried as she pushed past him.

"It's never too late. I want you. I always have," Cameron said, his voice husky and hoarse with desire.

"Is it me you really want, Cameron, or is it the Duncan lands? Can you deny that you want to carve them up into pieces, too, and sell them to more of your friends?" Blair accused, so distraught and confused that she didn't see the hurt her words had wrought as they were reflected in the handsome nobleman's expression.

"Maybe we've done too much talking for one day," Cameron said, his voice carefully void of the defeated weariness he felt. "I think it best that I leave now, but we'll talk again . . . we have to."

"Go! I want you to go," Blair said. Close to sobbing, she used a delicate fingertip to brush away a fresh tear.

"Will you say it for me before I leave?" Cameron asked, unwilling to depart until the ritual that had been special between them had been completed.

"What?" Blair demanded suspiciously.

"The Highland farewell. Didn't you always use it? Have I ever left this house without hearing it on your lips? I'd like to listen to it once more."

Blair's continued silence induced Cameron to prod her gently.

"I can remember it still, and the girlish sincerity that rang in your voice at the saying of it. Come on, love...'Wouldn't it be a fine thing now, if you were coming instead of going?'" he prompted. "Can you say it for me still, Blair?"

"Only, Cameron, if you wish me to lie," she replied, anguish mixed with tears that flowed freely down her face at the sweet memory he had evoked, of a time and a relationship that no longer had any place in her life.

"Ah, well, never mind then. I'd never want you to lie to me, Blair...not to me," Cameron said soothingly, unwilling to upset her further. Hiding his disappointment, and vowing to change things between them, he bent to place a feather-soft kiss upon her forehead.

But the sensation of Blair's flawless skin beneath his lips made Cameron forget the solace his brotherly kiss was meant to bestow. In fact the scent of her, fresh and wild like the Highlands themselves, and the taste of her, sweet as honey, made him forget himself completely. Unable to stop, Cameron's greedy mouth descended on Blair's. His kiss spoke so eloquently of all the passion, all the yearning, she refused to allow him to put into words.

However, emptying his heart through his kiss brought Cameron little satisfaction. It only inflamed him further, so that he wanted Blair Duncan now, this moment, completely. Wrenching himself away from Blair, Cameron looked at her, his eyes hard and intent.

Blair, who had been completely encompassed by the sensations Cameron had summoned, returned his stare with bewilderment. He appeared to be silently asking her something, but before Blair could ascertain what, he had turned away, and the spell was broken.

Then he was gone, his sudden departure making the lonely old house seem emptier still.

Chapter Three

"You've done naught but fidget and sigh since I came back from Glenmuir. What has gotten into ye, lass?" Mrs. Brown asked, sealing the last of the marmalade. It was unusual for her self-possessed mistress to be so restless, and the older woman didn't mind voicing her observation.

"'Tis nothing really, I'm just a wee bit tired," murmured Blair, her dark lashes lowered as she placed the pot of marmalade on a tray. "I hardly closed my eyes all night... thinking about the Christmas baskets and all...."

"It would seem to me that if ye had so little sleep ye'd slow down your pace and not be so full of unspent energy," Mrs. Brown said. She suspiciously eyed Blair, who appeared to be exhibiting excessive concern with arranging the contents of the tray.

The young woman felt Mrs. Brown's sharp gaze upon her. Since the laird's death and the departure of most of the servants, theirs was a small, close-knit household. And if they didn't have money aplenty, there was warmth, caring and honesty. At least there had been honesty, until this moment when Blair was loath to relate the story of the morning's provocative visitor.

Though concealing the fact from Mrs. Brown did not actually constitute lying, the girl felt guilty none-theless, and the emotion sat upon her uneasily. Blair Duncan was the sort who usually said what she meant and had little to hide. But Cameron Montgomery had changed that. Unused to keeping things from Mrs. Brown, Blair sought to put an end to the misery she felt by toting the pots of orange treat into the dining room. There she settled them on the large table amid the bas-kets and other bits and pieces she had collected for distribution to those poorer than she. However, Blair soon discovered that escaping her housekeeper's scru-tiny had little effect on her troubled spirits.

Cameron's lips had left hers burning, and now, hours later, the blazing sensation had yet to subside. The steam coming from the stove in the kitchen and the fire in the hearth had not been half so hot as the lin-gering touch of Cameron's mouth upon her own. Nor did the chill of the unheated dining room cool the flame Cameron Montgomery had started. Try as she might, Blair couldn't banish the bold, handsome En-glishman from her mind.

Cameron had changed. Through the years she had been able to control the sweet longings awakened so long ago by his youthful declaration of devotion and his tender kiss; this Cameron was another matter en-tirely. He was not the boy who had captured her heart in childhood. He was quite definitely a man. There was something dangerous about him now, a wild, reckless air that clung to him even in so domestic a setting as her own kitchen. Certainly Cameron's recent kiss was not the sort she had remembered. This morning he had seared her lips if not her soul, scarring her memories of the gentle, tentative touch of his mouth planted softly on hers, a recollection she had kept alive all these years. He had replaced it with a feeling that couldn't be ignored but besieged her still, keeping his presence and demands alive in the old house though he had departed hours ago.

Blast him, Blair thought crossly. Only this morning, a glance at the trappings of Christmas and the baskets spread across the table had filled her with happiness and satisfaction, sweeping away the tediousness of day-to-day existence as she anticipated the joy these small tokens would bring. But she no longer rejoiced in the bits of ribbon, sacks of walnuts and the other bundles that littered the surface of the table, waiting to be apportioned into each basket. Now, no matter where she looked, it was Cameron she saw, his green-gold eyes haunting her so that even visions of Christmas cheer could not dispel his image.

The audacity of the man, to return to this place, to intrude upon her quiet life! How dare he ruin the Christmastide for her, her most pleasant time of year, the Daft Days, which usually helped her to forget the troubles and toil of the other eleven months? More importantly, how dare he kiss her as he had?

What was worse, Blair considered, was that the villain had probably not been affected by the incident one whit. Their kiss had meant no more to Cameron than the one that had accompanied his false vows so long ago. After all, this morning, hadn't he stopped abruptly and left without a word, as though it meant nothing to him?

Why didn't he take that handsome face of his with its roguish smile back to London? Blair swore softly beneath her breath, her mild burr becoming more pronounced as she vocalized her wish that Cameron Montgomery might pay for the trouble he had caused in the Highlands, and for the tumult he had set loose in her own, previously tranquil life. She hoped that the Spirit of Christmas would attack the bounder most heavily this year. It would serve Cameron right if his losses were great. Perhaps he would even close down his house and return to England, never to set foot in the Highlands again! Who said Christmas wasn't a time for adults to wish and dream, Blair thought wickedly.

Then she became ashamed of such musing. Writing out labels for the crocks of marmalade, Blair sighed as she wondered what had happened to her own ability to find peace on earth as Christmas approached. What type of man had Cameron become that he could unsettle her so with one kiss?

Blair refused to search for the answer. To purposefully think about that virile devil, to dwell on his attributes, would only destroy what small amount of reserve she had left.

Drawing boughs of evergreen on the corners of her labels, the dark-haired Miss Duncan knew that she had to stay away from Cameron Montgomery. It was not a decision that arose from anger. It was merely a matter of self-preservation.

Blair looked up from her task to see an anxious Mrs. Brown wiping her hands on her apron and observing her from the doorway. It was enough to make Blair determined to thrust aside her own problems and attempt to put the woman at ease. She smiled prettily and began to chat about the coming holidays, placating the older woman somewhat. After all, if Cameron wasn't spending his time thinking about her, if her lips beneath his hadn't disturbed his peace of mind, why should she allow him to make her miserable? Because she couldn't help it, she thought as Mrs. Brown finally left the room, and Blair's bright smile faded with the housekeeper's departure.

Under the inky blackness of the night sky, the air was crisp and cold. Cameron removed a piece of straw from his hair and shifted quietly while he waited for the man of the house to give up his search and take himself and his pistol back inside.

Though his heart still thundered, the rugged-looking English aristocrat breathed quietly. His roguishly attractive features appeared to be cast in stone and gave no clue to the emotions that claimed him, just as his barely moving chest belied his recent physical activity.

Cameron heard the man shout orders directing the search when his pursuer came nearer, and the fugitive cursed silently, berating himself for this night's folly when he could have been home, sipping a whisky before a roaring blaze in his own hall.

In his irritation at his present situation, Cameron asked himself what he was doing here, damning the straw that dug so ruthlessly into the back of his muscular neck. But even as he asked he was aware that the answer was a simple one: Blair Duncan, and well he knew it!

That he was here and in such circumstances was her fault! Not that he hadn't indulged himself in such adventures often before, he admitted, trying to be fair as his hand stroked the prize held tightly against his side. However, he really hadn't planned on such an excursion tonight. It was his encounter with Blair that had sent him out restlessly into the night, bent on taking what wasn't his to take, what belonged, in fact, to another man.

But this night, he thought, careful not to let the sigh of exasperation he felt escape his well-formed lips, had been less than satisfactory. He was very much aware, as he moved closer to the dark shape beside him, that the evening's activities certainly hadn't made him forget his desire. Too late, he was wise enough to know that after his meeting with Blair, nothing would have brought him much solace.

All he'd ever wanted was that blue-eyed temptress, yet here he was lying in a haystack in the dead of night. Gentlemen, he thought irritably, were supposed to be merry and to enjoy God-given rest during the Christmas season. At least that was what the carol promised. Yet all he had received was longing of a sort that was likely to drive him mad before Christmas morning ever dawned.

Pursue her, Cameron fumed, a lock of his raven hair falling across his forehead as he recalled Harry's advice. Like a fool he had listened and where had it gotten him? He'd gone rushing off, upsetting Blair and making himself appear like the village idiot. Not only that, he decided, his frustration mounting in proportion to his anger, he had probably ruined any chance he had possessed of setting things to rights with Blair and winning her heart.

Sound the horn and begin the hunt, he thought scornfully. It appeared that the fox had gone to ground. And as a result, he was in this odious haystack with a member of the gentry hunting him!

Yet even as he heard his pursuer's voice only a few feet from his hiding place, Cameron was more concerned with what he was going to do about Blair than he was with his present predicament.

As a boy he had adored her, but it was as a man that he wanted her, desiring the sapphire-eyed beauty as he had no other woman. The tenderness he had felt for her in his youth had become an entirely different thing that morning. It was harder, fiercer, more demanding. And worst of all, there wasn't a damned thing he could do about it. The sensation had taken hold of him, controlling him so that the more he fought it, the more it possessed him.

But to what end? Blair had been a childhood friend and nothing more, he tried to tell himself. And even that was something she no longer wished to acknowledge, if her behavior this morning was any indication.

As the man who was seeking him moved off in another direction, Cameron mourned the loss of his dream, the end of the carefree, laughing young lass who had dressed so prettily in frills and expensive frocks, the girl who had given him a place in her heart. In her stead was a serious young woman who had lost almost everything and wanted no more to do with him.

Yet like a costly jewel, Blair Duncan did not need an elaborate setting. Her beauty shined and glistened all the same. And while this womanly Blair might not bubble with laughter, she smoldered with sensuality. And, God help him, Cameron wanted to be the one to fan the spark of passion that burned deep within her.

Blair, with her reddish brown hair and sparkling eyes. She was a Highland siren and not the Christmas angel she pretended to be, her baskets be damned! If she were so intent upon giving, there was something she could give him, all right, Cameron thought, shifting in discomfort yet careful not to upset the dark shape resting beside him. A wicked gleam lit his eyes when he thought about what he would like to give the enticing Miss Duncan in return.

It was a haunting realization. For a long time he had thought her reticence to renew their acquaintance was rooted in her newfound poverty, that her damnable pride had prompted her to avoid him. Not knowing how to overcome such an obstacle, he had relied upon patience and overtures of friendship. It had all been to no avail. This morning he had learned the depths of her disdain.

Besides condemning him, Blair had exhibited no trust, no feelings for him at all, and certainly no shyness in her accusations, he thought, his own pride wounded. She had blamed him for something he hadn't done, and been unwilling to listen to explanations. In fact, for all her beauty, Blair had been nothing short of unreasonable, charging him with all sorts of ridiculous things. He *did* care about this land and those who lived upon it, and, by God, someday Blair Duncan would learn she had been wrong about him.

Certain he was alone now, and that it was safe, Cameron stood, brushing himself off, and then he reached down for the shape he had been cradling in his arms. Taking hold with a firm hand, he slung the sack of apples over his shoulders and struck out across the deserted field for the woods.

With each step he longed to go to Blair, to tell her what his feelings for this place, these people, had led him to do. Though the knowledge might cause her to see him in a different light, Cameron knew, too, that such an admission was impossible. No matter what his intentions, his actions were illegal ones. If Blair learned that he was the man the locals called the Spirit of

Christmas, it would only implicate her should he ever be caught. And no matter how things stood between them, he could never knowingly place her in danger.

Frustration nipping at his heels, the rugged looter allowed himself a muttered curse and then the luxury of a sneeze. His cloak was a heavy one, made of good English wool, but it had proved ineffectual against the cold Highland night, just as his English charm had been unable to warm a cold Scottish heart. Another sneeze followed by a sniffle made Cameron realize that the night's folly might very well see him ailing. And for what, he berated himself as his self-pity reached new heights of recrimination. A sack of apples stolen from Lord Fairfax's root cellar? It had been his poorest take of the season and had caused him the most trouble. Bloody hell, but life was an unpredictable affair!

After a long trek, Cameron approached the isolated hunting shack where he lardered the goods he would begin to distribute soon to the needy of the district. And damn her proud nature, that included Blair Duncan, Cameron thought, his mood little improved as he entered the shack and he thought of the gowns he had ordered her from London. Not that he'd ever see her wear them if she had her way, he grumbled. And damn it all, he thought, dumping the apples onto the floor, maybe she was right! Maybe he should leave her alone. She had told him that she wanted little to do with him, and he surely didn't want to spend his life loving a woman who felt nothing for him.

Locking the door behind him as he slipped from the weather-worn building, his body cold and his ego wounded, Cameron Montgomery cursed his appetites and decided to forget Blair Duncan. Though he had

promised her they would speak again, he was certain
that this was one promise Blair would not mind his
breaking. It was better for both of them that he stayed
away. Why with any luck, if he avoided the village and
the locals, he would probably never have to see her
again.

Late the next morning, Lord Haverbrook's driver
brought the earl's coach to a stop in front of Duncan
House. Soon Harry had made his way to the main entrance. Lifting the heavy knocker, fastened in the shape
of a thistle, the nobleman noticed the peeling paint of
the wooden door and clucked reprovingly.

Ah well, if he could convince the vixen to leave her
den, he was certain the enticing creature would soon be
hunted down. Perhaps not by Montgomery, but certainly one of their band would be capable of cornering
Blair Duncan. And with a few coats of paint and other
surface improvements paid for in English pounds, this
rambling old house would become the finest of hunting lodges for some lucky English husband.

In the midst of these thoughts, the door was opened
by a stern-faced old man, his grizzly beard and hair
making him appear very fierce indeed in spite of the
festive armful of holly boughs he held in his arms.

An inquiry as to Miss Duncan's whereabouts
brought no response from the brutish fellow other than
a silent gesture to follow him. Harry did so, thinking it
would take more than garland and ribbons to make this
a cheerful Christmas setting if so sullen a man was part
of the household.

He discovered Blair in the dining room, artfully arranging sprigs of evergreen and holly in an ancient

vase, while great trays of shortbread sat nearby, cooling before they were cut into wedges.

"Good day, Lord Haverbrook," Blair said. Though surprised to see him, she remained regally composed, with no trace of a smile lighting her lovely face. "What is it that brings you here today, an offer to buy my lands?"

"Lord, no!" Harry protested with a laugh, delighted by her forthright manner and sharp tongue. Watching Montgomery attempting to woo such a firebrand would be amusing in the extreme. "I was in the vicinity, having visited our friend Cameron this morning, who by the by is a bit under the weather. But that is of little consequence. . . ."

"No consequence is more like it," Blair interjected, her lovely cheeks reddening and her soft burr becoming more emphatic as her temper rose at having that man's name mentioned in her house so soon after she had vowed to rid herself of him forever.

"Be that as it may," Haverbrook continued, "I thought that as we had been introduced I would take advantage of the situation and call to politely pay my respects."

"Then in the name of politeness," Blair said dryly, looking at him with suspicion, "allow me to inquire after your wife's health."

"Lady Haverbrook, Estella, is quite well indeed," the earl said, stifling a laugh at this woman's impudence. "Actually I am here to solve a bit of a mystery. But I say, that shortbread smells marvelous. I don't suppose I could have a nibble . . ." he said hopefully.

"Of course, it would be my pleasure," Blair replied, working to keep the insincerity from her voice.

Wiping her hands on the apron she wore, the attractive young woman rang for tea, grating at the fact that the hospitality of her homeland forced her to offer some of the shortbread intended for the villagers' Christmas to one of the rogues who had caused them to go hungry in the first place. Was there no justice in this world? Yesterday Montgomery, this morning Haverbrook, would she be expected to feed every Englishman in the Highlands this Christmastide?

Still Blair was the perfect hostess when Mrs. Brown placed the tea things on the sideboard. The young mistress of Duncan House, fetching though her heather-gray gown was a few seasons old, cut a large wedge of shortbread and then prettily poured her guest a cup of tea.

Settling herself across from Haverbrook, she eyed him over the rim of her teacup. "Now tell me," she said, very much the old laird's daughter and very much in command of her house, "what is it that has brought you here? You spoke of a mystery."

"Actually I wondered why I never see you about in local society. Cameron told me that you ignore the English, turning down invitations from him as well."

"There's nothing mysterious in that, Lord Haverbrook. You English have no place in the Highlands," Blair replied, replacing her teacup in its saucer so that it clanked sharply.

"But surely you don't think that snubbing us will help your cause, nor that of the people you profess to care about," Harry pressed.

"I doubt that if I talk with you, sir, and attend your parties, you will abandon your holdings on the old Connery estate," Blair commented shrewdly.

"Of course not, no more than you would give up Duncan House. But I could be persuaded to do something else to help the locals in their plight, and so could the rest of the English landowners hereabouts."

"And what is that?" asked Blair cautiously.

"Why, my dear, if I knew someone who could honestly recommend them, I could hire a number of Scots rather than bring up servants from England. In fact I would like to be able to do such a thing. And I daresay many of my friends would, too. While it wouldn't solve the problem entirely, it would put food on quite a few tables, and keep many of the villagers here in their homeland. It would certainly lessen the number of people you'd have to worry about," he said smoothly.

"What have I to do with this hiring?" Blair asked in spite of herself.

"You must understand that as we are absent so much of the year, we could not entrust these duties to just anyone. We would have to be assured of a man's character before we took him on, and to know that he would be willing to indulge in honest work for us rather than participate in dishonest activities against us. You know these people well. Your recommendation could do a lot of good...if the rest of the English landowners could get to know you. In order to make their acquaintance, though, you would have to come out into society."

"I don't know," Blair responded doubtfully, shaking her head so that a rich, burnished brown curl fell against her cheek.

"Well, think about it, my dear," Haverbrook suggested in his most kindly tone, consulting an extremely elaborate and expensive-looking pocket watch before he stood up to take his leave. "I am having a small gathering tomorrow evening to begin the Christmas activities. I would be pleased if you would join us."

"Will Cameron Montgomery be there?" Blair asked as she considered attending.

"I doubt it, Miss Duncan. He was invited, of course, but his health this morning makes me think he will be unable to attend," Harry lied easily. "However, don't allow his absence to keep you away. I shall put you in the care of Lady Haverbrook, and you might find that you have a merry time indeed, even though that would not be your purpose in attending. Think of what a fine Christmas present employment would make for some of your villagers," the earl concluded convincingly. "Now say you will attend."

"All right, your lordship. I will try it this once," Blair agreed before she could change her mind. Watching a contented Haverbrook depart, the lovely Highlander attempted to persuade herself that this was all for the best. She might be able to help some of her fellow countrymen, and Cameron Montgomery would be nowhere around.

Chapter Four

Blair stood dutifully still as Mrs. Brown adjusted the folds of the tartan flowing from her employer's elegant shoulders. The *arisaid* she wore was still beautiful, timeless in its appeal. But as fetching as Blair looked, Mrs. Brown was not at all happy with the occasion for the girl wearing her Highland finery. Though the older woman didn't voice her disapproval, it was there in the soft clucking of her tongue as she fixed her charge with a critical eye and then moved to fuss with the Duncan colors once more.

"No need to wait up, Mrs. Brown. Robbie will see me home safely, I'm sure," Blair said, the faintest edge of defiance sharpening her words. Did the woman actually think she wanted to socialize with the English invaders? Blair had explained to her that she was going only to obtain situations for the inhabitants of Glenmuir. Certainly circumstances demanded that the housekeeper show at least a degree of sympathy here for the sacrifice her employer was making, Blair thought, pique dusting her cheeks a dark red.

However, Mrs. Brown misconstrued this physical manifestation of Blair's emotions and read it as a young girl's romantic blush. Her own suspicions of a lurking English suitor grew. Still the older woman did nothing more than draw her lips together grimly, concluding it was not her place to say anything about the matter... at least not with words. And so she heaved a mighty sigh and flounced from the room, a terse goodnight her only reprimand.

The ride to Harry Rogers's hunting lodge was not a long one, and still Blair felt she had arrived at the place much too soon, her emotions still a jumble. She was not at all sure she had made the right decision in accepting Haverbrook's invitation, a qualm underscored by Old Robbie's mood. Under normal circumstances his conversation was terse when he was at his most loquacious. But tonight, any attempt to draw him to talk had elicited no more than a grunted response.

Perhaps the old man and Mrs. Brown were right, maybe she shouldn't be here, Blair worried, her mouth puckered daintily with uncertainty. However, the time to change her mind and return to Duncan House had passed. Her small, rather shabby carriage had turned onto Harry's property, where the approach to the house was lighted cheerily with scores of lanterns along the gravel road.

The main building, more like a manor than a hunting lodge, was ablaze with light and welcome, and before she realized it, Robbie had handed her down to a waiting servant, who escorted her to the impressive stairway leading to the Earl of Haverbrook's sometimes residence.

Surely it was naught but the chill of the December air that had her shivering, Blair told herself. Nevertheless, she had to fight an urge to pick up her skirts and dash back down the stairs into the security of her own carriage. Apprehension at mingling with the English was daft, she told herself sternly, forcing herself to remain where she was. After all, these people were the outlanders, and this country was her homeland. She had nothing to be either frightened or ashamed of.

Squaring her shoulders, she reached out to assertively announce her arrival with the metal cherub adorning the door. Her summons was answered immediately, and as Blair stepped into Haverbrook's purloined piece of Scotland, she did so with no less bravery than her ancestors had demonstrated when they strode into the fray at Culloden so many generations before.

At the worst, the blue-eyed Highlander thought while a very proper butler took her plaid, this evening could be nothing more than a few hours in the company of people she detested. That was but a small price to pay for seeing to the welfare of any one of the families who called this part of Scotland home. Besides, the Englishman she despised the most would not be present, and there was quite a bit of solace in that.

Stepping into the elaborate ballroom, Blair was struck immediately by the opulence of the place, so different from the humble homes of those born and bred in the area. There was a roaring fire in the hearth, and cascading crystal chandeliers bathed the room in a brilliance that contrasted sharply with her own enforced thrift and the dim atmosphere of Duncan House. Here, expensive furnishings that spoke of money if not taste lined the walls and spilled over into the half-dozen small alcoves set into the walls. Evergreen garland decorated with sprigs of holly and plush velvet ribbons was arranged in graceful swags near the ceiling. But the most magnificent ornament of all stood at the far end of the room, and the sight of it caused Blair's breath to catch in her throat.

It was an evergreen, tall and full and fragrant. Its clean scent greeted her where she stood while dozens and dozens of candles winked merrily from its sweeping branches. But even that beauty had been enhanced with numerous decorations. These were plentiful and gay, crafted to appeal not only to children but to the child sleeping within every adult, evoking and celebrating the desperate desire for magic that dwells within each human, from the most austere monarch to the most downtrodden of men.

Heedless of the curious stares of those assembled in the room, Blair moved closer to inspect the treasure trove adorning the evergreen tree. There were gleaming foil cones of every hue, lined with lace and filled with sugarplums. Gilded walnuts danced on the tips of branches, and marzipan fruits seemed suspended in midair, while cherubs fluttered everywhere. Blair had never seen, had never dreamed, of a creation so enchanting, and she was hard put to contain her awe as Harry Rogers rushed over to greet her.

"My dear Miss Duncan, how very good it is to have you here. I see you're admiring our Christmas tree. They've become quite fashionable in England since Prince Albert introduced one into the royal household. It's a German custom really, but charming nonetheless, don't you think?" Haverbrook asked congenially, taking the luxury of the room for granted. "However, what am I doing monopolizing your company? Come and join the others. Everyone is anxious to meet you."

Led forward on Harry's arm, Blair allowed her long lashes to sweep down over her brilliant, sapphire eyes.

It created a lovely and demure effect while actually allowing her to study the others gathered for the evening. The young woman was gratified to note that Cameron was indeed absent. And though she had seen one or two of the faces within the confines of Glenmuir, all of these people were strangers. Ironically, she was the foreigner here tonight, a fact she was hardpressed to ignore when Haverbrook concluded his introductions and left her with a small group.

These English proved polite, but it was obvious that they regarded her as a curiosity, a bit of indigenous decor come to give the gathering some local color. Emphasizing her soft burr as she replied to a question asked by one of the noblemen, Blair decided wickedly to make this a colorful evening indeed.

Cameron sat before the fireplace in an oversized chair, sipping whisky. Despite the furniture's size, his large frame and long, outstretched legs made the thing seem diminutive. He reminded himself that he didn't much like parties as he brought the glass to his lips and savored the warmth of the amber liquid when it settled in his mouth and then slid down his throat. Besides, colds such as his were meant to keep people at home, he decided, suffering as much from ennui as from his inconvenient, minor ailment. Then why, Cameron asked himself, as he looked around at the tables of cardplayers, had he made the effort to attend Harry's festivities?

The games going on in this room didn't interest him. Nor did the merriment and dancing in the ballroom, with which Harry hoped to usher in a lively Christmas season.

Cameron knew he had come there tonight for only one purpose—to disassociate himself from the activities of Glenmuir's elusive Christmas thief. A failure to partake in the revelries of this temporarily self-exiled English community might arouse suspicion. And his absence while thefts took place would surely be noticed sooner or later.

But that wasn't the only reason he had come out tonight, Cameron reluctantly admitted with a scowl as he tossed down the remainder of whisky. If he were going to be honest with himself, he had to own up to the fact that he had come here because he hadn't wanted to spend the evening alone with only thoughts of Blair Duncan for company. Damn the girl! After the incident with her at Duncan Hall, he no longer dreamed of the sweet innocent lass he had left behind. No, he wanted the sensuous woman whose lips he had plundered so recently. And no matter how much he tried to forget her, the little sorceress held him tightly in her spell, so that wanting her was a constant ache.

Perhaps she had been right, he mused, when memories of the kiss he had stolen evoked no feelings of shame or remorse. He was definitely no gentleman. The longing that had obsessed him when his mouth had found hers left no room for manners and civil behavior. It was too primitive a thing, raging at being restrained and just waiting for release. And as for having stolen the kiss, that was quite in keeping with his character of late. Hadn't he already been a thief for quite some time?

No, he told himself, his handsome, brooding face illuminated demonically by the flames of the fire. His activities had merely been to return to others, in one form or another, what had been taken from them in the first place. He felt no remorse for that, either.

Initially, upon his return to the Highlands, he had sought to ease the burden of the locals through conventional charity. However, he had learned quickly that the people of Glenmuir wanted little to do with his money and less to do with him.

So he had begun a campaign of making anonymous gifts, practical presents sorely needed by those who resided here. But such unexplained largess would have quickly been traced to him as he was the only one present during the holidays who could have afforded such generosity. Then, the necessities he wanted to give these stubborn Highlanders would have been stoically returned.

Instead, he had hit upon the idea of reporting a theft before unexpected bounty began appearing at the doors of Glenmuir's most humble houses. He knew the Highlanders would associate their gains with his loss and delight twice as much in their newfound wealth.

With his resources, he could have sustained the cost of his charity, but anger had driven him to take from others. He had grown tired of watching his countrymen take advantage of the Highlanders and never pay for their crimes. What the English were doing here amounted to thievery with the full approbation of the law. And so, Cameron Montgomery had set out to administer his own brand of justice.

Hearing the clock strike ten, Cameron decided to join the majority of guests in the ballroom. Supper would be served soon, and then he would depart, using his cold as an excuse to leave early. Irritating as sniffles might be, however, they would not preclude him from making a surreptitious stop, a stop one of the guests would have cause to regret. He smiled grimly as he got to his feet and set the glass down upon a table. At least the evening wouldn't be completely dull, and by the time he arrived at his own door he would be too tired to moon over Blair. That would be a welcome relief. After the havoc his last encounter with her had caused him, Cameron never wanted to see or think about her again.

A peckish Cameron was halfway across the dance floor before he noticed her. There stood Miss Blair Duncan in all her Highland finery, like some ancient warrior queen among fading English blossoms. The sight of her drove Blair's childhood sweetheart to the brink of rage. Despite all of the invitations he had issued and she had ignored, all of the times he had wished her in his home and she had remained absent, Miss Blair Duncan had chosen to grace Haverbrook's gathering after meeting the man but once. Or had it been more than that, Cameron wondered jealously, recalling how Harry had been taken with the girl...and her property.

Was he pursuing the lass despite the fact that he was married, or was he perhaps actually going through with his absurd plan to cultivate Blair's acquaintance in order to introduce her to his nephew? Neither answer was one Cameron liked, and he crossed the room like some charging lion, shortening his stride and dropping a bemused mask into place only when he reached the group and stood behind Blair, out of her line of vision.

"So Hogmanay is your major celebration during the Yule season?" Estella Rogers, Lady Haverbrook asked. "How odd!"

"But I'm sure delightful," Harry interjected as he saw Blair's brow draw together in irritation. And then a smile spread across his face as he looked beyond his Scottish guest to see Cameron Montgomery and the deadly glare emanating from his predatory eyes, despite the man's expressionless features. This evening might contain some excitement after all, Harry thought with self-congratulations.

"Yes, delightful..." Estella murmured, feigning interest in Scottish customs rather poorly.

"Ah, that it is, but I have a prejudice in the matter," Blair said. "I suppose, though, that everyone is fondest of their own Christmastide traditions. Which is why, I confess, I found it beyond my ken that all of you chose to remain in the Highlands for the holidays, rather than return to your homes."

"Yes, my dear, I must say it is beyond my understanding as well," Lady Haverbrook said, delivering a sharp glance to her husband. "But the men would have it no other way, I'm afraid."

"Now, now, sweetest, you know why we must stay here this year. We've got to catch the villain who has been pilfering from all of us," Harry said, attempting to soothe the petulant woman he had married.

"Why I detest the Spirit of Christmas," Estella Rogers continued to pout. "If it weren't for that dastardly fellow we would be in London right now, celebrating the Christmas season in familiar luxury rather than having to make do with so little."

Blair bit back a retort. If the woman's London home were more richly appointed than this one, the Rogers could afford to lose the sort of things the Spirit of Christmas took. And besides, the beneficent Christmas phantom was a hero, not a common criminal, sharing his wealth, stolen as it might be, with the poor of Glenmuir. However, Blair knew she could say no such thing and still hope to influence these English into hiring her people.

"Ah, my dear, perhaps the bounty we have placed on the thief's head will aid in his capture," Harry said, his mouth growing grim. "But enough talk about that thief. We'll have a jolly Yule in spite of him. Won't we, Lindsay?"

Blair's face turned pale at the sound of the name, and then flushed red when she heard Cameron's rich, deep voice rise in response.

"Indeed we shall. Good evening, Miss Duncan. What a pleasant surprise to find you here," the nobleman said smoothly as Blair whirled around to face him. "If I had known of your presence, I would have left the card room an hour ago."

"There would have been no need to forgo your pleasure," Blair replied, her honeyed voice not hiding the insult she intended.

"Ah, but one game is as good as another," Cameron said softly, noticing a smug, bemused smile plastered across Harry's face. "But that is neither here nor there. At the moment, I find that I'm famished. Surely supper hour is almost upon us. What time is it, Harry?"

Haverbrook reached mechanically across his expanding stomach to his vest pocket before he recalled that the thing he sought was no longer there. The resulting scowl was very out of place amid so many cheerful decorations.

"You'll have to ask someone else," the earl grumbled. "My watch seems to have disappeared last night while I slept."

"You misplaced it?" Cameron prodded, enjoying his revenge on Harry. The man had not only offered a reward for the Spirit of Christmas, he had also invited Blair here tonight, as if winning her was indeed no more than a hunt.

"No, in all likelihood it was stolen," Harry mumbled.

"Stolen! The Spirit has had the audacity to strike your very bedroom?" Cameron asked, managing to look aghast while he relished the anger such a bold move had caused Harry. Not that the blighter didn't deserve it. The earl had bragged to everyone that he had bought the watch with money that had been saved by evicting two tenant families this year. The price of the timepiece was minimal, but Cameron hoped that the lesson of having it stolen from his room while he slept a few feet away would be worth much more to Rogers.

"How tiresome!" Cameron exclaimed at Harry's miserable nod. "Really, this fellow must be caught. I, myself, have been informed by my servants that a few hams and yards of sausage are missing from my smoke shed. The fellow has no shame!"

"That's right, he doesn't," Blair retorted in a voice so low that only Cameron among the entire gossiping group could hear. "Shame, sir, is a trait which belongs entirely to you! Had I known you were to be here, I would never have come. Haverbrook told me you were ailing."

"Ah, feisty Blair," Cameron said in a hoarse whisper as supper was announced and he took her arm without permission to lead her to the refreshment tables. "You're fiery enough to make any man's blood boil... with anger if not passion. Sorry to disappoint you, but I'm on the mend. You won't hear the kirk bell tolling anytime soon for me.''

"I wouldn't swear to it, Cameron Montgomery. Keep up with your impudent remarks, and I'll kill you myself," Blair hissed, her eyes burning like twin blue flames.

The only response her threat brought was that the rogue holding her captive popped a dainty into her mouth and then threw back his magnificent head and laughed more heartily than he had in quite some time.

Blair swallowed the confection quickly, and when she was able to speak once more, her words contained no trace of the sweetness still lingering in her mouth.

"You're everything I abhor in a man."

"Then you hide your feelings admirably, my love. Towards the end of my visit to Duncan House the other day, I could swear you didn't find me all that repulsive," Cameron stated, his blood thickening at the recollection. But damn, what was he doing, he thought in surprise. He should be apologizing to this enchanting woman for the liberties he had taken.

Yet Blair's smoldering eyes served to ignite something deep within him that made him forget every lesson in proper behavior he had ever learned. And the fact that Harry was nearby, and most likely watching them with amused interest, tempered Cameron's reaction to Blair not one bit.

"I don't know what you're talking about," Blair said over her shoulder as she turned her back on him and began to place food on her plate.

"Shall I remind you?" Cameron asked in spite of himself, his silken voice so low that no one could possibly overhear. "There are alcoves aplenty that would give us privacy."

"No gentleman would say such a thing to me," a blushing Blair whispered in response.

"But I can't be a gentleman when I'm near you," Cameron persisted, bending his handsome head to hers and deciding to share the truth. "No, when I'm with you, Blair Duncan, I become something much more primitive."

"Then why not do as I have already suggested and stay away from me?" Blair asked, her face almost as red as the holly berries decorating the base of the punch bowl. What he had suggested should be considered an insult, yet she was struck by the tenderness in Cameron's tone all the same. It called to her, enticing the pretty Highlander to forget all of her objections to the man standing by her side.

"I find I can't do that," Cameron said simply.

"Then I'm afraid I shall have to help you," Blair stated quietly. Before she could change her mind, she walked off to join Harry and the others, even as something in Cameron's expression, insufferable though he was, beckoned her to stay.

Chapter Five

The Highlands never failed to weave their spell, no matter how overcast the day, marveled Blair thankfully as she finished gathering the extra evergreen sprigs and small branches of holly. The air had become misty, and small droplets were gathering on her lashes while she tied the greenery together. The rolling hills and craggy heights were magnificent in their isolated grandeur amid the blue-grey shadows of late afternoon, their very desolation spurring the heart to appreciate the splendors of unspoiled nature, a land where man was subordinate not only to his God but to the very earth on which he toiled. There was nothing like an afternoon in the countryside to renew her affection for Glenmuir and its rugged people.

Life in the Highlands was not for the weak of heart or spine, the young woman reflected, brushing her long hair under her plaid for protection against the moisture. Yet the pride and promise of generations past held her and the others here, rewarding them with the surety of tomorrow. The salmon would again seek out their birthplaces to spawn and die; the heather would again bloom, briefly but gloriously; and man would again be tested by trials beyond his comprehension, only to come through the grief and celebrate his victory. Wasn't that the heart of the Hogmanay feasting, one year gone and another begun, despite the sorrows passing days incurred? That belief in the continuity of life was so indelibly imprinted on her soul that, unwanted English settlers or not, she'd see that the Glenmuir holiday celebrations did not suffer for their unwelcome presence, even if the intruders included one Cameron Montgomery.

Starting her trek homeward, Blair walked with a brisk purpose of spirit, striding confidently through the damp grass. This was the season of hope; things would yet work out for Glenmuir, especially given Lord Haverbrook's proposal of employment. And she did have her Yuletide baskets, she reminded herself, though today was December twenty-first and she hadn't nearly finished filling them, let alone decorating them. The contents were more meager than she would have liked, but at least the baskets' holiday look would be traditionally joyful, with a few sprigs of holly for color and evergreen for scent.

Over the years, her gifts to ease the plight of the less fortunate had been a source of pleasure and self-fulfilling delight. All the village knew she made up the baskets, of course, and there'd been a few anonymous parcels left on her doorstep of late, including a huge sack of lovely apples just the other morning. Yet for all her efforts, her gifts would be insignificant compared to those left by the Spirit of Christmas, the villagers expecting hers, delighted by the surprise of his.

That's if he even returns this Yuletide, said an unsought voice of doom.

And do you want him back? asked another stray thought.

For, in truth, as much as Blair appreciated the anonymous thief's generosity, perhaps his presents had somehow taken the joy away from her own contributions. Yet, he had been leaving much needed goods for the villagers for almost three years now. How could she resent his involvement, especially given the severe plight of so many?

Nonsense, she scoffed at the haunting questions; charity, no matter what the source, was nothing she could refuse anyone. But, undeniably, this year, her annual good works hadn't provided the warm pleasure she'd enjoyed in the past. This season, the task of soliciting the donations, preparing the marmalade, sharing the little she herself had, and incorporating everyone else's generosity had been more a chore than a challenge, an unwelcome obligation rather than a joy-filled enterprise, but that wasn't the fault of the Spirit of Christmas.

Probably, her good sense told her, the unfamiliar feelings could be traced to the insufferable Montgomery and his sudden appearance wherever she happened to be, from the paths of Glenmuir to her own kitchen. Never before had he been so persistent in seeking her out, so determined to court her despite her clearly expressed disinterest.

Even last night when she'd thought herself safe from his irritating presence, hadn't he been at Haverbrook's anyway, insistently attentive and provocatively handsome in spite of her pointed, if specious, immunity to his charms? Were she truly honest, however, she'd be hard-pressed not to admit she still found him attractive, despite his accursed lack of feeling for his Scottish heritage. It was just too bad that his mother had been an only child or perhaps the Connerys would still exist in Glenmuir, mused Blair, wiping the moisture from her face, and their former tenants would not be scattered to the far ends of civilization because of Montgomery's dismal judgment.

New Caledonia, it was halfway around the earth, according to Father MacKenzie, yet that was where the Macleods had headed when the fishing in the Sutherlands proved too poor to support the family. Lucifer, take the English—especially Montgomery; no hellfire could be too hot for him, decided Blair, though, if truth be told, he was a devil with heat of his own.

Glowering angrily as she stalked down the path leading to her small holdings, the lovely brunette paid no heed to the weight of her greenery, the chilling damp of the afternoon or the rapidly darkening clouds overhead. Righteous indignation sparked her Celtic temper and delightful thoughts of Cameron's inevitable damnation entertained her merrily as she descended Ben March in the steadily increasing mist. Then all of a sudden, he was before her, riding a large grey stallion, reaching out a long arm as if to pull her up into the saddle in front of him. The audacity of the man!

"And what do you want of me now, sir?" she demanded, moving out of his reach. "I assure you, I stole no Montgomery boughs."

"I didn't think you had," Cameron snapped in exasperation. Returning from taking coffee with the Enrights and inventorying the goods the Spirit of Christmas would liberate from them, he had seen her, half-drowned, crossing the meadow. But, bloody hell, the wench apparently didn't want to be saved from the elements—at least not by him. Reining in his temper as he held the stallion in check, he began again. "Blair, the weather is treacherous, I merely wanted to get you out of this downpour.''

''A bit of Highland mist never hurt anyone,'' retorted Blair, her voice as cold as ice though her rebellious blood ran hot at the sight of him. Last night she had no choice but to be civil; today there were no witnesses. ''But then I shouldn't be surprised you've forgotten how we once enjoyed running between the raindrops, imagining they couldn't find us.''

''We're both a bit larger now than we were then, Blair, and I fear there's not room enough between the drops to shelter us,'' he chuckled, surprised at the pleasure the sudden memory afforded him, despite his own growing discomfort. A sudden sneeze reminded him of the chill he had caught earlier in the week and he tried once again to hurry her. ''Come along, let me take you home and we can both dry off. Surely even Mrs. Brown wouldn't deny a wet Montgomery a place by your fire.''

''I'll not take you so far out of your way, sir. If my welfare truly concerns you, I'll take shelter in that cabin ahead and you can be on your way,'' the feisty brunette suggested, moving towards the small building half-hidden by trees.

''No! You can't do that,'' he objected loudly, moving his horse to block her progress. ''You can't go in there. I mean, it doesn't belong to you.''

''It's been abandoned for years. No one will mind. Besides, we Highlanders are committed to being hospitable, remember? Even if someone were there, he'd have to welcome me.''

''No,'' Cameron insisted urgently, dismounting so quickly he misjudged his footing, landing hard on the muddy path. ''Blair, I forbid you to go in there. If it's not been inhabited in years, it's not safe. The floorboards are probably weak, the roof undoubtedly leaks...why, there might even be squatters hiding inside—"

"Squatters? Unless they're Englishmen, I've naught to fear," she taunted him.

By now he was on his feet, mud coating his oncecreamy breeches, his dirty hands grabbing at her arms. His muscular body was rigid with purpose and his green and gold eyes burned with a peculiar intensity as he held her in place, recognizing the possible end to his masquerade as the Spirit of Christmas if she insisted on going into that cabin. How could the woman he craved betray him with her obstinacy? He had to stop her!

"Cameron Montgomery, take your filthy hands off me and let me go my way. You have no right to monitor my comings and goings, and I'll thank you to remember that!" Blair could feel the intensity of his anger, yet the answering heat in her own body had more to do with his preemptory touch than his words. Anxious as she was to be gone from him, a part of her ached to feel his arms around her, his lips on hers again. Oh, when would she learn to control her treacherous heart?

"Blair, I insist you stay away from that cabin," said Cameron. His voice had become husky, his eyes rather clouded, but his determination was undaunted as he released her and reached for her bundles. He would not allow her to discover his secret lair, no matter what means he had to employ. "Look, Lindsay Hall is closer than Duncan House. Let me take you there and we can talk—oh, damn, what the hell do you have in these baskets? Nettles?" he demanded angrily, dropping the offending parcel to examine his wounded hand. "I suppose they do suit your personality."

"I didn't ask for your assistance, sir. You have forced yourself on me—"

"Not to the extent I'd like," he muttered, wrapping a handkerchief around the burning cuts. "Then maybe you'd understand how I feel."

"What?" Picking up the holly from where it had fallen on the muddy ground, Blair hadn't quite heard his last words, drowned out as they were by resounding thunder.

"Nothing important. Just get on the blasted horse before I throw you over the bloody saddle," demanded Cameron, his tone as sharp as the finest English blade. "Regardless of what I've said in the past, I'll be the perfect gentleman. I cannot leave you out in this ungodly deluge." A loud sneeze punctuated his words and Blair weakened.

"Very well. If you stay out here much longer, you'll take to your bed for a month."

"Only if I take you with me," said Cameron as his overly familiar hand assisted her onto his horse.

"I remind you, sir, of your promise to be a gentleman," she retorted, settling herself uneasily astride his mount. Unhappy as she was at the prospect of Cameron's body pressed so close to hers for even a few moments, she was unwilling to prolong his soggy misery with further debate. By now, too, her woolen plaid was thoroughly sodden as was the thin gown she wore beneath it. Of course, had he not delayed her, she'd almost be home rather than shivering on his horse.

"Not to worry. Shadow will have us back at Lindsay Hall in a few minutes," Cameron promised, feeling her involuntary shudder. Wrapping his arms about

Blair's waist to share his warmth, damp though it was, he fought the urge to finger her luscious hair and rain kisses on her slender neck. He finally had her in his arms and he was not about to risk his success by moving too fast. "I am glad you finally agreed to come with me. It's been much too long since you've seen my home."

Blair said nothing, concentrating on the cold discomfort of the storm rather than the warming in her traitorous body. Maybe, if she were fortunate, he'd mistake the tears on her cheeks for rain. What might once have been between them could never be now, and more the pity of it.

"I can walk to Duncan House from here," Blair announced firmly as Cameron helped her down in the drive in front of Lindsay Hall, a large manor house, well kept and obviously well serviced as evidenced by the retainers who came scurrying to welcome their master and take charge of his horse.

"Nonsense, you'll do no such thing. Williamson, have Mrs. Pearson draw a warm bath for Miss Duncan, and send someone to her home to say she'll be dining with me this evening."

"I agreed to no such thing," protested Blair as he led her into a well-appointed sitting room usually reserved for members of the clergy or other prominent visitors. "Besides, it's much too much of a bother. This room? Cameron, I'm dripping all over the lovely carpet your mother chose. I belong in the kitchen, for heaven's sake."

"Nonsense, even wet and bedraggled, you're much too pretty for the scullery. Just because the parlor was off-limits when we were children, using it now shouldn't bother you. In case you haven't noticed, we're full grown.''

"Aye," murmured Blair, her heart in her throat as the tall brown-haired man who so reminded her of yesterday's love came nearer and removed her cloak. Even his fingertips seemed to set her on fire. What was wrong with her? Was it a chill she'd caught in the rain?

"Here now, have a dram of brandy to warm you while I see what is keeping Mrs. Pearson. Just because I've a bit of a cold doesn't mean you need to have one, as well."

Then he was gone and Blair took a deep swallow of the warming liquid, looking slowly about the once-sacred room. It was clear someone cared enough to properly maintain the spot that Mary Connery had loved best in Lindsay Hall. Little had changed in the past twelve years; from the dainty china figurines on the mantel to the prettily woven table covers, the lace curtains and the delicately embroidered fire screen. But that was a long time ago, reminded Blair's conscience, and too much had happened since for her to feel comfortable here.

"Miss Duncan, I am Mrs. Pearson. Come this way." The Montgomery housekeeper, a stern-looking Englishwoman whose disapproving expression spoke volumes, bustled in and out of the room so quickly that Blair had no choice but to follow her up the elegant staircase to the second floor, all too conscious of the watery trail she left with each step. "The only proper bath in the house adjoins his lordship's rooms, but he said that he would bathe in the kitchen. I've laid out dry clothes for you on his bed. I'm not certain they'll fit, but I'll be seeing to yours in the meanwhile. You just warm yourself as long as you like and when you come down, I'll have a hot meal ready."

"Please, don't go to any trouble. There's no need—"

"Hush, child. Enjoy Lord Lindsay's hospitality, rare it is he exercises it. Now give me those wet things. You know, you are the first guest he's brought without a houseful of others. Maybe it's a good sign."

Or maybe not, reflected the Scottish miss, sadly at a loss as to how to describe her feelings at being in Cameron's home, let alone undressed and about to step into his bath. He had treated her in such a cavalier manner, demanding she avoid that cabin, the English in him she supposed; yet, he'd seemed really concerned about her welfare in the storm. Was that pity or could the long-silent Connery blood be flowing in his veins again? No, the chance wasn't worth the taking, her good sense cautioned, though her heart held the question open for consideration.

Stepping into the tub, Blair emptied her mind of all but the delicate pleasure of the lavender-scented water warming her chilled muscles, soothing her aches and making her feel feminine again. It had been so long since she had pampered herself that the experience felt absolutely sinful it was so delicious. Throwing caution to the winds, she luxuriated lazily in the cozy comfort of the aromatic warmth, slipping completely beneath the water and allowing her hair its freedom as she gently washed its long tendrils with the perfumed soap Mrs. Pearson laid out. But suddenly the pleasurable sloth diminished, shattered by an unwelcome thought, and she bolted upright.

Why were there feminine scents and soaps in a supposedly male household, or was Cameron keeping someone? Not in Glenmuir obviously, but, from what she had heard, no one would look askance at such goings-on in London. And toiletries of this high a quality did not come from Mrs. Pearson's closet. *He* must have purchased them for someone.

Suddenly, in the utter quiet of the bath, Blair heard Mrs. Pearson's voice, apparently carried through the pipes from the kitchen below.

"She's a fair little thing, sir, she is. I fear those gowns from Miss Eloise may not be fitting her proper."

Miss Eloise! Who in blazes was she? Cameron had no sisters, and his mother's name had been Mary! How dare he give her another woman's clothes and expect her to wear them? Damn it all, her suspicions had been right all along. The friend of her childhood was gone, and this Cameron Montgomery was a no-good scoundrel!

Whatever he may have answered Mrs. Pearson downstairs was lost to Blair as she angrily exited the bath, determined to leave as quickly as she could. Still, she couldn't go back out in the storm without clothes.

Wrapping herself in a large towel, the indignant young brunette went through the door to Cameron's room, intent on drying herself before the fire. She certainly wouldn't wear the soft green gown so appealingly draped over the bed, no matter how attractive it was. As a gesture of defiance, she rumpled its silky fabric, enjoying its luxurious feel even as she resolved to avoid its temptation. Now, to find a shirt and tartan of Cameron's that she could wear; it seemed somehow fitting to borrow his finery rather than his lady friend's, Blair decided; let his clothes be ruined by the still-raging storm.

Though aware she should be ashamed of rummaging through Cameron's personal things, Blair felt only amazement at the fine fabrics and the fashionable cut of the man's coats and breeches. Given his own rugged good looks and clothing this dapper, he must cut quite a splendid figure in London society, she reflected, thinking back to the handsome lad she'd known years ago. For a moment Blair let herself imagine his long well-formed legs giving shape to the soft woolen trousers in her hands, his firm buttocks temptingly displayed beneath the taut fabric as he walked....

Then, as if her thoughts had bid him come, he stood in the doorway, clad in a long shirt. He came forward, apparently intent on fetching the trousers she held or another pair of equal quality, but instead, caught unaware by her presence, his step slowed, and his piercing eyes held her glance momentarily.

He hadn't expected to find her outside of the bathing chamber yet, and certainly not near naked in his room, though his imagination had often placed her there. Suddenly confronted by his pent-up passion, his years of desire for this woman, Cameron couldn't restrain himself. Slowly, gently, he reached out for the towel that hid her loveliness and lifted it away, exposing her to his view.

Fury coursed through Blair's veins at his presumption, turning her cheeks a ruddy pink, heightening the passion in her eyes as she lifted her chin defiantly, daring him to make the next move. For an eternity, neither said a word, each absorbed by the other's unexpected presence in the shadows of the flickering fire.

I should hate him, she told herself; he'd abandoned her and Glenmuir, all the people who'd trusted him; he had never answered her letters or come home till the queen had made the Highlands fashionable, but yet . . . the damp curls on his forehead reminded her of the boy he once was and, without being conscious of her intent, she stretched out her fingers to brush the hair away from his devouring eyes. At her touch he rewarded her with a smile and took her hand in his, brought it to his lips and kissed its palm.

That innocent gesture so ignited her world, Blair suddenly realized there was no place she wanted to be more than in Cameron's arms, no place at all, no matter what prudence demanded. As if sensing her decision, he drew her close to him, his hands urgently massaging her shoulders, then her lower back and her buttocks even as his mouth murmured her name ever so sweetly before his lips closed on hers.

The rogue stole not only her breath, but all desire to exist apart from him, as her breathing turned to panting and their hearts seemed to echo in rhythm, the pounding louder and louder in her ears as she gloried in the taste of him. As his mouth left hers to pay homage to her breasts, Blair moaned at the bittersweet torment he delivered, wanting to enjoy every new sensation of her awakening womanhood.

How could she have ever doubted him, Blair wondered half-consciously as she pulled his head up to hers to claim his soul. Groaning at the effort needed to control his pleasure, Cameron lifted Blair into his arms and moved towards the bed. Enraptured by his blend of strength and gentleness, she nuzzled his neck as he moved. She was truly content with what was happening until she felt the cold silken gown beneath her. *Miss Eloise's gown!* In an instant, that sensual touch drew her back from the precipice, causing her to roll

away from Cameron and leap unsteadily to her feet.
Angry with herself and her tempter, barely able to
speak, considering the nearness of her ruin and the ease
with which she'd fallen prey to her senses, Blair was
highly distraught.

"You—you haven't a single tartan in your wardrobe," she wept, "but you've other women's ball
gowns! Call on Miss Eloise; maybe she'll entertain your
passions—"

"But, Blair, I didn't mean for this to happen; I just
wanted to give you—"

Rescuing the forgotten towel from where it had
fallen, the young Scotswoman wrapped herself in it and
left the room, ignoring his words. She knew all too well
what he wanted to give her! But she would be content
with her pride and her soggy gown and plaid as she
made her way home alone to Duncan House.

Chapter Six

The rest of the evening and the ensuing night were a painful blur in Blair's mind as she still lay abed at half past nine, too humiliated and angry to face the morning light, weak though it was. She'd accepted Mrs. Pearson's absolute insistence that Cameron's coach see her home through the storm, but the weather outside could no more compare to the raging fury in her breast than Lord Haverbrook could be likened to Father Christmas.

Yet, Blair knew her pain came not from her relative success with Haverbrook, but rather from the near failure of her moral code with Cameron. Again and again during the treacherous ride home and throughout her restless night, churning emotions labeled her *coward* one minute and *fool* the next. Was she afraid to yield to her body's demands or was she just too old-fashioned in a world that claimed its pleasure wherever and whenever it could be had, no matter how temporarily?

The knowledge that she had nearly succumbed to Cameron's overtures, in truth, had wanted to succumb, shamed her so, that the young woman wasn't certain she would ever find the stamina to leave her house again. How could she ever face her tenants or the villagers? For years, her father had resisted English offers of gold and promises of favor to preserve his honor while last night, she had practically volunteered to forfeit hers, all because her childhood sweetheart kissed her so thoroughly her senses took flight. What was wrong with her that she relished that demon's touch, that her lips and breasts could still feel the tormenting heat of his attentions?

"Miss Blair? Are you up?" called the housekeeper from the hall. In recent years, her mistress had taken to rising earlier than the elderly servants, seeing to the kitchen fires and the first pot of tea; her failure to do so today after she'd scurried off to bed like a whipped dog the night before had Mrs. Brown worried. Bustling into the room with a falsely hearty smile, the older woman carefully perused Blair's swollen eyes and tearstained cheeks before seating herself on the bed and handing her mistress a bracing mug of hot tea. "I fear more than a chill was bothering you last night, lass. Why don't you tell old Morag about it?"

"No, really. It's just the untimely weather and the baskets not being finished yet and..." offered Blair, halfheartedly.

"And?" prodded the servant softly. "You know you can share your troubles with me. And what?"

"And the blasted Englishmen interfering in our lives, taking over our holiday season, and disrupting our traditional Yuletide. They've even offered a bounty for the capture of the Spirit of Christmas when they are the ones who should be hunted down," confided Blair vigorously, thinking of one man in particular.

"Ian was by this morning and told Robbie the Spirit was at work, even in that tempest last night. Seems he took a couple head of cattle from the Enright herd, as well as a few lambs, and a side of venison from Montgomery, though why that man keeps such a well-stocked larder I can't imagine, him a bachelor and all.''

"Since our people may well be on the receiving end of what Montgomery had lost, I wouldn't question the matter. But, tell me, has anyone received the Spirit's blessings yet?''

"Mayhap you, miss, though 'tis more likely the things last night were intended for the baskets by some generous souls who can spare them," said Mrs. Brown, heading for the door now that her charge seemed to be her old self. "I can see to them.''

"What was left?" demanded Blair, throwing off her covers. No matter how miserable she might feel, she reasoned, she had a duty to Glenmuir, curiosity over-shadowing her own personal woes.

"A large sack of corn, two hunting knives, three hams and yards and yards of sausage.''

"Then, let's get to those baskets, Mrs. Brown." Blair grinned, remembering Cameron's complaints at the Haverbrook party. Nothing would make her day brighter than apportioning the Spirit's bounty, knowing Cameron was an unwilling donor.

Surveying her work later that afternoon, Blair couldn't help but be pleased at the sight of the food-stuffs and practical goods she'd managed to accumulate. Though there was always more needed than she could possibly supply, each of the baskets held provisions for a memorable holiday. It was unfortunate that she hadn't been able to scare up the extra woolens she'd hoped for or some new seed for next year's planting, but the twenty families would indeed have cause for thanksgiving with what she had gathered.

A sudden knock at the kitchen door made her jump. Could Cameron be so crude as to call after his most recent behavior? Hospitality would dictate his admittance, though she'd told Mrs. Brown she wasn't up to entertaining. Would he accept that?

"Cameron Montgomery sends his regards, miss—"

"I won't see him, Mrs. Brown. Tell him I'm unwell," Blair interrupted, a flush coloring her cheeks at the thought of just how much of her he'd already seen.

"No, miss. He didn't stay. He asked me to give you this note," said the housekeeper. "I'll be fetching your tea."

For a moment Blair's fingers trembled around the folded page as she contemplated tossing it into the fire unread. Yet, he *did* owe her an apology, she reflected; perhaps this was it. Breaking the seal, she opened the note slowly, still ambivalent about its sender.

My dear Blair,

   You left so abruptly last evening, you never asked after a donation for the baskets. If you will call personally at Lindsay Hall at your earliest convenience, you will find me most generous; I am a firm advocate of giving from the heart and the purse.

                          I await your pleasure,
                                        Cameron

"He awaits *my* pleasure? Doesn't he mean his own?" Blair demanded of the fire as she flung his note into its greedy tongues of flame. Damn the man anyway; who was he to think she'd come crawling back to him, whatever bait he dangled?

"Yet the snake extends an offer I can't spurn," muttered the angry brunette, pacing the floor in her anxiety. "How could I have ever considered trusting him? He's no different from the rest of the English, out to take advantage of the Highlanders for his own amusement! He doesn't care about his neighbors; they're just a convenient excuse to entice me to enter his lair. Well, he did say at my earliest convenience... dawn tomorrow should do quite nicely especially since he'll undoubtedly be out enjoying the Enright's hospitality tonight."

Pleading the necessity of staying home to guard his rapidly decreasing larder, Cameron actually spent the evening alone in his study, much as he'd spent the majority of his hours since Blair left—cursing himself and his animalistic response to the sight of her in his bedroom. He certainly hadn't expected her to be done bathing so quickly or he would have sent Mrs. Pearson for his trousers; other ladies of his acquaintance could spend hours amid the warm waves of silky bathwater, angrily resenting his suggestion they hurry.

His had been a simple errand to be accomplished in an instant, but when he'd seen Blair standing there, so fresh and rosy from her scrub, totally innocent and alluring, it was as though he'd become an amoral satyr. Damnation. He'd finally started to thaw her icy surface and now—now she'd never allow herself to be alone with him again. Of that he was certain, even if she didn't call out the old Scots of Glenmuir to horsewhip him, which was also a possibility, given her temper.

Idly he set Harry's watch on the desk, still pleased with the audacity of his theft despite the ostentation of the timepiece. Then he reached for the box of his father's papers, forwarded recently by the former earl's solicitors. Thumbing through the old correspondence, Cameron found a variety of things: receipts for goods purchased twenty years ago, his old school reports, letters from his mother and grandmother, tied with red ribbon. These he put aside, allocating the rest to the flames, but there was still another packet of letters from Glenmuir, letters that were addressed to him at the Montgomery's London address, letters that had never been opened.

Without hesitation, he cut the time-aged wax and began to read the softly faded handwriting, a script that told of love and longing, daily events and memories once shared. The next letter was the same and so too was the third and fourth. It wasn't until the fifth letter he felt her disappointment, the pain of his not answering. Even then, Blair Duncan had written once more, almost a year later, to tell him of her mother's death and to ask for his consolation. Of course he'd never replied, but then he had never had the message, mourned Cameron, saddened by his father's compulsion to deny his son's ties with Glenmuir.

But hellfire be damned, cursed the now-grown lad, pouring a large brandy and taking the bottle with him as he mounted the stairs to his room, the cost to Blair wasn't yours to decide, Father. And now, I fear it's too late. Even if she forgave the misplaced letters and your gambling with her friends' lives, I've hurt her too much to expect forgiveness. Otherwise she would have come tonight to claim my goods for her tenants. Abandoning the brandy snifter on a chest at the foot of his bed, Cameron drank straight from the bottle, wishing only for the land of oblivion, where Blair's sad blue eyes couldn't find him.

It was still dark when the determined young woman left Duncan House carrying a small lantern. The air was heavy with moisture and the villagers still abed as she skirted Glenmuir heading toward the old Connery lands, but the haunting solitude of the dew-laden fields appealed to her Celtic soul, calling forth memories of sun worship in a land so often dark and grey. This morning, if she had timed her journey properly, the sun's arrival would coincide with hers at Lindsay Hall. While she didn't expect any ancient ritual, she'd at least have the satisfaction of discommoding Cameron Montgomery at an inhuman hour.

The servants were not even about, discovered the young woman, dressed in her warmest plaid, as she hammered on the door for the fourth time. Finally the hewn oak door opened and Williamson, hurriedly attired in less than meticulous fashion, looked askance at her presence.

"Miss—Duncan, is it? His lordship is not yet awake, nor is the rest of the household," he chided. "It is barely six."

"I've no time for sluggards, sir. The earl asked me to call at my earliest convenience, and this is it," she announced archly, moving to enter. "Aren't you going to invite me in while you fetch him? I won't steal the silver."

"No, miss, but perhaps you'll take some tea in the kitchen. Lord Lindsay really doesn't like being awakened so early."

"His lordship's preferences are of no concern to me. If you won't awaken your master, I shall be forced to do so."

"No, no, miss. He certainly wouldn't appreciate that," exclaimed the butler. "If you will wait in his study, I will tell him of your arrival. This way."

"Blair Duncan here? Now, at this ungodly hour?"

"Yes, sir, in your study."

"I can't believe she came." Cameron knew he was blathering, but why had she come so damned early? *Early,* that was it! He'd invited her at her earliest convenience, by heavens. His sudden eruption of laughter startled the butler so that the man backed away from his employer, wondering if he should perhaps seek help.

"Very well, Williamson, fetch my clothes at once. I can't keep a lady waiting," he instructed, grinning from ear to ear. *This* was the Blair Duncan he remembered, devilish, impudent, and absolutely maddening one minute and purely angelic the next. With a smile of pleasure that she'd come to him, he wondered which Blair awaited him below.

Left alone in the clearly masculine room, Blair couldn't help but notice the cluttered mass of papers on the desk. Approaching out of curiosity, she was astonished to recognize her letters, the youthful missives of more than ten years past. The boy hadn't cared enough to answer them, yet the man had saved them to read again? Unwilling to deal with the puzzle of Cameron Montgomery, Blair sternly put her pages to one side, examining the other papers about.

There! She knew it, an accounting from a woman's shop in London, Miss Eloise's of Regent Street. Well, she'd been wrong the other night; the gown hadn't belonged to Miss Eloise, it had been made by her, but for whom? From the size of these bills, Cameron might be outfitting any number of women in London, probably a different one each night of the week. No wonder he stayed in the Highlands so long; he and his purse needed the rest!

Well, if he could be so generous to relative strangers, he could certainly afford to do twice as much for Glenmuir, and she'd tell him so. Hearing footsteps on the stairs, she quickly placed the receipts back down, touching a round metal object as she did so, a man's pocketwatch by the feel of it. Good Lord, it was Haverbrook's! Without thinking, she slipped it into her skirt pocket and turned to face her bleary-eyed host.

"Lord Lindsay, you invited me to call at my convenience. I only regret it is not at yours, as well." How she kept her voice calm, Blair couldn't imagine, the stolen watch burning hot against her thigh. Could Cameron be the thieving Spirit of Christmas...or had Harry merely forgotten the watch at Lindsay Hall? She couldn't very well ask, but it didn't take a fool to see that Cameron was both delighted and troubled by her presence in this room. Awkwardly he came to stand between her and the desk, gesturing towards her age-old letters.

"Blair, I—I must apologize to you," he said softly, reaching out to take her hand, only to see her move farther away. "First, for my inexcusable behavior the other night and second, for my never answering your letters...but, please believe me, as odd as it might sound, I only received them last night."

"I came to accept your donation, Mr. Montgomery, not to discuss personal matters, no longer of consequence," rebuked the stubborn Scotswoman. He'd drawn her into his lair and only coldhearted vigilance would allow her to escape unscathed, Blair reminded herself, refusing to hear his words of explanation.

"Of course, Blair, and I will abide by your wishes," he conceded, opening the bottom drawer of the desk and extracting a cash box. "I thought perhaps a gold piece might be a practical addition to each basket and allow the families to purchase whatever they might want most."

"Highlanders understand the futility of wanting, sir. It's needs which concern them," admonished his visitor, surprised at her own vehemence in view of so fine an offering.

"As you say. Will twenty do?"

"Thirty would do better, and be more apt," pressed Blair, curious now to see just how guilty Cameron felt.

"Here you are. And Blair, buy something for yourself, too."

"Thank you, sir, but I'll see to those whose needs are the greatest. On behalf of them, I appreciate your generosity, and I hope the Spirit of Christmas leaves you untouched from here on."

Was that a flush her last remark elicited, or was the light in the study too uncertain to tell?

Then she was out of Lindsay Hall, her mind and heart a jumble. Thirty gold pieces! Had any Scot seen such a fortune in years? Was Cameron trying to assuage his conscience for abandoning Glenmuir? Or was he trying to win her favors after his attempt to take them had failed? What other reason could he have for such unprecedented charity?

Maybe he is the Spirit of Christmas, argued a niggling thought...remember the way he behaved to keep you from that old cabin? And his having Lord Haverbrook's watch was certainly odd.

Blair knew she had no choice; she'd have to go to the abandoned cottage and explore it. If it were the Spirit's hiding place...well, then she'd consider what to do next.

It was nearly teatime when she returned to Duncan House, still amazed at the bounty stored in that apparently forgotten cabin. Undoubtedly the place was the Spirit's treasure trove; even the missing lambs had been tethered behind it. But how could she really connect Cameron to the place—or the Spirit? Yes, he'd worried about her entering the dilapidated building, but couldn't that have been real concern? Harry's watch, she'd already decided, could have been merely misplaced, regardless of what Harry claimed. After all, how could she credit Cameron with caring so much for the people of Glenmuir that he would steal from his fellow countrymen when he chose to live in London nine months of every twelve?

He did tell you he tried to reclaim the lands his father lost, chided a small voice. Maybe he really did. And maybe he had only received her letters last night, twelve years after they'd been written.... He certainly had tried to communicate with her when he first returned to the Highlands, acting astonished at her refusal to see him. Perhaps he hadn't known how much she'd needed him...and he had given her thirty quid for the baskets today, a very generous gift from a man who had no feeling for the Highlands.

Yet, did she trust him enough to believe he would risk his reputation and, this, perhaps his life for those who wouldn't associate with him? Blair's mind roiled with the questions and queries she couldn't answer, her heart offering him forgiveness even as her head refused a pardon. For now, the issue would have to wait. Tomorrow was Christmas Eve and she had to add these coins to each basket. They glittered in her palm, but their sparkle couldn't compete with the bright hope shining in her heart that perhaps she had misjudged Cameron Montgomery.

Chapter Seven

Blair climbed into her well-traveled coach, assisted by Old Robbie as Ian Ferguson's resounding thanks echoed in the chill evening air.

"You're a wonder, lass," the old man called from his doorstep, his glance sweeping the contents of the overflowing basket delivered by the former laird's daughter. "Christmas Eve morning will be a sweeter occasion for that jar of marmalade. And with apples, sausage and walnuts for holiday feasting, this Yuletide will be a grand one indeed!"

Blair smiled prettily and waved before Robbie set the coach in motion once more. Then, the lovely benefactress of Glenmuir issued a contented sigh that she had delivered the last of her Christmas baskets. All the work, the time, the scrounging for goods had been worth the effort, she thought with satisfaction, recalling the pleased reactions her gifts had brought from her tenants and the other needy families in the vicinity. Now it was time for her own holiday to begin.

Leaning back against the seat as the coach continued its slow, rhythmic movement, she happily envisioned the clutter in her kitchen tomorrow as she and Mrs. Brown immersed themselves in final preparations for Christmas Eve and the dinner to be served the following day.

Christmas and the ensuing Daft Days had always been Blair's favorite season. But these past few years, the holidays had been more than that. It had been a time when she could cast aside her problems and relish the happiness of Christmases past, luxuriating in the recollections of a time when her family had been intact, her friends still in Glenmuir, and money no problem. In quiet moments, Blair could close her eyes and hear her father's laughter, feel the warmth of her mother's smile and smell the delicious aromas of the Christmas feasts prepared so long ago.

Basking in these memories was a gift she always allowed herself, and it was more precious to her than any number of new gowns or costly pieces of jewelry. But this Yuletide, Blair discovered to her discomfort, the memories did not appear so readily when she attempted to summon them. Her mind was preoccupied with thoughts of a more current nature. Cameron Montgomery! His image materialized unbeckoned whenever she was least ready for it. The handsome Englishman's presence made it impossible to dwell in the past. Instead it teased her with present possibilities and future promises.

Not that such musings were altogether unpleasant, Blair had to admit, recalling the kisses she and Cameron had so recently shared, and the encounter in the bedroom at Lindsay Hall. Lord, but the man's good looks had been enticing! Clothed, Cameron was a handsome enough rogue, but half-naked, he had been temptingly seductive. The effect this virile man continued to have on her sent Blair's heart racing. The Cameron of the bedroom had been so unlike her youthful sweetheart. There had been nothing childlike or innocent about him. No, he had been all full-grown male and deliciously sensual.

Even now, thoughts of what had very nearly occurred in that room warmed Blair much more than the old plaid wrapped tightly around her. It had been her fear concerning another woman that had allowed her to escape...and then only barely, though certainly not unscathed. But Blair's present suspicions that Cameron could be the Spirit of Christmas eclipsed her condemnation of him as the man who had destroyed the Connery estate. In spite of herself, she had to admit that Cameron Montgomery was quite a man, outside the law though he might be. After all, hadn't he but recently stolen her heart?

Yet this revelation, while unspoken, did not sit easily with the pretty Highlander. After all, he might look after the welfare of her friends, but what sort of man would steal from his own kind? Then, too, how could he act as if he cared for her when in all probability he was keeping another woman? Perhaps the bills she had found while rifling his desk could be explained by the existence of a ward or some dependent female relation, but how likely was that? Cameron was, after all, very much a red-blooded male. His kisses had taught Blair that.

No, she couldn't respond to his overtures and give in to her own desires until she was sure of his sincerity. Her honor was not something to be stolen along with her heart. It was a gift she would bestow freely once she learned the truth of the matter. And doing so before Christmas was an unlikely prospect. It was evident there would be no peace for her this Yuletide. Cameron Montgomery had seen to that. At the thought,

Blair's holiday mood fled, and she leaned her head back against the worn cushion, lapsing into pensive speculation.

Cameron wrapped his ineffectual greatcoat about him, swearing that he really ought to get himself a warm Scottish plaid. He watched Blair's carriage pull away slowly, glad that he had not met her upon Ian Ferguson's doorstep while they were both about the business of delivering their respective holiday gifts. Just such a thing had very nearly occurred, with Cameron scarcely managing to avert it. It would not do for Blair to learn his secret. It might color her feelings for him and he was stubborn enough to want her because she loved *him,* and not his charitable deeds.

As the chilling cold nipped at Cameron's muscular body, the plodding horses pulling the ancient coach finally reached the main road and turned. A few minutes later, the carriage disappeared entirely. Teeth chattering, Cameron lifted a bulging sack tied to his horse's saddle and carried it to Ian's front door. The bold Englishman set his load down gently, careful not to break the bottles of whisky packed inside along with a small purse of coins and a good-sized ham. Not that a salty bloke like Ferguson would appreciate the taste of the ham anyway, Cameron thought with a wry smile. Still, it would fill his belly during the holiday and that was what mattered.

Quickly the Spirit of Christmas arranged his offerings then stealthily returned to his horse. Intent upon his hasty departure, Cameron did not hear the door open. Nor did he see old Ian venture out upon his doorstep, thinking Blair might have returned.

With eyes trained on the figure retreating into the darkness, Ian Ferguson stooped and picked up the bundle left by his visitor. His sharp ears noted the clink of bottles within, and a broad grin lit the old Scot's weathered face as he shook his head in amazement.

"So that's the truth of it, is it? Well, I'm no surprised. He is Mary Connery's son after all," he muttered to himself, the tinkling of the glass as he shifted the sack more pleasing than any symphony. "Och, but I always did find Mary's bairn to be a likeable laddie."

The following evening, Christmas Eve, Blair greeted her neighbors as she made her way into the small kirk sitting at the edge of Glenmuir. The happy faces surrounding her made Blair's spirits soar. Without a word being spoken, the cheer of the parishioners was evidence enough that the Spirit of Christmas had once more visited the isolated Highland village.

A small smile settled on Blair's attractive mouth as she took her seat and relished her delicious secret concerning the hamlet's benefactor. She suspected what not one of them would ever guess. Cameron Montgomery might very well be the man to whom they should be grateful. Such a thing would mean that he did care for Glenmuir and its people, even if he didn't really care for her. Seeing Cameron as the distributor of such largess made his story about the destruction of the Connery estate more palatable. And that, Blair realized, happily erased many of her doubts concerning her childhood friend. Whatever his behavior in London, the people of Glenmuir had nothing for which they could reproach him.

Still, seeking more evidence of Cameron's secret identity would have to wait. With the exception of this hour to be spent in quiet prayer, the evening promised Blair little rest. She still had another duty to perform. And doing so meant she would not be at home to wait with Mrs. Brown for the MacNab lads to come along. Following Highland tradition, Mrs. MacNab's brood would laughingly abduct Mrs. Brown as their Christmas witch, and bear her to their hearth, where Mrs. Brown would be seated in a place of honor and expected to entertain the family with tales of days gone by. It was a merry tradition to be sure, but Blair's plans for the evening would force her to forgo the fun.

Patting the glorious reddish brown hair that curled from beneath her bonnet, Blair almost regretted having accepted Harry's invitation to partake in a cup of Christmas cheer following her Christmas Eve service. Still, she could not have declined. The nobleman had told her quite frankly that the Fairfaxes would be returning to London the day after Christmas, and, while they were willing to consider hiring a local as groundskeeper, they needed some reassurance from Blair about his reliability. The opportunity to secure employment for Mr. MacNab was reason enough to call at Harry's lodge. Besides, it would keep her mind from dwelling upon Cameron and the confusion she felt whenever she thought about him.

Stirring in the church wrenched Blair from her musing. Looking up, she expected to see Father MacKenzie entering the sanctuary, but she saw someone else instead. Cameron Montgomery had come to church and was slipping into her pew.

So much for her hour of tranquillity, Blair thought miserably. Prompted by Cameron's nearness, she prepared to fight off thoughts that could only be considered sacrilegious in a house of God. Yet the Englishman's presence and warm smile did not make the service as torturous as Blair had feared. Rather, his proximity felt natural and brought with it a sense of peace.

After the final blessing, the locals stood watching the old laird's daughter being escorted from the kirk. Cameron had been prepared to meet their disdain in order to spend some time with Blair despite the fact that the church was not his own. But disapproval was not the emotion these Highlanders were silently communicating. It was almost as though they felt that a man who attended the kirk on Christmas Eve could not be all bad, even if he was English.

In truth, a few of the villagers gave every indication of regarding him agreeably, while Mrs. MacNab's soft glance hinted at her speculations concerning the bonny bairns he and Blair would produce. As for the cousins Ferguson, the usually dour duo appeared almost friendly. Why Cameron could swear that old Ian had even sent a nod in his direction! Could Blair have told them about his monetary contribution to her baskets?

The Earl of Lindsay felt distinctly uncomfortable with the truce the people of Glenmuir seemed to have declared. Was it perhaps a new tactic meant to make him so uneasy that he kept out of the village and away from Blair in the future?

Shaking off his doubts, Cameron looked down to see Blair offering him a shy, tentative smile, and the villagers were immediately forgotten. His thunderous heart flared with hope that perhaps she was coming around. After all, she had accepted his donation for her charity baskets. And though she had arrived at his house the other morning practically at dawn, in a rather impersonal mood, she hadn't been overly antagonistic.

Losing himself in Blair's beguiling gaze, Cameron was vaguely conscious that he should question this woman's sudden geniality. But when a dimple appeared near the corner of her delectable mouth and she reached up to place her hand on his arm, the virile Englishman found that he didn't care about the reason for Blair's change of heart. The fact that she seemed to accept him at last made him feel as if the long years that had separated them had never occurred.

"Happy Christmas, Blair," he said, stooping to plant a tender kiss on her cheek before he could stop himself.

"Happy Christmas," Blair whispered in return, blushing a becoming shade of pink under the watchful curiosity of the other churchgoers.

Then a devilish glint lit her deep blue eyes. Perhaps this was her opportunity to learn why Cameron had purchased gowns from a London dressmaker. What decent man could lie while standing on the steps of a kirk? And, if his answer could allay her concerns, then her own Christmas might prove to be very happy indeed.

"Are you going to Haverbrook's this evening?" Blair asked coyly.

"No. What with the Spirit of Christmas taking everything that is not nailed down, I thought it best to spend tonight at Lindsay Hall. I take it that you'll be attending Harry's gathering," Cameron said gruffly, his attractive face marred by a frown. His unhappy expression was meant to be part of the role he was playing as a worried English aristocrat, but he quickly realized that it was real enough.

Hadn't he visited Duncan House last week to invite Blair to sup with him on Christmas Eve? And hadn't she told him she would be too busy to join him? Yet here she was, prepared to go off to Harry's without a word of explanation. Oh, he knew what she was doing all right, associating with Haverbrook and the others in hopes that it would benefit the villagers. And to be honest, he couldn't chide her for such noble actions. But when would she realize he needed her, too? And most important of all, when would Blair understand that she needed him in return?

"Yes, I am calling at the lodge on my way home. How unfortunate you won't be there," Blair replied, a small pout lighting on her lovely mouth. But then, she thought to herself, craftily, it could be that you have too much to do yet this evening, Cameron Montgomery. While my deliveries are all made, perhaps you have a few secretive stops to make?

"May I drive you?" Cameron asked.

"No, Old Robbie will do that before he goes off to join Mrs. Brown and the MacNabs for a bit of merry-making. But tell me, Cameron, don't you find yourself lonely spending Christmas up here?" Blair asked, ready in earnest to find out about that damnable slip of paper her foraging had uncovered.

"It's not all that bad, Blair," the rugged earl replied, pleased by her concern for him. "The Highlands are beautiful at any time of year."

"Yes, they are. But don't you miss the other members of your family during the holidays? Isn't there a

Christmas dinner waiting for you somewhere, host-
essed by some loving aunt, or cousin or ward?" Blair
asked, holding her breath as she waited for his answer.

So that's it! Cameron thought exuberantly. The little vixen is trying to issue an invitation to dinner tomorrow without actually having to swallow her pride.
Well, I'll play her little game. I'll be the miserable loner
languishing for family and hearth so that her charitable instincts can be the excuse she needs to invite me
to her table.

"No, Blair. I've no family left to save me a seat at
their holiday feast," he replied, looking at her expectantly and waiting for the invitation that was sure to
follow.

"Is that so?" Blair asked, her words suddenly curt
and her smile fading as she envisioned some other
woman wearing the gowns.

"Why, yes, I'm afraid it is," Cameron replied, confusion at her behavior rapidly taking the place of his
happy expectation.

"That's really too bad," Blair said, her voice tight
in her chest. And with that she whirled around and entered her carriage, leaving a baffled and disappointed
Cameron to deal with the curious stares of the inhabitants of Glenmuir.

The Earl of Haverbrook had promised that tonight
would be only a small gathering, but the magnificent
lodge was ablaze with light as usual when Robbie
halted the Duncan coach before its doors. Knowing
Harry would see to her transportation for the trip
home, Blair instructed Robbie to join Mrs. Brown in
the evening's festivities, before she turned to deal with
her own commitments.

The butler who greeted her and took her plaid was as decorous as ever, yet Blair couldn't help but notice the great flurry of activity that seemed to be taking place for an evening when only a few guests were expected.

She followed the butler to a large sitting room, which was the source of loud guffaws and boisterous laughter. It would seem these English had already downed a few cups of Christmas cheer, Blair thought while she stood waiting to be announced.

The butler went forward immediately, but as he opened the door the lovely young Scot caught a snatch of Harry's conversation.

"Yes, it was I who advised Lindsay on the way to capture such an elusive creature. And it would appear that my words have done a lot of good. The lady is practically his, and I understand he can't wait to show her off. What is it, Thompson?"

"Miss Blair Duncan has arrived, milord," the butler intoned solemnly.

The man's implacable demeanor contrasted sharply to Blair's emotions as she seethed just outside the doorway. So it *was* true! There was no escaping this proof. That bounder Montgomery did have a woman in London and everyone but she was aware of it! How dare that bastard toy with her and speak to her of love! Did he think she deserved to be nothing more than a holiday diversion during his sojourns to the Highlands? The idea shouldn't surprise her. He had demonstrated the same mentality in his youth. That insufferable, arrogant Englishman! Well, she didn't care how much he did for the people of Glenmuir. She would continue to sleep alone. Her honor was not available as recompense for his charity.

"Ah, Miss Duncan, we've been waiting for you," Harry said with a conspiratorial wink to the others as he changed the subject and headed for the doorway to escort his guest into the room himself. "None of us had any notion of what time your church service would conclude, so there was no way of informing you that there has been a change in plans for this evening."

"Change, milord?" Blair managed to ask. In her struggle to keep her rage at Cameron under control, her voice took on a breathy, demure quality that quite belied the bitterness she felt.

"Yes, I'm terribly sorry, but an emergency has come up that makes it impossible for Fairfax, Enright and myself to remain here attending you ladies, as lovely as you might be. Still there's time to raise a glass before we must leave. Come, my dear, allow us to wish you a joyous Christmas."

"What has happened, Lord Haverbrook, to spoil your holiday eve?" Blair asked, taking a cup of mulled cider from her host. "I hope it is nothing gone terribly amiss."

"No, my dear, nothing wrong at all, in fact things are finally right. Come along and allow me to leave you with Estella and the other ladies while we men go off to do what we must."

Soon Blair found herself with a bored Lady Haverbrook, Lady Fairfax and Mrs. Enright while the men hovered excitedly in a far corner of the room, speaking in low muted tones. Using the pretext of wishing to inspect the Christmas tree once more, a curious Blair moved closer to the men's group and was able to make out bits and pieces of their talk. Conversation about ammunition and blinds and waiting under cover caused her to think that, odd as it might be, these men were going out hunting on Christmas Eve. No wonder their wives were so put out.

And then, a muttered phrase almost made Blair's heart stop.

"...return to that deserted cabin tonight...it's where he has stored the stolen...."

Good Lord, they weren't tracking any animal! They had found the place where the Spirit of Christmas had cached the things he had stolen from them. And should Cameron be the person they were seeking, he was in terrible danger!

Visions of the handsome Englishman killed or wounded or even trapped and sent to prison whirled around Blair's head, completely eradicating the hatred she had felt for him only a moment before. Cameron might have betrayed her heart, but that was not a crime which demanded his death. Blair only knew that she had to leave as quickly as possible so that she could warn him.

The fetching Scotswoman found that Lady Haverbrook readily accepted her excuse of a headache and made no effort to stop Blair's departure. Though the woman was impeccably polite, there wasn't any doubt that Estella had no desire to entertain this local beauty. Blair had just made her goodbyes to the others and Harry, who apologized profusely for his inability to entertain her properly without telling her why, when more Englishmen arrived.

Growing desperate, Blair hastily took her leave, but not without noticing the pile of hunting rifles in the corner of the spacious vestibule. Spurred on by her worry for Cameron, Blair knew she could reach Lindsay Hall quick enough by foot if she ran across the fields and through the forest. She only hoped she would be in time to prevent his leaving for the cabin.

Fifteen minutes later, a bedraggled Blair pounded on Cameron's front door. The butler raised his eyes in exasperation when he saw who had come calling. Didn't Scottish women know anything about what the civilized world accepted as proper visiting hours?

It took all of his powers of persuasion to make the young woman believe him when he informed her that his lordship was not at home. And then did the odd creature leave a message of any kind? No, she just raced off again, without a word of explanation.

Striking off up the hillside, a rapidly winded Blair struggled for breath. She knew that what she was doing was foolish, but it didn't matter. If anything should happen to Cameron because she hadn't warned him, she would never forgive herself. All she need do was reach the cabin before the English, to tell Cameron to flee if he was there, or to assure herself of his safety if he was not.

Despite the growing pain in her side, Blair ran onward. She was amazed at how much she could endure in order to save the man she loved. No sooner had the idea entered her head than a cry escaped her lips. It was true, then. She couldn't hide it from herself any longer. Despite the woman Cameron evidently had in London, Blair knew that she loved him as she could never love any other man. Damn, but she never did have any sense where Cameron Montgomery was concerned.

Soon Blair neared the cabin where the English intended to trap the rogue who had laid claim to her heart. The dilapidated building gave no sign of any occupant. But that did not mean that Cameron was not inside even now, filling one of his sacks for distribution. Anyone who was stealthy enough to elude capture for the past few years could certainly avoid the detection of one woman half-crazed with fear.

After circling the cabin quietly and seeing no signs that the English had arrived before her, Blair stepped onto the porch and reached for the latch. Slowly she pushed the door inward, the creaking hinges singing more loudly than any choir. She advanced on tiptoe into the center of the small room, and was about to call Cameron's name when a match was struck and a voice called out.

"We have him, chaps. Take aim!"

Chapter Eight

"Heavens above," exclaimed Enright as the lanterns exposed Blair's features under their harsh glare. "Lower your rifles, men. Our thief is none other than little Miss Blair Duncan. Amusing, isn't it, Haverbrook, that the criminal is the woman you were so busily touting as the epitome of Scottish loyalty and honesty? I guess that shows how far we can trust your judgment."

"Don't be absurd. I—I'm certain that Miss Duncan can explain her presence here tonight," said Harry Rogers, looking hesitantly at the comely female who stood her ground without flinching, though her deep blue eyes seemed to spark with annoyance.

"I think we already know why she's here," chimed in another of the Englishmen, "to collect more of our goods. No wonder she was able to fix such fine holiday baskets for her Highland neighbors year after year. The provisions she steals from us don't cost her much."

"And who would ever suspect a woman of such underhanded skullduggery in the name of charity?" asked Lord Fairfax, whose apples had graced the holiday gifts.

"I hardly think Blair Duncan would—" started Harry.

"Gentlemen, if I might have a word here, what in heaven's name do you imagine I've done that's so terribly wrong? Obviously something has upset you, but taking a solitary walk on Christmas Eve has never caused such consternation for me before," said Blair softly, trying to mask her breathlessness. Caught in the very trap from which she'd sought to protect Cameron, she had no choice but to pretend ignorance of what was left of the cabin's significant contents. Yet she offered up a silent prayer of thanksgiving for having left Harry's watch at home; her case certainly wouldn't be helped by its chiming the hour at this moment. "Have I stumbled on a secret meeting of English husbands whose wives don't know their whereabouts? If so, I'll gladly take an oath of silence and depart at once, I assure you."

"Don't be in such a hurry, Miss Duncan. Take a seat on that crate and maybe you can allay our suspicions that *you* are the Spirit of Christmas who has been wreaking havoc with the inventory of our lodges every Yuletide."

"Me? The Spirit of Christmas?" The very absurdity of the notion made Blair giggle. It wasn't that she wouldn't have enjoyed every minute of raiding the storerooms of these pompous fools, but how could they imagine she'd then distribute the proceeds so openly? "Gentlemen, be reasonable. The Duncan family has been donating holiday baskets to their tenants and neighbors for almost fifty years. Your thefts only started three years ago."

"Aye, but times weren't so hard earlier. And, besides, we've heard you speak out on the injustice of the

English taking Scottish lands," objected Lord Fairfax.

"It *is* unjust, but these little thefts won't correct that misfortune," declared Blair.

"No, but it might improve your way of life," interjected Enright.

"Lord Haverbrook, you've seen the sad state of my house. No matter how charitable I might be, wouldn't I at least have kept that keg of nails for repairing my own residence? That is if I truly were in charge of the thievery," reasoned Blair.

"Actually, I don't know what to think," admitted Harry Rogers awkwardly. It hurt him to see the lovely girl trapped so, but if she were guilty, he had no choice but to see justice done. "What reason would a young woman have for coming to this cabin so late at night if she weren't involved in matters of a criminal nature?"

"Exactly so, Miss Duncan, so don't bother to deny the reason you came here tonight was to gather another family's Christmas bounty to deliver before morning," sneered Enright. "I even found my lambs tethered out back."

"But, I give you my solemn word, I had no such intention at all. I was merely enjoying the crisp clear air and the brilliant sky of the Highlands," offered the brunette, uncertain as to whether righteous anger might serve her better than logic. The Scots temper was infamous and, perhaps, if she were significantly indignant—

"Now, Blair, I know you're concerned about your good name and mine, but shouldn't you tell these kind gentlemen the truth?" Cameron's voice came from the open doorway where he lounged against the doorpost in a relaxed pose. "I fear the time is past for maidenly secrets."

"Cameron!" For an instant, Blair knew only panic; her palms grew damp and her breathing quickened as she tried to find meaning in his words. He wasn't going to confess to being the Spirit of Christmas, was he? As generous as such a move might be, that would be the foolhardy gesture of someone in love, someone who'd risk his reputation for the woman he adored.... Did Cameron Montgomery feel that way about her? Maybe twelve years ago, she would have believed him capable of such emotions, but now?

Shaking her head in confusion, Blair could do no more than watch silently as Cameron slowly crossed the cluttered wooden floor of the abandoned cabin, skirting the piles of purloined goods, until he stood directly before her. Then, in a gesture so quick she could almost believe she imagined it, he winked at her, kissed her gently on the lips and wrapped his arm around her shoulder, turning them both about toward the curious faces of the gathered Englishmen.

"The truth is, Blair was meeting me here tonight," he offered with a sheepish grin. "Harry, you know I've been pursuing her for years. You even told me to be more aggressive. Well, finally the lass agreed to a Christmas Eve rendezvous here after your party, which I didn't attend to avoid talk of our leaving together. I truly thought I'd won her heart, or at least a small piece of it, until I find all of you here ahead of me. Blair, did you promise each of them a kiss under the mistletoe?"

"No, Cameron, of course not, I—I didn't expect to find anyone here, except you." Cameron had thrown her a lifeline, perhaps one that might fray her reputation, but a lifeline just the same. "Cameron couldn't come to Duncan House at this time of night and the townsfolk might not understand if I went to Lindsay Hall," Blair explained in a very quiet voice, as if embarrassed to admit her actions too loudly.

"So, I suggested this old shack, on the fringes of my land," continued Cameron, his greenish gold eyes daring anyone present to call him a liar. "As far as I knew, it's been abandoned for years. I brought a few blankets, some firewood, a few candles, even a bottle of spirits, but what do I find? Every appearance of a party to which I wasn't invited—and I must say, this is a pretty rocky beginning to the first Christmas Blair and I intended to share together. Harry, if this is your doing, I may never forgive you."

"No, Cameron, no. A few of the fellows stumbled on the place and found some of our stolen goods, and we, well, we thought we could catch the Spirit of Christmas tonight," Lord Haverbrook explained rapidly, envisioning Lindsay's forbidding him to hunt the Duncan lands once he took possession of them. In any way possible, Harry had to assuage the man's anger. Cameron seemed a bit too protective of Blair as it was. "I mean, if he didn't come tonight, when would he show up? No, no, son, really, this had nothing to do with you or your lady. Come on, gentlemen, let's be going and leave the lad alone."

"But what about our goods, Haverbrook? I, for one, am not leaving without my lambs and those blankets over there in the corner," declared Enright.

"We can't go home empty-handed or our wives will skin us alive for leaving them alone on Christmas Eve," exclaimed Fairfax.

"Well then, take what's yours and be off with you," instructed Cameron. "Blair and I would like a little time alone while there's still a moon in the sky. Oh, and our meeting here is not to be mentioned to the ladies, my friends, or Blair will never be able to face them, even though she has unofficially agreed to be my wife. I expect, however, that we'll make our betrothal public any day, so you won't have to remain silent too long."

"Cameron Montgomery, how dare you tell—" began the outraged Scotswoman as his lips descended swiftly on hers, ending all vocal protests by diverting her passionate fury into more pleasurable avenues.

Motioning the men towards the door with one hand, Cameron drew Blair's very breath from her body, taming her fiery anger into sparks of irrational desire. His wondrous lips alternately caressed and pressured hers, rewarding and demanding responses until she no longer cared who was in the cabin with them or why, her senses completely sated with the taste and presence of the enigmatic man who had so easily revived her childhood dreams of "happily ever after."

Then, when the wooden door slammed shut behind the departing noblemen, Blair suddenly remembered the outrageous lies Cameron had told and the reason she was at the abandoned cabin in the first place. The man was a thief. He had not only stolen the real property of others but he had robbed her of her good name, as well. In the blink of an eye, she forced herself from his imprisoning embrace, freeing her soul from the invasive temptation to which she'd nearly succumbed.

"Cameron Montgomery, you are the world's lowest, most vile, disgusting animal! How could you possibly utter such blatant falsehoods about us?'' she cried angrily. ''If you were the last man alive, I would never have agreed to be your wife, nor will I do so in the future, no matter how boldly you lie about it.''

''Och, now, my sweet one, be careful of what you say. Fate has a peculiar way of serving up our words in humble pie when we least expect it,'' said the handsome Englishman, clearly uncowed by her fury. ''Besides, when I first arrived, you didn't seem to be faring too well with your tale of an innocent stroll in the moonlight. Another few minutes and I fear Enright and Fairfax would have been taking you into custody until they could scare up a magistrate. What were you doing here anyway?'' he asked speculatively.

''The magistrate? *I'm* not the guilty one. *I* didn't have Harry Rogers's stolen watch on my desk two days after he missed it,'' retorted Blair with an insolent toss of her head, sending her long curls free of their restraining pins. ''As for my business here tonight, I came to save the Spirit of Christmas, though why I bothered, I do not know.''

Bending to gather the fallen hair pins, Cameron shook his head regretfully, considering the options open to him. Life would be so much simpler if Blair would just admit the two of them belonged together and let it go at that. As it was now, with the others involved and the price on his head, he did not dare trust her with the truth about the Spirit of Christmas, since she could be considered an accessory. Besides, given her mood, Christmas Eve or not, she'd be more apt to turn him in to his neighbors and claim the bounty on his head than applaud his charitable efforts.

"Well, Lord Lindsay? Have you no ready explanation for possessing Lord Haverbrook's watch? Don't tell me he lost it in a card game and was afraid to tell his wife," taunted Blair, feeling oddly bereft at Cameron's refusal to defend himself. One thing she'd never doubted was his firm commitment to truth, whatever the consequences. Yet now he hesitated; why? If he couldn't share his secret identity with her, how could she trust him regarding anything else? In the chill of the abandoned cabin, the lingering sensation of his demanding mouth on hers and the memory of his arms holding her close threatened to smother her. What was wrong with her? Unless he spoke soon, she was afraid she'd yield to the increasingly provocative silence. "Certainly you can create a better tale than that, sir."

"Actually, Blair, the only story I have is the real one," he lied. Reaching out to grasp her hand, he turned it palm up and slowly returned her hair pins, one by one, his long fingers dancing gently over her soft flesh as he deposited them. "I am not the man you seek. You must have noticed that Harry has a sad tendency to overindulge in drink. Well, he stops by my house almost daily for a chat over a brandy or two. I suppose he must have left the watch behind accidentally and forgotten his visit. I'd only just discovered the timepiece the night before *you* stole it from me."

"I—I was going to return it to him," defended the blushing young woman, "but I didn't know how without incriminating myself...or you."

"Ah, see there, Blair? You do care for me after all," Cameron rejoiced, lifting her off her feet and swinging her in the air. "I swear that you'll be mine before the Daft Days are through and the new year begun."

"And I swear you're daft if you truly believe such nonsense. Now, set me down and let me be on my way." Rearranging her skirts as he complied with her demand, Blair acknowledged to herself that she didn't really want to return to the emptiness of Duncan House, but she knew she couldn't trust herself in Cameron's presence much longer. Each time the lantern light reflected the golden flecks in his eyes, she wanted to run back into his arms and peer more closely at the mysteries buried deep in those bottomless green and gold pools.

"Very well then, let me take you home. I've my horse outside and this time, there's not a cloud in the sky."

"That's not necessary, Lord Lindsay."

"Of course it is, Miss Duncan," he corrected softly, his formality at odds with the twinkle in his eyes. "It's much too late for you to be wandering about alone, especially since half the English population of Glenmuir believes us to be betrothed by now."

"And whose fault is that?" she demanded angrily. "You'll have to tell them the truth."

"I give you my solemn word of honor, Blair Duncan, if you've not accepted me by Hogmanay, I'll admit it to the world. Until then, however, I fear that I'm your best defense against a visit from the magistrate."

Suddenly too weary for further argument, the Scottish lass nodded slowly and left the cabin, waiting beside Shadow for Cameron to assist her up. The ride back to Duncan House was a silent if companionable one, each occupied with their own thoughts.

In some ways, Blair mused, the evening had been successful; she had kept Cameron from being taken prisoner as the Spirit of Christmas, even if she had cast suspicion on herself. And if he weren't the mysterious benefactor of Glenmuir, at least tonight the English were no longer out hunting for the real Christmas thief. Perhaps, whoever that generous soul was, he'd have other hiding places and would still visit Glenmuir this year. She knew she, for one, could use a bit of extra cheer after tonight's revealing temptations.

For his part, Cameron felt only warm satisfaction. Blair had proven her love for him tonight, whether she realized it or not. She'd risked being taken by the English in order to warn him. And then of course, there was the remarkable way in which she'd returned his kisses; her body had warmed to his, anxious to answer his affection in kind. Now, all he had to do was make her stubborn Scottish mind accept what the rest of her already understood: they belonged together. Tomorrow he'd begin his campaign of betrothal in earnest, he pledged silently as he left his passenger outside the dark gloom of Duncan House.

The morning arrived more quickly than Blair imagined possible, but then she'd slept so little in recent weeks, perhaps she needed a tonic. Nonetheless, it *was* Christmas morning and, if only for the sake of Robbie and Mrs. Brown, she had best attempt to enjoy the day. Completing her toilette quickly, she descended to the kitchen and stopped in utter amazement at the sight that greeted her eyes.

There, on the broad worktable, sat a plucked goose, already cleaned and stuffed, and all the appropriate fixings for a true holiday feast. A small handwritten card was propped up amid the fresh fruit, candies and vegetables.

From the Spirit of Christmas to one who shares my love of the season and of Glenmuir. Enjoy.

Enjoy? She certainly would, as would her household and Father MacKenzie, her traditional holiday guest, who only expected a small chicken. Cameron had outdone himself! But what was she thinking? He never would have had time enough to prepare this after he'd seen her home, let alone deliver it. For a moment, the vision of the proper Cameron Montgomery plucking a goose made her giggle, but she quickly cast aside the image as pure foolishness. Well, wherever her Christmas bounty had come from, she thought this was one meal Duncan House would indeed relish.

At Lindsay Hall, Cameron was thinking much the same thing although Mrs. Pearson's constant nattering was beginning to irritate him as he finished his breakfast in the large, lonely dining room.

"Woman, I don't know what you expect me to do at this hour of the morning. I realize you have every right to be angry at all the time and effort you put into the holiday preparations only to have the entire meal pilfered right out of the cold room, but you know my appetite isn't particular. If you've nothing better, we'll eat poached eggs," he soothed.

"On Christmas Day? Glory be, my sainted mother would spin in her grave," sputtered the housekeeper indignantly. "No, I'll fetch a venison roast and make do with that, if that damned rascal hasn't emptied the meat shed, too."

"Do as you wish for the staff then," instructed Cameron as he adjusted his cravat in the mirror near the door. "I'll be dining at Duncan House, so you needn't fuss for me."

"You? But, I didn't expect—" Blair stopped before her tongue betrayed the Scottish tradition of unfailing hospitality. "Do come in, sir, though I thought Father MacKenzie would be my only guest for dinner."

"Dear Blair, surely you noticed the smiles and grins directed at us when I appeared in church again this morning. You certainly can't send your intended away on such a holiday as this," challenged Cameron with a devilish grin, "even though you did vanish rather abrupty after the service. Besides, I've brought some fine wine to enjoy with our goose."

A sudden rapping on the door prevented Blair from replying, though she couldn't help but note that Cameron had known the menu of the day…was this his way of telling her she had been right about the Spirit of Christmas?

"Come in, Father, and a happy Christmas to you," she said with a smile. "Lord Lindsay will be joining us today."

"Aye, Father, I was telling Blair how much I enjoyed your sermon. Sharing the love in our hearts as well as the goods in our cupboards is surely the real spirit of Christmas.''

Again there was the faintest twinkle in his eye as he spoke of sharing, Blair noticed. Could he really have meant . . . ? It seemed so.

Chapter Nine

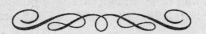

Returning homeward through the crisp cold air from his Christmas night visits, Cameron debated stopping at Duncan House. Since his cache of holiday gifts had been discovered, the goods he had delivered tonight were from his own home, though there was no reason for anyone to ever know that, given the size and stock of Lindsay Hall. But as he rode along, charity was not uppermost in Cameron's mind; what concerned him now was the lovely Scot who had captured his heart.

Blair had been a truly charming hostess today, even if she hadn't exactly invited him, but he'd probably be overplaying his cards to call on her again at this late hour. Yet as much as he begrudged the necessity of leaving her while the priest had lingered, the Spirit of Christmas had had work to do, and he couldn't regret that.

Concentrating on the delight of tonight's recipients when they opened their doors tomorrow morning, he felt truly warm inside despite the chilly December night. Charlie Ferguson and his family could certainly use the coal to warm their small croft against the coming winter, especially with his old mother living with them; and, of course, the MacNabs deserved more than they ever had. When he envisioned Mrs. Mac-Nab's excitement as she unwrapped the bolts of cloth and bags of wool he'd left, Cameron honestly couldn't begrudge the time he'd stolen from Blair. Given her large family, poor Mrs. MacNab always had another grandchild, niece or nephew who needed a layette or trousseau, and little enough means to provide one. It seemed only fair that the Spirit of Christmas lend a hand.

Peculiar how much the people of Glenmuir had invaded his heart this year, the tall Englishman reflected. In previous Yuletide seasons, his acts of charity were certainly as well planned and generous, but he hadn't felt so personally involved. Of course, be it years ago or today, no one in Glenmuir concerned him nearly as much as the lovely dark-haired Miss Duncan.

Indeed, as infuriating as it was to have been so close to Blair this afternoon and unable to run his fingers through her glorious hair or plant provocative kisses on her long slender neck because of the visiting priest and the ever-present housekeeper, Cameron was wise enough to realize that the presence of the others probably contributed to Blair's willing acceptance of him at her table. Despite his wishes otherwise, Cameron strongly suspected that she did not fully understand the depths of his feelings or his sincere commitment to a life with her. That was something he'd have to change.

Even so, her soft hand had once lingered on his as she passed the meal, and she had seated him on her right at the table. Also, Blair had not refused Father MacKenzie's toast to her betrothal, saying only that she and Cameron hadn't quite settled all the details. Given the Montgomery persistence, the matter appeared quite promising, Cameron decided, turning his horse toward Duncan House after all. Even though it was unseemingly late, all she could do was turn him away and, somehow, he didn't think that she would, not if he'd read the message in her deep blue eyes correctly.

Despite Mrs. Brown's protests, Blair had dispatched the housekeeper to an early bed, preferring to linger quietly by the dying fire in the kitchen with her cup of tea, puzzling once more over Cameron Montgomery. Each time Blair thought she'd deciphered the mystery of her neighbor, he did something to set her wondering again.

Lying for her sake in the cabin was unexpected, but hadn't it also been self-serving on his part, she pondered, a trick to turn the Englishmen's attentions away from him if he were the Spirit of Christmas? Because of Cameron's protests, the question of Harry's watch was still unanswered, but it was definitely curious how those to whom the Spirit was especially kind were the people that she particularly worried about. Was that just a coincidence . . . or was it Cameron?

Even today, his gift of the soft blue shawl for Mrs. Brown and the woolen mufflers for Robbie and Father MacKenzie had been thoughtful gestures in and of themselves, and his effort had certainly pleased her. Then Cameron had gone one step further and presented her with fruit, flour and extra sugar for her Hogmanay preparations, all wrapped in a huge cotton apron, twice as large as she could ever wear. When he had sheepishly admitted that he would like to attend her Hogmanay celebration, what else was she to do but invite him, although occasional thoughts of his woman in London still haunted her?

Of course, with her freshly stocked larder, this year's holiday would be more lavish than those of more recent days, but she wouldn't have minded including Cameron if she had much less. He was no longer the selfish lad who'd hurt her so by not answering her letters; perhaps, as he claimed, he'd never gotten them. Aware even then of the four-year difference in their ages, Cameron had only promised to write to her after she wrote him first, and if he never received her notes.... Yet, did the mere absence of guilt in this matter mean that Cameron was the man for her? Did he love her as she needed to be valued or was she just a convenient local attraction since his English lady wasn't at hand?

The flickering fire held no answers though she searched its design most carefully, almost mesmerized by the play of light and dancing shadow on the hearth. No one could read another's heart, she mused, but did she even know her own?

The soft tapping coming from the kitchen door took a moment to penetrate her thoughts, but then Blair felt her heart beat suddenly faster and sensed the quickening of her breath. Somehow she had no doubt about her visitor's identity and she moved quickly to admit him before he awakened her servants. It was one thing to have male callers during the day, but quite another after dark.

"Cameron, come in. But, tell me, whatever can you want at this hour?" she asked quietly, stepping back to allow him to enter and smiling warmly to take the edge off her words.

"Just to wish you a proper good night," he replied, "one your priest might not approve of if he had witnessed it when I took my leave earlier this evening."

"Speaking of that, where did you have to go in such a—" she began, only to be halted in midsentence as the broad-shouldered Englishman drew her into his arms and attempted to take full possession of her heart and soul. His ravenous mouth demanded answer in kind, and Blair found herself resisting his advances. But it was only a momentary defense on her part as her traitorous body became more than willing to echo his devouring need with her own. Clinging to him, she relished his roving kisses and the gentle nips of his teeth as he awakened her passion and made her feel cherished and, at the same time, loved. Running her fingers through his dew-dampened hair, she cared not about his past transgressions, wanting only to share fully in the pleasures of today. Wordlessly they exchanged heartfelt dreams and yearnings, igniting each other as surely as flint calls forth the flame on kindling. Blair realized suddenly that this, not her cold rejection of last night, was what Cameron truly deserved.

As she reveled in his artful loving, Blair found the cold draft of night air against her legs barely sufficient to keep her from exploding into flames, his touch enkindled her so, his hands giving such pleasure. Then, just as she began to grow faint with excitement, he released her, guided her back to her chair, kissed her on the cheek and turned towards the door, as if meaning to leave without another word.

"Cameron—" But what could she say to let him know that she understood, that she'd forgiven him his years of silence? As he waited for her to continue, she recalled his words of last week and she smiled, affecting a heavy burr in her unexpectedly hoarse voice.

"Wouldn't it be a fine thing now if you were coming instead of going?"

"Aye, my love, that it would," the English Scot answered with a happy grin, thrilled at this evidence of her growing trust yet unwilling to push her further tonight. "But not to worry, the Daft Days have just begun and the craziness of life won't disappoint you, I promise. I'll be back tomorrow to help with the baking."

"The baking?" she echoed in amazement. She wasn't baking tomorrow, but he'd already gone, closing the door behind him and leaving her lips swollen and tender from his fervent kisses, even as she craved more.

What a wonderful Christmas Day it had been.

And the days that followed were equally marvelous, with Cameron nearly always at hand, excusing his presence by explaining that he had to keep up appearances as far as the English were concerned since the two of them were unofficially betrothed. He'd taken her walking in the morning mist, riding in the moonlight, and had even had her to dinner at Lindsay Hall, much to Mrs. Brown's disapproval. Yet he'd never permitted their conversation to become serious, turning away her queries about his life in London or the identity of the Spirit of Christmas with a quick smile or silly comment. Just when she'd be ready to trust him fully, his reserve would appear and make her wonder if perhaps he did have unpleasant secrets to hide. As much as she might want to, unless Cameron trusted her, could she really give this man her heart?

"I received a silver bonbon dish from Lord and Lady Haverbrook today, for our betrothal, I suppose," she said, the day before New Year's Eve as they worked together at last in the kitchen. These had to be Daft Days indeed. Imagine an earl helping her with the baking! Why, in all likelihood, the man hadn't seen his own kitchen since he was a child.

Unable to resist the urge to tease her handsome assistant, Blair reached up and tweaked his nose as he floured the boards for her shortbread. "But, tell me, sir, just what would I want with such a strange creature as yourself? No Scotsman I know would stoop to do woman's work even if they're all more than happy to eat the results."

"Aye, and no intelligent Englishwoman of my acquaintance would dare to provoke me when I've flour on my hands," he retorted, playfully wagging a white finger in her direction.

"Not even the ones who wear fashions by Miss Eloise?"

"Aye, not even those," he responded mysteriously, circling the table quickly and placing a dab of flour on her pert little nose while she giggled at his fierce expression. Before he could move away, she'd dusted his face with the white flour, intending to dash beyond his reach. But Cameron, finding himself lost in the carefree happiness reflected in her eyes, drew her close and kissed her deeply, relishing the ease with which she accepted his gestures of affection, clearly allowing herself to relax in his embrace and enjoy his overtures.

Only Mrs. Brown's loud cough brought them back to their senses as the indignant housekeeper bustled about the room.

"In my day, such things were done in private, and without leaving telltale signs, sir," she muttered, swiping at the clearly floured handprints on Blair's backside. "I'll thank you to clear out of this kitchen and let my mistress alone."

"Not until she tells me that is what she wants, Mrs. Brown," Cameron said firmly, sending a questioning glance in Blair's direction. One delivery to this very house and the Spirit of Christmas could retire. Hopefully, Cameron Montgomery could remain a welcome visitor. Now was as good a time as any for her to declare herself since today was New Year's Eve, the deadline he had set for winning her hand. "Well, Blair, tell me that you wish me to stay."

But it was too soon, too abrupt. He shouldn't be asking her to decide like this, her mind protested. They still hadn't discussed the Spirit of Christmas, where they'd live if she accepted him, or the love that should exist between a man and a woman. They'd played, they'd laughed and teased each other, been riding and skating, and had even had breakfast on top of Ben March, but these were the Daft Days. How could she trust herself to decide rightly? And how could she answer truly with Mrs. Brown watching, Blair worried.

However, Cameron had grown impatient waiting and was already untying the great white apron, folding it and placing it on the chair with an air of finality.

"I'm sorry I misunderstood, Blair. I had thought— well, at least I've given you some help with your preparations for Hogmanay," he said abruptly, donning his jacket and heading for the door.

"Cameron, I'm sorry, but—"

"Don't bother to say it, Miss Duncan. I expected too much and I am the one who should be sorry. Goodbye." His voice had become coldly formal, that of a stranger. Then he was gone.

For a long while, Blair looked at the closed door, hesitant to go after him. Yet, if she weren't truly certain of her heart, would it be fair to either of them if she did?

Blair passed the remaining hours of the day in an agonizing eternity of self-recrimination while Mrs. Brown scurried about, directing last-minute cleaning chores and cooking tasks for the night's festivities. Not really caring how she spent her time, Blair wordlessly followed the housekeeper's instructions. After all, since she hadn't spoken up earlier when it was important, what was there left to say now? The question seemed to resound unendingly in her mind, no matter what she did or how she tried to distract herself from the vision of Cameron's walking out on her.

Yet, what choice did you leave the man? her heart inquired. *You didn't invite him to stay.*

When early evening came and Mrs. Brown was busy readying the dining room for tonight's feast before the Hogmanay celebrations commenced, Blair found herself alone before the fire, tears coursing slowly down her cheeks. It was the first evening since Christmas that Cameron had not stopped by to say good-night.

But did that mean that she couldn't go to him? For, as irrational as it might be, the young woman realized now how deeply she needed that maddening English Scot. If his talk of betrothal had been just that, talk, and he had another woman in London, so be it. But, whether as wife or mistress, Blair acknowledged, she *would* be a part of his life. Her stubborn pride had prevented her from confessing her heart earlier, but now there was no time to lose. In a few hours, it would be midnight, and she couldn't envision starting the new year without Cameron at her side.

Plucking her plaid from its hook by the kitchen door, Blair quietly slipped outside and headed across the fields to Lindsay Hall, determined to admit her unquestioning love for the man who'd stolen her heart.

Williamson put his punch cup down on the table, muttering under his breath as he headed upstairs to answer the loud rapping at the front door. Didn't the locals have better things to do than interrupt the staff's merriment on New Year's Eve? His disdain only increased when he saw Blair on the step, her face flushed from the cold, her hair in disarray.

"The earl's not here. He's already left," the butler announced curtly, beginning to close the door.

"Left?"

"Yes, he's gone," said Williamson.

"Back to London?"

"It could very well be. Lord Lindsay is not in the habit of always informing me of his destination," snapped the servant, firmly shutting the door.

Blair couldn't bring herself to believe he'd gone without calling on her again. Yet, what encouragement had she ever given him? She had denied him by not speaking her feelings when he asked, and she had no one but herself to blame for his departure from her life. While she had begun to dream of his being her first-footer at tonight's festivities, her symbol of good fortune for the coming year, Cameron Montgomery had apparently surrendered his campaign for her heart and escaped to London.

She, however, was not so fortunate; she had to face the entire village of Glenmuir and celebrate the holiday when all she really wanted to do was weep for the love she had tossed aside. Squaring her shoulders and taking a deep breath of cold December air, Blair recalled the old laird's lectures on tenacity and courage, no matter how bleak life appeared.

Well, perhaps she could avoid joining the townsfolk in the village waiting for the sound of the church bells, the sighting of the Candlemas Bull and the riotous parade. But she would have to return to Duncan House to open her home as her family had always done, sharing the Highlands hospitality with all, even though, for the first time in her life, her enthusiasm for Hogmanay would be forced.

Nearing her kitchen door in the quickening darkness, Blair almost stumbled over the parcels left on the step. Now, who on earth? As she carried the bundles inside, Mrs. Brown appeared.

"Now then, lass, that's more like it. I've been wondering when the Spirit of Christmas would get around to you with something other than that goose, good as it was. But, I suppose it's only right he leaves you for last," the housekeeper said with a chuckle. "Men are like that. Go on now, open them up."

"No, I don't think these could be from him," Blair said, not when I've prompted him to return to London.

But before Blair could protest further, Mrs. Brown had cut the string and drawn away the wrappings, revealing three fashionable silk gowns, one of them the very dress that had been on Cameron's bed that fateful night. Immediately, the older woman proceeded to undo the other package, and lacy undergarments came into view.

"Well, the Spirit of Christmas is getting a bit personal, now, isn't he, lass?" asked Mrs. Brown with a broad wink. "Still, with you nearly betrothed, and him Mary Connery's son, who would say anything?" Especially, she thought, after my conversation with Ian Ferguson but an hour ago.

Mrs. Brown knew? The implication amazed Blair almost as much as the exquisite wardrobe, the one whose bill she'd misunderstood. How could she be such a fool that even the servants understood what she was reluctant to admit, that Cameron Montgomery did love her, love her enough to order these gowns months ago in the hope that she would accept them? Instead, she had rejected them, and him.

"I—I don't think I'll go to the village, Mrs. Brown," the unhappy young woman said quietly. "I'll change and finish preparing things here."

"Oh? Well, whatever you wish," agreed the housekeeper, assuming from the gifts that Blair's earlier spat with Cameron had produced no lingering effects, and speculating that the young ones undoubtedly wanted time alone.

The soft green gown fit Blair perfectly, its bodice uplifting her bosom and cinching her waist so the figure in the cheval seemed too fine, too beautiful to belong to Blair Duncan. For an instant, she wanted only to tear the dress from her body, ashamed at the way she'd misjudged its giver, but then thoughts of Cameron soothed her as she imagined the care with which he must have chosen the color and fabric for her. No, the gown would serve as her penance tonight, a reminder of what her foolish pride had cost her, a vision of what might have been.

Hearing the far-off tolling of the kirk bells begin, Blair quickly descended the stairs to the first floor. She didn't have much time to light the candles in each window that signaled Duncan House's welcome to the New Year and Glenmuir, but somehow, she managed. Just as the final tone chimed, she lit the last taper and turned expectantly toward the door.

There was only one dark-haired man she wanted to cross the threshold as her first-footer, though in Cameron's absence, Ian Ferguson would have to do, more interested in the refreshments than the traditions, but a dark male nonetheless.

The expected knock came before Blair was ready to face her guests, but opening the door, she realized she'd always be ready for this man.

"Cameron, I do love you," she cried, the traditional Hogmanay greeting forgotten as she threw herself into his arms.

"Your wearing that gown told me so," he admitted, bringing her inside with him and kicking the door closed behind them. "Let me put down your coal and salt, and I'll show you just how thoroughly I concur with your sentiments."

"I thought you had returned to London," she began.

"How could I ever leave you behind again?" he chided tenderly.

Then the night took on a new glow as Blair's heart erupted with pleasure. She was overjoyed at being where she belonged, in Cameron's arms, sharing Hogmanay kisses all the more fervent for having nearly lost him.

There was an intensity to their behavior that admitted without words, the depth of their commitment. Still, reflected the Earl of Lindsay, he did want to make her acceptance of him official. Gently he pulled back from Blair's embrace just long enough to extract the wrapped piece of jewelry from his pocket.

"This was my mother's, Blair, and her mother's and grandmother's before her. Will you wear it as a sign of our love?" he asked, softly unwrapping the heirloom.

"A Luckenbooth brooch?" she said in wonderment, her slender fingers tracing the intricate pattern of the traditional design, once outlawed by the English but highly valued by the Highlanders as the ultimate symbol of commitment between a man and a woman. That Cameron had kept it meant he truly treasured his Scottish heritage and his giving it to her meant he prized her even more. But still, she had to be certain he understood its significance. "Cameron, if I wear this, it means we're officially betrothed."

"Haven't I been telling you that for days?" He grinned, reaching out to pin the ornament onto her gown. "You will marry me, won't you?"

"Of course," she conceded, sealing her fate with a heartfelt kiss as Ian Ferguson entered the house without knocking.

"Bliadhna mhath ur, agus moran diubh, Blair, Cameron. A good New Year and many of them. Don't let me trouble you. I'll just sniff out the whisky," the old man volunteered. He deposited his coal and salt on the hearth and headed for the dining room without a second glance at the embracing lovers.

The other villagers were not so considerate, however, insisting on congratulating them both and admiring Blair's telltale brooch. While the bride-to-be seemed to shine amidst her rejoicing friends and neighbors, Cameron grew increasingly uncomfortable under the scrutiny of all of Glenmuir. It was clear that the entire town valued Blair and wanted to share her happiness but, damn it all, when would he enjoy the pleasure his betrothal should bring him? Just as he was suggesting to the MacNabs and the Fergusons they might be off to the next open house, however, Harry Rogers appeared in the door.

"Happy New Year, Miss Duncan, Lindsay. Before we leave for London, I wanted to stop to wish you both well and announce to the villagers that I'm personally tripling the reward for the Spirit of Christmas. I realize he's probably stopped his deliveries this year, but surely one of you townsfolk know who the devil is. I'm certain you could use the money."

Suddenly the party revelry ceased and an uncomfortable silence descended. Blair felt her blood run cold and she found herself examining the faces of her neighbors for some indication of their intent. If Mrs. Brown knew, certainly they all did. Would one of them betray Cameron, given such hefty temptation as the purse Harry offered? When Ian Ferguson stepped forward, she shivered, grasping Cameron's arm for support.

"Well now, lord, sir, I fear we canna be helping ye. You see, we captured the real Spirit of Christmas in Glenmuir years ago, and any others just do na matter," the dour Scotsman announced to cheers of approval from the rest of the crowd.

"Harry, will you join us in a drink, anyway?" Cameron invited, with a calm Blair could only admire. "I have just announced that Miss Duncan has agreed to be my wife."

"At least your pursuit was successful," said the Earl of Haverbrook. "You know, I did tell you you could win her if you tried hard enough."

Suddenly the words she'd overheard at Haverbrook's lodge made sense to Blair. *She* was the woman who was "practically" Cameron's, but now it was time to become "completely" his.

As soon as she could, Blair echoed Cameron's earlier suggestion that everyone be off for the trek to the next house, pleasantly urging them to go. When the last person had finally departed, Cameron stood near the still-open door, his eyes wearing that haunted look Blair had seen after they'd exchanged their first kiss as adults in her kitchen.

"Should I leave too, Blair?" he asked softly.

"No, Cameron. Your place is here with me," she replied, taking his hand and leading him up the stairs.

Starting here and now, Blair decided, she and Cameron would make their own merriment. What better way to begin the new year than in each other's arms? She couldn't think of one, and judging from Cameron's performance a short while later, neither could he.

* * * * *

Dear Reader,

For us, Christmas has always been a special, magical time of joy and hope, when the child within is celebrated and nurtured, and those we care for are remembered with love.

During this warm and wondrous season, there is nothing quite so pleasurable as enjoying the company of those who are dear to us. Therefore, no matter how many gifts remain to be wrapped, regardless of how many bicycles still have to be assembled, the two halves of Erin Yorke make it a practice to put aside time on Christmas Eve to spend with each other.

If it is cold enough, there is a blazing log in the fireplace. The scent of evergreen mingles with the festive aromas of the evening's meal, which can be as simple as steak and salad or as elaborate as a roast goose dinner with all the trimmings.

What is important is that we have some time to share together as friends, observing the season's rituals. Susan's children are amused by Aunt Christine's presence as well as her presents. And in turn, she is "entertained" with renditions of Christmas carols played as duets on the cello and electric guitar. Stockings are hung, cookies and milk are left out for Santa, along with a carrot for Rudolph, and the crèche is readied for the next day's observance. In a quiet moment, gifts are exchanged and memories steeped in friendship are recounted.

It is a time of year that we happily anticipate, because it signifies so much of what is good and joyous and beautiful in life. And so, our special wish for you this holiday season is that your lives, too, are rich in love and joy, now and throughout the coming year.

Merry Christmas,

Erin Yorke

A PROMISE KEPT

Bronwyn
Williams

The incident of the table is true.
The table made by the Union soldiers for Rebecca
Jones is now in the possession of one of Becky's
granddaughters.

This book is lovingly dedicated to our great-
grandmother, Rebecca Smith Jones, and to her seven
surviving grandchildren, Lina, Becky, Howard,
Jack, Grover, Mabel and Gilbert.

Sara's Christmas Cake

This is not a rich cake. I first made it during the Second World War, when there was no butter and little sugar, milk or shortening, and what there was required ration stamps to buy. It's been called Poor Man's Cake and Hatteras Cake, but I like to think it's not very different from the cake Sara would have made for her loved ones.

1 lb raisins
2 cups flour
1½ cups sugar
2 tsp cinnamon
1 tsp nutmeg
1 tsp baking soda
1 tsp salt
2 eggs
½ cup shortening
1 cup nut meats

Cover raisins with water and boil gently for 10 minutes. Sift together dry ingredients, add raisins and mix with water from raisins. Add beaten eggs, melted shortening (Sara would have used lard) and chopped nuts. Pour batter into greased loaf pan and bake at 350° F for about 45 minutes, or until done.

Chapter One

*Five Mills, Camden County, North Carolina
December 1863*

Sara would have liked to wait until Becky, her five-year-old daughter, was asleep before slipping away, but with the river full of patrols and the roads full of strangers, she didn't dare. Annie Walston, her nearest neighbor, had come soon after the noonday meal and stayed forever, and she'd been forced to bide her time, listening to Annie's laments over things that couldn't be changed.

If the woman had brought so much as a scrap of encouraging news, it might have been worth the wait, but she'd gone on and on about General Wild's men stealing every turkey, chicken and goose they could lay hands on, raiding smokehouses and even taking a washtub full of new-made lye soap from old Miss Gilbert.

"At this rate," Annie complained, "we'll all be lucky to have journey cakes and leather-britches for Christmas dinner!"

With her younger brother Jimmy hiding on the edge of the swamp, in danger of being seen by both the river patrols and the blue-bellies using the Shiloh Road, Christmas dinner was the least of Sara's worries.

"I reckon you're wanting to get back home before dark," she'd said time and time again, but Annie had just nodded and then launched into another tale, always coming around to the same thing.

The war. This wretched, unending war that had taken the best of the men and still demanded more!

Jimmy was only sixteen now. In spite of Sara, he had joined the Home Guard in the winter of '61, soon after they'd heard that her husband, Robert, had died at the fall of Fort Hatteras. Becky had been only a baby, Jimmy little more than a child, but he'd gone anyway, claiming that as head of the family, it was his place to protect the women and children now that all their own troops had been ordered north to protect Virginia.

Sara could have done with another hand on the farm, for she'd only her own two to work with. But farming wasn't near as exciting to a sixteen-year-old boy as fighting Yanks, and when the farm they had both grown up on had been burned to the ground, he'd insisted on going.

One man was enough for any woman to give to the cause. There had been times after Robert had marched off, so handsome in his uniform, his buttonhole sporting a sprig of lilac from the bush outside the kitchen door, when Sara had wished she'd never heard of the Confederacy, the Union, or any blessed government at all outside the pecking order of her own henhouse!

But with the Yanks occupying the entire northeastern part of the state, determined to rout out and exterminate every member of the Home Guard—or the guerilla forces, as they called them—she had quickly become a staunch partisan. Mills, homes—even churches had been ruthlessly commandeered, neighbor turned against neighbor, as the Yanks had set about playing on old enmities to draw as many locals as possible over to their side.

The handbill had been only one more injury added to a growing list. Sara had read it when she'd gone to the mill that morning to have her corn ground and see if she could trade some for a peck of flour, which was all but impossible to find. "'Any person or persons known to have consorted with, comforted or supplied a member of the Guerilla Forces will be dealt with most harshly,'" she'd read aloud.

And that, as old Abigail Gregory had stated at the time, had plumb tore the rag off'n the bush!

Sara, along with many others, had kept watch on the roads and rivers, reporting all activities to the Home Guard, who in turn had raided Yank supplies and passed them on to the families who were in sore need of food. Sara was in an excellent position to help, with the farm being located on a well-traveled road so close by the river.

But fear and worry, even more than hunger, were taking a toll. With Papa and Robert gone, all she had left were Becky and Jimmy.

And as much as she hated leaving Becky at home alone, she daren't risk waiting any longer to meet her brother. "Mama has to go out for a little while, dumpling. Can you be a big girl and look after Emma while I'm gone?" Emma was Becky's doll.

"Are you going to go find Daddy for Chris'mas?"

Kneeling on the wide-planked floor, Sara tucked a loose strand back into Becky's gleaming brown braid and put on a cheerful smile. "No, baby, I'm afraid not." Mature for her age, Becky could barely remember her father, though Sara had done her best to keep Robert alive in her daughter's memory. Sometimes even she had trouble calling to mind that special way he'd had of smiling when he'd first come courting—the way he'd had of nodding his head and tapping his foot when he was preoccupied. Which had been more and more often after the newness of their marriage had worn off. Robert had been a serious man, not overly given to laughter though he'd never actually been gloomy.

"Will you bring me a pretty?" Becky teased.

Sara racked her brain for something that would qualify as a pretty in the eyes of a child who had been forced to grow up too quickly. The few small things she had managed to make, she'd set aside for Christmas, only four days away. "We'll see," she promised, hiding her despair. "I'll leave the lamp lit so that you and Emma can have a tea party until I get back," she said, crossing to draw the curtains. They were kept tightly drawn at night against any passing Yank patrol. While the farm could not be hidden, by day it was hardly prosperous enough to invite further inspection. But Sara well knew that a light glimpsed at night might be taken as a signal and arouse unwanted attention.

"Don't open the curtains," she warned, and Becky nodded vigorously.

"I know, Mama, on 'count of the buff'loes and blueberries."

Sara's quick smile made her look years younger, but it faded almost instantly. "Blue-bellies, pun'kin, not berries."

"Is Daddy an' Cousin Joe an' Uncle Jimmy called gray berries?"

"I'm going to have to hurry if I want to be back before dark, Becky. Now you mind Mama and stay right here in this room with Emma until I get back, you hear?"

The child nodded, her big brown eyes solemn in her small angular face. "Yes, ma'am."

"And don't poke up the fire, it doesn't need it."

"No, ma'am."

"And don't let Emma get into our Christmas cake, or there won't be enough left to feed a sparrow."

Becky giggled, her eyes dancing, while Sara turned the single lamp down as far as she dared, gave the faded curtains a final twitch and told herself nothing could happen in the few minutes it would take to hurry down to the river and back. If only the child were older. If only Robert were still here . . .

If only this terrible war had never happened!

Flinging a heavy and much-mended shawl about her shoulders, Sara Bell Jones hurried across the yard, let herself through the gate and cut across the field. The smell of frost-withered weeds rose to her nostrils as her footsteps crunched over the partially frozen ruts.

"You're not to worry," she whispered over and over, like a litany. It was almost a habit by now, not that it did any good. She knew Jimmy wasn't truly reckless, not like some of the wilder boys who had joined up, eager to get into the fray. Besides, he'd been hunting since he was eleven, doing a man's job on the farm until Papa had died.

''Oh, Lordy, Sara, don't start sniveling now!'' she chided herself as she hurried over the half-frozen mud. Jimmy despised tears, and Sara had vowed never to use them to try to hold him back.

Truth to tell, she probably couldn't have squeezed another one out if she'd had to now, her heart having long since bled itself dry.

Sometimes, laughing with Becky over some silly bit of nonsense as she sat before the fire, turning a gown or letting out a hem for the growing child, Sara could almost convince herself that it was truly but a dream; that any minute now Robert would walk through the door, sail his hat across the room and sweep Becky up in a rough-and-tumble embrace that would have the child laughing until she was in tears. He had been rough at times, her Robert, but he had been a good husband.

Hearing a sound, Sara froze. Sometimes the river patrols came ashore. A detachment of blue-bellies prowling through the edge of the swamp in search of guerilla camps was the last thing she needed now, with Becky home alone and Jimmy hiding under the honeysuckle, waiting for her to meet him.

At that moment, a possum waddled across the trail as if she weren't even there, and Sara clasped a hand over her mouth to stifle a gasp of relief. If she had a gun, she might even have risked firing it, for meat was scarce. Possum was too fat for her taste, but food was food.

The smell of smoke lay heavy on the air tonight. The rich layer of peat just under the surface of the swamp had been ignited months before, either by gunfire or campfires. It could smoulder for years, one more danger for those poor brave boys who made the swamp their home for the duration.

Off in the shadows, the sound of a night bird shivered on the cold air. Sara clutched the shawl tightly around her shoulders with icy fingers, her own woolen gloves having been unraveled and redyed to make a pair of red mittens for Becky's Christmas.

"I'd about given you up," came a terse whisper from the shadow of a lightning-blasted oak.

"I couldn't get away any sooner," said Sara breathlessly. "There were patrols on the river all morning, and then Annie came over."

James Edwin Bell, small of stature but wiry, was as much at home in the swamp as any muskrat. With a pang of tenderness, Sara reached up and brushed a lock of dark blond hair behind his ear, smiling when he ducked away. He was still her baby brother, for all he toted a liberated rifle near as tall as he was. "Is there news? Is that why you sent the signal?"

"We raided a Yank storehouse two days ago for weapons and ammunition. I'd thought to be bringing you a ham, but things have happened since."

"You're all right?" she demanded anxiously.

"'Course I'm all right, Sara, but things are heatin' up too much for my likin'. Has there been much traffic on the road today?"

"Not as much as usual. Some on the river, though. I counted seven boats in one hour this morning while I was hanging out the wash."

He nodded, frowning. "Bringing in more supplies to make up for them we took. Ever since the Fifth Pennsylvania blew up the bridge at Indiantown, Wild an' Lewis has been puttin' it around that there's more'n three hundred of the Guard holed up between Old Trap and Shiloh. Ol' Beelzebub's foamin' at the mouth!''

''Three hundred! Where did he get that notion?'' Sara knew of General Wild's devilish nickname and considered it fairly earned.

''From gettin' his feathers singed one too many times, I reckon. He don't dare let on to headquarters that he's being run ragged by no more'n a handful of swamp rats armed with squirrel guns, and him with enough firepower to blow the whole country to kingdom come. You heard about that howitzer o' his we captured?''

Sara nodded. ''Though if it's as big as they say, I don't see how you plan on dragging it through the swamp,'' she said tartly.

Jimmy grinned. ''I'd give a pretty to see the look on ol' Wild's face when he heard about it, though.'' And then the grin faded. ''Sara, why I come—you and Becky had best lay low for a while. Word is that General Wild's gettin' up what he calls an Army of Liberation. They're freein' an' armin' all the Northern slaves and sendin' 'em down here with orders to do whatever they have to do to wipe us out and put an end to the Guard and the blockade running. They say he's joining forces with Draper's Second, and they're out to burn everything from Shiloh to Indiantown.''

Sara uttered a small cry of distress. ''But why? There's only women and children left, and a few men who are too old or sickly to fight. What good does it do to burn our homes?''

''They reckon you're keepin' us supplied.''

''But it's the other way round! With the river blockaded and those devils stealing everything that isn't nailed down, we'd all starve without what the Guard can provide.''

"Yeah, well...they know where we get it, too. Anyways, that's not all I come to tell you. Last night a scoutin' party from the First Pennsylvania followed one of our men back to camp. First thing we knew, the whole detail was on our backs.'' Jimmy swallowed hard. "Sara, they burned us out, cabin, tents, arms cache and all. Besides them that was killed outright, nine were took prisoner. They're puttin' out they wiped out the whole nest, but they know better.''

Sara felt a coldness that had nothing to do with the weather. "Who?'' she asked, feeling guilty relief that Jimmy was not among the casualties.

He named seven boys and one old man as being killed outright, his voice suspiciously rough. Two of the boys, brothers, had been his boon companions, growing up on the next farm over from the old Bell homestead. "We're agoin' after them that was took prisoner, so don't worry if you don't hear from me for a while.''

Eight killed and nine taken prisoner. How many were there left to fight? "Oh, Jimmy, do you have to go?''

"Sara, they took two Guard families last week, and they're holding them hostage. Two women and five children, Sara.''

She nodded. Of course he had to go back. All the same, she couldn't help but think of what had happened to others who had tried to free prisoners from the heavily guarded stockades. "I'm sorry. I know better.''

Jimmy patted her awkwardly with his free hand. "The rest of us'll be meetin' up and moving out tonight soon's the moon sets. Once we make camp again I'll try to get word to you."

He embraced her awkwardly, smelling of wood smoke and musk and other less salubrious things, and Sara steeled herself not to break down. "You be careful, Sara, you hear me? You'll probably be safe enough at the farm long's they don't know about me, but if you have to leave, don't worry none on my account. I'll find you, one way or another."

"I don't know where we'd go, even if we left. Besides, we've already put up a Christmas tree. Becky would never stand for it." Her attempt at humor failed miserably.

Jimmy nodded. Gruffly he said, "I know. Hug her for me and wish her a happy Christmas. Likely, you'll not be bothered, but I thought I'd better let you know not to look for the signal for a while. I just wish I could've brought you a few supplies, but..."

"We still have a few hens, and Annie's got her rooster. I thought if I kept back two for setting come spring, the rest would see us through for a spell."

"Keep 'em real close to home, you hear? The word is that Wild and Draper split forces this morning. Wild's bunch is movin' on toward Currituck Courthouse, burnin' everything in sight. Lord willin', they won't be comin' back this-a-way."

"Amen," Sara breathed reverently, but Jimmy shook his head.

"Don't drop your guard too fast. Some of Draper's men are still hanging around these parts, so you stay real close and keep the doors latched, you hear? You know how to use Papa's rifle, don't you?"

Sara nodded. She had used it on snakes, and once on a hawk that was pestering her chicks, but she could never use it on a person, not even a Yankee, and they both knew it.

Unless Becky was in danger. Then she didn't know what she was capable of doing. God willing, she would never have to find out.

It was just before dusk when Lieutenant Rolph Mallory and a detail of seven men split off from the main detachment of Federal troops, taking a small detail south along the Shiloh Road. They had already searched four farms on the way, finding nothing incriminating, but the order had been to burn out any home they suspected of harboring one of the damned guerillas.

The lieutenant was tired, discouraged and sickened by much of what he had seen over the past few days. General Wild, he concluded, had been aptly named. His so-called Army of Liberation was little more than a ruthless, undisciplined mob, due partly to a lack of training, but mostly to a lack of decent command. A man could abide only so much pillage and destruction, even for the most noble cause, without turning sick to his belly.

And God help him, sometimes he wondered if the cause was all that noble. If the seceshes were so hellbent on self-government, why not leave them to it?

Treasonous thoughts, Rolph told himself, knowing full well what lay behind them. So far his luck had held—to the best of his knowledge. He'd taken his share of prisoners since he'd come south, but at least he'd not yet had to look down the barrel of his Enfield and wonder if the poor devil on the other end was his own father.

Could he pull the trigger, not knowing?

God help him, he was no longer sure. All he knew was that he was tired of fighting a war, no matter how just, that had set brother against brother, father against son. Sometimes he wished his uncle had never told him the truth of his birth.

Rolph had been too young to remember when his mother had taken him away from his father in north-eastern North Carolina, to live with her family in Boston. His earliest memories were of a dark and cavernous house where he had been forbidden to laugh or play for fear of disturbing some nameless dying relative.

The Mallorys had been a sick and dying lot. After what had seemed an endless series of funerals, his mother's included, Rolph had been left in the care of an ancient uncle who had unwittingly named his sire and the place of his birth. It had lodged in his gullet and stuck like a bone ever since he'd come down here— the fear of meeting and killing the father he'd never known.

Not that Rolph had any great liking for the man. Any man who would allow his wife's delicate health to suffer by refusing to give up a family farm didn't warrant a second thought. The very fact that he had allowed her to leave, taking with her their only son, spoke louder than words of his character.

"Light up ahead, Lieutenant," his corporal said quietly. "Flashed on and off, like a signal. Want me to move out ahead and investigate?"

"Looks like a farmhouse. Cecil, take four men, one to a side and two to the back. I'll take the front. Burden, you and Smith cover the outbuildings. Easy, now, we don't want any trouble unless they start firing first."

"This close to the river, it could be a nest of them swamp devils, sir," one of the men muttered.

But Mallory was already waving his men into position. Silently he moved around to the front of the small clapboard house, noticing incongruous details like the lopsided wreath on the front door and the scraggly, winter-bare shrubs surrounding the front porch.

No dog. Thank God for small favors. Sliding into position between the door and the front window, Rolph eased his face alongside the glass pane and tried to see through the narrow slit in the curtains. Someone was in there. Someone had shifted the curtains, possibly sending a signal to another person on the outside. They weren't all that far from where Wild's men had routed that nest of guerillas last night.

"Lieutenant," came a loud whisper from behind him, and he sliced the air with an impatient gesture. He heard the click of a hammer and swore silently. "Move back, men. I'm going to try the door. Give me two minutes and then come at the ready, two by two. If they try to sneak out the back way, cover them, but I don't want any shooting unless they start it, is that clear?"

It wasn't even clear to Mallory himself. All he knew was that he couldn't take any more killing. Not this day.

"Let me go in, Lieutenant," begged an eager young private. Newly blooded, he was spoiling for another fight.

"Get back out of the line of fire, son. This is no picnic."

The men faded into the darkness, and Rolph, flattened against the side of the house, leaned toward the window again. If he could get the lay of the land before he went in, it would help, but either way, it was his duty to go.

His face was pressed against the glass, his right eye aligned to the sliver of light that shone through, when suddenly the sliver widened. Rolph froze, still in a crouch, as a large brown eye met his own from a distance of mere inches. The two eyes, both brown, one wide and the other narrowed, caught and held as Rolph swore silently.

What the bloody hell was he supposed to do now?

"Lieutenant?" came a whisper from the darkness behind him.

Rolph gestured violently for silence. It had to be a child. Why the hell would a full-grown man—or woman, for that matter—be crawling around, peering out windows?

Why would a grown man be peering *into* a window? he asked himself with a bleak sense of irony.

"You want we should go in the back way and jump 'em, sir?"

"Dvorski, just shut up, will you? All I can make out in there is a child, and I don't want it frightened."

At that moment the child edged away from the window, and Rolph dropped to one knee, his face still pressed against the glass. He could see more of the room now, for the curtain had been tugged awry. As far as he could tell, the child was alone. It was a girl, and she was quite small. He had no idea of her age, not being all that familiar with children. There was a Christmas tree, a small, scraggly thing trimmed with bows that looked as if they'd been fashioned from corn husks and dyed a sickly shade of red.

As if she saw strange men peering through her windows every day of her young life, the child continued to stare at him. They faced each other for what seemed an eternity, and then the child rested her small arms on the windowsill and smiled at him.

She ought to know better than that! He was the enemy!

Rolph could hear his men shuffling their feet. They were cold and hungry, having been on the march since daybreak.

Ah, the devil! What was he supposed to do now? Forget his orders and move on, risking a court-martial? Or go in and scare the hell out of some poor secesh family a few days before Christmas?

Abruptly he stood and made his way quickly to the door. The door was unlocked, making it easy to slip inside. Too easy.

A trap? He froze, the door partially open. The back of his neck prickled, as if he was being watched. But then he saw the little girl again and his thoughts took an abrupt turn.

Where had he seen her before? She looked so familiar to him...the way her hair grew away from her brow. The tilted set of her eyes under those surprisingly dark brows.

Where could he have seen her before? He hadn't been in these parts very long, having been sent down from South Mills only a few day ago.

Rolph considered the handful of children he knew. Cousins, mostly distant, all either freckled and redheaded or fair and round as little buttertubs.

This child was slight, her cheeks thin instead of round. Not precisely pretty, but pleasing for all that, with her merry brown eyes so at odds with her absurdly stern-looking eyebrows. Before he could think of a way to announce his presence without frightening her, she smiled again, revealing a dimple in one cheek.

''Um . . . how d'you do, miss,'' said Rolph. How the devil did one address a child? Was she old enough to talk?

''I thought you was Sandy Claus. Mama said you wasn't coming, but I knew you was. Did you bring me a pretty?''

''A pretty!'' Damn! She thought he was Santa Claus? So that's why she was peering through the window. ''A present, you mean?''

''Mama said she'd try to bring me one, but sometimes she forgets, and then she cries, on'y I'm not s'posed to hear her, 'cause I'm s'posed to be asleep.''

Rolph glanced at the meagre Christmas tree and back at the child. ''What would you like to have for a, uh—pretty?'' Where the hell was her mama? Who in their right mind would go off and leave a baby all alone at a time like this? ''Where are your people, child?''

''Gone.''

Two of his men appeared in the doorway, and Rolph signalled them to silence. Before he could think of a way out of the uncomfortable situation he found himself in, two more entered, and then two more.

He sighed. The child looked up at him expectantly. ''Aren't you going to give me some sugar?''

Sugar. Sweets? Cakes? Rolph was sweating, in spite of the meagre fire in the chilly room. A bit desperately, he knelt and picked up a tiny cup and saucer, balancing them in the palm of his hand. ''Is this your— uh—dolly's teacup?'' he asked. How the dickens do you talk to a child no bigger than a cricket?

"Her name's Mary Manie Marjorie, but I call her Emma."

"Oh. That's a pretty name. Is your, uh—daddy at home?" He could feel the tension emanating from the four men standing near the door. Then Burden came in through the back way and stood quietly against the wall. Stanley and Dvorski slipped in behind him, until the small room was lined with blue uniforms.

"That's a pretty Christmas tree."

"I helped tie the bows," the child said proudly.

"Very nice job, too." Rolph tugged at his collar. "My name is—Mallory," he said. Lieutenant Mallory was probably too big a mouthful for her to handle, he thought. "What's yours?"

She gave him a speaking look. "You forgotted already! I'm Becky. I've growed and growed till I'm almost as big as Mama."

Rolph knelt and replaced the tiny cup on the floor. He had never felt so out of his element in his entire life. Helplessly he glanced over at Burden, whom he knew to have been a family man, and the gruff old trooper took the hint.

"What's Santa Claus going to bring you, little girl?"

Becky seemed not at all put out by the roomful of strangers. She had sidled over to lean her back against Rolph's knee, and he was afraid to move for fear of dislodging her. "I asted him for a table for my dolly," she confided. "But Mama says he's awfu' busy right now, an' he might not come to see me if he gets sick or something, but it doesn't mean he doesn't love me anymore. I told him and Jesus about the jam jar, an' they said it was awright 'cause I di'nt mean to break it.''

A log settled in the small fireplace, sending up a flurry of sparks. Burden cleared his throat, and another man swore softly, breaking off at his lieutenant's glare of disapproval.

"How big a table do you think it would take?" Rolph asked. Somehow he found himself seated crosslegged on the floor. His men had settled themselves around the room, and Burden, an inveterate whittler who was the only Southerner among them, was examining the wooden limbs of Becky's doll, one of which had been crudely mended.

The child extended her arms. "'Bout this big, I reck'n. Emma likes to have comp'ny sometimes.''

"We wouldn't want Emma to be disappointed, would we?" He glanced up at the corporal. "You heard the lady. Head on up the road and see what you can round up."

"You mean go looking for a toy table?" the startled young soldier exclaimed.

"I mean you're to secure whatever supplies you need to build a table large enough for Emma and her friends!"

Corporal Stanley's eyes bugged out. "But Lieutenant—"

"Now!"

The lad jumped to his feet, clicked the heels of his muddy boots and slammed the hard edge of his hand against his brow. "Yes, *sir,* sir! You, Burden, you Smith, you, Dvors—"

"Take 'em all, boy. Just go."

"Sir, permission to guard your rear?"

Rolph looked at the man who had offered to stay behind. He looked at the child, at the barren, if surprisingly cozy room, and said, "Go, the lot of you. Forage for whatever you need and get on back here. Don't go looking for trouble, though."

They filed out, and then the only sound to be heard was Becky, humming to her doll. Rolph leaned one shoulder against the doorway to the kitchen and sighed.

God, he was tired. He had joined up at the first call to arms, earned his commission three months later and been soldiering ever since. In the early days, he'd been filled with zeal for his mission, determined to force the backward secessionists to throw in their lot with the union. There were Northern mills rusting in idleness while the stubborn Southern planters continued to ship their cotton to England.

The Mallorys' fortune, once large, now modest in the extreme, had been built on Southern cotton. "By God," his uncle was fond of railing, "they *won't* go on shipping their damned cotton off to foreign markets when we need it to keep our mills running! One way or another, Lincoln'll see to that, don't you think he won't!"

But the punishing tariffs had not cured the problem, it had only caused the stubborn rebels to dig in their heels. When Lincoln had proposed freeing the slaves, Rolph had cheered along with all decent men, but that had not brought the intransigent rebels to their senses, either. They had only fought harder, until now not only their cotton fields, but their entire way of life, lay in ruins.

Now Rolph only wanted it to end, so that he could go back to Boston, to an ugly, empty old house, to the handful of ancient servants who were all the family he had left.

What the devil was he doing here, anyway, playing dolls with some skinny little rebel baby? God, he was tired!

Chapter Two

Sara had just let herself through the side gate when she caught sight of a small group of men. Edging behind the woodshed, she peered through the gloom, trying to recognize them. It couldn't be Jimmy and his fellows, for she'd just watched him slip away into the swamp.

They were carrying something...a box? A table? Oh, my mercy, it *was* a table! A *large* table—and they were toting it up onto her porch, one man at each corner and another three following along behind!

But why? And who? And what in heaven's name were they doing at *her* house?

"Becky," she breathed silently. Sweat suddenly beaded her body, chilled instantly by the frosty night air. Sara ignored the cold. The nearest house was Annie's, but what could two women do against seven men, even if she dared take the time to go for help?

Oh, God, where was Jeff Davis's army? Where was the Guard? Where was Robert when she needed him?

The rifle! It was in the pantry by the back door. If she could just open the door and slip inside without being discovered ...

Keeping to the shadows, Sara sped silently toward the back of the house. How could she have left her baby alone that way, even for a minute? Becky was good and obedient, but she was still only a child. If anything happened to her, Sara would never forgive herself. She would die! She would—

They had to be either Union soldiers or Buffaloes, and of the two, she preferred the soldiers. Too many of the Buffaloes were of a low type, drawn into the Union cause for less than honorable reasons. Blood feuds, spite and envy too often rose to the surface under the guise of patriotic convictions.

Sara had nearly reached the back porch when the door opened again. Instantly she dropped down behind the woodpile, not daring even to breathe.

Were they leaving?

They were! Dear Lord, if they took Becky—

She counted the dark figures emerging from the lighted doorway. Two, and then three, and one more...and then another one. Seven had gone in. Seven had come out. One was carrying Robert's toolbox. The other four picked up the table and set off.

Robert's toolbox?

Oh, God, her poor baby! If those devils had harmed a single hair on Becky's head, she would see them all roast in hell, Sara vowed.

Trembling from fear and cold, she forced herself to wait until the men had moved on beyond the turn in the road. Then, rising quickly, she raced toward the back door. She had just reached the bottom step when she heard the sound of laughter. Becky's high voice, giggling the way she did when someone tickled her. Relief made her knees buckle, and she grabbed at the porch post just as another voice joined in.

The sound of a deep masculine chuckle made Sara's blood run cold, and she eased back toward the wood-pile. A moment later she approached the house silently, her shoes in one hand, a long split of pine wood in the other. Oak would've been better. Hickory better still, but pine was closest to hand.

Leaving her shoes on the stoop, Sara dropped her shawl to allow her arms the needed freedom and slipped silently into the house. From the doorway, she could see along the short hall into the front room, still lit by the light of a single lamp.

Becky was on her knees and elbows, pretending to sip from Emma's cup. A black-haired devil in a dark blue Union officer's coat was seated in the doorway, his back to the hall. Dear God, could it be a trap? Sara glanced warily over her shoulders, half expecting the whole swarm to be there, but there was nothing to see but the scarred old pine table, a corner of the range and the sackful of clothes pegs hanging beside the door.

Jimmy had warned her that the blue-bellies were combing the area in search of the resistance fighters. How much had Becky told him about her Uncle Jimmy? Sara had been careful not to let on to the child that Jimmy was with the Guard, but an uncle who lived in the swamp and never came to the house anymore told a tale of its own.

Halfway along the hall, Sara hesitated. The gun? No, it was too noisy. Besides, two screws were missing and loading it was such a messy business. It would have to be the log. She flowed silently past the two bedroom doors, thankful that she'd left only the mantel lamp burning, the wick turned low.

It was almost too easy. Just as she lifted the pine split over her head, Becky glanced over her shoulder, her

eyes widening. "But Mama," she wailed as Sara
brought down the log with all her strength.

Sara leaned against the wall as the man toppled
slowly over onto his face. "Baby, are you all right?
They didn't hurt you, did they?"

"But, Mama, why did you hit Daddy?"

If she lived to be a hundred, Sara would never forget the moment when she rolled her victim onto his
back and gazed down into that dear, familiar face.

Robert. It couldn't possibly be, yet it was. Miracu-
lously her Robert had come back from the dead—*and
now she had killed him again!*

Tears dripped onto his face as she knelt over him, her
fingers moving over his scalp. "I didn't know," she
cried over and over. "Lord help me, I didn't know. Oh,
Robert, why didn't you let us know?" she scolded,
emotions spilling out in all directions. He was leaner
now than he'd been when he'd left home more than two
years before, all bone, sinew and muscle. Before, he'd
been running a bit of a paunch. From her good cooking, he had claimed. They had laughed about that. In
the early days they had laughed so much together, but
then Robert had grown quiet and withdrawn. Bitter,
she'd always thought, because the farm hadn't pros-
pered as it had in his father's day.

"Oh, Robert," she cried softly. "Becky, lift his feet,
one at a time, and see if you can ease them onto the
bed. If not, I reckon we'll have to drag the feather tick
off onto the floor and roll him onto that."

But it didn't come to that. Robert roused enough so
that he was no deadweight, and they got him into bed,
with Sara doing most of the work and agonizing over
nearly killing him when she'd thought him dead these
two years and more.

He groaned but didn't open his eyes. "Why didn't you send word?" Sara fussed at the handsome man sprawled, muddy boots and all, across her hemstitched sheets. Tears were streaming down her cheeks as she turned her back, straddled her husband's leg and tugged at a boot until it came off, the same way she'd done a hundred times or more. "Oh, I know you couldn't, truly I do, I'm just so—so—"

Stunned. Delighted. Shocked. Relieved. There was simply no word to describe what she was feeling. She knew she was chattering like a guinea hen and Robert had never liked talky women, but she couldn't seem to stop. "Weren't you surprised to see how much Becky's grown? She was only a babe when you left, Robbie, but she asks about you all the time. I never let her forget, did I, pun'kin? Becky, go latch the doors, Mama forgot. If those awful men come back—"

"But, Mama—"

"Just do it, honey. Please?"

Sara needed a moment alone with her husband, now that he was awake. She had figured out what must have happened, but she needed to know for certain, and she'd just as lief not discuss it around Becky. The child heard enough of war, as it was.

"What happened, Robbie? How did you manage to escape?" And when he only groaned and felt for the growing knot at the back of his head, Sara, searching in the trunk at the foot of the bed for a nightshirt, said, "First we heard you'd been taken prisoner, and then we heard you'd been killed, and—" She swallowed hard, burying her face momentarily in the lavender-and-cedar-scented flannel garment. "Oh, Robbie—"

"Wha' happened?" he muttered. They were the first words he had spoken to her in more than two years, and even though they weren't terribly romantic, Sara thought she had never heard any sound so beautiful in all her born days.

"That's what I was asking you," she said tenderly, bending over to examine the lump on his head. "Size of a turnip already," she muttered. "Oh, my mercy, and to think I was wishing for oak or hickory. I'll fetch a cold cloth, and then we've got to get rid of that awful uniform. I reckon dressing up like a Yank was the only way you could escape, but now that you're home..."

Lord knows what would happen if those men ever discovered his true identity! Perhaps when he was well enough, he would tell her how he had managed to escape. Right now, she didn't much care how. He was home, and that was all that mattered. And if those men dared to come looking for him, she would take the rifle to them, herself!

Suddenly feeling unaccountably shy, she unbuttoned his coat, eased it off, and then removed his shirt. Next she unfastened his braces. Then, moving to the foot of the bed, she grabbed the legs of his trousers and started tugging.

Still dazed from the blow to his head, the man on the feather bed hadn't a clue as to what the woman was chattering about, much less who she was. Red-eyed, windblown and all, she was a lovely creature. He suspected, however, that she had no business removing his trousers. Not that he wouldn't have appreciated the attention under more favorable circumstances, but at the moment his head was fair splitting, he was seeing double—and there was something about a table. Something important...

"Table," he muttered, frowning at the effort it took to remember.

"Yes, and that was another thing I wanted to ask you about, but it can wait. Would you like a bite to eat?"

He shook his head and then grimaced at the added pain. God, what had happened to him? Had he come out the loser in a battle, and somehow managed to forget it? It was definitely a uniform the woman was trying to remove, which must mean that he was a soldier. An officer, judging from the coat she'd flung onto the chair.

"Robert, were you injured? In prison, I mean. Are you in pain?"

Hell, yes, he was in pain! Someone had tried to break his head, and damn near succeeded!

Robert. He tested the name on his tongue and found it strange, but then, so were the circumstances. "Head hurts," he managed.

And then she was all over him again, this bustling, chattering slip of a girl, this delicate creature with the light brown hair and the dark gray eyes, who smelled of wood smoke, woman, soap and violets.

"Does it hurt here?" She ran her hands over his shoulders, and he grunted a negative response. "Here?" Her small, capable hands moved quickly over his arm and then came down gently on his thighs, and he caught his breath.

"It does! They've hurt your legs! Oh, Robbie—"

He captured her hands in his own and removed them forcibly from his person. "Woman, the only hurt I've suffered is to my head, and I'm beginning to believe I— what happened?"

Tears brimmed her eyes, broke the barrier of thick brown lashes, and coursed down her pale cheeks. "Oh, darling, I'm so sorry, but how could I have known? It was the uniform—and those other men. Are you sure they don't suspect?"

Darling? His head was not only aching, it was reeling. He was her *darling?* What other men? Something about a table... "Where's the child?" he asked abruptly. He *did* remember the child. A taking little thing, full of laughter. She looked so familiar, yet he couldn't place her.

"Becky? Oh, hasn't she grown? Isn't she beautiful? She looks so near like you, Robbie!" Her hands were on him again, as if she couldn't get enough of touching him, and truth to tell, he found it not at all unpleasant.

She left him then, only to return a moment later with the little girl. Becky? Becky. And he was...Robert?

But who the devil was she?

"Is my table finished yet, Daddy?"

Daddy! The fallen warrior felt as if he were tiptoeing across a half-frozen pond, certain at any moment the ice would break and plummet him to a watery grave. Robert. He was Robert, and the child was Becky, and she had called him...Daddy?

"I asted the man to build it here so Emma and me could help, but he said he couldn't do that, 'cause he had to make a camp, too. Will he make Emma's table first? Could Emma and me see the camp when he makes it?"

Her name was Emma, then, the man thought with satisfaction all out of proportion to the small accomplishment. Evidently, the child knew more than the woman did. If he was to fill in the blanks in his memory left by this raging headache, it would have to be with the little girl's help.

"Becky, why don't you climb up here and talk to me while your mother, ah—"

"Fetches you some hot broth and a cold cloth for your poor head," finished the woman called Emma.

"Precisely," he said sharply, and fancied she gave him a strange look. So he softened it with a hesitant, "Please?"

"Now, child," he commenced once the bedroom door had shut behind the woman, Emma. "Suppose you tell me all about this table of yours, and the camp you mentioned."

Becky giggled, and the man winced as the sound stabbed through layers of dull pain. "You know, Daddy. Emma's tea-party table. For Chris'mas. I thought you was Sandy Claus when you looked in the window. I was lis'ning for him so I could tell him I was a good girl."

All of which told him nothing at all. "And the camp?" he prompted.

Shifting her minuscule bottom about on the billowing feather tick, the child lifted her slight shoulders in an exasperated sigh. "You tolded them to make a camp in the woods and to make Emma and me a table and 'liver it here at first lamp."

Liver and lamps. Uh-huh. "And did I say why I stayed behind?"

Becky tilted her head. "Don't you 'member *anything?* You tolded them you di'nt want to leave me by myself, but I stay by myself lots of times when Mama has to go see Uncle Jimmy, and I always b'have myself."

But the man they called Robert had stopped listening. Didn't he remember anything? No. That was the problem. He didn't. His memory began and ended with the sight of a child's smile, something about a table, and the sound and feel of a splitting skull that had evidently been his own.

Sara, her worry over her brother clean wiped out of her head, worked with her usual quiet efficiency to produce a rich broth from the meagre supplies she had on hand. The uniform . . . she would have to get rid of it, and quickly. If anyone should find it here, there was sure to be trouble.

She would have to burn it, that was all—one piece at a time, so it wouldn't smoke too much. As for the boots, they were just too blessed good to waste. She knew she could never bring herself to destroy them, with some folk going barefoot through the winter. Besides, who was to say whether they'd been cobbled for Yankee feet or Confederate?

She stole a molasses cake from the store she had put by for Becky's Christmas, set the old tin tray with her best dishes and added a sprig of holly for color. Perhaps instead of burning the uniform, she could cut it into sections and dye them with walnut husks. Good woolen cloth was hard to come by these days.

No, she'd better burn it. Robert's life, not to mention Jimmy's, was at stake. She would sooner go naked than risk a hair on either of their heads.

Just before she returned to the bedroom where she'd left Becky and Robert getting reacquainted, Sara paused at the small mirror over the dresser and smoothed her hair. Glory, she looked like the tag end of a rainy day, her hair every which away and her gown full of beggar-lice from racing across the field to meet Jimmy.

Biting her lip, she spared a fleeting prayer for her brother, who would be lucky to have more than a pinch of sagamite to sup on tonight. The Yanks would have retaken or destroyed all their supplies when they'd burned the camp.

Somehow she was going to have to get word to him about Robert and the blue-bellies who had unknowingly brought him home, before they realized their mistake—or Robert's trickery—and came back for him. However he had managed, he wasn't safe yet, not when the entire area was swarming with Yanks.

"There now," she said, reentering the cozy low-ceilinged bedroom to place the tray on the table beside the bed. "I've brought you a nice bit of broth and a sweet if you finish it all. Becky, you'd best go get ready for bed now. It's far past time, and Emma's getting sleepy."

Emma's getting sleepy? The man lying there, his lips curling at the smell of the abomination in the blue willowware bowl, took the time to study the woman called Emma and decided that she didn't look sleepy at all. She looked rather as if she were glowing from the inside, in spite of her pallor, the hollows in her cheeks and the shadows around her rainwater gray eyes. "You don't mean for me to actually eat that mess, do you?" he asked when she glanced up and caught him studying her features. "What's in it?"

Her face fell. "Onions. Turnips. A bacon skin and a handful of cornmeal. I know it's not your favorite, Robbie, but—"

"Nor anyone's favorite, unless I miss my guess."

"Well, my mercy, if I had better, don't you think I'd have done better? You know how it's been since the Yanks took control of the inlets and started scavenging the countryside like a flock of turkey vultures! The only fresh food we get is what the Guard can provide, and now the blue devils are driving them out and killing them!"

The man she called Robert caught himself on the verge of being bewitched by the golden sparks in her cool gray eyes. Flashes fire when she's angry, he thought. He should have remembered something so delightful . . . shouldn't he?

Sara laid a hand on his larger one, a look of guilt on her face. "Oh, Robert, I can't believe I'm scolding you already. How could you have known how it's been here at home, and you off in some filthy Yankee prison? Tell me how you even managed to—" She shook her head decisively. "No, don't tell me. I want you to forget the past, forget everything that happened, and let us take care of you. You're home again, my love, and that's all that matters."

If there was a bleak quality to his smile, Sara told herself, then it was no wonder, after all he'd been through. Oh, mercy, but he was good to look at! It seemed all wrong somehow, but she had to admit that never in all the years they'd been married had she ever felt quite so—

That is, he had never affected her quite so—

Flustered, and blushing all over, Sara lifted a spoonful of the cooling broth and took aim.

As for the man called Robert, he allowed himself to be fed the unpalatable stuff. Forget? Nothing easier.

The trick would be to remember, and he found himself, in spite of his aching head, wanting to remember all sorts of intimate details about this woman who seemed to be his wife, and the mother of his daughter.

Chapter Three

Her name was Sara. Sara Bell Jones, and they had grown up on adjoining farms, the Bell farm having been burned to the ground two years before. That much he had managed to learn, but little more. By persistently steering the conversation where he wanted it to go, he had learned the little she'd been told about his supposed death. He had learned that, save for one elderly great-aunt—his, not hers, and one younger brother—hers, not his—their families were dead.

Gradually Rolph's headache subsided, though the lump on the back of his head remained. Sara insisted on fussing over him and shushing Becky when she thought the child's chattering might be a bother.

"We'll have to get word to Jimmy somehow," she said now. She had taken her nightgown off the hook and was fixing to leave the room to bathe and change in the kitchen on the second night. His interest perking, Rolph wondered if she intended to share his bed. The first night he'd been too miserable to protest when she had dragged a chair into the bedroom and slept there.

Tonight, after watching her bustling around all day, bending and reaching so that her body was revealed far more than she could know beneath her limp, threadbare gown, he rather thought he might enjoy company. After all, if he had been taken prisoner in the late summer of '61, he had just come through a long, dry spell.

Hadn't he?

Damn and blast this persistent fogginess in his brain! For all he knew, he might even have forgotten what to do with a woman in his bed!

On the other hand, he had a notion it would come back to him quickly enough, given the opportunity....

Sara dragged the copper tub over near the range, spooned in a small heap of crushed purple blossoms from her precious hoard, emptied the steaming kettle and then added another kettleful of water from the pump. Tonight she would spread a pallet on the floor instead of sleeping in that miserable chair. She hadn't meant to fall asleep last night, but she'd been too tired to stay awake.

With her chin practically resting on her knees, she soaked and washed, her thoughts never straying far from the man in the next room as the scent of violets wafted up around her.

Robert. How could she have forgotten that certain way he had of cutting his eyes at her, not quite smiling, not quite frowning, but looking so intense. Was that the word? Yes, she decided, scrubbing her ears with the thin cotton rag—intense. As if he already knew a hundred secrets and wanted to look into her mind to discover hers.

And she had them, oh, my mercy, she did! The kind of secrets she would never have dreamed she could have, much less keep from her own husband. The kind of secrets no decent woman who'd been married as long as she had and had a five-year-old child should be having!

"Sara?"

At the sound of his voice, she shivered deliciously, hot color rising to stain her face. "I'm coming," she called in a hushed voice, not wanting to wake Becky.

What if he wanted her to—

But of course, he was too sick. He wouldn't...would he?

No, of course not, she told herself sharply as she stood, stepped out of the dented old copper tub and hastily blotted herself all over with the coarse cotton towel. The only light in the room came from a pair of candles on the table, and the curtains were securely drawn. There was no reason to feel so skittish.

All the same, she was dragging the billowing flannel nightgown over her head before her body was even dry, casting nervous glances at the door while she tugged the bathtub over against the wall to bail out in the morning.

"Did you want a glass of water before I blow out the light?" she asked breathlessly a moment later.

"No, dammit, I want a glass of brandy, but I suppose that's too much to ask," Rolph snapped. She had to come in here, smelling like a blasted flower garden and looking like a dying man's dream, with her hair spilling all over her shoulders and that hideous thing she was wearing stuck to her behind!

Her jaw, softer and rounder than her daughter's, dropped, and she stared at him as if he were the devil incarnate. "Brandy? But Robert, you *hate* brandy."

He did? "Oh—I meant medicinal brandy," he amended, not sure what he meant, suddenly all too sure what he wanted, though.

She slept on a pallet, insisting that he didn't need anyone kicking and squirming beside him, disturbing his rest. If she'd had any notion of just how disturbed his rest was, she would have run out screaming into the night.

Nor was the disturbance caused entirely by the questions that logjammed in his brain.

Lying awake listening to the sound of her slow, even breathing, Rolph tried to make some sense out of the situation. His name was Jones. Robert Jones. He was a farmer, a married man, a father, and a soldier in the Confederate army. The name, at least, felt familiar, although the fit wasn't quite perfect. A farmer? Not a very good one from the looks of this place. He'd been gone too long.

A husband and a father? He was obviously better at that, for they both seemed to like him well enough. As for being a soldier, what man wasn't in these days? Just his rotten luck to have been captured at the fall of Fort Hatteras and imprisoned at—

Where? God, he should remember that much, at least. Even more puzzling, how had he managed to procure a Yankee lieutenant's uniform, lead his captors to his own home and then trick them into leaving him behind?

Sooner or later the answer would come, Rolph assured himself. He'd heard of men losing their memory after a blow, a bad fever, or being caught too near an explosion. It seldom lasted long. No man he'd ever heard of had permanently misplaced his family, not to mention his entire lifetime.

On the other hand, it was not every day that a man had his skull caressed with a length of cordwood by a loving spouse.

Or perhaps it was. How could he know? A man who could forget a woman like Sara Bell Jones could forget most anything.

Now, by the gray light coming through the small window, Rolph watched as the woman who claimed to be his wife brushed her hair, rebraided it and coiled it on top of her head. Today he would add to his small store of knowledge. He had discovered, in trying to learn his wife's name, that he was clever enough, even if he didn't know turnips from tomcats when it came to farming. "Did I tell you I met another man whose wife has your name?" That had been his way of finding out who she was, once he'd learned that Emma was the doll.

"Another Sara Jones?" She'd been spreading his bed while he sat in the chair by the window watching her bend and stretch. "Well, I reckon it's not the most uncommon name in the world. I know three Saras, and there are certainly plenty of Joneses around. The ones over near Old Trap aren't even our kin."

"Maybe I should've taken your name when we married," he'd teased with a purpose.

"Would that've made me Sara Bell Bell?" She had laughed, and Rolph had savored the sound. Just as he'd savored the sight of her going about her household tasks, watching her through the windows as she fed and watered the mule, one old milch cow and the few chickens, all of which she kept penned up in the barn against predators. Two-legged and otherwise, as she'd told him.

There was something soothing about Sara Bell Jones. Something intrinsically warm and nurturing. He wished he could remember more of their life together before he'd turned into a blasted invalid!

Not that he was, only Sara insisted on making him stay in bed, telling him he was still too weak from the blow on the noggin, not to mention all the time he must have spent in prison.

Dammit, he didn't feel weak! He told her as much as he followed her into the kitchen for breakfast, which he refused to eat in bed again. All the same, he couldn't deny feeling a moment of weakness when she told him she'd burned his uniform.

"That was a mistake, Sara." He couldn't say why it was a mistake, or even why he felt the way he did. All the same, he wished she hadn't done it.

"I know," she said calmly, patting out a stiff batter of cornmeal and water into flat cakes. "It was such good wool, and Lord knows, wool's scarce these days, but I couldn't take the risk of someone's seeing it and recognizing it. They'd have taken you for a spy or worse."

"And what will they take me for in my nightshirt?" he asked with a rueful grin. The garment she had dug out of her trunk, claiming she'd cut down most of his clothes for Jimmy, was tight across the shoulders and did nothing whatsoever for his dignity.

"Depends on who they are." She answered his grin with a shy smile, and Rolph was enchanted to see flicker in her right cheek the same dimple that was such a delightful part of Becky's smiles. "If any strangers come around asking about my menfolk, I'll just tell them you're my poor half-witted brother."

And because it had nagged at him all day, he picked up the subject again that night after Becky had been put to bed. "Sara, are they likely to do that? Strangers coming around to question you, I mean?"

She shrugged and went right on braiding her hair. Then, finishing off the end with a strip of rag, she doused the lamp and knelt beside the bed. "How's a body to know what to expect in times like these? They've burned out every place they even suspicion might be connected to the Guard. They burned Papa's place, you know, not a month after Jimmy joined up."

Without missing a beat, she closed her eyes and said firmly, "Lord, we thank You for sparing our Robert, we surely do. I'll take over his care from now on, but I'd be much obliged if You'd keep an eye on Jimmy. He's not near as big as he thinks he is, for all he keeps one hand on that damn Yankee rifle of his and wears a knife sharp enough to whittle a railroad spike. Bless all our folks, Lord, and—" Here Rolph was bemused to hear her sigh mightily. "And I reckon you'd better bless the Yanks, too. Maybe then they'll go back up North where they belong. Amen."

She hadn't spread the pallet on the floor tonight, nor had she dragged in the chair. And she'd avoided looking directly at him for the past few hours. If he didn't know better—if they hadn't been married long enough to produce a beautiful daughter who, in all modesty, he had to admit, looked just like him—Rolph would have thought she was shy.

"Are you shy, Sara?"

Her eyes flashed with that delightful golden fire again as she cut him a sharp look. "Don't be foolish, why should I be shy?"

Heart pounding, he strived for a casual effect as he lifted the layered quilts for her to crawl in beside him. His mouth was dry, his palms wet. It was all so strange, and the strangest part of it was that it shouldn't be—it should feel like coming home. Instead, it felt like pressing his eye to the keyhole of the gates to heaven.

Lying stiffly near the edge of the bed, Rolph cleared his throat. Should he reach for her? Would she think he was indelicate if he pounced on her right off? It had been a long time for both of them.

It was all so deuced strange, this not remembering! His head was befogged with tangled memories, like remnants of a forgotten dream. Some of it—the land itself, his daughter's face, the pervasive smell of the burning swamp—some of it felt so right, so familiar.

Yet at the same time, it all felt so... alien.

They lay silently for several minutes. Rolph could tell by her breathing that Sara wasn't asleep. Odd, he thought—he'd never have taken her for a shy woman, yet it seemed she was just as uncertain as he was. With a fleeting glimmer of humor, he wondered if he'd made as miserable a showing on their wedding night.

Even if he had, surely in the years since then they would have grown accustomed to each other. Even if he'd gone to war at the first roll of the drum, they would have had more than two years together. Two years of intimacy. How strange, then, that they should be so acutely aware of each other now.

''Sara?'' he whispered tentatively. One of his hands crept across the space into the warmth of hers.

No answer.

His knuckles brushed against her hip, and his body leapt in response. Perhaps she thought him still too weak for the marriage act. Or perhaps she was only waiting for him to make the first move.

In the darkness, Rolph smoothed his hair and raked a nervous hand across his jaw.

Dammit, he should have shaved first! A dash of bay rum would not have come amiss, either. His body was reacting with increasing enthusiasm to the notion of lying with this woman who was his wife.

''Sara?'' he murmured again, and just as he turned to her, she rolled onto her side and into his arms. ''Ah, Sara, my sweetest love,'' he murmured. One of his hands smoothed over her hair until he came to the rag she'd bound her braid with, and he slipped it off and began to work his fingers through the thick silken rope.

Two and a half years! God, it was a wonder his parts hadn't shriveled up from lack of use! That was obviously not the case, however, and he reminded himself that he'd better go slowly. The first time, at least. If he could!

Easing her head onto his shoulder, Rolph slid his knee between her thighs and felt her heat burning through the double layers of flannel.

Nightshirts! Was there ever such a troublesome garment to remove? If he would do the job without strangling himself, he must first release her and climb out of bed to pull the blasted thing over his head, and then do the same for her. Where was the subtlety of that? Where was the finesse? Somehow, without knowing how he knew, he was certain that subtlety and finesse were a large part of his armory, where dalliance was concerned.

Chuckling softly at the fine state of affairs, he decided that henceforth, night garments would be banned in this household. "Sara?" he whispered when he had shed his own and slid back beneath the covers. "Don't be shy, sweetheart, this is nothing we haven't done before."

By the time he had gathered up a fistful of flannel and begun easing it up over her limbs, she had still not spoken a word. She seemed almost uncooperative. Surely she hadn't always been that way?

"Who would have dreamed," he whispered in her ear, "that the same woman who greeted her long-lost husband with a chunk of firewood would be so bashful when it came to... other things?"

He waited for a response that didn't come. Reining in his impatience, Rolph told himself that there was plenty of time. Perhaps she needed to be courted. For all he knew, his wife might be one of those women who took forever to come to a boil.

Strange, not knowing such a thing. He might have had trouble remembering his own name, but there were some things he could have sworn he would never forget, making love to a beautiful woman who happened to be his wife foremost among them.

Taking his time, Rolph explored her body, determined to allow her as much time as she needed to respond. As he traced the sloping hammock of her belly, his thumb and little finger touching her hipbones, and his middle finger just brushing the nest of curls between her thighs, he prided himself on his generosity.

Under the circumstances, it was nothing short of remarkable.

But damnation! he thought a few minutes later. If it weren't for the heat of her body and the soft, regular sound of her breathing, he might have been making love to a corpse.

The soft, regular sound of her breathing? His own was anything but regular! He was gasping for air, each shuddering breath torn from his lungs as his urgency increased, and she was lying there . . .

Asleep. Sound asleep!

Rolph swore angrily. Hearing him, Sara flinched. Why, oh, why, was she acting like such a ninny? Her heart was lodged in her throat, and she was burning up, and it was all she could do to keep her breathing even — and the worst of it was that she didn't even know why!

Robbie, oh, Robbie—give me time. It's been so long, yet I still can't forget the way it used to be.

She knew he'd never meant to, yet he'd always hurt her. He simply hadn't known his own strength, and it had always happened so quickly, with none of the hugging and kissing she'd always longed for. Of course, he'd been exhausted, poor darling, working so hard from dawn until dusk and beyond, but she'd been tired, too. He would come to bed, unshaven, unwashed, and flop over on top of her, and before she could find a way to tell him how she felt, he would grunt, groan and then collapse, nearly smothering her with his deadweight.

Forgive me, dearest—I always knew you loved me, but please, give me time to get used to having you back again.

In the darkness, Rolph's eyes narrowed. He knew she wasn't asleep. Damn her, she was lying there stiff as a board beside him, pretending, with him already so swole up he was about to explode!

Yet even as he tried to hang on to his anger, he wondered if he was being unfair. Willingly or not, he had lain abed while Sara had worked from sunup till sundown and beyond, grinding corn in an old stump mortar, frying up cornmeal cakes, scrubbing the kitchen, beating the mattresses, feeding the animals, keeping up with Becky's boundless energy. She had left the barn door open today, and he'd watched her, sensing her weariness, praying she wouldn't fall off the milking stool before she was finished. She had rested her forehead against the lank belly of that poor old cow while she tried to coax a pint of thin milk from her teats, and Rolph, who liked cream in his coffee, had taken it black so that Becky could have what little milk there was with her breakfast.

She was tired. So what if he was lying here like a damned tent pole? Sara had spent the day working, while he'd lain about and let himself be waited on. While he'd been shaving himself this morning, she'd been out splitting kindling, and before he could even climb into the homespun breeches she had unearthed from the bottom of a trunk, she was toting in the first armload to dump into the wood basket in the corner.

And tonight of all nights was Christmas Eve, which meant that before she could come to bed, there'd been carols to sing, Becky's stocking to hang, and then, once the child was asleep, she'd crept back to fill it with nuts and raisins, an apple that was only slightly blemished, and something wrapped in red tissue.

Rolph had felt like a cad, having nothing to give either of his womenfolk. He had lain abed and let her do it all, and now he was angry because she hadn't bounced into his arms and welcomed him into her body.

He was a sorry wretch for keeping her from her sleep... or trying to.

The next morning Rolph was awakened by a shrill squeal. Before he could gather his wits, Becky burst into the room. "Daddy, Daddy, it comed! My table, just like you promised!"

And then, of course, nothing would do but that Robert must get out of bed and hurry to the door in his nightshirt to admire the perfect child-size replica of a handsome mahogany dining table.

Becky alternately clung to his hand and stroked the gleaming surface of her table, ignoring the red mittens and the doll dress under the tree. "Now can we go see the camp?"

The camp?

"Becky, do leave off pestering your father, he's not well."

And then, of course, Rolph had had to set about proving that he was as well as any man. Certainly well enough to bed his wife at the very first opportunity. After puzzling over his supposed part in the appearance of the table on the front porch that morning— both Sara and Becky had taken his evasiveness for teasing—he had pitched in to help Sara with her tasks, over her loud protests. "If you come down with brain fever from that knock on your noggin, Robert Jones,

I swear I'll never forgive myself, and I've too much on my conscience as it is to add that to the heap!''

He refrained from asking just what sins lay on her conscience so heavily, other than depriving a husband of his marital rights. Instead, he set himself out to do his part toward making the Christmas as merry for his child as possible. He soon had both Sara and Becky laughing as he spun tales out of thin air, now and then catching a wondering expression on Sara's face.

Throughout the day, he managed to relieve her of her heavier tasks, cleverly distracting her with more tales dredged up from a source he hadn't even questioned.

''Robert, you never!'' she protested. He had put together some fanciful faradiddle about a dog, a flowered bonnet and his colonel's mother-in-law, and had them both giggling, even as he wondered what the man's name had been.

Draper? Howard?

Never mind. He was determined to conceal his loss of memory from his wife for fear she'd continue to treat him as an invalid. The last thing he felt was sickly, and once they'd bedded down the child tonight, he intended to prove it to both their satisfactions, or his name wasn't . . . Robert Henry Jones?

Rolph's headache returned in the afternoon, and he allowed himself to be talked into resting. Becky, who was tuned to a high pitch of excitement over the visit from Saint Nick, was persuaded to lie down, as well, and so the two of them settled down together.

When Rolph awoke, Becky was playing tea-party with her doll, and Sara was bailing wash water from the heavy tub over the scraggly row of collards beside the house. Christmas or not, the clotheslines were draped with sheets and towels, two of Becky's pinafores and several sets of smallclothes, including his own.

"Drat it, Sara, you didn't have to do that!" he protested. He'd wanted her rested tonight, not so worn out she would be asleep the minute her head hit the pillow.

"It rained all last week, and it's fixing to rain again from the look of that sky."

"It's Christmas!"

"Yes," she murmured distractedly. "I miss having church, but tomorrow's Sunday, so we decided to wait. I do hope..."

Rolph waited for her to continue, and when she didn't, he added dryly that he thought the Lord would understand, given the fact that so many of His children seemed to be at odds with each other.

Sara sent him a scolding look, and he shrugged. As far as he knew, he'd never been an overly religious man. As far as he knew.

"I do wish Jimmy could be here. Leastwise, I wish he knew you were back home. These days, good news is about the best gift a body could wish for."

"Can't you send word?"

"I don't know where to send it, much less how. They've moved, you know. He promised to get word back as soon as he could."

While Sara set out the Christmas feast—chicken, boiled greens, the dried green beans she called leather-britches boiled with a scrap of bacon rind, and more of the eternal corn cakes, Rolph worked at a project he had begun just that morning. The heavy cane vines that grew up into the trees near the river were a bit stiff for working, but he had managed to fashion a chair of sorts, scaled to Becky's new table. He intended to make a pair if this one worked out.

He wished even more that he had something to give Sara.

"I'm growing increasingly curious about this young brother-in-law of mine," he said idly while Sara put the finishing touches on the table.

"Jimmy? He's some taller, but he's still the same old Jimmy... although now that he's gone off and joined the Home Guard, he likes to be called James Edwin, only I can never remember. Lord knows what we would've done without the food he's managed to provide."

Robert could only hope the poor fellows did a better job of protecting their womenfolk than they did of providing for them. Sara had killed, plucked and drawn one of her few hens the day before so as to provide a festive meal for Christmas Day. The poor scrawny creatures scarcely laid enough to earn their keep, she had complained, but that was only to be expected this time of year.

He should know things like that, he reminded himself. Evidently he'd forgotten not only how to be a soldier and a husband, but how to be a farmer.

When the meal was ended, Sara proudly brought out a dark cake, its base garnished with dried apples dusted with cinnamon. Becky clapped her hands and practically jumped up and down in anticipation.

"Aha! Surprised you, didn't I? I've been keeping back flour and sugar for a whole year to make the Christmas cake." And with an apologetic look at Robert, she said softly, "It won't be what you're used to, love, for I'd no butter nor cream nor any candied fruit save for raisins, but at least we'll have cake for Christmas.''

Shortly after dark, Sara bathed and bedded the child, and then shyly begged a bit of privacy for her own bath. Rolph, wishing he had a cigar and a decent glass of brandy, took himself off to the front room, hiding the broad grin that threatened to split his face.

Another bath. Somehow, he was certain that tonight's bath would be put to better use than the one last night. Then, she had come to bed smelling of violets and her own sweet self, and he'd gotten himself worked up to such a high pitch he had lain awake for hours.

But there'd been hints today, starting with this morning, when she had come and stood in the doorway with her arm around his waist while Becky had emptied her stocking, making much over a pair of mittens, a doll dress, a crudely whittled dog and a handful of pecans and raisins.

Sara had looked up at him, her gray eyes glowing with that hidden fire he found so delightful. Her face had still been flushed with sleep, her hair tousled about her shoulders from where he'd unbraided it the night before, and two buttons at the neck of her flannel gown had been unfastened. Also his work, not that he had owned up to it.

She had reached up and touched the side of his face. ''Why, Robert, I do believe you're smiling,'' she'd teased.

God, that had felt good—her teasing him in that warm, familiar way. ''I know. Nasty habit, isn't it?''

"I must say, it's a strange habit to have picked up in a Yankee prison. You never used to smile before mid-afternoon."

And then her fingertip had strayed to a small thin scar that he'd noticed on his chin while he was shaving. "How did you get this?" she'd asked.

"Ice-skating on old man Holland's pond," he'd said without even thinking.

"Who?"

And then he'd frowned. Who indeed? Now why had he said that? "Sweetheart, you can't expect me to remember every little scratch I ever received, now can you?"

"I'm ashamed for even asking. No wonder you want to forget. We heard the conditions at the fort were awful, even before the shelling started, and that the men and supplies you'd been promised never came. Jimmy said word was that there was scarce enough to eat out there, even before the Banks fell. Robbie, if I have to kill every hen we have I'll not see you go hungry again, and that's a promise."

Rolph had been so touched he hadn't known what to say. She was such a fierce little partisan. He had replied something to the effect that he would gladly dine on corn bread and dried beans for the duration, as long as his other appetites could be assuaged.

The color that had rushed to her face had been purely delightful, but before he'd been able to take advantage of her disarray, she had joined in Becky's play and the moment had been lost.

Tonight was going to be different. He could sense it. It had been there in the soft glow in her eyes when she'd mentioned her bath. He had suddenly been glad for the extra material in his trousers.

Becky, exhausted from the excitement of the day, was already sound asleep in the room across from their own, and as soon as Sara was done in the kitchen, Rolph intended to claim the tub for his own use. He had waited a lifetime, he told himself. Two and a half years, in truth, but it might as well have been a lifetime for all the eagerness he was feeling.

Less than an hour later, Rolph wrapped a damp towel around his hips, wishing he had a splash of bay rum for his freshly shaven cheeks. He blew out the lamp and made his way silently along the plank floors of the hallway toward the bedroom where his wife lay waiting.

The damned nightshirt had been a miserable fit, anyway. Perhaps she could cut it down for the child. Come to think of it, every piece of his old clothing Sara had dug out of that trunk at the foot of his bed was at least a size too small across the shoulders and a size too large in the waist. Evidently, army life had been more strenuous than a lifetime of farming.

"Sara," he whispered as he closed the bedroom door quietly behind him. "Are you still awake?"

"I'm awake," came her soft rejoinder.

Surely, Rolph thought, his heart couldn't have pounded harder if the whole Union army had been nipping at his heels!

Chapter Four

Sara's marriage to Robert had not been perfect harmony. He was such a strikingly handsome man that she had failed to look beneath the surface. During the years since he had been reported taken prisoner and then dead, she had tended to glorify him in her mind, to forget that once their courtship had ended in marriage, he had grown—different. Not really cruel, but never again so loving. The intimate side of their marriage had all too quickly become no more than a duty to be performed on request, although fortunately, the requests had not been overly frequent.

Which made it all the more strange that she was so shudderingly aware of her husband now, had been almost from the first moment of his return. Sara had long since learned that she was not a passionate woman. Robert had demanded no more than a few minutes of her time twice weekly; less than that once he'd planted his seed beneath her apron, which had suited her well enough.

So why was she trembling at the thought of doing her duty once more? Why was her heart racing, her breath catching in her throat? Of course she loved him. She had always loved him, but why, after all this time, did the very scent of his body make her feel like pressing herself against him and . . . *moving?*

"Sara," Robert whispered as he lifted the covers to come down beside her. "You're not sleepy, are you, love?"

"No." Was that squeak of a voice her own? "Robert, are you certain you feel up to this?"

"Let me put it another way, wife. If I don't have you before very long, I'm afraid I might fall into a decline from which I'll never recover. Now, let's unwrap you, shall we? The night's not so cold you need to swaddle yourself in all that cloth."

And unwrap her he did, as if she were his own Christmas gift. He had never done that before. Not altogether, at least. As his hands skimmed down her sides, his eyes devouring her in the near darkness, Sara felt a blush start at the soles of her feet and burn its way up to the crown of her head.

"Oh, my mercy," she whispered, determined to allow him his freedom of her body, no matter what. It was the least she could do. "Robbie, what happened to your—oooh—" she sighed as his hands moved to her breasts "—your sense of modesty?"

"Modesty?" There was laughter as well as disbelief in his voice. "Darling, we're husband and wife, not strangers."

But he felt like a stranger. A wonderful, thrilling, forbidden stranger, which made it all the more exciting.

His hands moved again, and she caught her breath. "Oh, Robbie!" she gasped.

"How in creation did I get through all those years without you?" he whispered. "Without . . . this?"

Sara was wondering much the same thing, herself. Robert had never talked much in bed. When he had, it had usually been about the crops. Or the weather. Never, except perhaps in the very beginning, had he used the words he was using now, touched her the way he was touching her—whispered such delightfully wicked things in her ear.

No, not even then, she admitted silently. Now even his voice sounded different. It was as if he'd learned a whole new way of speaking from living amongst the Yanks all this time.

"I'm sorry my hands are so rough," she whispered, blushing again in the darkness.

Robert gathered them up in one of his hands, kissed them and placed them on his chest, where they curled in the thick patch of dark hair that grew there. "I love your hands. Someday, they'll be smooth as silk again. After this mess is over, sweetheart, I'm going to buy you one of those new rotary washboard machines, and we'll hire someone to scrub our floors."

Sara felt tears prickling her eyelids. As if they could ever afford such luxuries! All the same, she loved him for saying it.

He kissed her lips. He kissed her throat. He kissed each breast, lingering for endless moments before moving over her to kiss parts of her that had never been kissed before. Sara gasped.

"Stop wriggling, precious, I'm not going to hurt you."

She stopped, her breath catching in her throat. Soon there was another gasp, and another, followed by a shuddering sigh. The moon emerged from behind a cloud to spill its magic across the moving mound of quilts as muffled murmurs and soft laughter were heard.

After a while there were more low murmurs, soft whispers, and then several heartfelt groans before the thump of a headboard battering a wall could be heard.

Later...much later, there were still more murmurs and whispers and thumps. It was long past midnight when Sara's soft voice, drowsy and sated, could be heard saying, "Welcome home, my dearest love."

Not even Becky's energetic form clambering over their feet could dim the glow of the night just past. "Mama, Mama, Sandy Claus comed again! You said he wouldn't come this year, and he comed two times!"

Much was made over the cunning little chairs Robert had managed to make while Becky's attention was directed elsewhere, and set beside her table the night before. She exclaimed over the intricate pattern woven into the back, and Robert only hoped the canes wouldn't warp too much as they dried. Perhaps he'd better start drying more cane, in case he had to replace them.

Becky, barefooted and chattering like a magpie, was wearing a much-mended nightgown and her new red mittens, and Robert, seeing his wife's chapped hands, knew where the wool had come from. Once this war is over, he promised himself, there will be new kid gloves and fine silk gowns for both his ladies. And meat on the table every day! And God willing, no more of those damnable corn cakes!

Sara was already dressed by that time. She was wearing a necklace of buttons Becky had given her for Christmas, and Rolph had wanted to give her diamonds. Someday, he vowed, he would.

"She wanted me to help her make me a surprise," Sara had confided earlier. She had gotten out the button box, threaded one of her precious needles and allowed her daughter to select the order of the buttons to be strung: bone, glass and wood, with the few brass ones she possessed taking the place of honor in the center.

He had watched as she exclaimed over the trifle on Christmas morning, just as if she'd never laid eyes on it before.

His Sara. How had he ever got so lucky? She had the body of a houri and a face as guileless as a child, and the combination was driving him more than a little crazy! If it hadn't been for Becky, he would have taken her back into that bedroom and kept her there, Sunday or no Sunday—church meeting or no church meeting!

"Robert, stop looking at me," she whispered sternly, and then, "Becky, run wash your face and hands, honey. We don't want to be late."

Six years married, and she was still shy. Robert, amused and touched, found himself aching with an emotion he could never remember having felt before.

But of course, he had. Must have done, for he'd married the girl, hadn't he? Thank God he'd had the good sense to snatch her up before some other young jackanapes had claimed her. She was one in a million, his Sara. And Becky, for all she shared his own coloring and his features in miniature, had been blessed with her mother's calm, sweet nature and her laughing eyes.

He didn't want them to go off and leave him alone, but common sense prevailed. He promised to rest while they were gone, and not to show himself outside, and in case of trouble, not to be foolhardy.

''Papa's old squirrel gun is in the pantry,'' Sara told him. ''Your pistol is hid in the flour bin.''

Damn! He'd forgotten all about it, but of course, he would've had a gun. A side arm, more than likely. ''I'm glad you didn't try to burn it along with my uniform,'' he'd said, not quite in jest.

''Don't be ridiculous. If I'd wanted to get rid of it, I'd have dumped it in the river. It'll come in handy after the war. That old thing of Papa's falls apart every time I fire it. By now, half the screws are missing.''

Robert closed his eyes in brief supplication. ''Woman, I don't know how you managed to survive while I was gone.''

''Didn't have a whole lot of choice,'' she retorted, and then, blushing, she skittered a kiss off his chin.

Sara didn't want to leave, but once more, she had little choice. It was just over a mile to church, and the walk was not without risk, being right on the river road. Some of the churches—not hers, thank goodness—had been taken over to house and feed wounded Yanks.

She told herself she was going there to worship and give thanks for their many blessings, and to offer the Lord a birthday greeting only a day late, but she knew in her heart of hearts that the main reason she was going was to pick up any bits of news. She couldn't rest until she knew exactly how much danger her Robert was in.

The Gregorys were there, the Gilberts and the Stevenses. She greeted Ada Morris and old Miss Cherry and nodded to George Nixon's wife. Most of them, she knew for a fact, had someone in the Home Guard, if not the regular forces, so surely someone would know *something*.

Finally, after a brief sermon, a lengthy prayer and a hymn sung without accompaniment, their organist having joined the Thirty-second only a few months before, they filed out. Becky, after a nod from Sara, darted over to show off her doll's dress and tell her best friend about her new tea-party table and chairs, Sara having warned her earlier against mentioning her father's return.

"They say Wild's men has burnt nigh onto ever'thing 'twixt here and Currituck Courthouse," one widow whispered, and Sara nodded. That wasn't what she'd come there to learn.

"Are any of them still hanging around these parts?" she asked. Her greatest fear was that the men who had so unaccountably brought Robert home and left him would return. Goodness knows what he had told them to get them to leave him there. He refused to discuss it, and Sara, afraid of reminding him of the unspeakable things he must have endured during his captivity, dared not press him too far.

"River's plumb full of the devils, but I've not seen one on my place in over a week," Margaret Smith said, and her aged husband spoke up to say, "They took my last hog, may they rot in hell, begging the Lord's pardon, but how's a man expected to feed his family?"

How indeed? The Smiths had lost two sons at the battle of Roanoke Island, and their grandson hadn't been heard from in over a year.

"Did you hear about Miss Mary?" someone else put in. "Word is they arrested her and took her off to South Mills last week."

Glancing over to where Becky played with the two Gilbert girls, Sara turned back and said, "You mean *old* Miss Mary? But why?"

"Claimed she poisoned some Yank officer, and her eighty if she's a day!" Ada Morris offered.

"Did she do it?"

"Wouldn't put it past her if she'd thought she could get away with it," chimed in a close neighbor of the woman in question. "But the truth is, she was one of the women them devils took to the church and forced to cook, and when some blue-belly officer commenced castin' up his accounts right there at the altar after Mary'd done served him a feast fit for a king—"

"A feast? Where'd they get the food?" someone inquired eagerly.

"Off'n the Yankee supply boats, where else? I'd set a net for one myself if I thought I could fill my belly just once before I was hauled off to the stockade."

"But what about Miss Mary?" Sara steered the speaker back on course.

"Oh, they let her go after a few days in the stockade. She told the Yank in charge that any fool that didn't know no better'n to drink milk with his oysters deserved to get sick. But then, she'd prob'ly peeled the hide off every last one of 'em. You know Miss Mary's tongue."

Sara waved Becky back to her side. This was all very well, but none of it told her what she needed to know. "I don't suppose anyone knows if there're any Yank details still in the neighborhood?" she asked, and while there were suspicious mutterings, none could say with any certainty just where the blue-bellied devils were.

And wherever they were today, Sara reminded herself, they could be somewhere else tomorrow. She was simply going to have to get word to Jimmy somehow, as reluctant as she was to do it. She knew as well as she knew anything that the minute Robert learned where his own outfit was, he would insist on rejoining it.

Sara was in a quandary. As much as she wanted to keep him with her, she had to think of his safety. The only trouble was, she didn't know if he would be safer back with his unit, or hiding out in an area where he could be prey to either side, the Rebs taking him for a spy or a Buffalo if they discovered how he came to be there, and the Yanks taking him for a parolled prisoner—which he wasn't—or worse, a member of the Home Guard, which they were determined to exterminate.

Lord, she wished she could wrap him in a napkin and hide him under her flour bin along with that awful-looking pistol of his!

Sara clasped Becky against her side and said her goodbyes after Emma's new dress and Becky's new mittens were dutifully admired. All knew they were not really new, for every scrap of wool and cotton went to Raleigh, to be made into uniforms for Jeff Davis's forces, but with the harshest of the winter still ahead of them, no one begrudged the child a pair of remade, redyed, secondhand gloves.

It was by merest chance that Sara saw the signal on the way home. Becky was dancing along in front of her, singing snatches of the hymn they'd sung at church, and as the road swerved past a certain thicket, Sara glanced up by force of habit to check the river traffic. There, hanging from a limb, was a familiar knotted length of rope.

Her heart slammed into her throat. It was nearly a mile from their old place, but it had to be Jimmy! Smart boy, he had known she would be passing this way on her way to church this morning, of all mornings.

"Becky, I want you to sit right here with Emma and wait while I walk down to the river, will you do that?"

"But why, Mama? Emma and me could count the boats, too. Emma knows how to count almos' to a hundred."

The child was far too wise for her years. "Becky, do as I say, please. I'll explain later."

"Oh. I guess Uncle Jimmy wants to wish you happy Chris'mas. But I could—"

"Becky."

"Yes, ma'am."

By the time they got back to the farm, Sara was nearly bursting with the news, but she had to wait until after they ate what was left of yesterday's Christmas feast of greens, beans, boiled chicken and raisin cake. While she cleared away, Becky had played tea-party with her new chair and table, and then Robert took her onto his lap and read to her from her favorite book.

"Finally!" Sara exclaimed softly, having just settled the overtired child for a nap.

Robert, who had seen the frown on her brow more than once as she went about her tasks, opened his arms, and wordlessly Sara walked into his warm, strong embrace. How had she lived this past age without him? she asked herself wonderingly. How could she ever have forgotten his gentleness, his sweet strength, what a skilled and generous lover he was? Now that she had him back, how could she bear to let him return to the war?

But, dear God, how could she protect him?

Sara buried her face in the old blue muslin shirt she had not been able to part with, even though Jimmy could have used it. It had been Robert's favorite. "Robert, there's news," she told him, stepping away before she shamed herself by begging him to go to bed with her in broad daylight.

"I suspected that was why you'd insisted on going to church."

"I went because it's the Christmas season," she said with mock indignance.

"It's also wartime," he reminded her gently, and she moved back into his arms and sighed.

"Don't remind me."

Robert let her tell it in her own way and in her own time. She told him about an old woman's arrest and subsequent release, about the commandeering of someone's last hog, about the number of supply boats on the river, and who had recently heard from their menfolk. Unless he missed his guess by a mile, none of that had put the frown on her face.

"I saw Jimmy," she said then, and Rolph closed his eyes in momentary satisfaction. Now we get to the meat of it, he told himself.

"Did you ask him about my unit?"

"He says they're up in Virginia now, and that Yanks are thick as fleas all along the border. He says for you to stay here out of sight until he can make contact with someone to lead you through the lines, but Robbie, that's not all."

Robert waited, his face enigmatic, his pulses racing. For some reason—possibly having to do with a certain length of cordwood—his brain wasn't handling this information in quite the way he would have expected it to. "What else, Sara? Come now, it can't be as bad as all that."

"There's bad and good. The bad news is that the Yanks have got a hold of a list of the Home Guard. No one knows how accurate it is, or even if they really do have it, but word says they do."

His arms tightened. "Your brother—"

"And you, Robert!" she exclaimed, drawing back to gaze up at him with great brimming eyes. "If they come searching for Jimmy, they'll find you."

"Then I'll leave. But Sara, I can't go off and leave you and Becky here alone. There's no telling what—"

"You have no choice if they're right about the list. Jimmy's going to try and find out directly, and if it is, he'll get word to us somehow." She smiled, but it was a poor effort. Rolph wanted to take her a thousand miles away, to where there was no war, no Yanks, no Rebs, and shelter her in his arms forever.

"But there's good news, too. I left it for last," she murmured, and he sighed, burying his face in her fragrant hair. God, how could he ever have forgotten something so sweet, so precious to him? "Jimmy and his men surprised a Yank encampment no more than a mile away night before last. He said there were seven men. I'm sure it was the same seven men who brought you here." She waited, as if hoping he could add something to her story, but Robert was as mystified as she was as to why a detail of Yanks would lead him home, along with a large table, remove the table and allow him to stay. And although he was beginning to understand the source of Becky's tea-party table, he was damned if he could figure out the why of it.

"And?" he prompted.

"And? Oh. Well, Jimmy says the Yanks had left just one man on guard, and the rest were sleeping. They managed to capture four of the sleeping ones right off, but once the shooting started, one of Jimmy's men and two of the Yanks were killed, and another Yank got away. Jimmy thinks he'll probably get himself lost and they'll be able to recapture him—unless he makes his way to one of the Buffalo houses. The worrisome thing is that he'll know about you...where you are and all.''

Rolph was silent for a long time. Sara, her arms wrapped around his lean waist, neither moved nor spoke. He was thinking, she knew—thinking of the chances of making it up into Virginia to his own unit without a guide, with neither blue uniform nor gray.

She was tempted to hide his boots and burn every stitch of clothing he'd left behind when he'd enlisted!

Except, perhaps, for his nightshirt.

Chapter Five

The rains fell heavily. The fireplace sputtered and hissed, and Sara fussed over having to leave her shoes on the porch each time she went outside, the small complaints covering a much deeper anxiety. With the swamps flooded, there would be little likelihood of meeting with Jimmy anytime soon. Robert was growing restless. It was only a matter of time before he would insist on trying to rejoin his unit.

At least for now he was distracted by Becky. The Christmas tree was still standing, and Becky related at least once each day how they had selected it and chopped it down, how they had dragged it home on an old tote sack, nailing crisscross boards on the bottom.

"And do you know what we covered it with?" the giggling child would ask at that point. "One of Mama's—tee hee!—*petticoats!*"

Robert dutifully pretended shock at the mention of Sara's undergarment, which invariably sent Becky off into whoops of laughter.

There were nuts to crack and acorns to parch, and Becky, amazed that her father didn't know about such things, showed him how to make a whirligig with a loop of string and a large bone button.

But in between helping his wife with her chores and playing with his daughter, Rolph paced. Sara could feel his growing restlessness and wished with all her heart that he could be content to stay at home a while longer.

While he grumbled about clothes that no longer fit, she took in the seat and waist of his trousers to fit his new lean build. "Hateful devils must've starved you," she said, biting off her thread and shaking out the pair of woolen breeches when she'd finished.

Rolph, dressed in the infernal nightshirt, snatched them up and disappeared into the bedroom to put them on. The truth was, he had no idea whether he had been ill-treated or not. After an entire week, he was no closer to recovering his memory than he'd been the evening he had waked up on the floor with a splitting headache and a gray-eyed angel weeping over him.

But both Sara and Rolph admitted privately that the nights were the best. Once the child was asleep, they wasted little candle wax before seeking their own bed.

"How could I have forgotten all this?" Rolph marveled softly one night as he lay spent beside his wife's sleeping body. No man could ask for a sweeter welcome from his family, yet he felt like an imposter. If only he could remember! Each day brought more questions, questions he dare not ask for fear of being discovered.

Discovered? What was there to be discovered? He was who he was, wasn't he? Surely the child, if not the woman, could have no reason to pretend he was someone he was not.

Then why, he asked himself for the hundredth time, couldn't he bring himself to share this problem? To tell Sara about his loss of memory? There was nothing shameful about it, surely.

Of course, she might consider him an invalid and insist on withholding their vigorous nightly exercise. And that was one risk, he told himself with a reluctant smile, he was not prepared to take.

But damnation, a man grew restless! Memory or not, there could be no doubt about one thing. He was a soldier, and his country was at war. His place was with his men, not taking his pleasure each night in the arms of his wife and then lying abed late of a morning, rising only when his imp of a daughter brought him coffee in bed.

The corporal peeled away the wadded bandages from his shoulder and peered down at his wound. It was still proud but no longer quite so discolored. His head no longer ached, and he felt decidedly cooler. 'Strewth, he was beginning to think he might live, no thanks to that damned Johnny Reb and his blasted rifle!

Or that gouty old devil upstairs, Union sympathizer or no. Grumbling all the while, the old man had taken him in and instructed his manservant to dig out the bullet, smear some foul-smelling salve on the wound and bed him down in the cellar.

Fortunately, Cecil had soon passed out from the pain. He had roused once or twice, but for the most part, he'd even slept through the worst of the fever, according to the one-eyed servant. The wretch had forced diluted spirits down his throat instead of giving him the bottle as he'd requested, but at least he hadn't turned him in.

As soon as his mind began to clear after the fever had subsided, Cecil Stanley, a bright young lad who'd been apprenticed to a mercer before the war, began trying to piece together a most puzzling question.

What the bluebottle blazes had happened to his lieutenant?

Major Hallis had sent out a detail under Lieutenant Mallory in search of guerillas. Their orders were to locate the nests and burn them out, regardless of circumstances. They'd had several promising leads, but found no real evidence in any of the houses they'd searched. Mallory had insisted on leaving the houses untouched. Adam had been all for burning out a few as a lesson to the rest, but this close to Christmas, none of the others had been in much of a mood to burn women and children out of their homes.

Damn it all, something must've happened to the lieutenant! He could be all the way up to Richmond, rotting in Libby prison by now!

On the other hand, he might've found out the kid belonged to a family of Union sympathizers. Mallory had given them all the location of a friendly contact reported to live near Old Trap, instructing them to use the information only in the last extreme.

As far as Cecil was concerned, getting his left arm damn near blown off was extreme enough.

The trouble had come in trying to find the place in a land so flat and featureless that he'd damn near bled to death before he'd got himself out of the swamp. The only thing that had kept him going was fear for his lieutenant.

Something had happened to the man. Cecil was certain of it. Mallory was no cold-blooded bastard like some he could name. He would never have deserted his men that way.

They'd made camp and waited that first night, passing a few ribald remarks about lonely widows and warm, dry beds. They'd expected him to turn up bright and early the next morning. When he hadn't, Burden had insisted on cutting down the table, as ordered, and when the lieutenant still hadn't shown up, he had gone to deliver the thing just after midnight, taking three men in case things got sticky.

Back at camp, Cecil and Adam Dvorski had mulled over the possibilities.

"The way I got it figgered," declared Cecil, "them damned guerillas snuck up out of the swamp and caught him with his pants down."

"I never saw a man take to a kid the way he did, did you? She weren't even scared of him, neither."

"Damned secesh devils, they even use children to fight their battles!"

Burden had come back with no news, other than that there was a pair of familiar-looking boots beside the hearth in the front room. "I left the table outside the front door. Felt like a damned fool doing it, I can tell you, too!"

"Maybe he's on to something big, like maybe who them swamp rats answer to, and where they're holed up."

"I say we move in and take the place," Cecil declared.

"I say we wait till we know what we're up against."

"How bad could it be? A kid, a woman?"

"How about a nest of them damned guerillas? Something's sure as hell keeping the lieutenant there, and it ain't no Rebel kid."

"Hell, we got plenty of firepower. We go in just like the lieutenant said, two by two, front and back, and take 'em. They'll think they got the whole damn company on their backs."

Burden had looked at the young corporal, not bothering to hide his disgust. "You learnt fightin' behind the counter of that fancy rag-peddler's store, boy? Them guerillas learnt their fightin' behind the sights of their pappy's huntin' piece. I'd set back a while and consider before I go chargin' in there if I was you."

Cecil might be the corporal, but Burden, a grizzled old mountaineer from the western part of the state, was the undisputed leader in Mallory's absence. Age, experience and a wicked left cross had tipped the scales in his favor.

"What we're gonna do, boys, is we're gonna wait right here until tomorrow and hit 'em when they're least expecting it."

"Aw, hell, Burden, tomorrow's Christmas," complained one of the men, married and the father of four. "Think about that little girl."

The old soldier's face hardened. He had lost his own family, including a granddaughter about Becky's age, to a band of drunken Rebs celebrating a minor victory. After burying them, family and soldiers alike, he had started walking downhill to the nearest Yank outpost and offered his services. The officer in charge, thinking a local might come in handy as a guide, had accepted his enlistment and then, in his infinite wisdom, dispatched him to a Pennsylvania regiment that was headed some three hundred miles east.

Now Cecil stared out at the rain and sighed, cradling his wounded arm against his body. They should've listened to him. He should have led the men in and done what had to be done that first night, when Mallory hadn't returned. Now Burden and Adam and the rest were either dead or prisoners, and there was no one left but himself to go after the lieutenant.

If it wasn't already too late.

For a change, the day dawned clear. Sara, lying beside her sleeping husband, watched the sky turn from pewter to silver, and from silver to pearl. She would have to wash again today, for Robert had only the one outfit, which he'd worn all week. Not that she and Becky were in much better state. She hadn't had a new gown since the war began, and she'd had to cut down most of her older ones for Becky, as the child had recently begun shooting up like a weed.

Just like her father, she mused, too snug and warm in the cocoon of quilts and feathers to hurry rising. How strange it seemed to have him back after all this time. Strange and wonderful and—somehow different. Odd that it should take a war, and the separation of more than two years, to make her appreciate a man she had been married to for so many years.

In truth, Sara couldn't remember a time when she hadn't known Robert, although he was several years older than she. He'd told her when they began courting that his mother had died when he was a baby, and no one ever spoke of her. Robert's widowed great-aunt, Abigail Gregory, had lived at the Jones house and looked after father and son for as long as anyone could remember, and goodness knows, Miss Abigail had never been one to gossip. Closemouthed, some called her.

Mean as a half-skint snake, Robert had said once when she'd whipped him for stealing peaches off the Bells' tree. Sara would have given him the whole tree if she'd known he wanted them, but he'd been a grown-up eleven and she'd been only seven, and he'd tried his best to pretend she didn't exist back then.

Robert's father, Adolphus, had died several years before Sara and Robert had married. At sixteen, Sara had been exceedingly flattered when Robert had started paying her court, for he was generally conceded to be the handsomest man in Camden County, and she was no more than passable at best. Everyone had expected him to marry Julia Shaw, who was beautiful and bought all her gowns and bonnets in Norfolk, but then Julia had shocked half the county by running off with the Pritchard boy, and Robert had started waiting for Sara after church every Sunday and walking home with her.

He'd told her right off that he'd never planned on asking Julia to marry him, for she didn't have it in her to make a good farmer's wife. Too spoiled. Too vain.

Sara, on the other hand, knew her way around a barn, and while she might not be beautiful, her face had never curdled a single pan of milk, as far as she knew. More important, she was a worker, not too proud to turn a hand to any task that needed doing. And on a farm, there was never any lack of those!

Sara had never regretted her choice, nor did she think Robert had. He might not have loved her so much when he'd married her, but the love had grown slowly and steadily, even while he'd been gone and she'd thought him dead. And since his return . . .

Well, surely no woman had ever been courted so wondrously as she had this past week, not even on her wedding night!

Reluctantly Sara made to get up just as Robert mumbled something unintelligible in his sleep. She smiled at him, much as she would have smiled at Becky. For all her worries, all the uncertainty of the future, she knew she had never felt closer to complete happiness than she did at this moment, with her precious daughter across the hall in her own tiny bed, and her gentle, strong, handsome husband sleeping safely at her side.

"I've half a notion," she whispered to the sleeping man, "to forget the washing and make you forget all about the war, and going back to your precious old regiment." And I could do it, too, she thought smugly, for hadn't she learned more about the business of loving these past few nights than she'd learned in a lifetime before?

Without quite rousing from sleep, Robert muttered something and rolled over onto his side just as Sara eased the covers back to rise. Unable to resist a parting look at the beautiful naked body that had pleasured her until she could scarcely bear it, she glanced over her shoulder . . . and frowned.

Had it been on the other side? The scar from the time that hateful old bull of Lukey Stevens' had caught him trying to untangle that heifer from the fence?

No, it had definitely been on his right side, because he'd been so sore for weeks afterward that he hadn't been able to swing hammer or hoe without swearing.

But how—?

Sara reached out to touch his flawless skin but held back at the last moment. Instead, she brushed her hair away from her face and peered once more at the area where a deep three-cornered scar should have been.

And wasn't.

* * *

Somehow, she got through the day. In spite of her warnings that it was unsafe, Robert had insisted on dragging her wash boiler out into the yard for her, and toting the wood to build up the fire.

"All right, take in that one load of kindling while you're at it, but then you stay inside that house, Robert Jones, do you hear me? What if a Yank patrol should come by?"

"We'll tell them I'm searching the area for guerillas."

"Ha! The way you talk these days, they'll believe you, too. You sound just like a Yank, yourself."

Robert raked his dark hair back from his face, his brown eyes, so like Becky's, twinkling at his wife's anger. And that was another thing, Sara thought—he never used to laugh at her temper. He always snapped back, and they'd end up not speaking until Sara took the first step to making up.

"Well, anyway," she grumbled, "the Thirty-second can just do without you until I think you're ready to go back. And before you ask, that won't be until I can meet up with Jimmy and he can find some way to smuggle you through the lines."

"I thought you were going to tell them I was your half-witted brother," Robert teased, and she pretended to chase him back inside with her wash-stick.

The truth was, she wouldn't know what to tell anyone, when she didn't know what to think, herself. Robert was . . . Robert.

Wasn't he?

"Of course he is," she mumbled, slivering a chunk of soap into the heating water. Who else could he be?

Surely she knew her own husband, even after two and a half years! Even Becky had recognized him right off, and if a child didn't know her own father, why then, the whole human race might as well crawl back up into a tree.

Becky played noisily after being confined by the rain for three days. Sara kept her close, for though she'd seen no sign of soldiers these past few days, she had seen smoke over to the northeast. Thick, black smoke—the kind that came from a burning house.

"Lord ha' mercy on us all," she whispered as she commenced to poking the sheets down into the boiling water with her wash-stick.

By the time the wash was hung to dry and the tubs emptied and turned down over the fence posts, Sara knew what she was going to do. "Becky, go back inside now and keep your father company until I get back. I've an errand to do."

There followed the usual questions. "What? Why? May I go, too?" And then, "Why not?"

The questions ended when Robert appeared in the door with a greasy cleaning rag. It seemed he had taken apart her father's old rifle, cleaned it, put it back together again after some minor repairs and was now cleaning his own side arm. Becky spun away with no further pleas.

"I'll be back directly," Sara promised, and an unspoken message winged between the two adults.

Sara pushed away her guilt. She knew Robert was anxious to get back to his company. Her own anxiety was on an entirely different matter, but if he thought she was going to meet Jimmy to see about smuggling him through the lines, so much the better. She wasn't

ready to tell him that she was going to see old Miss
Abigail, who had moved out the day Sara had moved
in, claiming she'd done her do for her menfolk, and
that was that. Now she was going back to her own
house and rest a spell, and folks could fancy well leave
her be, thank you!

It was nearly three hours later when Sara let herself
into the kitchen. If it weren't for the fact that her
cheeks were red from walking so far in the cold, she
would have been pale as the sheets hanging on her
clothesline.

Even now she couldn't believe it! Didn't know what
to make of it, even if it were true.

But of course it was true. Abigail Gregory might not
be as sharp as she'd once been, but the record was right
there in the Jones family Bible, which she had taken
with her when she'd moved out.

Robert had a twin. What's more, if what Sara was
beginning to believe was true, he not only *had* a twin—
he *was* his twin!

Despite the late hour, she had lingered for ages on
the way home, wondering what to do now. Her first
impulse had been to charge him with the truth and see
if he denied it. Her next thought had been to take after
him with another chunk of firewood for what he had
done to her.

With her, not to her, she amended, because heaven
knows, he had had her full cooperation.

But why? Had it pleased him to make a fool of his
brother's wife? Rather, his widow? Had he done it out
of hatred for the Rebel brother he had never known?
How long had he hoped to get away with it?

As long as she let him, Sara told herself. And how long would that be, now that she knew the truth? She could face him with it and lose him, or she could pretend she didn't know and keep him for a while longer.

But how long? And to what end? God help her, she was so confused, she didn't know which way to turn!

It was at that moment that she became aware of the voices from the front room. A man's voice, higher pitched than Robert's. Only he wasn't Robert, she reminded herself even as she edged toward the door that separated the kitchen from the short hall that led past the two bedrooms to the front room.

She caught a glimpse of Becky's gingham pinafore, cut down from one of her own gowns. Emma, dressed in a scrap of the same material, dangled by one arm from Becky's hand, and another hand, much larger, harder and darker than the child's, rested on her shoulder.

The same hand that had mapped Sara's body from head to toe with such mind-shattering thoroughness, she reminded herself bitterly.

Taking a step forward, she leaned around to see who else was in the room and then clapped a hand over her mouth. A blue-belly! In her own front room! Dear Lord, how many of them were there? Were they armed?

Easing back, Sara moved silently to the pantry, where she always kept the rifle. It was not there. Evidently Robert—she still couldn't think of him as Rolph—had not put it back when he was done cleaning it. Or perhaps he was holding the Yank captive with it!

Unwilling to take the risk of barging in unarmed, Sara let herself back outside and hurried to the woodpile to select a length of firewood, a strange sense of irony echoing in her mind.

Had an entire week truly passed since she had played this same scene? Had Christmas truly come and gone? Or was this all no more than a dream born of fear and longing and loneliness?

Bracing herself, she stepped up onto the back stoop and reached for the brown china doorknob.

Chapter Six

Rolph was speaking, his voice sounding sharper, deeper. Almost harsh. Instinctively Sara moved to hide herself, careful to make no sound. If he had been playing some cruel game, she would—

"Lieutenant, I wanted to come ba—"

"Then why didn't you, Corporal?" Rolph snapped.

"Well, sir, it was like this," the other voice said. "Burden, he said—"

"Does a private outrank a corporal?"

"No, sir."

"Did I or did I not leave you in charge, with instructions to get started making camp and building the table until I could rejoin you?"

"Yessir, Lieutenant Mallory, you did that, all right."

Lieutenant Mallory?

"Then why the hell didn't you—?"

"Sir, an' begging your pardon, but I didn't wrap my arm up in this rag just to be fashionable. We did like you said, and we waited, and when you didn't show up, why—"

"I didn't show up, boy, because some woman who claims to be my wife split my skull with a length of firewood, and when I finally woke up, I had no more notion of who I was than a tadpole! It didn't come back to me until you burst in through the door, and then I was back at the beginning again.''

The familiar kitchen, with its smell of collard greens and raisin cake seemed to darken and drift away as Sara gripped the door frame to steady herself, her right hand still wrapped tightly around the split of pine. *Some woman?* Some woman who *claimed to be his wife?*

''Corporal, you have to underst—'' Rolph was saying when her fingers lost their grip on the splintery wood. It fell to the floor with a loud thunk.

''Behind you, sir!'' shouted the corporal. Moving swiftly, he shoved the taller man against the wall. Rolph, off balance, nevertheless managed to scoop up Becky and shield her with his body.

''Ouch! Daddy, you hurted me,'' the child wailed, and Sara, hearing her child's voice, was suddenly free of her momentary paralysis.

She rushed into the room to be met by a gleaming Springfield rifle in the hand of a perfect stranger. ''Beggin' your pardon, ma'am, but would you mind lifting both your hands and backing up against that wall?'' the boy asked politely.

Numbly Sara obeyed, her mind racing frantically. He looked to be about Jimmy's age, with Jimmy's open, youthful countenance. But there was nothing at all youthful about the gun in his hand.

''Mama,'' Becky cried.

''Sara! Easy, girl, it's all right,'' said the man she had known as Robert—the man who was also known as Lieutenant Rolph Mallory of the Federal forces.

Rolph deliberately softened his voice, using the same tone he had used so many times to calm a frightened mare. All right? he thought bitterly. Nothing was all right! After the bramble he had blundered into, how could anything ever be all right again?

Cautiously Sara lowered her hands, her eyes going from Becky to Robert—or Rolph, or whatever his name was—to the tense-looking boy in the dark blue uniform, his left arm in a fringed paisley sling that looked suspiciously like a lady's shawl, and his right holding the rifle pointed at her waist. "Who *are* you?"

Rolph started to speak, but the stranger clicked to attention and said, "Corporal Cecil Stanley, madam, come for the lieutenant."

"Lower that damned rifle, boy, before someone gets hurt!" Rolph barked, and the corporal, with an apologetic look, lowered the point an inch, then shrugged and leaned it against the wall.

Becky ducked away from Rolph's hand and hurried to hide herself in her mother's skirt, and Robert—that is, Rolph—looked as if he would prefer to be almost anywhere else in the world than where he was now.

"I'd best explain," he said quietly, and Sara's lips tightened.

"Yes, I think you'd better try." She knew, though. God help her, she knew and wished with all her heart she didn't.

"Wait outside, Corporal."

"But, sir, do you think—"

"Dammit, Cecil, outside! Now!"

The young man backed toward the door, eyeing Sara and her daughter suspiciously, as if expecting one of them to reach for the chunk of firewood the minute his back was turned. Slowly Sara expelled the breath she'd been holding. It was over. It had all been a dream, after all. Now the nightmare would begin.

"Do you want to tell me what happened, or shall I tell you?" she asked tiredly. At her side, Becky looked from one adult to the other, her small face puzzled yet not frightened.

"You knew all along?" Rolph marveled. "Then why did you pretend? Why the hell didn't you tell me?"

"I wasn't pretending. I honestly believed you were—" Her shoulders drooped. Turning to gaze out the window, she lifted a hand to the side of her face, shielding her emotions from him until she could get herself back in hand. No, she hadn't been pretending. Not any of it. And there was the shame, there the part she could never forgive herself for. She should have *known!*

"Sara? Please don't cry."

"I'm not crying, damn you! Becky, go play in your room."

The child clung tighter, her worried gaze going from one to the other, until Rolph knelt and placed a gentle hand on her shoulder. "Please, sweetheart," he said softly. "Your mama and I need to talk privately. It's nothing you need worry your pretty pigtails about, I promise you."

By the time Becky had closed the door behind her and Rolph had got to his feet again, Sara had her emotions more or less under control. "Why did you come here?" she asked despairingly. "Did you think that whatever had belonged to Robert would be yours now?"

"Sara, you have to understand—" Rolph began, but she waved him to silence, her eyes wild with grief and a pain that seemed to go beyond grief.

"No, *you* have to understand! If it's the farm you want, then take it! I won't fight with you. But Becky's mine, and if we never ever see you again, that will be a hundred years too soon! Just go back to wherever you came from and leave us be!"

"Please listen to me, Sara—"

She continued as if he hadn't even spoken. "Once this mess is over and done with, you can come back and claim your inheritance." She was shaking by now, her work-hardened hands clasped at her waist. "If there's anything left to claim," she added bitterly.

A frown drew his fierce dark brows together, as if he hadn't understood a single word she'd said. Ha! He hadn't counted on her discovering his little game, had he? Pretending to lose his memory. Pretending he didn't know about Robert! The despicable creature, had he no sense of honor at all?

But in all fairness, Sara reminded herself, Robert had never let on that he had a twin, either. Could it be—? Could it possibly be that, memory loss aside, *neither of them had known of the other?*

Oh, she didn't know what to think! Perhaps he'd never intended to do more than pay his respects to his brother's family, and things had just gotten out of hand.

"Sara, please listen to me," he pleaded.

Still shivering, Sara clasped her shoulders, her eyes too full to see more than a blur of color. Robert's old blue shirt. Robert's trousers. She drew in a deep, shuddering breath and blotted her eyes. "All right, I'll listen. For Becky's sake I'll do that much, for I reckon you're her blood kin, but for me, I want you to know that I'll never stop hating you for what you've done.''

His brown eyes—Robert's eyes, Becky's eyes—looked tortured, and Sara steeled herself against their spell. Even the timbre of his voice was disarming, for heaven help her, it affected her in a way that Robert's voice never had.

"Sara, I swear to you that I'm as mystified as you are by what happened. The child seemed to know me, and you . . .'' He let it drop when he saw the hot color rush to stain her pale cheeks. "And what's this about an inheritance? Are we kin, then, your Robert and I?''

Skeptically she let her eyes play over his familiar features. Robert's features. Now that she knew, of course, she could pick out the small discrepancies: Rolph's slightly more angular jaw, the intensity of his dark, liquid eyes. "You honestly don't know?''

"They say every man has a double somewhere in the world. I was told once by a relative that my father came from somewhere in northeastern North Carolina, and that his name was Jones, but how many Joneses do you think there are in the world? How likely was it that I'd stumble into the house of my own relatives? God, Sara, how could I know, when I didn't even know my own name until a few years ago?''

"Rolph Mallory Jones,'' Sara supplied.

"I grew up as Rolph Mallory. My mother resumed her family's name when we moved back home to Boston. It was only after she died that I learned about my father.''

"And your brother,'' she reminded him bitterly, only to watch the color drain from his face. "Rober—

Rolph?'' she whispered, ''perhaps you'd better sit down.'' Trickster or not, he had been injured by her own hand. Head wounds could be peculiar. ''Sit over there,'' she directed, indicating the walnut settee, and then she took her own place on the mule-eared chair beside the hearth.

A door opened behind them and Becky peered out, eyes fearful, cheeks streaked with tears. Sara opened her arms, the child dashed across the room and climbed up onto her lap, and Sara wrapped her arms around the small replica of the two men she had loved most in the world—Robert and his twin brother. And God help her, she loved this one still, no matter what he had done.

''Rolph, didn't your mother even tell you you had a brother?'' At the look on his face, she thought she had truly done him in. Perhaps she could have broached the subject more gently, but gentleness was the last thing she felt like offering.

Besides, there was that impatient young blue-belly waiting on the porch. She could hear him pacing. On every other turn, he peered in through the window, as if fearing she would suddenly leap up and begin to bludgeon his lieutenant again. ''Rolph, this afternoon I went to visit Abigail Gregory. She's your father's aunt—your own great-aunt. Miss Abigail's close to ninety years old now, but her mind is still sharp as a carpet tack.'' At least as far as the past was concerned, it was.

''And she told you that I had a brother?''

''A twin. Robert Henry. He was listed first in the family Bible, so I suppose he was the eldest. You were both born on the fourth day of November in the year of 1834, right here in this very house. Likely in the very bed where—'' She swallowed hard. Before her eyes, Rolph seemed to age, his face going gray where before it had only been pale.

Leaning forward, Sara made to catch him if he threatened to lose consciousness and slide off onto the floor. ''Rolph, it's true. It was written right there—the births and marriages and deaths of your great-grandfather, Lemuel, your grandfather, Josiah, your father, Adolphus—Robert's marriage to me, and Becky's birth. Miss Abigail said your mother tried her best to get your father to move north and go to work for her father, but Mr. Adolphus knew he could never abide working in a mill, being cooped up inside all day.''

Sara waited for a sign that he heard her, for the look on his face was so strange. After a while she went on, not knowing what else to do. ''Your mother never took to life down here. She didn't like animals or the dust that blew in when it was dry, or the long steamy summers. Miss Abigail says she missed all the paved streets and parks and fine shops, and all the fancy social doings. She cried all the time, and that made your father angry, and then one day when your father had gone to Suffolk to buy a bull, she took you and left.''

''What about—?''

''Robert? Your father had taken Robert with him, but your mother kept you behind, claiming you'd been fretful and might be coming down with a fever.'' With sudden insight, Sara knew why the woman had chosen to take Rolph and leave Robert behind. As the eldest twin, Robert had been his father's heir, but Rolph had been her baby, the younger of the two, even if only by minutes.

In spite of herself, Sara began to thaw toward the man who had inadvertently taken her husband's place in her heart. He was leaning forward, elbows braced on his knees, his face buried in his hands. "Dear God," he whispered.

The door opened a crack, and the young corporal poked his head inside. "Lieutenant? Everything all right?"

Sara glanced at him distractedly at the same time that Rolph lifted his head, his face still working, and dismissed the boy with a curt command. "Outside, Cecil. I'll join you in a few minutes."

"Yessir," the corporal said, shrugging.

"Rolph...why?"

"Why?"

"Why this particular house if you really didn't know? And why this pretense? Even if you'd lost your memory—even if you didn't know about Robert, why did you have to—"

"To try to take his place in your life?"

Wordlessly she nodded. The rest she could understand—not all of it, but enough. What she could neither forgive nor forget was his trying to take Robert's place in her bed and in her heart. Because in both cases he had succeeded far more than he could ever know.

"Sara, I swear to you I didn't know. I remember now that my detail was in the area checking out rumors of guerillas. We'd visited several houses, and yours was next on the list of those suspected of being connected to one of the guerillas. Then I met Becky, and she was such a taking little thing—she wanted a table for Christmas, and I reckon maybe I thought it might help make up for some of the..." He swallowed hard. "Anyhow, I sent my men on a scouting mission to round up supplies and build it for her."

Becky looked up at this, interest replacing the uneasiness on her face, and Sara waited for him to continue. So that was the story of the table. She'd thought perhaps Jimmy had brought it, although as far as she knew, whittling was the extent of his woodworking ability.

"I stayed behind because I didn't like to leave the child alone. Ours wasn't the only detail in the area, and I was afraid—well, anyhow, you came home and you know what happened next. When you called me Robert, I had no reason to believe it wasn't my name. After all, the child had accepted me. When I woke up lying on the floor with a knot the size of a cannonball on the back of my head, all I could think of at first was the pain. You were calling me Robert, and Becky was calling me Daddy. What was I to do? I accepted it."

He broke off, raking a hand impatiently through his tumbled hair, and in the process, surreptitiously wiping his glittering eyes. "Oh, hell, Sara, maybe it all happened because I wanted it to, I don't know! By then I'd come to despise the fighting, even though I still firmly believe in the cause. What made it even more hellish was the thought that I might have family somewhere in the area. I never went on patrol but what I didn't wonder if one day I might end up meeting a cousin across the barrel of a rifle."

"I expect you already have, but I'll not tell you more than that."

"I wouldn't ask you to," he replied, tacitly acknowledging the fact that they were now on different sides of a mortal conflict. "But, Sara, try to understand, I never set out to deceive you. All I know is that I woke up with a splitting headache and when you called me Robert, I accepted that as my name."

"And all the rest?" she asked quietly.

Rolph allowed his gaze to play over her now-familiar features, taking in the small firm chin, the clarity of her large gray eyes, the soft untidiness of her light brown hair, and he sighed. "And all the rest," he conceded. Including my heart and soul, for all the good it will ever do me, he added silently.

Once more they were interrupted by the agitated corporal. "Sir, if you don't mind, I don't feel real safe, standing out here on the porch in broad daylight, not with the swamp so close. For all I know, a dozen of them web-footed devils could be lining me up in their sights right this very minute."

"I'm coming, boy! Wait in the woodshed if you're afraid!"

"Afraid!" the corporal sputtered, but Rolph had risen and quietly shut the door in his face.

"Becky, would you mind very much giving your— Uncle Rolph a goodbye hug?"

"You're not my daddy anymore?" the child asked, her eyes as large as chestnuts.

"No, sweetheart, I'm your uncle, but uncles are good things to have, too." Were they? His own had been a wicked old skinflint who had allowed him to grow up believing a lie.

"Do uncles read little girls stories and play tea-party?"

"They do all that and more. Uncles write letters, and send presents and come to visit when they're invited."

"Mama and me'll invite you, won't we, Mama?" Now securely wrapped in Rolph's embrace, she looked to her mother for corroboration.

"Sometimes that's not possible, honey," Sara said gently. "Now go and get Emma dressed for supper, Becky. I'll have it on the table directly."

"Is Uncle Rolph staying to supper?"

"No, pun'kin, it'll just be you and Emma and me, the way it's always been."

"But you'll come back, won't you, Da—Uncle Rolph?" the child asked anxiously, and Rolph, meeting Sara's level gaze, nodded slowly.

"Yes, sweetheart, I'll be back," he said to the mother as much as the child.

Alone with his brother's widow, some of his assurance fled. "Sara? May I come back?"

"Don't promise her things you have no intention of delivering!" she hissed.

"This war won't last forever," Rolph said grimly.

"No, it won't. The sooner you Yanks go back home and leave us be, the better I'll like it."

"Slavery can't be allowed to continue, Sara."

"No? Well, for your information, I never owned a slave, and neither did Robert, but that didn't keep him from dying in some filthy Yankee prison. As for that, I'll vow there's many a Yankee shipowner who's lined his pockets in the trade, and none the wiser."

"Sara, I don't want to fight with you. There's been slavery in every part of the world for as long as there've been men. Still is, in most. At least in this country, we have a chance to end it."

"If you don't kill us all first, or tax us into our graves!"

"Dammit, woman, there's right and wrong on both sides, and good men and wicked wearing gray as well as blue! That doesn't have anything to do with us, Sara, and you damned well know it!"

Sara was devastated, but she was far too proud to let him see what he had done to her. "You'll want to take your pistol in case you meet any wicked Rebels along the way. I'll go and fetch it for you. Where did you put it, back under the flour bin?" She had to get rid of him before the dam broke, because once the tears began to flow, they might never cease.

Rolph caught her as she went to move past him, swinging her around to slam her up against his hard body. "Dammit, Sara, would you *listen to me?* I'm not your Robert! I can't help that. But I swear before God that I love you as much as he ever did—more than I've ever loved anyone in my entire life. I promise you, you've not seen the last of me!"

Sara stood still as a stump in his embrace. Her heart nearly stopped beating when he ground his mouth into hers, lifting his lips after long moments had passed to swear at her under his breath.

"Stubborn woman," he muttered against her wet cheek. "Maddening, hardheaded female, if you think we're done, you're daft. I'm coming back here the minute I'm free!"

"I won't be here," Sara said flatly.

Rolph's arms tightened, and she was nearly overwhelmed by the clean masculine scent of his body, so familiar, so very dear to her after the week just passed.

"You'll be here," he told her. "And I'll be back. And that's a promise, Sara. Now, kiss me proper before that damned young hotblood comes in here and drags me off."

And to her everlasting shame, she did. Lifting her face, Sara parted her lips just as Rolph covered them with his own. All the pent-up loneliness of the past few years, all the love, the longing and the passion of a lifetime, newly awakened, was his for the claiming, and they both knew it.

Finally, his unsteady hands putting her away from him, Rolph lifted his head. "I have to go now, Sara, but know this—your house is safe. I'll pass the word, and you'll not be bothered. And as soon as I can, I'll be back."

Chapter Seven

At the door, Rolph paused and looked back. She was still standing there, her back impossibly straight. Even as he watched, she turned her head and lifted her hand to the side of her face again in that singularly telling gesture. He couldn't see her tears, didn't need to. The brief glimpse he'd caught would be etched on his heart until the end of time.

Taking one last look around the small room, Rolph memorized its shabby warmth—the lopsided Christmas tree that Becky refused to allow them to take down. The hearth with the bellows, the battered copper kettle and the poker that had been bent and straightened too many times.

There was the small round table where Sara's workbasket stayed, and the smaller one that had been liberated from some poor devil's dining room and cut down for Becky's Emma. Beside the hearth was Sara's favorite mule-eared chair... and his brother's armchair.

With a sharp and wrenching sense of loss, Rolph quietly closed the door. "I'm ready, Corporal."

As if sensing his lieutenant's mood, the young soldier fell in silently behind him. Not until they'd left the house did he speak. "Uh—sir, it might be better if you was to hand over your gun. Meaning no disrespect, but if we was to come up on a patrol, and you not in uniform, there wouldn't be no trouble if it looked like you was my prisoner, sir."

Numbly Rolph complied. What difference did it make? What difference did anything make now?

Inside the house, Sara stared at the cup at Rolph's place at the table. It still held the dregs of the coffee he'd had earlier. There was a smudge of grease on the handle, likely from cleaning the guns. His lips had tasted the rim, just as they had tasted . . .

She reached for the willowware cup and held it against her breast, dry-eyed and determined. She would not weep. Dammit, she would not! She had grieved for a mother, a father and a husband, and that was all the grief she had to spare.

January turned out mild after all. There were Yankee patrols about, but none ventured near the farm. Sara put it down to luck, refusing to credit Rolph with keeping his word.

Annie's youngest came down with a bad case of boils, and Sara took over the last of her sugar to treat him with, knowing Annie would've done the same for her had it been Becky.

February brought rain, a dusting of snow and the confirmation of Sara's worst fear. Worst fear and secret delight. Lord knows it was the very last thing she needed. She'd be shunned and whispered about, and Becky would likely bear the brunt of it, not understanding her mother's shame. Yet, with all that, she couldn't deny the small thrill she felt whenever she laid her hands on her still-flat belly and thought of the tiny life sheltered there.

"Robert, you'd have loved him, too," she whispered as she turned a rope tied on to the gatepost for Becky to jump one mild morning. Surely he would have understood that she'd had no way of knowing until it was too late, she told herself.

More than likely, she thought a week later as she waited for the persistent nausea to pass, he would have the stamp of the Jones men on him, same as Becky did. Dark eyes, dark hair, angular features. It would be up to James Edwin to populate the county with sandy-haired, gray-eyed little Bells once this awful war was over.

The tide was turning against the Confederacy. They had lost so many men, and those who remained were hungry, ill clothed and, as often as not, fought barefooted even in the bitterest winter weather.

Oh, the Yanks had food and clothing aplenty, but with their stranglehold on every port and waterway, they made sure the South went begging. The gristmills, those that hadn't been destroyed, lay idle, for who could grow corn with no seed and no mules to plow? Flour, even when it could be had, was upwards of two hundred dollars a barrel, and shoes were not available at all, even for children who outgrew a pair before the soles were worn.

Sara found herself resenting friends who had food only because they'd agreed to work for the blasted blue-bellies. Including her best friend, Annie Walston!

But then Annie got herself arrested, and Sara forgot her resentment. Several weeks before, the Yanks had decided that the big old Walston homeplace, situated right on the river, with its own boat dock and all, would make a mighty fine Camden headquarters. Given no choice but to agree or pack up her children and leave, Annie agreed to cook, clean, wash and mend for the Yanks in exchange for food and two small, unheated rooms on the third floor for all eight Walstons.

Sara hadn't seen her since then, and she'd worried about them all, especially Margaret, who at thirteen was shy and pretty and turning into a young lady. And then nine-year-old Matthew had come racing into the yard, breathless and big-eyed. "Mama's gone! Can you help her, Miss Sara? They took 'er away yes'dy morning, an' they won't tell us when we kin have her back," the boy had panted, his eyes enormous in his pinched face.

Sara felt sick, and it had nothing to do with the changes in her body. Her first thought was of Jimmy. Could the Guard free Annie before she was forced to suffer all manner of indignities?

But with young Matthew, the spitting image of his late father, pulling on her hand and pleading with his eyes, Sara knew she couldn't wait for the chance to contact her brother. Somehow, she was going to have to tackle a whole houseful of blue-bellies on her own. Could she take on a whole detachment with Papa's old gun?

Did she have any choice?

Her mind flew to Becky. What would happen to her? Her next thought was for the precious new life she carried. *Damn you, Rolph Mallory Jones!* "Matthew, you stay here with Becky. If I'm not back by dark, you take her and go to Miss Abigail over by the burnt mill, you hear me?''

Sara set out, mentally rehearsing her arguments. Even Yankees had mothers, sisters, wives and daughters, didn't they? They were men, like all other men, even if they did happen to be on the wrong side of this bloody damned war.

She had worked up enough rage to ride roughshod over an entire regiment by the time she arrived, gun in hand, only to see Margaret riding the youngest Walston on her hip and hugging Annie in the front yard by the Cape Jasmine bush, under the watchful eye of an armed blue-belly who didn't look a day over fifteen.

''Sara, are you all right?'' Annie called, eyeing the scarred old squirrel gun.

''Me! The question is, are *you* all right? Matthew said you'd been arrested.''

''He's over to your place then?''

Sara nodded, warily eyeing the armed guard, who seemed much more interested in Margaret than he did in the dangerous criminal, Annie. ''He came for me. I left him with Becky and told him if I wasn't back directly, to take her and go to Miss Abigail's. Are you sure—?''

''It's all right, all settled. Send him on home, will you, Sara?''

''You're *sure?*'' Sara had been all charged up to tackle the entire Union army. Now she felt let down, not to mention slightly foolish.

''I'm sure. We'll be all right, Sara. How are you and Becky faring?''

"We're not starving. Yet," Sara replied, staring accusingly at the young soldier, who had the temerity to blush. To *blush!*

"Lord, deliver us," she swore as she strode off into the dusk. "Women fighting children!"

Not until several weeks later did she learn that it hadn't been the commandeering of her house, nor the endless hours of cooking, cleaning and washing for a houseful of strange men—nor even the ruination of her hardwood floors and her fine mahogany furniture by all those damn Yankee boots and spurs, that had brought about Annie's rebellion.

It had been her dishes. When a bunch of the younger soldiers had discovered a forgotten case of her late husband's liquor in the woodshed, drunk themselves stupid and commenced to throwing her precious wedding dishes into the air for target practice, Annie had had enough. Armed with only a skillet and a cooking fork, she had charged the lot of them, managing to inflict several serious wounds before she'd been brought under control.

"Lord," Sara murmured on her knees by the bed that night, "I know you don't have time to oversee every pesky detail, but couldn't you please look after the children? It's not their fault we older folks have made such a botch of things."

The fourth day of March brought the last and the prettiest snow of the season. Nearly an inch fell before the skies cleared, and Becky managed to roll up two hard knots of icy, muddy slush into what she called a snowman. Sara gave her a pie tin for a hat and slogged on out to the barn with a handful of cracked corn for the animals. She had only two hens and Cow left. Jimmy had come for the mule, and she'd surrendered it willingly rather than have him to feed.

Poor Jimmy... wherever he was tonight, she hoped he had a good warm fire and a belly full of liberated Yankee beans and bacon.

By July, every family in Camden County had suffered losses. Sara's own cousin Jack Bell, a member of the Home Guard, had been shot down in cold blood while he crossed a log footbridge, and Annie's brother, poor Sticky Jarvis, had been murdered on the road to Indian Island, his body tied to a tree and left to hang there. The worst of it was that most of the killing was being done by Buffaloes!

The Guards had quickly retaliated against one of the most notorious of the Buffaloes when they'd caught him at the Going-Over Place near Sandy Hook. They'd dispatched another one near the Casey Oak, but the losses on both sides brought grief, and as often, shame, to their own neighbors.

On and on it went, the killing. Yank against Confederate, Buffalo against Confederate—strong spirits against the lot of them, for few on either side could resist the escape provided by liquor.

Sara was far too worried over Jimmy to concern herself with what her neighbors thought of her condition. She'd considered telling them that Robert had been paroled and come home, and then returned to fight again, only to be killed in battle. No one would ever believe the truth, even if she'd found the courage to tell it.

But with one thing after another—barn roofs caving in, cows drowning when a riverbank collapsed—stray bullets killing the Snowdens' goat and Margaret Walston marrying that Yankee soldier, and her only thirteen years old and a Confederate, to boot, why Sara's condition was the least of anyone's worries.

Seven weeks went by with no word from Jimmy. Sara found herself weeping more than was healthy. She cried when the last of the raisins turned wormy, cried when a windowpane fell out and broke. Cried when the roof leaked, wetting the last of the leather-britches she'd had strung in the attic and causing them to ruin.

Becky had patted her on the back and said, "There, there, it's not so bad but what the sun won't shine tomorrow, Mama."

How many times had Sara's mother said those very words to her? How many times had she said them to her own daughter? So she'd cried some more, but she'd laughed, too.

At night she cried over Rolph. The Camden Home Guard was forced to secrecy by the large number of Federal troops quartered in the area—she knew that. Even so, if anything had happened to Jimmy, she would hear eventually. But if anything happened to Rolph, she would never know about it.

She told herself that the man wasn't worth a single tear, that he was a blasted blue-belly, a usurper and a pretender, no matter that he had lost his memory—told herself that he'd found a soft bed and a willing woman and thought to take advantage of them both, but none of it did any good. She would grow still, one hand stealing over her rounded belly as she recalled each look, each touch, each precious, never-to-be-forgotten kiss.

Becky grew taller. At nearly six, she was reading quite well under Sara's instructions. Sara grew enormous. She had finally gotten over her anger so that only a deep sadness remained, and now even that, thanks to the baby, seemed warm and distant.

The fighting that had raged around them for a while moved on, yet with enemy forces in possession of the whole northeastern part of the state, no one felt really safe. There were still skirmishes between the Yanks and the Guard, and never any telling where the next one would take place.

In the first few weeks after Rolph had left, Becky had asked several times a day if Uncle Rolph had written her a letter yet, until Sara finally explained that with travel so uncertain, letters often got lost. Most likely, she told her daughter, Uncle Rolph had written a dozen letters, and they were lying forgotten somewhere in a way station.

She didn't believe it, not for a single moment. Tall, handsome Northern men like Rolph Jones—or Lieutenant Mallory, as his corporal had called him—didn't give a second thought to dirt-poor Southern widows whose best gown was a faded, mended thing that had lost all shape and color, and whose hands were hard as a hickory hoe handle.

Pretty words and false promises. She knew all about those, as what woman didn't? Robert had dealt in pretty words when he'd come courting, too. When a man needed a woman in his bed and in his kitchen, pretty words were a cheap enough price to pay.

But for all that, Sara was no longer bitter. She had Becky, didn't she? And now she would have the child just under her apron, who kicked like a mule, keeping her awake far into the night, until it was all she could do to drag herself out of bed come morning.

On the morning of September the eleventh, Sara sent Becky after Annie. In truth, she'd thought to before now, for she was as big as a sow in a watermelon patch. For two days, she'd had a low backache, and that morning, when she'd gone out to feed Cow, her water had broke, scaring poor Becky half to death.

"It's nothing to fret over, pun'kin. You remember when Cow had her calf, don't you?" But Becky didn't. She'd been too small at the time. A sharp pain caused Sara to catch her breath. She hung on until it passed and then sent Becky on her way, cautioning her not to dawdle. "Just tell Annie I said it's time, and then you stay with Margaret until I send for you, you hear?" Margaret was increasing, too. Her soldier husband had left, promising to return once the war was over.

Sara had bitten her tongue to keep from offering her opinion of that particular faradiddle. Leastwise, Annie had her house to herself now, for the regiment had moved on, some said to Currituck Courthouse, some said back to South Mills.

Meanwhile, Sara bore the fierce pains, thinking of names. She considered Adolphus, after Rolph's father, or Abner, after her own. Of course, it might be a girl, in which case she'd decided to name it Nancy after her own mother.

Or she could call him Robert. Robert Henry... or maybe Walter.

In the end, she chose both Robert Henry and Walter Mallory.

Rolph propped his crutch against the wall and eyed the door on the other side of the room. He could make it. He damned well knew he could! He hadn't fought half the doctors in the Union army to keep them from hacking the damned thing off just to drag it around like a blasted log!

One step—and then another. He swayed, recovered his balance and bit his tongue to keep from crying out at the pain. A few more feet and he'd be halfway across the room. Twelve feet. That would be a record without the crutch.

He made it all the way to the leather wing chair before the damned thing buckled under him. "More than half, Sara," he murmured. "Maybe, just maybe one of these days..."

And then, sprawled in the chair, well out of reach of his custom-made crutch, he yelled for the ancient butler who'd been a fixture at the Mallory mansion for as long as Rolph could remember.

"Carruthers! Where the hell are you, man? Bring me my brandy! I've earned it!"

Sara wept when she opened the box. It was four days until Christmas in the year of '64, a full year to the day since Rolph had burst into her life. She was furious, hurt, excited and hopeful again, and she'd sworn never to hope.

"Is it from Uncle Rolph?" Becky asked excitedly.

Sara nodded. ''I expect so, pun'kin. I don't know who else would be sending us a Christmas parcel, do you?''

Wisely Becky refrained from mentioning Sandy Claus. She was older now. A big sister, in fact. Big sisters knew about things like that.

Sara lifted out two flat boxes containing the finest kid gloves, one pair in a woman's size, the other only slightly too large for Becky's small hands. There was a length of silk in a wonderful sea green color, and another in bright red, both finer than anything Sara had ever owned. There was a box of candies from a store in Boston, and a jar of scented cream that was ''guaranteed to soften and beautify the complexion,'' and to ''remove ugly liver spots like magic.''

Sara laughed through her tears. How on earth had he got it through? Mail was impossible these days, much less boxes like this! Truly, he must have bribed Mr. Lincoln himself!

''Oh, Rolph,'' she whispered. ''A few lines just to let me know you're all right would've been more than I'd hoped for.''

But there was no letter, not so much as a single word. And so Sara was left to wonder why he had bothered to send anything at all if he didn't intend to keep his promise.

''What's wrong, Mama?''

''Nothing, honey. I think I hear the boys waking. You go throw a handful of scratch to the chickens while I get them up, will you?''

Chapter Eight

1865

Another Christmas passed. Grant's Federal forces, having left Atlanta in ruins, set out for Savannah, leaving in the wake a trail of devastation unlike anything this country has ever known. After taking Savannah, he burned and plundered his way north, through both of the Carolinas.

By March, the South had been bludgeoned to its knees. It would survive, but it might never fully recover. Sara's only hope was to hang on with enough strength to rebuild on the ashes of the past, for the sake of her children, if not herself.

Becky had grown tall for her age, and far too thin, a result of too little food for too long. However, she remained a cheerful child. From time to time she would take out her length of red silk, admire it and then fold it back into the trunk, along with Sara's piece. There was no thread to sew either gown, much less lace for trim, and besides, as she told her mother, she would far rather wait until Uncle Rolph came back, so he could see it, too.

Emma finally lost her mended leg and Jimmy replaced them both with a pair whittled from cedar. Cleverly articulated with wooden pegs at knee and hip, the doll could now sit properly at her table.

Jimmy, forced out of the Guards when a minnie ball had torn through his left arm, leaving it largely useless, was cautiously courting Margaret Walston, whose Yank husband had died in Libby prison in Richmond about the same time Margaret had lost the baby she carried.

The twins, Henry and Walter, took their first stumbling steps, Henry first. He made it all the way to the hearth before tumbling and cutting his chin. Walter grabbed hold of Becky's table, which quite naturally overturned. Instead of crying, he proceeded to gnaw on one of the mahogany legs.

With Jimmy's help, Sara butchered Cow and they divided the meat. She would miss the poor creature, but Cow was too old ever to freshen again, even if a bull could be found. On the second day of April Sara traded Papa's rifle for a sack of dried corn, a rooster and three hens, two for laying, one for setting. Life went on.

Word got through that Grant was on his way to meet up with Sherman. Lee retreated westward, hoping to join forces with Johnston, but it was already too late. Realizing that prolonging the fight would only mean a useless sacrifice of lives, Lee wrote to Grant to arrange the terms of surrender.

And then, finally, it was over. The South lay in ruins. Families on both sides had suffered devastating losses, but particularly the South. And particularly North Carolina, which had lost more men than any other Confederate state in a cause that many of her sons had never truly believed in.

As for Sara, her hope resurged despite all reason. Rolph had said he loved her. He had promised to return. It all seemed a lifetime ago, yet she couldn't look at a single one of the three children without seeing his dark eyes, his angular jaw.

Robert she mourned afresh, but it was Rolph her heart ached for each night as she lay awake and stared into the darkness, unconsciously listening for the thunder of distant gunfire.

Oh, she had gone through every argument a hundred times or more. He was a Yank. At first she had told herself that the risk of being caught in Confederate territory, no matter that it had been occupied by his own forces for much of the conflict, was too great.

Or he had been taken prisoner, and for some reason, never parolled. Or having been parolled, he had been forced to return to his home for the duration of the war.

Oh, yes, Sara knew all the reasons why he might have stayed away for more than two years, including a reason that her mind refused to accept. He could *not* have been killed. She would have known. Somewhere deep inside her, where logic ended and instinct took over, she would have known if he were dead.

A mile from the house, Rolph got down and looped the reins over a cypress branch. He had ridden too far. Should've taken a carriage, but dammit, he refused to go to her an invalid this time! If he couldn't make the journey under his own power—and that of his roan gelding, Moses—he wouldn't make it at all. It wasn't a matter of pride, he assured himself. It was more a matter of consideration. Common decency had kept him from writing to her, from any contact at all outside that one Christmas parcel, until he was damned sure he could take care of her and Becky.

Flexing his leg several times, Rolph inhaled the pungent fragrance of evergreens and swamp. Through the bare cypress branches he caught a glimpse of moonlight reflected on the dark, still waters of the Pasquotank River. There was not even a hint of frost in the air. He'd left snow on the ground back in Boston.

Stiffly he remounted and turned south along the Shiloh Road.

Instantly awake, Sara sat up in bed and listened, her heart pounding in her throat. For one wild moment she was terrified, but then she reminded herself that the fighting was over.

"The henhouse," she whispered, sliding out of bed and reaching for the shawl that hung over the bedpost. She and Jimmy had just finished the new henhouse, but she was by no means certain it was proof against racoons, stray dogs or even the hungry stragglers that roamed the countryside, looking for work or food or just a place to curl up and rest for a little while.

Instinctively she turned toward the pantry before remembering that Papa's gun was no longer there. Instead, she reached for the broom, and was halfway to the back door when she heard it again. First the stomp and whuffle of a horse, then a low voice, and then hesitant footsteps on the front porch.

Silently she hurried through to the front of the house, wondering if in the darkness, a broom handle could pass for a gun. Perhaps she'd do better to go back for a skillet and a cooking fork. They'd served Annie well enough.

She made to turn, and the broom handle whacked the corner of the door. She froze.

"Sara?"

The voice was deep, male, without a hint of a drawl. That didn't necessarily mean—

There was surely no reason to stop breathing, no reason at all for her heart to set up such a ruckus.

"Sara, are you awake in there?"

A thousand years from now she would still remember the way he looked, standing so stiffly in her doorway, as if uncertain of his welcome. As if presenting himself for inspection. By the time she had come to her senses enough to reach out and pull him inside the house, tears were running freely down Sara's cheeks. The cold night air cut through her flannel gown and shawl as if she were naked, and her breath came out in little clouds of vapor.

An eternity passed before she remembered to close the door. While he stood there, she lit a lamp and poked up the fire, hiding her face until she could gain control of herself.

"If you want me to go, you've only to say the word," Rolph told her, his voice devoid of any emotion.

Sara was struck anew by how much he resembled his twin. Oh, they weren't truly identical. Put them side by side and the small differences would have been easily discernable, yet it never entered her mind that this was Robert, come back after five years. Her heart would have known the difference even if her eyes played her false.

"What are you—I mean why are you . . . ?" Hardly a hospitable greeting, but she dare not let herself hope too soon. "I mean, were you only passing through?" she whispered.

"If you want me to."

Oh, dear Lord, he was so beautiful! He looked older, yes, and thinner. There were new lines in his face, and his eyes shone with an intensity that seemed to burn right into her soul.

Sara's heart had never been so full—nor so uncertain. If he had returned only to leave her again she would die, no two ways about it. The heart would go right out of her.

"My horse is tied up out front. I, uh—didn't unsaddle him yet, so if you want me to go, you've only to say so."

"You could put him in the barn. There's no hay, but Jimmy cut some sedge grass, and I could spare a handful of dried corn. I—would you like some coffee? Something to eat? I expect you're hungry. How far have you come, Rolph? Are you just—passing through?" she asked again.

Rolph was achingly aware of the question behind her words, just as he was achingly aware of everything else about her. The way her hair slid out of her nighttime braid. The way her gray eyes could look shadowed one moment and flash with warm golden lights the next. Her face was thinner, her breasts fuller, her mouth still more tempting than the sweetest fruit he had ever tasted.

"Sara, I—" he began.

"Rolph, I—" she said at the same time, and then they were in each other's arms, Sara laughing and weeping and Rolph praying his leg wouldn't give out on him before he could get her over to the settee.

Shyness set in once they were seated. They both commenced speaking at once again, both laughed, and then Rolph laid his hand over her mouth, extended his stiff leg to ease the pain and turned to face her. "Sara, hear me out, and then if you want me to go, you've only to say so. I'll understand, and I'll never bother you again, although from time to time I would like to see Becky, if you wouldn't mind. After all, she's my closest kin." His gaze strayed to the corner where the Christmas tree stood. Like the one he remembered, it was slightly crooked. As Sara would later explain, the same Yanks who had delivered him to her doorstep had stolen her toolbox and never returned it, and she was still making do with her grandfather's old dogwood mallet.

"No, Rolph."

A light seem to go out of his eyes. "No?" he repeated softly.

"She's not your closest kin."

It took him a moment, and then Sara saw him wither before her eyes. "Robert's back, then? I'm glad, Sara."

Glad wasn't the way he sounded, Sara thought, resisting the urge to gather him into her arms the way she often did her children. Their sons. "Robert didn't come back. What I'd been told was true. He was taken prisoner at Fort Hatteras and died of his wounds on the way to prison."

"Then who—?"

Sara rose and took his hand. Puzzled, Rolph stood and followed her across to the smaller of the two bedrooms. It was only then that Sara noticed his pronounced limp. Several things fell into place in that moment, but there would be time for that later. First he had to meet his sons. If she'd dared, she would have kept them secret until she knew if he could love her for herself, but she could never be so selfish. Whether or not he still wanted her, Rolph deserved to know that he was no longer quite so alone in the world.

On one side of the room, Becky lay sleeping on her stomach, her head half-hidden under a pillow. It was the way she always slept, and Sara thought it might be so she wouldn't hear any sounds of gunfire in the night. Come summertime, she was going to have to break her of the habit, but for now it did no harm. For a long time Rolph gazed down at her, and then he laid a hand ever so lightly on the braid that dangled over the edge of the narrow bed.

Sara covered his hand with hers and turned him toward the wide crib. She felt him stiffen, felt his fingers tighten convulsively on hers. "Sara?" he whispered.

She smiled, the light from the lamp just outside the door seemed to glow right through her eyes. "I named them Walter Mallory and Robert Henry. I hope that's all right."

Henry was stretched out across the foot of the cradle, limbs spread wide, a wooden pig his Uncle Jimmy had carved clutched in one fat fist. Walter was on his belly, his bottom reared up in the air. He sucked twice on his thumb without waking, and Sara adjusted the covers. She'd made sleeping suits of old blankets, finding it impossible to keep them covered, and already they were threatening to burst through the seams.

Silently she slipped out to start a pot of coffee brewing, leaving Rolph to get acquainted with his sons.

Before the coffee was even ready he rejoined her, his dense lashes glistening with moisture. Pulling out a chair, he straddled it, extending his right leg under the table. "When?" he asked, and Sara quirked an eyebrow.

"Can't you guess?" She set out a plate of cold corn cakes, a pitcher of wild honey and a saucer for dipping.

"September?"

She nodded and poured the coffee. Still looking slightly dazed, he asked, "Who? I mean, how?"

"Rolph, I'm pretty sure some things are the same, North or South. Henry was born just before midnight on the eleventh, Walter just after on the twelfth."

"God, I can't believe it." Absently he bit into a corn cake. Sara happened to know he detested the things, but it was all she had to offer at the moment. Tomorrow, if she had to beg, borrow or steal, she was going to find some white flour for biscuits!

"I won't give them up, you know," she said softly. It had to be said. "I'll share them, but I'll never give them up."

Stricken, he stared at her. "You think I'd ever ask you to?"

With the heat from the cast-iron range, the room had warmed up, but Sara wrapped her arms around her as she sought to put all her uncertainties into a single statement. "I don't know, but if you're married now— that is, if you wanted to take them back to—"

He was around the table before she could even finish, the chair clattering to the floor behind him. "Dammit, Sara, don't do this to me! It took all the courage I could scrape up just to come back to you like this—" He spared a scathing glance for his own right leg. "I don't have time for riddles, so I'll just come right out and ask you." His eyes, the color of black opals, glowed with internal fire. "Will you have me? I don't know a damned thing about farming, but I can learn. I'll never be able to dance again, and there might come a time when even walking's too much—without a stick, at least. But if you'll have me for a husband, I'll see that you never want for anything money can provide, and I—"

She waited, her heart in her eyes, for him to say the words she needed so desperately to hear—the words she had clung to all through the years when she didn't know if she would ever see him again. "You—?" she prompted.

Hands braced on the table, he leaned over her. Sara thought for a moment he was going to lower his head and kiss her, and she lifted her face.

Instead, he stood up and turned away. "Sara, I considered not coming back at all. What happened between us—well, it was crazy. It was all a mistake." Her heart plummeted, and she covered her chin with her hand to keep it from crumpling. "You thought I was someone I wasn't, and I thought..."

Thought you loved me? Sara finished silently, pain a wild thing inside her. Thought I would forget a careless promise made under duress of war?

And then he turned to her, and his eyes were as wet as hers. As wet and as tortured. "I thought you might possibly be able to love me for myself, and not because I bore the image of another man. You can't know how many times I wanted to write—to beg you to wait for me, to give you a chance to court you as myself.''

''Why didn't you?'' Her voice was commendably steady, her hands white knuckled as she gripped them together at her waist.

Rolph laughed, but the sound was filled with bitterness. ''Maybe because for the first eight months, I wasn't sure I'd survive long enough. Once I was reasonably certain I wasn't that easy to kill off, I was too busy fighting off a platoon of army surgeons who wanted to carve me up like a side of beef.''

Through silent tears, Sara stared at the man who spoke so dispassionately of living through hell. For the first time she noticed that he was dressed in civilian clothing, in saddle-worn but finely tailored breeches, a coat that had obviously been custom-made to accomodate those broad shoulders, and a pair of expensive boots that supported more than a light coating of road dust. How little she knew of the man who had occupied a large part of her mind for so long.

''Where were you?'' she asked when she was sure her voice would not betray her.

''Boston mostly. An army hospital in northern Virginia for a while first, for I was wounded two days after I rejoined my regiment. Once the fever left, I was sent home to the tender mercies of a man named Carruthers, who stood guard by my bed with a pair of dueling pistols when the doctors wanted to cut off my leg. He weaned me from the bottle before I could drown in brandy, and then threatened to beat me over the head with my own crutch if I didn't damn well get off my duff and take charge of my life. May God bless him.''

"And are you? Taking charge, that is?"

He turned then, his gaze plumbing the depths of her heart. "That's up to you, Sara. I can walk out of here tonight if you want. I told you that. My lawyers can set up a fund for you and the children, so that you'll never know a minute's need, and you won't have to worry that I'll try to take advantage."

"But what if I want you to... take advantage?"

She could actually feel the heat of the flame that leapt in his eyes. "Don't say that unless you mean it. Sara, this time there'll be no leaving, no backing out, no second chance to change your mind. If you can't love me, then tell me now while I still have the decency to try and behave like a gentleman."

Sara could wait no longer. At the door they had embraced, clung to each other for long, wordless moments and then sprung apart again, neither certain enough to risk a rebuff.

But now she knew. Rising, she reached him just as he opened his arms, and then the waiting was over.

A long time later they lay in bed, not so much as a scrap of flannel between them. The door was open, for Sara had taken to sleeping with both bedroom doors open so she could hear the boys if they woke in the night. They could see the tip of a branch of the Christmas tree without moving, and moving was the last thing either of them wanted to do.

"Looks like the same tree," Rolph murmured.

"Same decorations, at least. Becky wanted candles, too, but there's hardly enough tallow for soap, much less candles. Same petticoat wrapped around the base, though. Henry spit up on it after he tried to eat the tree. I'll have to find something else next year, I expect."

Rolph stroked her hair off her shoulders, leaned down and placed a kiss in the hollow of her throat. "Sweetheart, we're going to have to get married, you know. Becky's old enough to notice, and I don't particularly want the neighbors knowing that Uncle Rolph sleeps in Mama's bed."

"Would Uncle Rolph rather have a bed of his own?"

Mouth against her throat, he growled, and Sara shivered in ecstasy. "Try putting me out of your bed now, woman, and you'll have a whole new war on your hands."

But for Sara and Rolph, the war had finally ended. Only time could heal the wounds. There would be lasting scars, but the future was theirs. It was their gift to their children.

* * * * *

Dear Reader,

You might think it strange that someone would choose to write a Christmas story set in the midst of one of the world's most tragic wars. Wars have been fought since the beginning of time—fought and ended, only to be fought again. Sometimes I wonder how men who profess to believe in the Prince of Peace can create war. Yet they do, for reasons just or unjust. How many wars have been fought in the name of religion itself?

Our only hope of survival lies in the fact that the instinct to love is even stronger than the instinct to fight. Love knows no reason, no season...it simply is. The only hope for a lasting peace lies in the ability of mankind to love—love something, if not everything. Someone, if not everyone. It's a beginning.

And from such a beginning, miraculous things can grow. So celebrate this holiday season. Celebrate love. Celebrate our common humanity, and perhaps in time we can forget our differences and join hands in a true and lasting peace.

Sincerely,

Bronwyn Williams

ROMANCE IS A YEARLONG EVENT!

Celebrate the most romantic day of the year with MY VALENTINE! (February)

CRYSTAL CREEK
When you come for a visit Texas-style, you won't want to leave! (March)

Celebrate the joy, excitement and adjustment that comes with being JUST MARRIED! (April)

Go back in time and discover the West as it was meant to be... UNTAMED— Maverick Hearts! (July)

LINGERING SHADOWS
New York Times bestselling author Penny Jordan brings you her latest blockbuster. Don't miss it! (August)

BACK BY POPULAR DEMAND!!!
Calloway Corners, involving stories of four sisters coping with family, business and romance! (September)

FRIENDS, FAMILIES, LOVERS
Join us for these heartwarming love stories that evoke memories of family and friends. (October)

Capture the magic and romance of Christmas past with HARLEQUIN HISTORICAL CHRISTMAS STORIES! (November)

WATCH FOR FURTHER DETAILS IN ALL HARLEQUIN BOOKS!

HE CROSSED TIME FOR HER

Captain Richard Colter rode the high seas, brandished a sword and pillaged treasure ships. A swashbuckling privateer, he was a man with voracious appetites and a lust for living. And in the eighteenth century, any woman swooned at his feet for the favor of his wild passion. History had it that Captain Richard Colter went down with his ship, the *Black Cutter,* in a dazzling sea battle off the Florida coast in 1792.

Then what was he doing washed ashore on a Key West beach in 1992—alive?

MARGARET ST. GEORGE brings you an extraspecial love story this month, about an extraordinary man who would do anything for the woman he loved:

#462 THE PIRATE AND HIS LADY
by Margaret St. George

When love is meant to be, nothing can stand in its way... not even time.

Don't miss American Romance
#462 THE PIRATE AND HIS LADY.
It's a love story you'll never forget.

PAL-A

HARLEQUIN®

Temptation®

the Fortune Boys

A funny, sexy miniseries from bestselling author Elise Title!

LOSING THEIR HEARTS MEANT
LOSING THEIR FORTUNES....

If any of the four Fortune brothers were unfortunate enough to wed, they'd be permanently divorced from the Fortune millions—thanks to their father's last will and testament.

BUT CUPID HAD OTHER PLANS!
Meet Adam in #412 **ADAM & EVE** (Sept. 1992)
Meet Peter #416 **FOR THE LOVE OF PETE**
(Oct. 1992)
Meet Truman in #420 **TRUE LOVE** (Nov. 1992)
Meet Taylor in #424 **TAYLOR MADE** (Dec. 1992)

WATCH THESE FOUR MEN TRY TO WIN
AT LOVE AND NOT FORFEIT $$$

HARLEQUIN®

Temptation®

Rebels & Rogues

Jared: He'd had the courage to fight in Vietnam. But did he have the courage to fight for the woman he loved?

THE SOLDIER OF FORTUNE
By Kelly Street
Temptation #421, December

All men are not created equal. Some are rough around the edges. Tough-minded but tenderhearted. Incredibly sexy. The tempting fulfillment of every woman's fantasy.

When it's time to fight for what they believe in, to win that special woman, our Rebels and Rogues are heroes at heart. Twelve Rebels and Rogues, one each month in 1992, only from Harlequin Temptation.

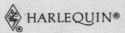

The most romantic day of the year is here! Escape into the exquisite world of love with MY VALENTINE 1993. What better way to celebrate Valentine's Day than with this very romantic, sensuous collection of four original short stories, written by some of Harlequin's most popular authors.

ANNE STUART
JUDITH ARNOLD
ANNE McALLISTER
LINDA RANDALL WISDOM

THIS VALENTINE'S DAY, DISCOVER ROMANCE
WITH MY VALENTINE 1993

Available in February wherever Harlequin Books are sold.   VAL93